Morning Light
and
The Heavy Wait

Morning Light and

the Heavy Wait

JARED STANGER

JEST/CRY PUBLICATIONS

KENT, WASHINGTON

Published by Jest/Cry Books

ISBN 978-0-557-68815-9

Printed in the United States of America

First Edition

Book design by Jared Stanger

For TD...
Cause it already is

CONTENTS

∞

Preface

In the early days of 2009, I was single with no kids, collecting unemployment checks, and struggling to make my mortgage payments. Months earlier I had been laid off from a career I truly loved, working in the radio industry as a programmer and DJ. I decided to make the most of all the free time I was then "given", and to spend as much time as I could writing.

I had been a writer off-and-on since junior high. I had written sports for a local newspaper, music for an online website, and commercials and production pieces for various radio stations. Once, I had even taken a stab at writing a feature-length movie script. None, other than the 10 years I spent in radio, had ever led to anything lasting or profitable. But everything I did always came back to writing. Now, I wanted to write a book.

When it came time to decide what and how to write, the former came instantly, and upon deciding the subject, the "how" of the subject evolved. I wanted to spend my unemployed days productively, I wanted to force myself to write something every day. To insure that could happen I needed to be able to write from any location at any time. I would write the book on my Blackberry smartphone and email the contents of my daily writing to myself. And further, I liked the idea of each day's writing being in the form of a letter.

When it came time to decide "what" I would write, the subject was already in my mind. I discovered my sister had recently moved into a house that was a block away from the house where my high school sweetheart, my first (and only) love, now lived.

This was a woman that had broken my heart years before when she married someone else. Before she married I went to her, asked her to reconsider, and to marry me instead. She didn't. I think I only saw her once after that night...after she had married...after she had birthed a baby. Seeing her with that baby, conceived with that man, was too real and too overwhelming. I spent years after that trying to avoid seeing her.

But then came this day when my sister told me of her new neighbor, and the curiosity was overwhelming. I went online and searched for her on Myspace. After cross-referencing her through her sisters, I found her page. There she was...still as beautiful as I remembered, but now a mother of three. There I was...far more confident and experienced of the world than I had been when she knew me.

And I could contact her. She was a mere mouse-click and a few keystrokes away. My mind raced with all the possibilities. She could ignore me completely. But, then again, she could have missed me. Maybe she could embrace some form of friendship with me. Could that friendship build to something else? What could it build to? My imagination answered each question only to ask its follow-up, and then to repeat it again, and then again, and again...until a year had passed...and...

"April 2009

∞

...It Ended

April 19, 2009 – 9:09 PM

Dawn, My Love-

Let me begin where I had left off...I love you so much. I miss you every moment of every day. I am so incomplete without you in my life. I hope and I pray that you will come back to me.

A year ago...we were strangers...oblivious to what had become of one another's life...ignorant, or simply ignoring, the impression we had left on one another's heart all those years ago.

Six months ago...you became my best friend...the shining light in one of the darkest periods of my life...you were my rock and my inspiration...my soulmate...and I couldn't let any days go by without you knowing how much you meant to me.

Three months ago...we were having an affair...at the height of our affair our discussions had intensified to the point of thinking of a marriage for us, a future together, and the divorce it would take to make that possible.

One month ago...the plans of our future together became dashed...my heart broken by your decision to overlook the love we share in favor of working on your marriage...a job you are committing to for the next year.

A week ago...this years' Easter Sunday also marking the 13th Anniversary of our first date...the day I first knew I was unequivocally in love with you...Red Hot Chili Peppers, April 12th, 1996.

A day ago...I entered into my third decade on this planet...I was fortunate to celebrate with my family and many of my friends...but there was a void...an absence...a vacancy in my heart. There was no candle to blow out, but had there been, my only birthday wish would be to be with you...it is my wish regardless. No...I would settle only to know of how you are...and I'd ask that wherever you are that you are happy. All I've ever wanted is your happiness. For a time this year I thought that happiness would be with me.

April 19, 2009 – 9:09 PM

      Today...I've decided to create this journal...this notebook if you will. Every day I will write you a letter. Every day I will attempt to express my love for you. To show you the depth of my love...the breadth of my commitment...my faith and belief in a greater power behind our greater love. This is a love that has stood the test of time...eight years without you ...let me have the strength to wait for you another year.

      And in that time I will mark each day with a letter...each letter a mark of my love...my love for you forever. And in that year should you find in your heart the want, the need, and the will to be with me, I will mark in my notebook a new chapter..."Chapter 2: Our First Year Together"!

      I miss you! I love you always!

-Jared Christopher

April 20, 2009 – 10:05 PM

Dawn, My Love-

     I woke up this morning with a beautiful sunlight sneaking through my blinds. My thoughts go immediately to you. For I always love to see you with the sun on your face. In part because the sun so loves to swim in the oceans of your eyes. In part because it reminds me of the first time ever I saw you. A lovely golden dusting in the dusky magic hour. We didn't know each other then, nor what would become of us. But then again…maybe we did.

     Maybe our souls have known each other before. Maybe in another life, in other bodies. No...that's not it. Our souls have known each other...perhaps for an eternity...but our bodies are new. After a lifetime of knowing and loving your soul only in the ether, in the great unknown, or the space between...my soul came to this body now so as to finally know your touch.

     And do you remember that first touch? The miracle of an instant. The delight of an idea. The beauty of a sunrise breaking the horizon. The power in a bolt of lightning. All these things from your hand to mine. Surely I have reached for the car stereo a hundred thousand times before, and since, but only that time do I remember. A moment of such concentrated thought, emotion, and truth we both recoiled from the touch... for fear that to prolong the contact time would stop, the atom would split, and we would risk losing the chance to feel that touch again…if only for a millisecond at a time.

     And oh, what I wouldn't give for a millisecond more...

     I long for your touch. I no longer fear it...I only fear a life...no, a day...without it.

     I miss you so much! I love you always!

Love,
Jared Christopher

April 21, 2009 – 10:57 PM

Dawn, My Love-

Today was the third day of not hearing from you. The silence is deafening. I long so much to know what you are doing. I want so badly to tell you about my days.

Today, again, I awoke to sun. I try so hard to busy myself...to occupy my mind. A morning workout, a light breakfast, a late morning bike ride along the river, a shower, lunch, homework and a philosophy quiz I ace. As a reward I relax some in the afternoon sun. Later I will drive to my parents' to keep my mom company. She gets a little scared when my dad works nights and she is left alone.

I wonder if anyone worries about me when I am left alone. At the end of the day I am always left alone. It is the end of the day. This is not a feeling I would wish upon an enemy.

I miss you so much! I love you always!

Love,
Jared Christopher

April 22, 2009 – 8:45 PM

Dawn, My Love-

Today was a rough day. Where yesterday I managed to find so many little activities to distract me from thinking of you, today I could not. I found myself in the quiet times dwelling on thoughts and memories of you. There were so many.

The one that hit me most deeply today was the idea of how you were raised. The idea that your parents raised you in the Christian Church, with a strong Christian value system. The idea that those values created in you a fear that to love me...a non-Christian...was to do wrong. A fear that your family would not accept me, and us together, because of my lack of belief, and the thought that those beliefs kept us apart.

Although you've recently expressed to me the tension, the anxiety, and the frustration being raised in that manner caused you...although you've recently expressed that you feel similarly anxious in your marriage...although you have recently admitted you feel none of those anxieties, nor any pressure to "perform" to some lofty expectation, when you're with me...conscious acknowledgment of these facts have not given you cause enough to actively seek a path to me, to us.

It is very tempting for me to be frustrated with your parents or family for laying the groundwork to any part of this situation...but I really can't. I know little of parenting, but logic and observation tell me it is the hardest job in the world. Parenting is not only the creation of a snowflake (and no two snowflakes are alike), but it is also the idea that even very similar snowflakes will never take the same path as they fall from the clouds.

What I know of your parents' parenting...call them strict, call them protective, call them perhaps close-minded...but the truth of the matter is they created a snowflake...pure and beautiful. Then again, perhaps a snowflake is really a tiny angel...dressed in white and dropped from the heavens. That is what you are to me.

April 22, 2009 – 8:45 PM

You are this incredible beacon of warmth and light in my life. Whatever fault or objection I could find with your parents would be ignorant of this: they created an angel. They created the woman I love. I can't express how much respect I have for that. I can't hold any grudge.

I love your parents. I love your family. I love you! I love you! I love you!

I miss you so much! Come back to me!

I love you always!

-Jared Christopher

April 23, 2009 – 5:33 PM

Dawn, My Love-

Late last night my phone buzzed. It seemed odd at that hour. I open the message...it was from you. You were announcing that you would be bringing me a birthday present today. My heart leapt into my throat. It had been several weeks since I had heard so much as one word from you. My eyes began to well...I thought of how much I miss you, how sorry I am at how things ended...the tears began to roll off my cheeks and onto my pillow.

Then I began to wonder...will you silently drop a package on my front porch and then leave without saying a word? Will you wait long enough for a "hello" and a brief embrace? Will you come in so that we can talk?

It was the second..."hello" and a brief embrace.

You still take my breath away. I couldn't have sculpted a more perfect face had I made you myself out of clay. This is the face I want to wake up to every day. To grow old with. It still baffles me that you ever took interest in me. I am so undeserving of a woman like you.

On top of your physical beauty is the beauty of your soul. Exhibited today by the thoughtfulness of the gift you've given me. The idea that you take notice of every little detail of every conversation we have...you remember them...and you work to create them. I love you for these things. They say it's the thought that counts and your thoughts count tenfold!

Our visit today was mere seconds, but I will feed off the happiness you've given me for days.

You are an amazingly thoughtful woman.

I love you so much!

Yours Always,
Jared Christopher

April 24, 2009 – 8:18 PM

Dawn, My Love-

Last night I tossed and turned...waking up alternately feverish and then with a horrible chill. When chilled I would bury my head under the blankets. When feverish I would push the blankets away and turn my pillow over and over, looking for a cool spot for my head.

In between, I dreamt. Never has so restless a night produced so many dreams. In each there seemed to be a common theme...you. In one, there was a party at your house, it got too rowdy so I kicked everyone out, and then you and I cleaned the house together. In another dream the plotline was less memorable...the lasting thought was hearing your laugh.

I've often wondered if other people hear things the way I do. I've always felt I have sensitive ears...obviously, for work, hearing which new songs will be hits on the radio...but also to everyday sounds and voices.

I can honestly say your voice is the sweetest I've ever known. Your laugh its perfect partner.

I miss them both. I miss you!

I love you so much!

Forever yours,
Jared Christopher

April 25, 2009 – 7:29 PM

Dawn, My Love-

I am sitting at my house in the dark. Only this is not for dramatic effect...the electricity to my neighborhood has gone out. Funny how life and the senses seem to intensify when we turn off the white noise of modern society.

This blackout has been just another oddity in a very strange day. Earlier today you and I had been communicating by text message. Your sister Bonnie is holding a housewarming party and there has been much drama and confusion about my attending. Even though I had previously been given an open invitation, I am now expected not to attend until I get an "all-clear signal" that you and/or your husband have gone. This bothers me greatly.

Firstly, I am so envious that it is not me that will be there by your side. But then the idea that it will be okay for me to be there after you have left...like some kind of social sloppy-seconds...it just feels deceptive and degrading.

I realize I am "the other man" in this situation...some will say "home-wrecker"...but from within this situation I see it so differently. I see a woman who I love dearly, completely...who has been stuck in an unhappy, unfulfilling marriage for 8 or 9 years...who finds in me the things she never knew she wanted, or needed, or could find...and with these discoveries she finds peace. These are your words.

I can think of no greater priority, no greater obligation than to bring happiness to the heart of one's soulmate. So although our present situation breeds negative judgments...from within I believe in our love, I believe in our future...and with these things in mind I overlook the labels and the judgment and promise to change the negative views to positive if given a chance.

Now I just wish you would give me that chance...give us that chance. I will do the work. I will charm the skeptics.

I miss you. I love you so much.

Love Always,
Jared Christopher

April 26, 2009 – 9:20 PM

Dawn, My Love-

Oh, today was hard. I have days where I know the love we found with each other will be rewarded, fulfilled...someday. Then there are days when I feel my stubborn optimism will be overruled by your stubborn passivity. Today was the latter.

I am so at a loss for why you continue to fight for a marriage that continually disappoints you, and why you continually ignore your heart's longing for me and a love that continually inspires you. I try to see it objectively and I find so little understanding for what you are doing. This isn't a case of you having a "bad day" with your husband and wanting to run to me on said day. And since I'm on the subject...why does it seem your bad days are most often Saturday and Sunday? The days when your husband doesn't head off to work and you are instead forced to feign a healthy relationship for an entire day, rather then just for a few hours in the morning and night.

Am I the only one that recognizes these things? Or am I simply the only person you've been honest about these things with? Either way I am bothered.

Would I be correct in theorizing that you fill your days with as many activities...with your children, with babysitting your sister's kids, with get-togethers with your family and/or in-laws...so as not to have to spend much, if any, time alone with your husband??? I'd also guess you wear yourself out with all these activities so as to have an excuse NOT to be intimate with him.

Am I wrong?

I'm sorry if these questions are too blunt...I had a bad day and am very frustrated.

I miss you so much. I love you even more.

Love,
Jared Christopher

April 27, 2009 – 10:26 PM

Dawn, My Love-

Another day of silence gives me pause for thought. There is, of course, my overwhelming desire to be your husband. To live a life with you openly, and in a way very much acceptable to your family. But some days I find myself wishing we were still in the midst of our secret affair.

At least then I could hear from you. In fact, then, we spoke almost every day. Some days we would even find a way to be together. And at one point those visits became physical, and the physical became bliss.

What began with a 'hello' or 'goodbye' hug, became a lingering embrace...the embrace became a kiss...the kiss bred more kisses...and then one day, my hands on your hips, your lips on my lips...my love for you took new form...I picked you up, your legs wrapping around my waist...I carried you to my bedroom...I laid you upon my bed...and we began to undress...

The further details of that day I won't recreate now.

I only mention it because...well...oh how much I long to recreate that day now. It both haunts and inspires me. I want you. I want all of you.

I lay no claim to being an expert at pleasing a woman...I know not enough of what makes a woman good at pleasing a man...I only know the contact of your body to mine...from fingertip to fingertip, lip to lip, or hip to hip...or any combination therein...would produce electricity. It is the greatest feeling I have ever known.

I miss the touch of your hand. But even more I miss the love in and of your words. For surely it pained me to think of you nightly in the bed of another, but a new day would always bring new words, and your words would always bring me hope. And hope can do quite a lot.

April 27, 2009 – 10:26 PM

These days I am left to create my own hope...and it grows harder and harder. My greatest help is the knowledge that I will always love you...and if our love is the same (as I believe it is), you will always love me too. And a love that never dies will always have a chance.

Well...that is my hope.
I will love you forever!

Love,
Jared Christopher

April 28, 2009 – 8:15 PM

Dawn, My Love-

The silence of yesterday has been forgotten.

Today you have responded to my text messages. We have spent the day in this glorious back-and-forth of digital chatter. You ask of my classes and I of yours. We discuss gardens and cooking and your daughters and more.

It is a little thing, but it is so huge. It means the world to me.

In the course of this conversation you exhibit thoughtfulness, intelligence, humor, sex appeal (well, the last I may have intuited)... so many of the things I love about you. You are a complete woman and I love you completely.

I don't know why today happened, I don't know if it will last...but for today...I am dwelling in the joy of knowing you and thanking God for who you are.

I love you so much!

Forever Yours,
Jared Christopher

April 29, 2009 – 8:42 PM

Dawn, My Love-

It seems strange to be writing you these letters, of which you don't yet know about (and won't know about til I have completed all 365 of them a year from now), while in real-time we are corresponding by text message.

Regardless, today was the second day that we spent typing back and forth on our little cellphone keyboards. A second day of wonderful anticipation that my phone will buzz at me, and within each message, the wonderful thoughts and ideas you've sent will leave me laughing and smiling and delighting the day away.

At one point I make a joke and I can just picture you shaking your head and thinking, "oh, silly boy". But in my imagination you're also smiling. I type you a request, "Just tell me you smiled." Moments later your answer..."I've been smiling the whole day." And my heart is full!

I am living for days like today...I am living to give you a lifetime of "smile-filled days"...I am living for the days my arms join my heart in being filled by your love!

I love you so much!

Yours Always,
Jared Christopher

April 30, 2009 – 8:04 PM

Dawn, My Love-

Today was our third consecutive day of a day-long texting conversation. I don't know what we're doing. You're not supposed to be talking to me because you're supposed to be working on your marriage, and supposedly you can't do that whilst interacting with me. And I am not supposed to talk to you, so as to make you miss me enough that you will decide to make a major change in your life...to divorce...which will then allow us to be together.

What does it say that neither one of us can stay away from the other for long? Is it a demonstration of the power of our love and foreshadowing an inevitable reunion? Or is it merely delaying our eventual pain? Am I reminding you daily of what you are missing? Or am I giving you love and support that then makes it easier to tolerate your marriage, and delays you from taking the actual step to change?

And what happens when the people in your life find out we're still continuing, whatever this is we're doing, even after we've been discovered? Do you want to be discovered? Do you want our discovery to cause your husband to make the decision you won't...to separate?

Tonight I had many questions...many things I don't know. What I do know is that seeing you respond, reading your thoughts, knowing you're thinking of me...it all makes me feel better...you make me happy! Even long-distance...through the wonders of technology...on my little two-inch screen.

Thank you for today! I love you so much!

Yours Always,
Jared Christopher

26

May 2009

∞

Motherhood

May 1, 2009 – 8:27 PM

Dawn, My Love-

Today marks the 13th consecutive day I have written you a letter, and the 4th consecutive day we've spent texting one another. I think we're both avoiding the elephant in the room, but I also feel like we're (once again) building toward a rendezvous. I'm okay with that because something occurred to me...

You spend your days talking to me, you spent last night out with a girlfriend, you raved about your two trips to Eastern Washington earlier this year (one with only your sisters, one with only your daughters), and it begs the question...where is your husband in all of this? If you were to poll your memory of the last 12 months, the last 10 years...how many of your favorite memories in those timespans involved your husband? How many involved exclusively your husband? I'll bet the number is low.

And of course it would seem at first glance that this would be his fault. But upon further thought, it is also yours...

Maybe he doesn't like to do the things you enjoy, and refuses to compromise and do them if only to please you. Or maybe he is ignorant of the activities you enjoy. But either way you are responsible for allowing him to continue his arrogance or ignorance. And you are responsible because, my intuition tells me, you would really rather not spend that kind of time with him...with any kind of intimacy. You are not insisting your marriage involve the activities you love, because even an activity you love would be wasted if spent with a man that you don't.

I'm sorry to be blunt about this, but as we know that is my nature. And I have to talk my way through this process...if only so that I may someday talk you through this process.

I want so badly to see you again! I love you so much!

Yours Always,
Jared Christopher

May 2, 2009 – 9:40 PM

Dawn, My Love-

Today I am slowed...brought down by not feeling well...perhaps it was something I ate. I just want to get back in bed and rest. More than that I wish you were here. I know you would take care of me.

You are such a caring, nurturing woman. You take care of so many people in your life. I know you would offer to make me some soup or some of the hot chocolate you gave me before. But really all I want is your arms.

Today I just want to lay in bed holding you. Me on my back, you on my left snuggling in the crook of my arm, your left arm resting across my chest. You kiss my shoulder, I pull your hand up to my lips and kiss the back of it, we both exhale and sink into sleep.

You take care of me. You heal my soul.

I love you so much!

Yours Always,
Jared Christopher

May 3, 2009 – 8:03 PM

Dawn, My Love-

Just before the stroke of midnight this morning you wrote me that you had an awful night yesterday. I didn't have time to ask what happened...I only had time to try to make you feel better. I told you I loved you and you said you felt better.

Today I found out you had run into my mom at the grocery store...you had told her that you would be talking to your parents last night. Was the conversation about your marriage? About our affair? Was the conversation their idea or yours? Were they supportive or critical? I don't know. Is this what made your night awful? Or was there a conversation that took place afterwards (perhaps with your husband) that was the awful part? I don't know.

What I DO know? I'm proud that in your time of stress you turned to me and you felt better. I know I've been thinking about you all day...wanting for you to be happy...worried about why you were upset and unable to sleep. I know I've spent today trying to find a song that will speak to how much I love you, and to do it in a way that will soothe you to sleep if ever you're in that position again. A calming lullabye from my heart to yours...

I think I found it. Tomorrow I will send it to you. Along with all of my love, my thoughts, my concern.

I want so much for us to move forward into a place where you don't have these awful nights...where I'm not missing you so much for so long...where we can live as man and wife.

I love you with everything I am!

Yours Always,
Jared Christopher

May 4, 2009 – 9:01 PM

Dawn, My Love-

Today I've been thinking about you and us in terms of music. From the very beginning of our relationship there was a soundtrack.

There were the days at Dairy Queen I would catch you quietly singing to yourself. The first time we touched, the time I swear I felt a literal spark, when we were both reaching for the radio. There was our first date...of course at a concert. And all along the way there were mixtapes and guitar serenades and slow dances and beautiful melody.

Two days ago you were having an awful night...after I did my best to ease your mind, and you told me you felt better, the next day my mind went immediately to finding a song. A song with lyrics that expressed my love for you. A song with a soothing sound that would help you to sleep. A song with a history, a meaning that is special to only you and me. It must be all of these things. It must be perfect. A perfect song for the woman perfect for me.

I think I found just the one, and you have now heard the song. I hope you liked it. I hope it will be something you will keep...to remind you of our past, to give you peace if the present should go awful again, and to give you hope and determination to make the future one where we're together.

Like my favorite albums, you bring me comfort and joy. Like the song I will play you at our wedding, you make me feel as though my heart will burst. Like music, you nourish my soul.

I love you so much!

Yours Always,
Jared Christopher

May 5, 2009 – 9:46 PM

My Lovely Dawn,

Most mornings I wake up and hate the emptiness of my bed...wishing I could turn to my right and see you there...put my arm over you and pull you closer to me. Tuesdays are the worst. Mostly because they used to be the best. Today was especially rough. I wanted you so bad.

And then a couple of hours later, there you were at my door...and I couldn't hold you tight enough...I couldn't hold you long enough. And your eyes...oh, they are so amazing. Everything you say, everything you do makes me feel amazing. Like I'm already the man I want to become. The man that deserves you.

All that goodness in such a brief encounter. And I still have to wonder what we're doing. I know I love you and living without you makes me sad. Seeing you for even a brief time lights me up for hours or days. There's a writer I like who once said, "If we resist our passions, it is more due to their weakness than our strength." Surely the inverse would be, "The passions we can't resist are due more to their strength than our weakness." And surely that is how I feel about you...the love I feel for you is so strong I can't resist seeing you.

As for what you're doing...I can't figure out. Are you trying to keep me from being depressed? Are you using our limited contact as some kind of crutch to get you through your day, but long-term you still won't make the change to be with me? Or, after the time we spent with no contact, are you now realizing how much you want and need me, and this is an early step in building toward our legitimate relationship.

I don't know. I just know I love every moment I get to see you or talk to you. And today I got to hold you.

I love you!

Yours Always,
Jared Christopher

May 6, 2009 – 9:00 PM

My Lovely Dawn,

Tonight some of your words are replaying in my head...in reference to your parents, "They see the world through their religion." Religion, of course, has played a huge role in our relationship (or lack thereof) since we were kids. This has always been a huge frustration for me.

The essence of religion, after all, is what a man believes, who a man prays to, while alone in the dark with his thoughts and his God. Or at least this is what it should be. Religion should be the thing that people turn to for hope, for encouragement, for uplifting. It should not be for judgment, for division, for war.

For some time now I have been enamored with the concept of choice...and offended by instances of it's lack. More recently I have come to believe that I want there to be choice, but I don't want to make them. An example: When I think of choosing a university, I am also thinking of that choice then making me an enemy of alumni of my school's cross-state rival. People who I could otherwise share many interests with. And the same is true of religion. To choose which religion is right, is also to choose that all the other religions are wrong, which is to risk absorbing the entire acrimonious history of religious rivals.

At the risk (and hope) of sounding elitist...I am interested in a greater truth. And the greater truth is that I can't hate my high school's cross-town rival, because my equal from that school will someday become my college roommate. It is silly to despise the New York Yankees and their fans, because when a plane crashes into a New York skyscraper those same New Yorkers will become "my fellow Americans" and they will be in my prayers. It is incomplete to want the United States to crush Iraq in war, because the greater truth is; borders are man-made...without borders, we are the same...we are all children of Earth...and, by the way, our Mother is dying.

I guess my earlier statement wasn't true...I do want to make choices. And I choose not to recognize our smaller differences, and instead to live for our greater commonalities. We are all the same. We are good and we are bad. We are cruel and we are kind. We are Christian and we are Muslim. We are Christian and we are undecided.

May 6, 2009 – 9:00 PM

   I wish the rest of the world could see this...could live this...in all its sizes and forms. And then one day when a boy unsure of his God loves a girl with many, many blessings, the parents of that girl will judge their relationship not by the books on their shelves or the bumperstickers on their cars, but by the respect in their communication and the affection in their kiss.
   And isn't this, in turn, what any and every God would love most of all? To see two of His children loving each other truly and completely. And they, in turn, paying that love forward to family, to city, to country, to humanity. And that love will manifest and multiply.
   And in the end we will not see the world through our religion, but see our religion through the world.
   I love you with all my heart!

Yours Always,
Jared Christopher

May 7, 2009 – 9:01 PM

My Lovely Dawn,

Today silence.

We've spoken to each other many times daily for over a week now, every text a blessing, every thought cherished...and today silence.

One of the last things you said to me yesterday was, "Listen to how wonderfully we communicate!"...and today silence.

Today I wrote you a text, proud of an essay I'd written, asking if you would read it because your opinion means the world to me...and today silence.

If I have two loves in this life...two is music and one is you...you are the music of my soul...and today silence.

I don't know if I can take this...this cycle of days of joy and then weeks of pain...I need you to decide to fight for us, to get a divorce...if this is not your decision tomorrow...then tomorrow silence.

I miss you already. I want to be your husband. I wait for you in silence.

I love you so much.

Yours Always,
Jared Christopher

May 8, 2009 – 4:09 PM

My Lovely Dawn,

It's been a tough day. I'm pretty sure I bombed a biology test. Still no sign of work. And earlier today I shaved off most of my beard. I can't wait til it grows back.

It's been so long since seeing my face. I forget how much that beard is like a security blanket. It's instances like this that show why I need your love. As conditional as our relationship was, I never questioned that the love behind it was unconditional. And that kind of love wipes away any and all self-doubts.

I think of the day I told you why I always wear a hat...because I'm losing my hair...and your response was that my revelation was sweet, and you backed that up saying that you loved everything about me. What a perfect response. How instantly my insecurity dissipated after those comments. I've never known that kind of support. That kind of love. Well I've never known that kind of love as recipient. I know that kind of love as giver. This is how I love you.

Every time you doubt how amazing you are, I see only loveliness. When you wear the clothes and exhaustion of a mom...I see only beauty! When you see the curves of your body as too curvy...I see the sexiest woman I've ever known! When you doubt your skill as student, or wife, or mom...I see the most balanced, capable woman I've ever known!

I just can't see these flaws you claim. Or maybe I'm okay with them because I'm so worried about my own flaws. Maybe subconsciously I think that if you have flaws, even imagined ones, then maybe it makes you more likely to tolerate me and all of my flaws? Maybe it lets us cancel out each other's flaws, and we can just be a couple of average people? Average people with an uncommonly perfect love?

May 8, 2009 – 4:09 PM

      I don't know. I just know when I'm with you I feel like a better man. I want to be a better man. I want to deserve you. I want to be with you. I want to hold your hand again...like the day we walked a college campus as though we were a couple of kids, when in fact we were the oldest two there. No...I had it right the first time...we WERE a couple kids...two kids in unconditional love.

      I miss you. I love you so much!

Yours Always,
Jared Christopher

May 9, 2009 – 2:14 PM

My Lovely Dawn,

  The sun came out today. I grabbed my sunglasses and headed out on my bike. First I challenged myself with a short ride up a steep hill. I made it to the summit, but it took a lot out of me. I'm not in midseason form just yet.

  After coming back down the hill I cooled off with a leisurely ride along the nearby trail. So many people out today. Some are fellow bike-riders, some joggers, and then many dog-walkers. I try to guess the breeds as I pass. Maybe a Schnauzer here? The unmistakable shape of a Dachsund. There, what I guess to be part Chihuahua, part Jack Russell.

  I notice other wildlife. There's a raven hovering against the breeze...and then suddenly it dives into the tall grass along the river. Seconds later it is airborne again only now there, in its talons, a writhing garter snake. I glance behind me to see the bird drop its meal on the pathway and then pick it up again. At one point I watch a dozen or so ducks slowly making their way up the river. I don't know which must look more tedious, the ducks against the river current, or earlier me against that hill.

  I find a bench and put it to use. Sitting fully-encompassed in the afternoon sun. I watch the people as they pass. I listen to the river flowing a few yards in front of me, and the birds singing all around. I can occasionally catch the scent of a barbeque drifting to me on the wind. I can finally feel the full warmth of the sun.

  I wish you were here. You would complete this peacefulness. You would make it perfect.

  I love you so much!

Yours Always,
Jared Christopher

May 10, 2009 – 1:35 PM

My Lovely Dawn,

Happy Mother's Day.

It has become apparent over this last year that I love you even more than I did when we first met all those years ago. One of the reasons for this, I think, is that I have now seen you as a mother. It is the loveliest thing. It is all the emotions of life in a rapid recycling process. I have seen the way motherhood frustrates and drains you. But I have seen the way it fills and completes you. And I have seen how each of your three daughters are little pieces of you.

I have seen your brilliant mind reflected in your oldest, L. I'll never forget you beaming with pride as, at six, she was bilingual...speaking more Spanish than I do...and, in turn, her face filling with the same proud expression at the acknowledgment of her impressive ability.

I have seen your affection reflected in your youngest, J. I'll never forget the day I sat with you at the kitchen table...exhaustion on your face and in your body language...you held J. on your lap...mustering enough energy for tickling and cuddling...and your reward was her squirming and giggling with delight...and later J. would smother her sisters with hugs.

And I have seen your unspoken grace and support reflected in your middle daughter, A. I will never forget the day I was visiting you...we both sat on the couch...you on the left, me on the right...without a word A. sat down between us, and after a moment she leaned her head on my shoulder. It seemed, for her, an unconscious gesture, but for me I recognized it fully and deeply. It touched my soul. To this day, to think of that moment, it makes me well up with tears. There is a certain expectation of love between family of blood, but to bestow love on an outsider...well, it isn't required...and to find it offered makes it feel all the more honest, all the more special...I cherish that memory.

For a man who has so long feared the responsibility of being a father...my only fear now is never getting a chance to be a father with you. I grew quite fond of your girls and, as I miss you, I miss them. They are the loveliest girls, and it is because you are the loveliest mother...the loveliest woman.

May 10, 2009 – 1:35 PM

I don't know what I can offer to you as a partner in parenting. I don't know how I would be as a father. I only know I will work, I will try, I will learn, I will love...all as much as I can. And I would have the best friend, the best teacher, the best partner, the best mother to learn it all with.

You are an amazing mother! I love you so much!

Yours Always,
Jared Christopher

May 11, 2009 – 11:50 AM

My Lovely Dawn,

There have been some events over the last few days that have given me pause for thought.

There was a birthday party for my younger sister's boyfriend. Occasions like that never cease to make me feel so out of place with my own family. I have little in common with my siblings, and the distance is even greater between me and their significant others. I don't like to party like they do, I'm quieter than they are, and I'm much more private than they are. Add to that the fact that I am always the odd-man out...the only single one...and it's very isolating.

I often worry about how you would react to them if we were together. We already know that your family and mine were raised completely differently...and while you and I have found a happy medium that would leave little to no problems in the privacy of our home...I wonder how your family would react to me (I feel I could rise to the occasion)...and I don't know how you would react to my family (I don't want you to lower your morals, or feel peer-pressured to). I don't know if it's normal to feel embarassed by your family. I don't know if I'm not giving you enough credit for being understanding. I've never brought a girlfriend home and I don't know how these things play out. Do people generally like their in-laws? Is "chemistry" (for lack of a better word) with in-laws important? Or do we just focus on our partner...make them the happiest they've ever been...and let extended family issues work themselves out?

The other event this weekend was Mother's Day. It's the one day each year where my mom shouldn't have to do anything. No cooking, no cleaning, no babysitting. But shortly after returning home from a shopping trip with my sister, there my mom was...cooking an early dinner for my dad, and packing his lunch before he headed out for his overnight shift at the hospital. It frustrated me to see that. This one weekend, this one day, he should have taken care of himself.

I never want to be a man that is dependent on anyone. Well, I'll never stop needing your mental and emotional support. But I never want it to be your "duty" to cook or clean or work or anything. I want to take care of you. There will always be jobs that we naturally fall into on a regular basis, but I want to be able to "pinch-hit" for you in whatever you normally do if needed. I want you to have days off. I want to be a complete man, because in so doing I think it will allow you to be a complete woman. I want you to always have time for your passions. Because passions refuel our souls to make it easier and more worthwhile to perform our duties.

I love you so much!

Yours Always,
Jared Christopher

May 12, 2009 – 4:40 PM

My Lovely Dawn,

Actually today my letter should be addressed to L, A, and J.

You see girls...yesterday your mother asked me not to contact her and promised that she would not contact me. In spite of the love I feel for her...the love I think she feels for me...she asked that I allow her to give her marriage a chance...to see if she can find complete happiness and fulfillment within it. And her reason for this? I quote, "I believe my kids will be happiest if they can have their dad and their mom under the same roof."

This is the woman that your mother is. She is the most incredible, selfless, loving woman I have ever known. She adores you all so much. So while she and I may have done something selfish that may some day hurt or embarass you...while she may partially want or need to continue it...it is important to note her effort to end it and the motivation for that end...which is you.

You are all the innocents in this. Victim to the actions of adults with great flaws...making mistakes. For this, for my part...I am sorry. I wish I could explain thoroughly enough the 'how' and 'why' these things have happened, but I am not owed your understanding or forgiveness. But I want them. I am entirely ashamed of the possible affect my actions could have on you as you grow. But in my heart of hearts, I sincerely thought (and think) that after the weathering of the storm...there would be tremendous benefit of your mom and I being together. I still feel such optimism about the limitless possibilities that come when your mom and I are together...and I know this would transfer down to you.

But today I am without optimism. I am terrified of your mom's decision. I fear she won't find the happiness she seeks, and that she deserves with this decision. I fear she will live indefinitely unhappy as a gesture of principle. I fear I will never see her again. I fear I will never see you again.

May 12, 2009 – 4:40 PM

     I know as I write this all three of you are quite young...you may forget me quite easily (if I made any impression to begin with). But I won't forget you. And if by some miracle I can someday be a part of your family...I will never try to replace your father, but instead I will only try to be another figure of love and support in your lives. Think of it not as losing a dad, but as gaining a step-dad. Someone of strength and thought that you can lean on when needed. Someone who would love your mom with every breath in his body. I promise you that.

     Your mom is my angel! I miss her and I will always love her!

Sincerely,
Jared Christopher

May 13, 2009 – 1:35 PM

My Lovely Dawn,

Today I was thinking of our first date. We were in Seattle, walking to a concert...you asked if I liked your fingernails...they were some kind of artificial, press-on nail. I didn't care for them. You immediately proceeded to rip them off.

I tell this story because, like everything else about you, I love your hands and I love them in their natural state. You need no adornment. You need only to show up to be spectacularly beautiful. Your hands are the loveliest I've ever seen. You keep your nails short, and your fingers are slender, delicate, and entirely feminine. I can't recall noticing a woman's hands before yours, but I think I've noticed every pair since.

Many women have short, stumpy fingers. Some have broad, muscular hands. Others keep long, painted nails. For whatever reason, all of these qualities go against my taste. And hands are important because hands are a microcosm of who a woman is. Ray Charles was said to have felt a woman's wrist to know of her beauty...but I want to see her hands.

A slender proportioned hand equates to a slender proportioned body. A simple, natural nail treatment equates to a simple, natural woman...and the opposite; a high-maintenance hand is a high-maintenance woman.

Now I am thinking of the night we went to the movies with your youngest sister. Afterwards your sister left and we lingered in wonderful conversation. You drove me back to my car. I couldn't say goodbye...I didn't want the moment to end. I leaned over to hug you goodbye. At that point our moral boundaries wouldn't allow us to kiss...but I wanted to kiss you...I had to kiss you. I took your hand, held it between both of mine. I kissed your hand. I kissed it again. I kissed your fingers, I kissed your palm, I kissed your wrist. And then, my eyes closed, I brought your hand to my face...held it against my cheek. Don't let this moment end. Don't let me wake up.

I love you so much!

Yours Always,
Jared Christopher

May 14, 2009 – 3:32 PM

My Lovely Dawn,

The fourth day since we stopped communicating. I've spent a lot of that time wondering about the reasons for your decision.

You say you want your kids to have their mom and dad living under the same roof. Of course a noble intent. But I wonder if things would be different if we weren't in the midst of the biggest recession since the Great Depression...if I wasn't laid off months ago and living week to week on these unimpressive unemployment checks...fighting like crazy to finish my college degree and find a new job...wondering if I should continue schooling to earn a better degree, or perhaps go to film school and pursue my true passion. Without question, I am at a crossroads.

We've spoken before about how much I want to work and be able to support you and your daughters (in whole or in part). You've always downplayed this...saying that you have some money saved, or you could go back to work, or...I don't know what. Basically you don't want the responsibility to all fall on me. But I wonder if me being unemployed with an uncertain future truly scares you away from considering your future with me? Or is it not the future...you just can't consider your present with me? Will you quickly and gladly reopen our relationship when my life is back in order?

Then I wonder if I'm right about this...would this be something you wouldn't feel comfortable telling me? Are you trying to protect my ego and feelings? Is this year you've given yourself to work on your marriage serving multiple purposes? To fully and honestly assess your marriage and it's future...to continue your schooling and prospects for your eventual return to working...and for me to rebuild my career? Or, is it not about protecting my feelings, but about not revealing these calculated, and somewhat cold, plans? Cause, although I can see how it is cold, I can also see a certain amount of sense in it. I, for one, would prefer to know if what I'm describing here is what you're thinking. Ignorance has always been scarier to me then knowing a displeasing truth.

May 14, 2009 – 3:32 PM

      If my theory is correct could this also explain why you said you're scared that I will find someone new in our time apart? Because secretly when you said "goodbye" you were really saying, "I'll see you later," and hoping I would find that in the subtext of your letter and wait for you? And you hide it in the subtext because you think how selfish it would be to openly ask me to wait?

      Oh, I have so many questions. So many questions and no one to ask. And no answers.

      Well I have one answer...I love you! I truly, truly do! Forever!

Yours Always,
Jared Christopher

May 15, 2009 – 8:53 PM

My Lovely Dawn,

In this time of my personal recession I take great comfort in time with friends. An invitation of any kind is to be accepted if only for welcome distraction.

Last night I was invited to a bar near my house with some of my brother's friends for a trivia night. The prize for winning was $65. A couple of drinks and I become more social. I tease the waitress a little and she mocks me right back. Toward the end of the evening she asks if we're ready for our bill, and I tell her, "we're gonna win, so you can just take what we owe from our winnings," (that we hadn't won...yet). She retorts, "so I'll just bring you your bill?" She's no fun.

After the trivia challenge had been given and each answer sheet been scored, the judge reads off the scores from lowest to high...and team after team is read off before us...the judge says the words, "...and finally...", and knowing we haven't been called yet, we expect to hear our team's name, "...in first place...Team Whiskey and Coke!" Our table erupts into cheers!

I don't recall which arrived at our table first, the bill or our prize...but they're both almost an identical amount. We each throw in a dollar to increase the tip, and when the waitress returns I make sure I get to hand her the money. When she arrives I look her straight in the eye and say, "I told you we'd win!" She replies, "Yeah, but I thought you were crazy!"

"Crazy like a fox!"

And speaking of foxes...I miss you!

I love you so much!

Yours Always,
Jared Christopher

May 16, 2009 – 8:51 AM

My Lovely Dawn,

     I awoke this morning to the buzzing of my cellphone on the nightstand. From behind my closed eyes I could feel my bedroom awash in a glow of early morning sun. I lay there a bit longer in hopes of dreaming...to see you in my thoughts.

     And then there I was, knocking at your door. Only it wasn't your house. This was a house I've only seen once before...in a dream...of you.

     The door opens and there you are. Your clothes, your hair seem different, but still it is you. You let me in. I embrace you. I try to pull you with me as I fall onto a couch, but you pull away. My eyes scan the rest of the room and find two tiny witnesses, your babysitting tasks for the day, sitting on a blanket on the floor.

     When you pulled away I felt a great disappointment, so I walked out the door. The outside world is now colder than when I arrived and I pull the collar of my coat tighter as I walk away, into the city.

     And then I'm awake. Now consciously disappointed that my dream of you had not been a bit more intimate. For when you can't be with your love in flesh, how wonderful to be with them in dream.

     I dream to be with you in the flesh...in marriage...in sickness and in health.

     I love you so much!

Yours Always,
Jared Christopher

May 17, 2009 – 8:39 PM

My Lovely Dawn,

   I saw something today that made me smile. I saw a young black boy cruising down a sidewalk on a skateboard. I see this more and more lately, but it wasn't always the case. There was a time skateboarding was almost exclusively white. But it made me happy because it represents the fall of a stereotype.

   I just love to see a stereotype fall. I love to see Eminem excel in hip hop music. I love to see Tiger Woods dominate golf. I love to see Steve Nash win MVP's in the NBA. And I love to see the United States of America elect Barack Obama president. And not just because I'm so proudly contrarian.

   Let the poor become prognosticators of taste. Let the nerds become first-picked. Let the man become more sensitive. Let the woman become more logical. Let us all become bi-racial, or to redefine what it means.

   Let it not only mean half black and half white, but also half Irish and half Italian...half Moroccon and half Samoan...half Dutch and half Chinese. And then let the halves become quarters, the quarters become eighths and sixteenths and so on...until we lose track. Let us continue to blur the lines of culture until there are no defining characteristics, or even common traits. We destroy all the stereotypes and then the judgments that so often follow them will wither and die. Eventually we will lose all sense of race and country, and when this happens the world will see itself as Martin Luther King always dreamt...a place where a man is not judged by the color of his skin, but by the content of his character. Bios will not read 32 years old, black, American, male, brown hair, brown eyes...but rather; 32 years old, good father, good husband, organ donor, veteran of war.

   Let the reasons for division end. Let black become white, white become black, and all become grey. Let young black boys enjoy the hell out of riding a skateboard on a sunny spring day, and let us realize that we are all the same. Let us be the same.

   This is the future I hope for and I can see. A future I want so much to share with you. A woman who loves the potential of mankind as much as I do...no, more. I love you so much!

Yours Always,
Jared Christopher

50

May 18, 2009 – 10:03 PM

My Lovely Dawn,

This letter will be the 30th consecutive I've written you, and it marks one month since we've begun our respective year-long trials-by-fire. It feels like a bittersweet milestone. And it is not even a legitimate marker as I heard from you as recently as one week ago...I saw you in-person as recently as ten days ago. As excruciating as this month has been, I am terrified of how a month of absolute silence, of your complete absence, will feel.

Silence is a cruel, cruel teacher. And today it doesn't teach me anything new. The lesson is a refresher course in the appreciation of thought...your thoughts. As staggering as your beauty, as incredible as your touch...nothing fills me, challenges me, or inspires me like your thoughts!

Thoughts of imagination, thoughts of support, thoughts of religion, thoughts of science, thoughts of compassion, thoughts of tenderness, thoughts of unconditional love. To that list add an element of surprise, because I often don't know what you're thinking. But oh how I love to ask what's on your mind so I can find out.

I was asked recently what I did for fun and I didn't have an immediate answer. But as I've been writing you tonight it dawns on me how much I love good conversation. And I don't think I've ever known a better conversationalist than you. I just love talking to you. I don't think we've ever had an awkward silence. In fact, I don't know that we'd ever have a moment of silence if not for how much I love kissing you. But I have to be careful how much I say. When I'm careless, I risk deepening the void, the loss I am feeling without you in my life.

I miss your voice. I miss your thoughts. And I love you without measurement...without equal...without end!

Yours Always,
Jared Christopher

May 19, 2009 – 9:46 PM

My Lovely Dawn,

Today I have nothing.

No ideas for this letter. No deep thought on the world. No silly anecdote of my day. No rememberance of our past. No dream of our future.

No job interviews. No college acceptance. No progress on my screenplay.

No questions. No answers. No leads. No luck. No love.

No girlfriend. No lover. No partner. No confidante. No better half. No wife. No best friend. No you.

I have only faith. And maybe that's enough.

I love you. I want you, I need you, and I miss you. But above all else...I love you!

I am Yours Always,
Jared Christopher

May 20, 2009 – 3:34 PM

My Lovely Dawn,

On the news today they spoke of a toddler that had been found drowned in a pool. I didn't feel sad. I immediately thought an innocent child would now be in a better place.

It makes me wonder if mankind doesn't make too much of death. If we don't fear it unnecessarily. And I wonder if fearing death doesn't contradict the faith that so many in the world say they have.

In my limited knowledge of religions, it is my understanding, there is an afterlife in most (if not all). To fear death personally is either to show the hollowness of one's projected "faith", or it is to suspect one has lived a life unworthy of an ascension upon dying (or, more accurately, fear of accountability/punishment for a life lived wrongly).

Similarly, when people fear the death of others, of loved ones, are they fearing that family member cast into damnation, or are they merely being selfish and worried about the pain they will feel themselves upon death and the tribulations they may encounter subsequently without said relative in their life? Is this why the mother of the drowned girl cries?

At this point I would like to make a distinction. I am not questioning the fear of dying...the process by which one dies (whether sudden or prolonged). I, too, am scared of that. I am scared of dying painfully.

But shouldn't we all be rather accepting of death? The actual moment after last breath, when a soul leaves it's earthly vessel and transcends to whatever may exist in the great beyond? The Heaven we've been taught to expect.

I think of my only personal glimpse of death...November of 2008...my maternal grandmother...my Mimi...had taken quite ill. Her condition inoperable...her body too weak to recover...the family's only option to medicate and minimize her pain until she passed.

We drove from Washington down to her hospital in Oregon. We all crowded into her room. We all took turns walking to her side, taking her hand, saying a few words. Her body, her voice were so frail...her spirit was still strong. "Do you need more medicine?" someone asked. "Just a twinge." See how tough she is? But her thoughts came and went incoherently. One of my sisters tried to give her a hug and Mimi visibly grimaced in pain from the pressure. She was putting on a tough façade.

At one point everyone but myself left the room. Mimi's eyesight was almost gone and I could sense she felt the quiet as abandonment. I moved to her side, took her by the hand and whispered, "I'm still here." We spoke for a few minutes...we remembered our summer together many years before, driving cross-country...she remembered the foot massages I would give her...I remembered the breakfasts of cheese-eggs and sticky-buns she would make. She said she was ready "to go see father". As we sat there, just the two of us, her hand in mine...I closed my eyes and prayed. I wanted her to go. I wanted her pain to be over. I knew she was a good woman, she had lived a good life...I knew good things awaited her on the other side. A few days later she was gone.

And now my worry can transfer from the pain my Mimi was feeling while dying, to the pain some still feel in her absence. My mom had a rough Mother's Day...openly because she was tired from babysitting grandkids the night before...but quietly, I think she was missing her mom.

While my pain for losing her is comforted by thinking Mimi is in a better place, I think of another woman...someone who I fear is in tremendous pain...who also wears a tough facade, but whose pain has no known end in sight...I think of her and I worry and hurt.

I'm thinking of you. Please don't be in pain. If you are, please come back to me and cure us both.

I miss you! I love you!

Yours Always,
Jared Christopher

May 21, 2009 – 9:03 PM

My Lovely Dawn,

...and after dark comes light.

Only two days ago I complained of not being accepted to the college of which I've applied. Today, I open my mailbox, and inside a large envelope with purple lettering... "Welcome To The University of Washington". But I can't dwell in the accomplishment for long. This breeds further questions. Will I be able to afford attending? Will I be able to attend and work full-time simultaneously? Do I still want to attend? Meaning do I want to be practical and get my Bachelor's Degree from UW, or do I change my mind, follow my heart, and attend film school?

Only two days ago I complained of having no job interviews. Today my phone rings with an offer to interview for a job tomorrow. This breeds further questions. Will I get the job? Will it pay enough to cover all my monthly bills? Will having a job cut too dramatically into my time for homework and writing?

And speaking of writing...that was my third complaint two days ago..."no progress on my screenplay". So I guess I'll have to write something tonight just to make myself seem like a total turn-around today (and a total whiner two days ago).

Well...not a total turn-around. I still don't have you. And that might be the greatest trial of all.

I miss you! I love you!

Yours Always,
Jared Christopher

May 22, 2009 – 3:56 PM

My Lovely Dawn,

It was a stunningly beautiful day.

I began the day with a job interview, and as soon as I was done, before I even reached my car in the parking lot, I was tugging at the knot of my tie. I opened the car door, tossed the tie on the passenger seat, and undid the top button of my shirt.

Once at home I immediately trade tie and slacks for shorts and sandals. I sit in the sun on the patio for a few minutes. It is just now noon and the barbecue grill to my left is begging to be used. I'm no great chef, but I can grill a mean steak or, in today's case, a double burger with cheese.

After lunch, cleanup, and a couple chores, I realize I had skipped my morning workout to get ready and attend the job interview. I grab my sunglasses, crack the garage, and head out on my bike. I head straight from my condo, near the river in the valley, to the top of the nearby East Hill. I think it's close to a mile-long climb and today I make the trip up and back twice. My endurance is improving. After the climb I cool down by riding along the river trail. I stop at a nearby park to replenish fluids, relax, and wonder.

I wonder where you're at, what you're doing, how you're enjoying this beautiful day. I wonder if you'd like sitting at this picnic table, and under this tree, and near this river...and maybe with me. I wonder how you will be spending this upcoming Memorial Day weekend. I wonder if you'd like to spend it hiking, and fishing, and camping...and maybe with me. I wonder how you'll spend the rest of your life. I wonder if you'd like a life of music, and movies, and books, and walks, and talks, and kids, and hard work, and romance, and passion...and maybe with me.

I know I'd like all these things. That part I don't have to wonder.

I miss you every moment of every day. The dark days and the bright.

I love you so much!

Yours Always,
Jared Christopher

May 23, 2009 – 9:36 PM

My Lovely Dawn,

I am trying to transform myself. Like the bionic man, I have the technology to rebuild myself...only instead of becoming faster and stronger, I am focusing on wiser, more sensitive, a better cook, a more complete person...and of course stronger.

I am trying to improve the fitness level of my body. In part because I am taking a PE class that requires it, but also because I just want to look good with my shirt off. I think you are so incredibly sexy and I want to make my body something you will find sexy in return. To reconstruct the old adage, "Do unto others as you'd have them do unto you"...I want to be for you as you are for me. I want to give you reason to be eager to have some fun, as you are more than reason for me to want to have some fun!

I've been pretty pleased with my first two months' results. My arms feel better, my shoulders feel better...my skinny legs need work. I wish you were here to see. To encourage and to critique. Or to work out with me. I would insist you don't need to work out but I would also cheer you on in the very next breath if you insisted on exercising. I can imagine so clearly us taking turns holding one another's feet while we did our respective sit-ups.

My other physical goal is to put on some weight. I've always been thin and never been able to gain, but I'm trying. I just know you would help me with that as well...with the way you talk about your love of cooking and baking, and the snacks you've made for me already...you could just fatten me right up.

I think you're a wonder of a woman...of fittest body and skilled chef...and of support and thoughtfulness and an honest voice.

I miss you! I love you!

Yours Always,
Jared Christopher

May 24, 2009 – 1:44 PM

My Lovely Dawn,

I think it will take tremendous discipline to remain vigilant in my promise to write you every day this year. As I consider my life, there are very few things that I've ever had the dedication or passion to fulfill on a daily basis. But the one other I can think of, also has your influence all over it. For many years now, it has become a priority of mine to take a few moments each night...to pray.

It began in high school...in part because of a couple events in my life that felt quite miraculous...but in larger part, due to you coming into my life.

For a long time I wondered if I was doing it "right", if I had to begin with the Lord's Prayer, or end with 'Amen'. Now I don't care about form. I only care that I take the time every night before I sleep to say my piece and say my peace.

I have stopped worrying if I'm praying to the "right God". I no longer want to participate in that debate, or defend my personal belief. I only want to say "thank you". Just like a parent on Christmas, whose child thanks Santa for the gifts she's received...as that parent I would know the "thanks" were for me. So it is that I believe the true God...whatever or whoever He may be, and however I send my "thanks"...He knows they are for him. And God knows these things without us saying them. But we say them again to show our respect.

I prefer to spend my prayers saying "thanks" than to spend them in requests or in needs. This is a constant battle, but I am always trying. And when I do use a prayer to ask of God, I try to only ask that He make me a better man.

I want to be a man worthy of your love. And in your absence I continue to work to that goal.

I miss you. I love you!

Yours Always,
Jared Christopher

May 25, 2009 – 9:43 PM

My Lovely Dawn,

There's a show on television tonight...one of my ridiculous reality shows that I love and you love to tease me about. Which is okay cause I know they're bad. But this one is about a young family that is going through a divorce.

Where once the couple would do interviews in front of the camera together, they now speak individually. Scenes where they are seen together the tension is palpable. The camera speaks volumes. Body language says many of the things their words will not.

But I also started to study the children of this family. And to my surprise there isn't much noticeable stress, or drama, or sadness in the words and actions of the kids. Whatever is going on between the parents is not transferring to the kids. In fact the kids seemed better behaved and happier than when the parents were together and unhappy.

I can't watch this show on this topic and not think of you. And then the girls. I wonder what all four of you are thinking and feeling on a daily basis. Are you still feeling the anxiousness and unease you've told me you feel in your own home? Do those feelings transfer down to the girls? Does the very act intended to provide the best life for the girls, both parents living under one roof, actually create two parents living unhappily, and therefore cause more stress and dysfunction for your daughters? Could a separation/divorce, contrary to logic, actually be a better solution because it gives the girls the possibility of two individually happier parents? As I said it's contrary to what most would find logical. But it's what I'm wondering.

And I know it's easier for me to dwell in these thoughts. It would seem I have only to gain. But why does it feel I have everything to lose...and I am losing?

May 25, 2009 – 9:43 PM

I've said it before and I'll say it again...I want to marry you, I want to become a step-dad to the girls. And if one knows anything about me, all I need is a desire to accomplish something and I immediately lose any fear of doing it. With desire I can learn. And where I can learn I can do. And what I can do I can do well. Therefore, when I realize I desire to be a parent with you, I believe I can do it well...I can be a great dad.

I miss you very much! I love you even more!

Yours Always,
Jared Christopher

May 26, 2009 – 9:21 PM

My Lovely Dawn,

I was at my parents' house tonight to take a test for my Philosophy class and to write a new article for my online column. Afterwards I stayed for dinner. The conversation reminded me of one of the last things you wrote to me...the line about not believing in your parents' life-philosophies. Tonight I am definitely relating to that.

My stepdad and I basically disagree on everything. He recently asked me to research this name he gave me. I looked into it and it turned out the man was a German sociologist/philosopher who tried to write music. There were some articles online that suggested he had something to do with the writing of the songs of the Beatles.

He just loves his conspiracy and media manipulation theories. But his filter is completely dislodged. Does the media try to manipulate the public? Of course. But it isn't a consistent message. The one message that trumps all is capitalism. Money. But there is money to be made in both Republican AND Democratic messages. There is money to be made in popular culture AND there is money to be made in counterculture. AND there is money to be made selling conspiracy theory. And he is BUYING!

Like so many things we've discussed recently, it comes down to choices. There are reasons to believe left and right of any issue...life comes down to which side do we CHOOSE to believe. We can choose to believe CNN, we can choose to believe Jon Stewart, or we can choose to believe some internet blogger who we know nothing about. We can choose to believe in God, we can choose to believe Allah, we can choose to believe atheism. We can choose to believe just like our parents teach us, or we can choose a path of our own.

May 26, 2009 – 9:21 PM

I think I've lost my train of thought repeatedly, and some of the points I intended to make when I began, so I will close. I guess I want you to know that I appreciated when you said you didn't want to follow your parents blindly. Although I'm confused, because what you're doing is what they want you to do anyways. But I think, if I'm reading between the lines correctly, you're not doing this for your parents, you're doing it for your daughters. Which is far more noble, but which will be far more difficult to go against in the future.

I am tired tonight. I will sleep soon. Come visit me in my dreams? I miss you! I love you!

Yours Always,
Jared Christopher

May 27, 2009 – 7:25 PM

My Lovely Dawn,

As I was beginning this letter I had this idea of what I wanted to write, but just as I wrote the words, "My Lovely Dawn," I changed my mind. It only occurred to me today, after beginning many letters to you this way, that it is a presumptuous thing to say...to say that you are "mine". I hope you know that I only want of you the same that I will give. And as I have said, and will say, "Yours Always," that is what I mean...that is what I give. I am yours.

When you have homework that you want an opinion on or proofreading of...I give you my mind.
When you have a tough day and the girls have misbehaved...I give you my ear.
When you get tired on the return trip of a hike...I give you my hand or my piggy-back.
When you allow yourself a cry...I give you my shoulder.
When there is no reason or special occasion at all...I give you my arms and my kiss.
When you decide to start your own bakery or write your first book...I give you my support.
When you do all the thoughtful, little gestures you always do for me...I give you my thanks.
When you take a breath...I give you my love.
When you are ready, willing, and able...I give you my life.

I am yours.

I miss you! I love you!

Yours Always,
Jared Christopher

May 28, 2009 – 5:15 PM

My Lovely Dawn,

Watching the news this week there is a lot being said about President Obama's Supreme Court Justice nominee. It began weeks ago when Suitor announced his retirement and Obama said he would look for an "empathetic" Justice as his replacement. And now the Republican right have latched onto that word as some kind of disagreeable trait.

First of all if you're going to pay so much attention to one word, you better know its definition. Empathy is to intellectually identify with the feelings or thoughts of another. It isn't to agree with those feelings, but merely to acknowledge them and the reason behind them. It is merely the attempt, with class and grace, to understand the position of another.

It would seem the right has mistaken "empathy" for "sympathy". Sympathy is the naturally existing feeling of shared tastes or opinions between people. Sympathy is, "I know being unemployed sucks because I've been there too," whereas an empathetic response would be, "I don't know the struggles of being unemployed, but I imagine they're difficult and I'm sorry you're going through it." Neither of which, by the way, is a negative quality.

If sympathy or empathy were to exist without a filter of logic and reason then there might be a problem. But I'm pretty sure there's a degree of wisdom required of a candidate that comes far earlier in the process than empathy. To empathize with a participant of a legal trial or hearing is merely one tool in the extensive skillset that should be required of a Supreme Court Justice. A justice must be able to consider how their interpretation of law will affect all walks of American life. And when a justice him/herself belongs to one set of economic/ethnic/social class, the only way to consider the thoughts and feelings of the other classes is to empathize with them.

May 28, 2009 – 5:15 PM

    To say we shouldn't have justices with empathy is like saying we should have justices without feelings or emotions. And to say that, is only a step away from suggesting we shouldn't have female justices because they are more emotional than men. No, the fact is, justices are human and we should only expect that they can use all facets of their humanity to conclude what interpretation of the constitution is best for the country.

    And now I shall step down from my soapbox.

    I wish I could share these thoughts with you in real time. I think you would get what I'm saying. Of course you would...you're tremendously empathetic.

    I miss you! I love you!

Yours Always,
Jared Christopher

May 29, 2009 – 10:18 AM

My Lovely Dawn,

The weather was incredible today. Warm and sunny. But as night fell the temperature did not. I lay in bed more restless than usual. Even with the window open and a small fan pointed at the bed I am uncomfortably warm. I turn the pillow over again and again, searching for a cool spot for my head. The restlessness of my body pales in comparison to the restlessness of my brain. My mind is working late tonight, and the job is thinking of you.

I think of our past...the impending one-year anniversary of our reunion. I think of our present...how every day I fight the urge to drive to your house and wrap my arms around you. I think of our future...please let there be a future.

I think of what it would be like if you decided to get a divorce...what would be my first words to you. I would want to know if you were okay. I would want you to know I still loved you. I would let you know whatever you needed of me I would give. I would fight the urge to immediately ask you to marry me...for I have a better, proper proposal already in mind.

I think about what it would be like to sleep beside you. I've never slept beside someone before...not for an entire night, let alone every night. All attempts I've made have resulted in me moving to a couch or going without sleep. On a few occasions I've found I even struggle to sleep when there is someone else in the same room. But I wonder, could you be the cure to my sleeplessness? A sort of backwards tale of Sleeping Beauty, where the beautiful princess is the prince charming, and her kiss brings sweet, peaceful sleep.

These are the things I think about in between turns of my pillow. Forever in search of the cool spot for my head...forever in search of the peace and comfort only you have brought to me. You...the cool spot for my heart.

I miss you! I love you!

Yours Always,
Jared Christopher

May 30, 2009 – 1:54 PM

My Lovely Dawn,

I took a walk along the bike trail today and a thought occurred to me: Where do all of these bicyclists come from and how do they all have biking outfits of spandex bike shorts and zip-up spandex bike tops? They all look like wanna-be Lance Armstrongs. Do the shorts come with the bike? Is there some law that says spandex must be worn on a bike just like there is for the helmets?

And what purpose does the spandex serve? Does it make the rider more aerodynamic so as to enable them to win the race they're not actually in? Does it cause the thigh muscles to work harder or sweat more thereby providing a better workout? Or does it just make them look like they fit in?

What about the number of bicyclists? In the middle of the afternoon on a weekday...why aren't these people at work? Sometimes I'll see a huge pack of 12 riders...how do they all coordinate their off-days so as to be able to ride bikes together?

And lastly, how are there so many bicyclists but I don't know a single one personally? Where do they all come from?

I know today wasn't a very romantic letter. If you were here beside me I know I would be more romantic.

I miss you! I love you!

Yours Always,
Jared Christopher

May 31, 2009 – 6:57 PM

My Lovely Dawn,

Do you remember that present you got me? The t-shirt with the Superman symbol? As I was folding it today after doing the laundry I was thinking...I wonder if there's more to the analogy that inspired you to get it for me than just silly pillow talk.

Like Superman I feel like an outsider. Like Superman I feel I carry a responsibility to care for those around me. Like Superman I walk through the world in disguise. And unlike the comic book characters who put on a disguise to do their good deeds, when Superman goes to save the world he actually takes his disguise OFF.

He appears as mild-mannered Clark Kent. I appear as this skinny, nerdy guy from the suburbs. But inside Superman has all these incredible, innate abilities. While I can't leap tall buildings in a single bound, I feel very few people know what I am capable of beneath this outer shell. People don't know how smart I am...how creative I am...that I'm good with pen and camera and guitar...or that I've got abs of steel (well, they're getting there...let's just say the skinny guy is getting pretty cut up).

Superman has this desire to use his abilities to better the world. And that's what I want to do. If ever I get to leave a mark on the world, let it be one of wisdom, inspiration, creativity, and compassion. I want to be remembered for something great...a great piece of art, a great piece of wisdom, or the greatest love that I've found with you. Or if I can somehow combine all three.

And, lastly, there's the matter of how Superman and I gain our power. This is where we differ. Where the dawn of Earth's sun's light enhances Superman's strength, my strength is enhanced by the light from a Lovely Dawn. A slight, but important, difference.

I want you to know how much your presence fuels me. It does give me a strength that I don't know otherwise. And now with that presence gone, I am reduced to a mere mortal. And I feel the change.

I miss you! I miss your presence and your presents! I love you!

Yours Always,
Jared Christopher

June 2009

∞

Dry Spell

June 1, 2009 – 7:30 AM

My Lovely Dawn,

Happy Birthday!

Not only is today your birthday, but those are also the very same words I first wrote to you 365 days ago...the words that reunited us...the words that we couldn't have known would begin our affair.

I wonder how you feel today about the last year. Do you regret the relationship we came to share? Is it something you wish never happened? Or do you look upon it as something important...a collection of lessons on life, on love, on who you are, and who you want to be? Will this year be forgotten? Or will it someday be repeated, expanded, enriched, fulfilled?

For me it has been a year of the highest highs and the lowest lows of my life. The highs owed almost exclusively to the exquisite joy of every moment with you...every new discovery and experience and thoughtful gesture and passionate embrace. The lows due to the loss of my job, my grandmother, and, most recently, you.

I can no longer remember who I was before loving you and I don't want to imagine what I'll become without loving you. I just want to return and stay in the perfect realm of your love. Where I am never out of sight of the amazing blue of your eyes. Where I am never out of reach of the tenderness of your embrace. Where I am never out of range of the beautiful melody of your laugh. Where I am never out of mind of your thoughtful, caring spirit. Where I am never out of inspiration to create and return all this love back to you every day, and eternally.

Although we aren't together on this day, you are on my mind and in my heart, and with both I am wishing, hoping, praying that your day is consumed with happiness and love. And should there be a lack I implore you to return to me with haste.

Happy Birthday!

I miss you! I love you!

Yours Always,
Jared Christopher

June 2, 2009 – 4:59 PM

My Lovely Dawn,

As yesterday was your birthday and we couldn't spend it together, I tried to do something you would enjoy, something I would have planned for you had we been together. So I took a trip down south to a beautiful lake where I spent the afternoon quietly thinking and fishing.

It was such a peaceful scene. The water so clear, the weather so warm, and the mountain in the distance a fantastic, imposing backdrop. I stood at the end of the dock, casting into the shadowy spots where the fish love to hide. It wasn't very surprising that I didn't catch a thing as my thoughts were far away. My thoughts were of you.

I couldn't help but imagine you there with me, your fishing skills likely surpassing mine. The girls playing on the lawn back by the house in their beautiful summer dresses...L. leading A. and J. in the schoolhouse of pretend. The hours would pass and we'd eat dinner outside, under the trees...the waves lapping against the bank. You'd make salads of pasta and fresh fruit and I would fire up the grill, perhaps cooking our catch of the day. And then, after the girls had been put to bed, we would slip away in the rowboat for a moonlight cruise just for two.

I still don't know whether these thoughts and wishes and dreams are coming closer or falling further away. I hope it's the former. And hope is all I have...well, hope and promise. I will remain their friend as long as they will have me. The hope I will keep and the promise I will give. The promise to love you in good and in bad, in laughter and in tear, for ever and for always. And the promise that every day will be for you, but your birthdays will be for your dreams, and the dreams to come true. It is only fair, as a life lived with you would be my dream come true daily.

I miss you so much! I love you forever!

Yours Always,
Jared Christopher

June 3, 2009 – 8:56 PM

My Lovely Dawn,

Today I was wishing to again be on that lake and by your side, but instead I found myself rather in solitary confinement. I soon grew weary of my own four walls and took to the bike trail to find some escape.

Immediately out the door I found that summer had arrived...one step into the light and I was struck by a wall of heat. The sun beating down on the black asphalt path, on this hottest day of the year, made the nearby river, rushing at a deceivingly swift current, seem cool and inviting. But I labored on, my clothes sticking to my body from the instant perspiration.

The world around gave further proof of the heat of the day. The breeze blew quite consistently, but brought no relief. Rather it only stirred the buds of the cottonwood trees to fly from their homes. They would tickle some as they'd land on my brow or my nose. Here by the river their parent trees were so plenty that in places the banks of the trail more resembled a snowy, winter scene than this day of enscorchment. A second, silent clue about this incessant heat...there are fewer fellow riders and I find myself quite alone...it would seem this day the sun's partner: heat, has scared away those that generally love the sun on its own.

Halfway through my ride I came to a park where I had my choice of tables at which to sit and rest. I choose a shaded spot beneath a tall, fir tree where I sip my water and begin to write. The quiet is impressive, and it allows for new discoveries. As when the breeze shows itself again, this time sounding like the faintest, bamboo wind-chimes rustling through the pinecones on the branches just above. Further away the quiet gives stage to one of the greatest sounds Mother Nature ever sang...the breeze through the tall grasses near the river. If a person gets to choose his heaven let mine, in part, have a field of waist-high grass, that gives both voice and a moving body to the breezes that blow.

June 3, 2009 – 8:56 PM

     And in my heaven let there be a bed placed just inside large, twin French doors. And outside one of the doors the field of grass, and outside the other the ocean waves lapping at the shore. And every day a perfect sunset. And every day, beside me in that bed...my Lovely Dawn. Just to hold you as close as I can, and as the sun kisses the water, I kiss your lips. That would be my heaven.
     I miss you! I love you!

Yours Always,
Jared Christopher

June 4, 2009 – 7:07 PM

My Lovely Dawn,

Have you ever noticed how the famous actresses and supermodels of the world all say that they were "such a geek" when they were a teenager? And people generally take them at their word and accept that there must be some kind of "ugly duckling" transformation that commonly takes place. But lately I've begun to wonder if it's more a question of confidence. These beautiful women all share this same story, not because they all share the same physical transformation, but because they all share the same transformation of confidence. Perhaps these women's idea of "geeky" or "awkward" would seem exaggerated if taken in context relative to many girls of the same age, but perhaps their confidence is worse.

Or maybe it's not even a change of confidence...but rather an acceptance that the compliments and attention they begin receiving in their teen years may have a factual basis. But that acceptance may only arrive after repetitious occurences. This is to say that even in adulthood, when paid for their beauty, models and actresses still lack self-confidence, but recognize intellectually that they are perceived as beautiful from an established pattern of behaviors.

As a man I doubt my appearance regularly. I can, however, recognize that although I don't have a natural confidence in my physical appearance (which is an emotional response), I can also recognize that some really beautiful women (first and foremost you, when we were in high school) have found me attractive enough to date. Therefore I can recognize my emotional, self-doubt is simply that...emotional, subjective, and therefore wrong (this is a logical analysis of my emotional response). It is the confidence of logic...or the logic of confidence.

June 4, 2009 – 7:07 PM

    And as I just alluded, this confidence was first born of our relationship. The idea that this geeky, inexperienced guy working at a fast-food restaurant could be going out with a beauty as incredible as you...well, in moments of doubt I would try to remind myself of that in the years that followed. The unfortunate, parallel realization was that my frequent single status was not because of my looks, but rather because no other woman since has matched your character, mind, and heart. I've seen many a beautiful face, but I've never known a beautiful face in such perfect union with a beautiful soul as when I sit and talk with you. You are the consummate and complete beauty!
    I miss you! I love you!

Yours Always,
Jared Christopher

June 5, 2009 – 2:44 PM

My Lovely Dawn,

I am entering my ninth month of unemployment. When I'm not looking for work I try to remain productive with school work, my freelance writing, and the movie script about our teen years. But every additional day without a job grows increasingly frustrating, increasingly terrifying.

The frustration because I don't understand what I am doing wrong. What is it about my resume, my work history, my application process that is not yielding any job offers, and only the occasional job interview? Is there a way to express my innate abilities that my resume is not or cannot? Is the problem only mine indirectly? Am I being victimized by some flaw of the bureaucracy of internet job boards and HR departments who only see X's and O's, but lack the ability to read between the lines? Or is it perhaps the opposite and my resume makes me seem over-qualified for the jobs I'm currently applying?

All this frustration breeds fear. The fear of the day coming when I can't scrape together enough money to make the mortgage payment and all my other bills. The fear of the giant setback this presents to my career and my life. The fear that being broke and possibly soon homeless is a huge factor in your decision not to be with me now and fear of "now" lasting indefinitely. The fear of making a poor choice as to how to make my future the most secure, while finding a way to be fulfilled emotionally in a future career.

I went through a similar process six years ago...I had the toughest time finding a job then as well. Once I did I started below my ability but quickly climbed the ladder to the highest point my career had ever reached. When I'm given an opportunity I show people my ability is exceptional. I just need that opportunity.

June 5, 2009 – 2:44 PM

    And the same applies to you. If you gave me the opportunity I would show you that I can love you in an exceptional way. I would show you my attention to detail, my attention to romance, and my desire to ease the workload of household and family that may fall on you so as to give you more time to be loved. It's a cycle I think I know the pattern to, and I like to break from so as to set a new standard. A standard of love that recalls the great romances of all-time. That is what I want you to have...an epic, complete, and fulfilling love.
    I miss you! I love you!

Yours Always,
Jared Christopher

June 6, 2009 – 7:46 PM

My Lovely Dawn,

I was at a baseball game today...trying desperately to distract from missing you. But instead I found a woman sitting in the row in front of me with two young daughters reminding me of you. Her youngest must have been quite exhausted. She sat on her mother's lap leaning against her chest. The mother holding her so tenderly, patting her back to help her fall asleep, kissing her on the top of her head. It was such a beautiful, loving moment. It reminded me of you with J.

Later in the day I joined my family to celebrate my mom's birthday. My nephews all were there in their usual rawkus behavior. Lots of fighting over the same toys and "he started it". My younger sister sarcastically commented how she "SO wants kids". Even amongst such chaos I actually felt the opposite. I do want kids.

Because I know there are the moments when they just need you to hold them and all the stress and misbehaving of the day can be forgotten for a while. The times when they first discover a new word or phrase, and the delivery of said phrase, from such a young mind, is nothing if utterly charming. The times when a simple lean on a shoulder can show the love their innocent hearts can deliver unexpectedly.

Today, I sought out to not dwell in missing you, but instead I found myself missing you AND the girls, and wishing for a day when we may add a child of our shared creation. A little boy perhaps...to teach how to ride a bike, to love and respect women, and to throw a baseball. A little boy with the heart of his mother.

I miss you! I love you!

Yours Always,
Jared Christopher

June 7, 2009 – 9:35 PM

My Lovely Dawn,

Today I made tremendous strides toward finishing my screenplay. I've written roughly 10 pages in the last few days putting the total length now at an even 100. I may write some more later tonight after sending you this letter.

The pages I've written today surround the time you left me for the college in Minnesota many years ago. The event that surely caused most of our "drifting apart". They have been some of the hardest pages I've had to write. I've incorporated lines from letters you wrote me back then and some of the notes you gave me on the script when you read it last summer. There is something especially pleasing in finding ways to use your actual words to create this new work of art. There is certainly a higher degree of realism as a result.

There will need to be ten to twenty more pages written. It is mostly connecting the dots, as the ending has been written for some time. Years in fact. When those pages are done, I will allow a few select friends and family to read the completed script to verify it's quality, clarity, and continuity. When I am entirely satisfied I will take the step of copyrighting the finished script with the United States Copyright Office and the Screenwriters Guild West. Following copyrighting I will begin submitting the script to screenwriting contests, as well as managers and agents for screenwriters.

The biggest remaining question will be whether or not, at some point, I can attend film school. Attending film school would increase the possibility of directing my own film as opposed to simply selling the script. This is preferable as I am so close to the material and want such a specific finished-product. The problem with that is there will be fewer, if any, studios that would put the power and responsibility of directing in my unproven hands. It may require finding my own, independent financing. On the other hand, simply selling the script may be the fastest way to a fairly substantial payday, which could then pay for film school at a higher caliber institution. But I may be too idealistic to sell my vision to an outside party.

June 7, 2009 – 9:35 PM

      Regardless, when I do finally finish the script, I will be torn on whether or not to ask you to be one of the "friends and family" I ask to read it. I know I will want you to, but I may also want to respect your wish that I not contact you. Oh how I wish I could contact you. There are many days that I can't bear not talking to you.
      I miss you so much! I love you!

Yours Always,
Jared Christopher

June 8, 2009 – 7:49 PM

My Lovely Dawn,

There has been a television program on this week documenting the inner-workings of the White House and President Obama's administration. It is a fascinating study. But the thing I enjoyed the most about it was the impression it gave me about the President and the First Lady, Michelle Obama.

It was not the first time I have noted the openly tender nature of their relationship. There was the fist-bump on the campaign trail, and then the slow-dance at the inauguration...and now, a series of candid photographs captured by the White House photographer. There was one picture where the President had seemingly grabbed his wife from the side, arms around her like a hug sneak-attack. And on his face...the biggest smile ever, his expression saying, "I got you". It is surely a man connecting with his best friend. It is surely a man in love. And it surely stirs my eyes to tears.

What a fantastic relationship. At once rife with an impressive balance of intelligence and an observable maturity, and then waves of playfulness and a youthful spirit. In my lifetime of observation it is an uncommon bond. In my personal opinion it is a divine and enviable relationship. And I do envy it. I wish for a relationship like that. But I know of the President's relationship's equal...it is between you and I.

When you and I stand together there is no partnership with deeper thought, there is no duo with higher ambition, there is no couple with greater passion. At the end of my day, the one thing that is certain...my life is not only full with you, but it overflows, and the excess is love. And when the cup overfloweth with love it spills all around...touching and nourishing many others. First your daughters, then your family, our friends, and some even trickles down to the rest of the world.

June 8, 2009 – 7:49 PM

But without you, the cup goes quite dry, like a desert without rain. The nourishment that could fill the whole of the world is left so lacking it can't fill the hole in my heart. These are not just words, they are the truth of my soul. You mean this much to me. With or without you, you are my First Lady, you are my first love.
I miss you! I love you!

Yours Always,
Jared Christopher

June 9, 2009 – 11:38 AM

My Lovely Dawn,

Out on the bike trail today there was a man walking his dogs (or were they walking him?). He had three dogs...three big, lumbering, panting, adorable English Bulldogs. Looking as though they had the combined strength, and will, to pull a sled in the Iditarod. As I passed them I had to look twice. And then I just flat-out turned around and went back to meet those gentle brutes.

There were two boys; one a very large fellow with a white head and brindle patches, and the other fawn-colored with a white belly. The smallest of the three was a young lady...an absolute sweetheart...also fawn and white. All three were very friendly...came right up to me and let me scratch their heads.

I don't know where my fondness for that breed comes from. But from all my firsthand experience I think I've chosen well. Every bulldog I've ever met has been quite confident, very relaxed, a tremendous athlete, and above all...completely friendly. (Kinda like me. Maybe a little?)

I want to get one. And if ever there was a time I could use that kind of a companion, it would be now. Now when I'm free of most obligation and able to devote lots of time to puppy potty-training and the like. Well...there's also this matter of feeling pretty alone lately.

I'm missing you so. I want so badly to marry you, to hear the girls excitedly shout out "J's home" as I walk in the door after a long day of work, to walk out to the backyard and have a catch with the puppy, and then to come in and help you with dinner. I can just picture it...you standing at the stove, stirring away on something smelling delicious. I sneak up behind you, placing my hands on your hips, and then a kiss on your neck. As romantic as the kiss is, it is surpassed by what I whisper in your ear, "What can I do to help?"

That's what I want for you...for us. Just a stunning passion and communication.

I miss you! I love you!

Yours Always,
Jared Christopher

June 10, 2009 – 7:49 PM

My Lovely Dawn,

I was speaking with a friend this week about my screenplay. She was saying how it seemed unlikely that a woman would marry someone she didn't love. And in my attempt to prove it's plausibility I stumbled upon this line of logic...

I believe divorce rates currently stand at roughly 50% of all marriages. We will ignore the affect serial divorcees have on the overall statistic as I have no idea of that number. So, out of the total number of divorces, what percentage of those end from one, or both, of the spouses "falling out of love" with his/her partner? Meaning it was, at one point, founded in love but something changed. Then, what percentage of divorces did not begin with love? Meaning one, or both, partners married with other things in mind (money/security, family pressure, pregnancy, or, more optimistically, a hope that love could be found once married). A third scenario could be not having a reason FOR entering marriage (either honorable or dishonorable), but rather an inability to turn down a marriage proposal (due to selflessness or weakness of will).

When I consider the very essence of love...what it means, what it should be...I find it difficult to believe that the percentage of divorces brought on by "falling out of love" could be the majority. A true and proper love would suggest a relationship founded with a yin/yang balance of personalities and with an abundance of common interests. This presents less opportunity for disagreement. And when disagreement occurs, true love suggests a relationship of more willing compromise. What better person to lay down one's own stubborn tendencies to, than the person they love and trust the most in the world? If these qualities exist at the beginning of a marriage, then there will likely be fewer problems, and any problems that do arise should be more quickly resolved. I believe, in a true love marriage, things would never progress to the point of divorce.

June 10, 2009 – 7:49 PM

There is also, probably, a low percentage of marriages that begin because one party didn't have the heart to reject the proposal. The possible percentage would immediately be reduced by the fact that this scenario would only apply to one half of each engaged couple (the one proposed to, rather than the proposer). And further reduced by the number who initially accept a proposal but eventually back out before the actual ceremony.

So, to my thinking, this leaves the majority of divorces caused by at least one half of a couple never being in love to begin with. As previously noted this is sometimes a conscious thing (the most obvious example being when someone marries for money). But, perhaps more importantly, how often does this occur unconsciously? How often does someone think they ARE in love when entering a marriage, but are mistaken? How many people are actually healthy and aware enough to diagnose their own emotions? And what would be the primary symptom of love? Or perhaps love is best diagnosed by a complete lack of symptoms. When a person feels the best they've ever felt. A certain sensation of invincibility and the confidence to match.

This is how I feel when I am with you. I believe it was Sir Shakespeare who once wrote something along the lines of, "With her I fear no death, without her I live no life." Without you food is not as rich, music is not as melodic, life is not as full, I feel lethargic and unmotivated. When I am with you I am happy, I am healthy...I am ready to take on the world. This is how I know I love you. This and the fact that in thirteen years I have never met your equal, I have never matched that feeling, I have never stopped thinking of and loving only you.

This is why I know I would marry you.

I miss you! I love you!

Yours Always,
Jared Christopher

June 11, 2009 – 6:17 PM

My Lovely Dawn,

A few hours ago I finished the last finals, of the last classes, of my last quarter, of my sophomore year of college. I will shortly have my Associate's Degree. And it only took me twelve years to do it. In my defense, there were ten years of working fulltime in radio sandwiched in the middle.

I won't get my official grades till next week, but I'm pretty sure I pulled 4.0 in Philosophy and a 4.0 in Culture of Film. I really disliked Biology so I probably only earned a 2.5. And then in PE maybe a 3.5 cause I missed a test that the teacher wouldn't let me makeup for partial credit. That comes on top of my English and Contemporary Mathematics classes from last quarter, my first college classes in nine years, that I finished with 4.0 in both. Kinda cool, kinda proud of that.

But enough about me. I've got some inside info that someone very special to me just finished her first college class in many years. And her result...a 4.0! Congratulations! I'm so proud of you!

I'm proud that you decided to go back to school when others suggested you shouldn't. I'm proud to have walked with you on campus as you first pursued the information of the requirements needed to obtain the degree you are hoping for. I'm proud that technology allowed me to access video of you performing your speech assignments online. I'm proud of how natural you were performing those speeches. I'm proud I could participate in the preparation of one of those speeches, when you asked me to proofread it and make suggestions. And, more than anything, I'm proud that you feel proud of yourself and your accomplishment.

I had a feeling that going back to school would do so much for you. It would provide you some distraction from the monotony of daily life. It would give your girls a more varied impression of the modern woman and her capabilities. It would help you build toward your future career goals. And it would give you this sense of self and accomplishment that my words alone can't quite capture.

June 11, 2009 – 6:17 PM

     I just love that you're doing it. I love that I'm sure you're loving doing it. I love that you're doing it well! And I love you! You're just the most incredible, complete woman I've ever known, and you grow and blossom more and more every day!
     Congratulations! Keep going!
     I miss you! I love you!

Yours Always,
Jared Christopher

June 12, 2009 – 10:08 PM

My Lovely Dawn,

I'm remembering today the first time we saw each other last summer. I had made plans to come to your house to drop off a copy of my screenplay so that you could proofread it. Part of me thought it wasn't going to really happen. Or that I would show up at your door and you would be unaware I was coming and upset that I was there...both reactions the result of an online prank executed by your sister. This is the way my over-analytical mind works.

But I put those worries aside, drove to your house and knocked on your door. The first thing I see as it opens...your oldest daughter L...her long, wavy blonde hair a striking resemblance of her mother at 17. The door opens further to reveal her mother at 30. You wore a white sweater that day and held J. on your hip. Your blonde hair now brown, but the rest almost exactly as I remembered. You were even more stunning than ever.

The nerves I had felt on the drive to your house and the walk to your door had now taken over my tongue. I struggled to find words, and the words I found seemed to come in jumbles and stutters.

I wanted so badly to not have to say anything, but instead to simply wrap my arms around you and hold you. It would have been fitting considering how our relationship had ended all those years ago...you and I frozen in embrace, the dim light of your parent's porchlight revealing the fog of our breath, the cold of winter blocked out by the heat of our unrequited passion.

Later in our reunion year, you revealed to me how the embrace I was longing to share with you upon first glance of you that first meeting last summer, was secretly what you were wanting as well. And this was long before I rediscovered that I was still madly in love with you. Long before you consciously discovered you loved me as well. And long before our love became physical.

It is telling of the bond we created as naïve young kids, with a lack of life experience but an uncommon abundance of intuition. It is telling of the natural chemistry we shared and share. And it is telling of the people we are...fighting our selfish urges for sake of respecting others.

June 12, 2009 – 10:08 PM

Admittedly, the selfish urges eventually won out. But only after it began to seem that we were meant to be together, and would be together in the long run. I still hold on to this hope. I still know this love I feel for you will have no end. I still hope the love you once felt for me is the same as mine...unable to stifle itself for long and bound to rise up again and demand to be fulfilled. I hope this day comes soon.

I miss you! I love you!

Yours Always,
Jared Christopher

June 13, 2009 – 5:48 PM

My Lovely Dawn,

Today was a Saturday and I spent it working on some projects. I cleaned off my writing desk, I filled out some of the paperwork for my college transfer, and I designed a very rough draft of a logo for my film production company.

The logo involves the comedy and tragedy masks...an idea we've spoken of before. I have often felt that a laugh and a cry are two of the most honest gestures mankind is capable of...which I love. I love concentrated truth. In my design, the comedy mask stands foreground, illuminated by a single keylight. And on the wall just behind, it casts a long shadow. Only instead of the broad smile and twinkling eyes of "comedy", we find the shadow holds the downturned eyes and frown of "tragedy".

It is a subtle implication of the duality of man (that all men possess both joy and sadness...that one cannot exist without the other), and it bears reminder of "the tears of a clown"...a concept that I have often identified with. Add the obvious theatrical basis and it seems a fitting image for a film company.

Then, last night, a name for the company came to me in a dream. Rather than take the obvious name "Comedy/Tragedy Productions", I dreamt of a name that works on multiple levels. It will be called "Jest/Cry Productions". Of course it has the superficial meaning of laughter and tears. But I also like that when said quickly it almost sounds like "just cry"...something I feel like saying when I can tell you are stifling your emotions and fighting back your tears. And lastly, within "Jest/Cry" you can find "J.C.", and that is me. Kinda cool, right? Do you like it?

Now I just have to finish the screenplay, learn how to direct, and get financial backing. And probably a million other things. But I've lived a life so far where I have accomplished quite a few of my dreams, so I am optimistic.

June 13, 2009 – 5:48 PM

     That optimism would be even greater if you were here with me. You are such a tremendous example of support. You make me feel smart and talented and even attractive, and I love you for it. And in an interesting coincidence, you are the smartest, most talented, and crazy-beautiful woman I have ever known, and I love telling you these things at every chance I get.

     You are amazing!

     I miss you! I love you!

Yours Always,
Jared Christopher

June 14, 2009 – 7:26 PM

My Lovely Dawn,

As you know I spend a lot of time thinking about you. One of the things I am consistently thinking about, and constantly baffled by, is the seeming lack of love you have for your husband (your exact word in one email was that you felt so "unconnected" to him), and your contrasting deep and passionate love for me. I assume that the explanations you've given me for both of these things are true. And yet there still seems to be a disconnection for you on this topic. So it occurs to me that perhaps there could be a test of some kind you could give yourself to help you wade through the thoughts and emotions of this all. What is love, why is love, who do you love?

It is a series of scenarios and the likely conclusions for a) someone you love, and b) someone you don't love. As you read through them try to make a mental note of which of the conclusions best apply to your husband, and which to me.

If a guy writes you a letter every day for a year:
...when you do love him you think he is the most dedicated, romantic guy ever.
...when you don't love him you think he's being clingy.

If a guy does something he should be too old for:
...when you do love him you think he has youthfulness or a school-boy charm.
...when you don't love him you think he's immature.

If you have a bad day:
...when you do love him you escape to him.
...when you don't love him you want to escape from him.

If you're feeling frisky:
...when you do love him you initiate some fun.
...when you don't love him you make him earn some fun.

If you wear a new dress and he tells you how much he loves it:
...when you do love him the compliment puts you in the mood.
...when you don't love him you wish the man you love had said it instead.

June 14, 2009 – 7:26 PM

If you wear a new dress and he doesn't acknowledge it:
...when you do love him you give a compliment knowing you'll get one in return.
...when you don't love him you get upset that he doesn't notice.

If you decide to have babies together:
...when you do love him it's because you want to have his children.
...when you don't love him it's because children will allow you to hide behind a busier schedule.

If you plan lots of social events together:
...when you do love him it's because you have so much fun together and you want to show the world.
...when you don't love him it's because in social settings you won't have to be alone with him.

If he showers you with affection:
...when you do love him you are the happiest you've ever been.
...when you don't love him it's still not enough.

If you get fifteen minutes of his time:
...when you do love him it is the highlight of the day and leaves you longing for more.
...when you don't love him you would have been okay with only five.

If you don't see him for a week:
...when you do love him his absence hurts, but it makes your heart grow fonder.
...when you don't love him you really don't notice the time apart.

If you are at peace:
...when you do love him it is because he is holding you.
...when you don't love him it is because you are sleeping on the couch.

June 14, 2009 – 7:26 PM

If you were to lose him to an unfortunate death:
...when you do love him you mourn for a lifetime.
...when you don't love him you already know you will marry
again...and to whom.

If your stomach is a jumble of nerves:
...when you do love him it is because he still gives you the
butterflies.
...when you don't love him it is because he gives you an ulcer.

If you think of who you love:
...when you do truly love him his name is Jared.
...when you don't truly love him he is everyone else.

And when HE loves YOU; he still gets the butterflies
when he sees you, he is at peace when he is holding you, he hurts
when he doesn't see you for a day (let alone a week...or a year), his
life without you may as well be an unfortunate death, he cherishes
every fifteen minutes he spends with you, he wants to shower you
with affection, he wants to show you off to all his friends and the
world, he wants to have children with you, he is constantly wanting
to encourage your friskiness, he always notices how beautiful you
look in any new dress or old, and he will always be there for you to
escape to...no, to escape with...for you are his escape as well. And
he is I. And I love you!

Please know that these ideas are brought up because I
believe there are truths that are being ignored, and that, perhaps,
this exercise could help the truth come out. Please consider these
ideas, and if their answers should reveal that I am the one you love,
or love most, then we should be together and you should come back
to me. Please come back to me.

I miss you! I love you!

Yours Always,
Jared Christopher

June 15, 2009 – 8:56 PM

My Lovely Dawn,

I've spent a part of today corresponding with a couple friends of mine who are getting married this summer. It was somewhat comical as I was emailing the bride on my computer and text-messaging the groom on my phone almost simultaneously. It made me think though. It's so nice when you get along with both members of a couple. In part because of the obvious, but also because the only other option seems to be when you don't really get along with one of the members and you end up losing them both.

If I were to, for example, object to or dislike my friend's girlfriend, it would in essence be a death sentence for that friendship. It is any man's right, and perhaps duty, to spend as much time with his girlfriend as possible. If a man doesn't desire this then perhaps his relationship is lacking and should be ended for sake of both parties. But let us discuss a healthy relationship.

The man loves his partner, she is his best friend, they want to do everything together. This would suggest that his friends would generally have to hang out with her when wanting to hang out with him. This can present a problem when guy friends and girlfriend don't get along. In time one, or both, will ask not to have to hang out with the other, and the boyfriend will be forced to choose. Generally he will choose his girl.

I've had a few friendships end in these kinds of circumstance. I generally understand this decision as the girlfriend offers my friend something I can't...sex. Or even affection or romance. It is pretty much the way of things, so I don't fight it. Plus I recognize I'd make the same choice myself. And I've explained this to my friends before. I pride myself on being reliable, and if/when I cancel plans with a friend they understand it must be for a girl. And no girl has ever been more deserving of superceding my friends than you...my best friend. I would rather be with you than anyone else. It's not even close.

June 15, 2009 – 8:56 PM

And when I think of you as this best friend with benefits, I can also project to a future where we're together and see us socializing with all these other great couples. Quite a few of my friends already know you and love you...JP commented the last time he saw you, "she's a cool chick." And I would assume all my friends would react similarly. Because you are incredible. I can picture us having dinners with JP and LSP, going out fishing with BH and KW, sitting at a bonfire with JB and SM, or attending the upcoming nuptials of Paul and Holiday. And I would be so excited to meet all of your friends.

In reality I will be attending the wedding alone, but I will be thinking of you. I will be noting the ceremony, but dreaming of the wedding we would share. Especially our first dance...I've already got the song picked out. A song that would truly speak the truth of my heart at that moment. A song that would bring tears to our eyes...but in a good way. The way that makes the blue of your eyes all the more incredible.

I miss you! I love you!

Yours Always,
Jared Christopher

June 16, 2009 – 9:53 PM

My Lovely Dawn,

For as long as I've been aware of marriage...perhaps of procreation...I have been wary of being a father.

Perhaps it is because I am naturally a perfectionist, and there truly seems to be no perfect way to raise a child. No matter the route you choose to bring that child up, it seems they will inevitably rebel opposite (the child of strict parents wishing for freedom, the child of passive parents seeking discipline simply for the attention it would bring, etc). Plus doesn't every child think everything his/her parents do is the epitome of lame, the apex of embarassing? And eventually, and/or repeatedly, won't they come to hate you for a time?

Perhaps I fear becoming a father because I fear change (which I do). Not only the fear of a new being in my life with all THAT inherent responsibility and newness and unknown...but also the fear of a change in my relationship with my babies' mother. Will I still get enough of her attention? Will I give her enough of mine? Will there be changes I can't even imagine beforehand...until I am presented with them in action?

Or is the simple truth that I fear fathering a child because I don't want an innocent to be like me? My genes, my looks, my personality, my flaws. After dating a couple single moms in recent years, I've come to realize it IS this last fear. Whether by nature or nurture, I don't want to pass myself on to the next generation. There is a song that I love that says it like this, "son... you're so much like me...I'm sorry". This has been my own fear for all of my adult life...until last year.

For you see, I now know love. I love you. I love the entirety of you with every ounce of me. And once there in love with you, where you miraculously loved me too, I was hit by a moment of clarity. It dawned on me now why people are compelled to have children. I understand. On the occasions you mentioned thoughts of our "child together", it hit me quite deeply...it resonated...I felt a change. That change felt magnified tonight.

June 16, 2009 – 9:53 PM

     I watched a movie...a curious film with much I found impressive, and yet an equal amount that disappointed. But the one moment that hit me the hardest was between the onscreen couple...the man, who suffers from an unusual life, an unusual ailment...the woman, who announces she is pregnant with his child. The man's first thought, "what if the child is like me?". The woman's answer..."then I will love it all the more".

     It rocked me to my core. Even now, an hour or two since the movie ended, thinking of that one line and its' sentiment sends a tear streaming down my left cheek. Surely THAT is love. That is the reaction of an amazing woman in true love. And surely a man loved by a woman of that character and caliber, must be kind of an okay guy. With a partner like her, surely a child of their blood and their love would turn out pretty perfect!

     More and more I am finding I am not scared of being a father. Now the fear is, "what if I don't get the chance to be a father with you?"

     I hope you will some day give me that chance. I will love your daughters. I will love the son I will try to give you. I will love you.

     I miss you! I love you!

Yours Always,
Jared Christopher

June 17, 2009 – 12:31 PM

My Lovely Dawn,

As I was doing some cleaning this week I came across a note I had written months ago. I had been watching the TV show you had introduced me to, and one of the characters said some things that reminded me of you and your marriage, so I wrote them down.

"You're emotionally walking away instead of actually walking away. Which is stupid because only one of those is good for your heart." This is what you've done to your husband...instead of being honest and admitting you don't love him and ending the marriage (walking away), you have just walked away emotionally, leaving a shell of yourself to remain. Meaning neither you or your husband could possibly be fulfilled in that marriage. If your heart wasn't paying the consequences before, it certainly is now that I have re-entered the picture and your heart has felt what it is to be in love.

In another scene a woman suggests she never wanted to dump her boyfriend, to which the rebuttal is, "Absolutely, you wanted him to dump you. Much less guilt." You have openly admitted that you don't want to be the bad guy in the end of your marriage, you want it to be your husband's fault, or at least his decision.

Perhaps this is why you allowed yourself to have an affair. And why at one point you allowed yourself to get caught in the affair. You wanted to provoke your husband into doing what you cannot...ending the marriage.

It's the same reason you walk away emotionally. You want to give him as little of yourself as you can, so as to frustrate him enough so that he wants out, so that he can find a partner who gives him the emotional support most men secretly need. The problem with this is that your husband is probably not dumb...he knows what he has in you...he knows he will never do any better than you...and he would rather have half of you than to let you go to someone else.

June 17, 2009 – 12:31 PM

It is like the story of King Solomon and the baby being claimed by two mothers. While one mother is content to let Solomon cut the baby in half, the other would rather lose the baby entirely than to see it harmed. I let you go, so that you would no longer be torn between these two ideas; staying with your husband for your children, or finding personal fulfillment with me. But I know in my heart you won't be happy. I just wonder if being unhappy will be motivating enough to cause you to make the change to be with me. As we know, we are both somewhat of masochists...remaining in painful situations because they are all we know.

But at least one of us would like to leave those ways behind and give some intense happiness a try. Won't you join me?

I miss you! I love you!

Yours Always,
Jared Christopher

June 18, 2009 – 12:20 PM

My Lovely Dawn,

An old friend contacted me today on Facebook...Priscilla. She was a good friend and neighbor of JP's and then she worked with us at Dairy Queen for a while. You may or may not have worked with her. It reminded me how much I want to plan a DQ reunion. A few years ago I was supposed to go to my highschool reunion but didn't. There weren't many people from highschool I cared to see again (that I wasn't already still in contact with).

But I kept telling everyone that I would go to a DQ reunion in a heartbeat. Most of the best friends I ever had all worked there at the same time. We had that mini-reunion at my house back in November (with JP and MH and you and I), and that was so fun, but too short and too small. I want to see everyone together.

It still boggles my mind how there was something special about the group we worked with...something special in the water there. Just think of all the relationships that blossomed working there, and in time grew into marriages; KS and LS, DS and KS, MM and CM, WG and MG, JP and LSP. It wouldn't surprise if I was forgetting someone. I don't know what has come of most of those couples, if they're still together, but it's still so impressive that five couples met at a random fast-food restaurant at the same time and ended up married.

I really want to find out how many of them are still together and what the kids they have/had together look like. And of course I want to catch up with the co-workers I didn't mention, that married outside the DQ dating pool.

As anxious as I am to plan the reunion, I also want to wait. Part of me wants to be able to present a screening of a finished movie that was inspired by my days there (and perhaps filmed in the store). If not a screening, I would like to at least have a finished script. But more importantly, I want to wait to have the reunion until there are six couples that met at DQ that will be attending.

I want to be able to walk in to that reunion with my new girlfriend, or fiance, or wife; my Lovely Dawn, on my arm. Then they will all know that the movie will have a sequel with a happy ending.

June 18, 2009 – 12:20 PM

     And if we can't walk in to the reunion together, I want to be able to see you there. If not an excuse to show off our love, let the reunion be an excuse for us to meet once again under guise of an acceptable situation. And let our chemistry do as it may.

     Regardless of time, regardless of reason, all I want is to be reunited with you...the pure, shy girl making the ice cream cakes, who became the forever love of the nervous, funny guy, at the Dairy Queen on fast-food row just outside of Seattle in 1995.

     I miss you! I love you!

Yours Always,
Jared Christopher

June 19, 2009 – 9:01 PM

My Lovely Dawn,

I had a fairly productive day today. I began, as I do most days, with my workout. Lots of situps for my abs and today that was followed by working my legs; lunges, squats, calf raises.

After the workout I showered, made myself breakfast of an omelet, an English muffin with butter and jam, and two glasses of orange juice. So much for that ab work.

After breakfast I logged into my online college classes. My grades were expected to be ready today and I was excited to see if I had done as well as I thought. In two classes I earned 4.0's (as expected), but to my surprise I pulled a 3.7 in Biology. I did better on the final than I thought I would. I think you'd be proud of me for that one. It was the last chapter on genetics, alleles, phenotypes, etc. That helped me. It will be a couple more weeks before I receive my degree to make it officially official.

After checking my grades I started to write. I've been working for an arts and entertainment website doing some freelance writing while I look for a fulltime position. Today I finished two articles; the first a brief calendar of local concerts for the weekend, the second a review of a new album by a singer named Pete Yorn. The album is good, I think you'd like it. You might like some of the concerts too. Third Eye Blind and the Wallflowers are both playing...feels like a '90's nostalgia weekend, huh?

As I'm finishing the second article I receive an email from the website that my first paycheck has gone through. I guess I am now officially a professional writer. I'd be more excited if the pay was better. I'd also be more excited if the paycheck was for my screenplay or an advance from a book publisher for the book I'm working on.

Oh well. In these tough times we take what we can get and keep striving toward something better. Whenever you read this, please know I am always striving for something better. I want to be a great man and do great things. And my muse? You! A great woman!

I miss you! I love you!

Yours Always,
Jared Christopher

June 20, 2009 – 11:34 AM

My Lovely Dawn,

It has been a wonderfully warm and sunny Spring in Seattle this year. There have been record high temperatures almost daily and, at one point, so many consecutive days without rain that Seattle set a new local record dryspell. But as we near the official beginning of Summer, the Summer equinox tomorrow, ironically the skies have covered over, the clouds have opened up and here is the rain.

Without direct sunlight sneaking through the breaks in my window blinds, I find less motivation to get out of bed and work out. Instead I lay under the covers, silently dictating a letter. I am both author and transcriber. You are both recipient and inspiration. The letter will be complete within me before ever laying hand to keyboard.

Late last night as I lay alone in this same bed I began my nightly ritual...my daily prayer...my conversation with God. It isn't a formal prayer, it doesn't follow a consistent formula. It is often rambling, it is often interrupted by distracting thoughts, but it is always returned to, to leave as completed..."Amen".

My prayer is sometimes a request...wishing to be a better man, to find work, to have strength to overcome my recent challenges. But more often these prayers are a simple "thanks". Thanks for health, thanks for home, thanks for friends, thanks for family. And thanks for you.

Even with our current distance I am still immeasurably thankful that you came into my life; first as teenagers, and then last year as adults. And as I searched for the words to express this appreciation, I came upon this;

"God, thank you for bringing Dawn into my life. Thank you for giving her such incredible strength and character...an innate goodness that radiates from her like heat from a light. A goodness that has touched me, absorbed into the core of me, and inspired me to become worthy of it. Thank you for making her as you have, that she should influence me for the better. Thank you God for lovely Dawn."

June 20, 2009 – 11:34 AM

It is a prayer I have made before, with less eloquence, and will make again. It is a prayer I will hope to some day make as you lay peacefully beside me. And in the morning this silent prayer will become open praise...my vocal recognition that I am the man I am because of the love and support of the most incredible partner...the love of my life...my lovely Dawn.

I miss you! I love you so much!

Yours Always,
Jared Christopher

June 21, 2009 – 11:17 AM

My Lovely Dawn,

Another dreary day and I dwell in silent contemplation. Marriage. Gender. Intention. More specifically; I wonder if men and women don't have dramatically different intentions upon entering into a marriage. As a DJ, I once joked; "Men beware, women will try to change you. Women beware, men will try to watch you change." It is somewhat crass, but, as is often the case, there is also many a truth spoken in jest.

Men will generally enter into a marriage when they find complacency...a quiet security in their mental, emotional, and sexual compatibility with the woman of their choosing. They are finally satisfied, or at least more satisfied than ever before, with the state of a relationship and they would like that state to remain as it is forever. Whatever the sexlife before marriage, men believe it will continue after marriage, if not increase. So why then do we find husbands, when away from their wives, in the company of friends at sports bars or in locker rooms, will make jokes like, "What food is known to decrease female sex-drive?...Wedding cake."

Because where men feel a marriage is a way to "lock a relationship in place," women feel that a marriage is a stepping stone to greater heights of their relationship. Where men feel marriage is a reason to relax, having already achieved their goal of "locking down" their dream girl, a woman expects a marriage to increase a man's growth. This difference causes the conflicts of which withholding sex is sometimes a negotiating tactic.

Women choose who they marry based on what they feel that man's potential is. What he can become. They have plans for what they would change about their relationship, expect that marriage will obligate their partner to make those changes, and proactively attempt to complete the transformation. The question is; are these changes asked because a woman plans to ride the man's coattails on the uphill rise of change, or is it because she IS changing and wishes her man to "keep up"? Is it conscious or subconscious? Or is it neither and the changes are actually more a result of a woman marrying too young? Only in time does a woman discover who she really is, and what she should have looked for in a husband, and attempts, in vain, to make her husband fit her new realization of self?

June 21, 2009 – 11:17 AM

As a man myself, I don't understand the female tendency or experience. If a woman wants a well-mannered husband, then marry a well-mannered man. Don't marry a man who finds delight in the humor of bodily functions and then expect him to "grow up". The parallel point is that if a man wanted to marry a sexually reserved woman he would have married one. But he married a young, provocative woman and later found her changed to a more prudish form after marriage or children.

And you can't find blame with a woman for wanting upward improvement, but in reality you can't order a burger and expect to be delivered a steak. And you can't find blame with a man who is happy with things as they are, but where is your ambition or desire to improve, especially if it would please someone you love. No, the blame is with a couple who don't communicate, or know how to communicate, these ideals while in the midst of a burgeoning relationship. Halves of couples both constantly think their way is right, not just for themselves but also for their partner. But men and women are categorically different, and we all need to realize this.

Why this isn't a required course of study in high school I don't know. Or at least a certificate program in coordination with obtaining a marriage license. Women need to be more informed of the inability and/or lack of desire men have to change, to expect less change and therefore to work harder or wait longer to find what they want in a man before a marriage. Men need to be more informed of women's inclination to change and that women mature in bursts, and that an unexpected burst can leave him far behind, so they must always strive for improvement, especially once married.

Please know that I am constantly working towards this self-improvement. I truly believe once we're together you will find a man very close to a complete person. With a balance of mental, emotional, physical, and spiritual.

I miss you! I love you!

Yours Always,
Jared Christopher

June 22, 2009 – 12:42 PM

My Lovely Dawn,

I got to spend some time with my nephews this weekend. They are all growing up so differently.

LA, the oldest, currently loves to join the adults in games of croquet or charades. In fact, most family gatherings he is the gaming ringleader. In charades he is now able to come up with his own movie titles and give his own clues. And he's not bad at it. But he needs to learn more movies because he's used "Transformers" a couple times.

NP, the baby brother, is walking everywhere now. His favorite activity seems to be getting into whatever he's told not to get into. His second-favorite activity must be playing the drums...often on things he's told not to drum on. He would likely make a good actor someday as he is the most facially expressive baby I've ever seen. He would probably have to play mostly bad guys as he almost always has a scratch or bruise somewhere on his face from headbutting almost everything.

Then there is the middle boy, TJ. He's kind of the sweetheart of the three. Terribly finicky eater (like his uncle), but a sweetheart. At a recent family gathering it came time for him to go home...he usually goes around the room giving everyone a 'goodbye' hug. On this night he gave my brother's girlfriend, Kiley, two hugs. When asked why Kiley got two hugs and my brother, Jeff, got only one, TJ quickly replied, quite matter-of-factly, "because when you have soft hair you get more hugs." How sweet is that?

I'm sure TJ would have a couple hugs for you. Another way in which he is like his uncle.

I miss you! I love you!

Yours Always,
Jared Christopher

June 23, 2009 – 3:04 PM

My Lovely Dawn,

I've been thinking about something my sister asked me about you months ago...she wondered what I loved most about you. My first response was that I loved everything about you. Then as I began listing some of the things I loved, I mentioned how easy it was to be with you. My sister was puzzled by that idea. "Easy?" she asked. It turned out she was thinking of how difficult it has been, and will be, for us to be together permanently. But that's not what I was meaning. I was talking about the fact that when we're together, in the same room, things are easy.

There is the ease of communication that allows us to talk for hours at a time, shifting topics seemlessly from politics to sports to psychology and so many more. Truly amazing conversation where neither of us leads or follows for long.

There is the ease of affection where we can't seem to keep our hands off each other. Whether it's me wrapping my hands around your waist, or you sliding in next to me on the couch with an arm around my neck and your hand on my thigh. The only difficulty is deciding which is better...kissing you or you kissing me.

There is an ease of trust. This is the most important as it enables the ease in conversation and affection. When we're together we can trust that no conversation topic will be judged or off-limits. When we're together we can trust that no gesture of affection will be rebuffed or unappreciated.

Finally, there is an ease, or easing up, of my competitiveness. This is important because I often lose myself in the heat of battle and try to win at most everything I do, with most everyone. But when I'm standing beside you I don't care about winning. If the competition is with you, I can gladly and honestly hope that you will win. Or maybe I don't care about winning because when I'm standing beside you I've already found the greatest prize of all...my one and only true love, you. After a win like that a man will surely find a calmness...an ease.

You are my peace. I miss you! I love you!

Yours Always,
Jared Christopher

111

June 24, 2009 – 4:23 PM

My Lovely Dawn,

There are times that I hate the struggle I go through without you...I grow weary of keeping my hope alive. But other times, I think of all the couples I know, and wonder...what was their struggle? What is their story? And, would I trade this unfulfilled yet epic devotion for a completed mediocrity?

I doubt most couples have a story that anyone outside of the relationship cares to hear. The men never faced a fight to win the heart of their one true love. The women were never presented with an epic romance or swept off their feet by the soulmate they never saw coming. It is generally an acceptable union of those that can live together, and not the discovery of two people who cannot live without the other.

How many of the couples I know remember their marriage proposal? How many remember it with fondness or pride? How many with disappointment? How many women are robbed of a proper and beautiful marriage proposal by the lack of creativity and initiative of the average male?

I don't know.

What I know is that I can't settle for less than being with you. I can't be in an average relationship. I couldn't do it before knowing you loved me and I can't now, having touched the perfection we find together.

I know you are my muse. You inspire in me this incredible well of romantic desire and ingenuity. I will write you movies and books, poetry and letters. I will take beautiful photographs for you. I will cook you candlelight dinners. I will plot and plan every kind of detail of life that may bring you love. I already have plans of how I would propose to you, places I would take you on vacation, and speeches I would make at our wedding before our first dance (to a song I have also already planned). And all of these things will be both thoughtful and heartfelt so that you will always have layers of meaning to find and remember.

But more and more I begin to wonder if women truly want these things. They seem to love to visit with romance in bookstores and movie theaters, but it seems quite rare that they want that romance in their homes. It certainly doesn't seem required...save for a handful of designated occasions spread across a year.

June 24, 2009 – 4:23 PM

Is this lack of romance a result of a generally incapable male public that has conditioned the female gender not to expect much of us? Or is it not expected, and therefore not required, because it is not truly desired by women? If it is the latter, than what is desired in place of romance? Stability? Security? Control?

This last suggestion is an interesting one. Do women like to feel in control of their relationship? As the more delicate of the sexes women cannot control physically, so perhaps they have evolved so as to seek a partner that they can control mentally or emotionally. To control emotionally they must limit their loss of control.

Where the way to a man's heart may be through his stomach, the way to a woman's heart is through her heart. And when a woman's heart is found and exposed she is vulnerable. And maybe vulnerability is weakness, and weakness is loss of control.

So women take strides, consciously or unconsciously, to choose a partner who will never quite access her heart and make her feel vulnerable. Perhaps women have chosen to live in control of their unfulfilling lives, rather than to lose themselves in a man that makes them weak in the knees and out of "control".

Perhaps this is one of the reasons why you have left me behind? The willingness you found to break your marriage vow to be with me was a symptom of your loss of control...the loss of control that resulted from me seeing you truly and touching your heart.

I would not apologize for touching your heart, but I would apologize for making you feel vulnerable. I can only promise, with me, you are always safe. Because your security is mine, and when you find happiness only then can I find mine. This is the way it has to be and this is the way it is. Because you are my soulmate.

I miss you! I love you!

Yours Always,
Jared Christopher

June 25, 2009 – 9:15 PM

My Lovely Dawn,

Continuing or expanding some of the thoughts I had yesterday:

I'm wondering how often an epic love story is also true. Conversely, are the true love stories ever epic? Or are the true stories so common that they never get written? Replaced by a prettier lie...the poetry of imagination and fantasy?

What about the tragedies? Do the true tragedies more often find their way into the spotlight? Or perhaps there are simply more OF them? Or are the best stories both epically loving and epically tragic?

What will come of our story? Will it be love or tragedy? I know what my choice would be. I would choose that our story ends in tragedy. An epic Greek tragedy where characters are too stubborn to change and as a result lose their true love. And the tragedy becomes a film.

But in the sequel...

The story begins in affair, and an epic one at that...the affair turns to tragedy, and a year-long separation where the boy writes his girl a daily letter of love and devotion...and the letters become a book...and the movie wins an Oscar...and the boy wins back his girl.

An epic tale of life-imitating-art-imitating-life. An epic tale of perserverance. An epic tale of redemption. An epic tale of love.

Now if I could only think of a name.

I miss you! I love you!

Yours Always,
Jared Christopher

June 26, 2009 – 6:55 PM

My Lovely Dawn,

What strange hands of fate caused our reunion? It began when my sister and her family moved into a new house a couple blocks away from my parents' house. One day, while out on a walk, she ran into you and your sister, also walking in the neighborhood. It turns out you two live a block away from each other, which is, in turn, very near my parents' home. To this day I wonder what compelled you to purchase a house so near to my parents'...where I lived when we first met? Were you aware of this when you moved there? Or had you forgotten?

Word of my sister running into you came back to me almost immediately. It forced me to think of you and the love I once knew. And once I was thinking of you, curiousity would get the better of me. I was compelled to see you.

If I saw you, what would I see? Having occasionally spoken to a few of your sisters at various points over the years, I knew you had at least two children. Would those pregnancies have changed your appearance? Would it have mattered to me if it had changed?

First, I sought to see you from a safe distance, through the cover of the anonymous internet. I began to search for you on the website Myspace. I found one of your sisters before finding you. But from there it was easy to connect to you. Once at your page, I could see pictures of you, and see how your family had grown...three children...all girls...all beautiful...just like their mom...who looked just as stunning as I remembered.

Knowing your myspace page would also allow me to eventually contact you. I made the calculated decision to write you on your birthday. Technically it was the day after your birthday, as your birthday fell on a Sunday when I wasn't at work, on the computer. Not knowing if you would welcome my unexpected contact I decided to proceed cautiously...I merely wrote you, "Happy Birthday". I thought I would see if you responded to that before attempting anything more complicated. I had no idea then where it would go.

June 26, 2009 – 6:55 PM

      I had no idea what fate had in store for us. No idea that I would fall for you again. Or perhaps I had never picked myself up from the first time I fell for you.

      And as I sit here today, I have no idea what the hands of fate hold for us in the future. I pray that there is a future for us, and that our fate allows me to hold your hand...in love, in marriage, and infinitum.

      I miss you! I love you!

Yours Always,
Jared Christopher

June 27, 2009 – 4:46 PM

My Lovely Dawn,

Speaking with my sister, JLH, recently she revealed to me that she was at an end-of-year picnic at LA' elementary school. She tells me while she was there she saw you also enjoying the picnic with L. You approached her to say 'hello' and to share a brief conversation.

Simultaneously, I have been corresponding with two of your sisters who have been giving me advice on my screenplay...specifically helping me with the religious perspective that they are more educated in than I. This is a role I would rather was filled by you, questions I would rather ask you, but this is not currently possible.

It seems strange to me these parallel occurrences. I love that you and my sister speak, and I would enjoy you becoming friends. I also prefer to be on good terms with your sisters, if not friends. But I wish that both were done with you and I together and in witness to the building comraderie of our bonding families. I want to be there with you.

As it is, these second-hand accounts of your activities or your status only serve to frustrate and compel me to want to see you myself. It is like the cruelest form of a tease.

And now that I'm thinking about it, why would you initiate that conversation with my sister? Wouldn't there be some awkwardness since both of you know the pain of our separation? Wouldn't you assume that the word of your conversation with JLH would get back to me? Do you want me to know that? Do you want me to be reminded of you in hopes that I contact you (enabling you to hear from me while not feeling guilty of initiating the communication)?

Are you trying to see if JLH, as a "test sample" of my family, would hold a grudge against you for having hurt their brother/son? Are you trying to bond with her in hopes of our eventual reunion? Are you trying to reach out to me indirectly through her? Any of these scenarios seem possible.

June 27, 2009 – 4:46 PM

      If you are trying to reach out to me, how do I respond? Do I take on the responsibility, giving you a clear (or clearer) conscience? Would contacting you give you an emotional lift? Would that lift remind you of what we share and motivate you to be with me? Or would it give you energy and some degree of fulfillment without forcing you to do the hard, and honest, work of officially ending your marriage?

      Because, although I love even small pieces of your time and attention, ultimately that is not enough. I want to be with you forever. In a just and honest marriage. So how do I get to there? What actions can I take to best inspire you to sacrifice all and come back to me?

      I don't know.

      I just know I miss you! I love you!

Yours Always,
Jared Christopher

June 28, 2009 – 6:03 PM

My Lovely Dawn,

There are days when writing to you is harder than others. Today it is hard. It would be so much easier if I had a muse to spark my inspiration...do you know of any?

As it is, I have no cute anecdotes of my nephews...I have nothing deep, thoughtful, or provocative to philosophize on...I have no breaking news of what is going on in my life. I'm just blasé.

What is worse...today I've had less hope of seeing you, of being with you, again. I am aware that these things come and go in cycles, so I will shine it on as best I can today, hoping that tomorrow something may happen...my nephews may say something charming...a thought will cross my mind that is fascinating...I will get called for a job interview...and I will be compelled to share it with you in writing.

Let today be a day for catching our breath...recharging...so that for the next 290+ days I may give you more days and letters of exquisite thought and passion and poetry and love. The stuff that you deserve.

Oh how I miss you! I love you!

Yours Always,
Jared Christopher

June 29, 2009 – 12:18 AM

My Lovely Dawn,

Have you ever gone to a movie and been the only one in the theater? That happened to me tonight.

Was it because I chose the last showing of the day, late on a Sunday night? Was it my choice of theater...the one that is losing most of its business to the newer, bigger theater a few blocks away? Or was it the film? The answer is likely "all of the above", but the portion of blame falling on the film is undeserved.

At one point in the year of our reunion I told you of a film called "Brick". You borrowed my copy. You told me how much you loved it. The movie I saw tonight was from the same writer/director and it was called "The Brothers Bloom".

It was absurd and silly and smart and quirky and charming and...and just plain good. It's parts weren't necessarily unique, the influence from other films felt somewhat obvious, and yet it was still so original. A new, and somewhat surprising, packaging of classic features. As I thought about it, I felt the film was a little like me.

And like the film, that I watched alone in that theater, there may be only one person who has discovered ME...only one person who knows how good I am...only one person who loved everything about me, even MY flaws.

As I drove away from the theater I was trying to think of a way I could let you know of "The Brothers Bloom". I think you would like it. I think it would make you happy. I think I will consider my options further when it comes out on DVD.

In the meantime, I will hope to find more welcome distraction, and to stockpile more wonderful art to some day share with you.

I miss you! I love you!

Yours Always,
Jared Christopher

120

June 30, 2009 – 4:58 PM

My Lovely Dawn,

The news was all bad today. I just don't know how much more I can take. I just don't know if I am strong enough to continue in this world that I don't understand and that doesn't understand me.

I think I am a smart, hard-working employee...and yet I can't find work.

I am a responsible and respectful citizen...and yet I may soon lose my home.

I am a talented and creative writer...and yet the world cannot see the foresight of my vision.

I am a loyal and giving friend...and yet my friends don't have time or room for me in their lives.

I am a romantic and passionate man...and yet the love of my life has abandoned me.

The love of my life...the woman who, perhaps, sees these noble qualities in me better than anyone...abandoned me.

You abandoned me.

Where is justice? The justice due to a man of such intense ideals. A man who always gives you what you ask.

When I tried to end our relationship, when I began to see that it was headed toward something deep and complicated and immoral, and you asked me to come back...I came back because I love you.

When you showed up at my door because you were feeling the pressure of the life you have created for yourself...I let you in because I love you.

June 30, 2009 – 4:58 PM

When you asked me to hold you because in my arms you feel peace...I held you because I love you.

When you decided you had to return to your marriage for sake of your daughters...I let you go because I love you.

When I suffer through all the sun-less days and cry myself to sleep at night...I hurt because I love you.

And you are gone.

Why have you gone?

Tell me you will come back to me when our situations are less complicated. Give me this hope to cling to. If you can't tell me this...tell me nothing. For I fear I can't take any more bad news.

I miss you! I love you!

Yours Always,
Jared Christopher

July 2009

∞

Summer

July 1, 2009 – 7:33 PM

My Lovely Dawn,

      I was having a conversation with a colleague recently about art and art criticism...we were presuming the criticism my screenplay would receive en route to its production and/or upon its theatrical release. Although I often write critiques of new music for my online column, I feel it is one of the least honorable forms of writing (behind the tabloids). My only consolation is that I'm fortunate to be able to write whatever I want, and I generally am able to write only about records that I like and recommend. I want to turn people on to great music, not broadcast to the world the perceived shortcomings of the music I don't care for. And part of the reason for this is:

      Even an accurate, perhaps even poetic, judgment of the lack of quality in a piece of art, is less important than the attempt, successful or not, to create the art in the first place. The criticism cannot exist without the original work and therefore can never surpass the importance of the original. It may be of higher quality, but never higher importance.

      High art or low, good art or bad...it doesn't matter. The important thing is the sincere attempt by the artist to create something from nothing, and for that creation to express something of the artist's self to the world. For there is magic in creation.

      In terms of art, we, as humanity, should join together in celebration of common interest and common passion...not to unite in common negativity and dissent. This is not to say we cannot have a critical and dissenting opinion...it is just to say we should follow as our mothers have told us...when we don't have anything nice to say, we don't say anything at all.

July 1, 2009 – 7:33 PM

For, truly, what good comes from belittling those who are seeking their voice through art? And, quite frankly, how often are the critics of art proven wrong by the passage of time and the changing of societal taste and norms?

As we have discussed before, even Vincent Van Gogh was not a success in his life. Or remember in Amadeus, the film about Mozart, where the King of Salzburg (or whatever his title) criticizes Mozart's latest work as having "too many notes". Mozart's reply, "it has just as many notes as were required". And we cannot judge it, for it is his creation, and only the artist knows of how his art should be.

I miss you! I love you!

Yours Always,
Jared Christopher

July 2, 2009 – 4:01 PM

My Lovely Dawn,

My life recently has taken on the feel of living in prison. The closest I've ever come to prison anyways. Days of the week blend and blur until they become lost in the redundant meanderings of monotony.

And, as I suspect it is in prison, my outlets become two-fold; writing and working out.

My writing consists of screenplays, an online music column, and these letters to you. They all serve to keep my mind active and sharp.

My work outs consist of legs, arms, and core. They all serve to keep my body active and sharp. And to make me look kinda hot when my shirt is off.

I have this conscious desire to be the most well-rounded person I can be...a Renaissance man if you will. I want to be conversant on all topics; politics, sports, philosophy, entertainment, academics, etc. I want to surprise people with my physique and my athletic ability. And to cap everything off with an unstoppable heart and inconquerable soul.

I want to be all of these things so that I may always give you what you need. A strength when you are feeling unsure. A sensitivity when you are feeling vulnerable. A pride when you are feeling accomplished. A humility when you have proven me wrong. An uplift when you walk into a room. A love when you wake up every day.

I would give you anything for you are my everything.

I miss you! I love you!

Yours Always,
Jared Christopher

July 3, 2009 – 6:44 PM

My Lovely Dawn,

There are times when I try not to think of you. Because when I'm thinking of you I am missing you and longing to be with you again. And that can be saddening. But it is a useless endeavor. Everywhere I go, everything I do, rings of you.

To drive around the city is to see the many places we have been together...as kids and as adults. Places we have shared movies and walks and drinks and more.

To visit with my family is to be only blocks away from your home. Where we have met on many occasions and shared some of our best conversations.

To listen to the radio is to hear the songs that remind me of you. So many songs, each of which we share in love and memory.

Sometimes I turn the radio off, sometimes I stay away from my parents' house, sometimes I stay off of the streets hidden away from the reminders. But even this is useless.

For even to wake up in my room in the morning is to be reminded of you. To look at the empty pillow beside me...the pillow where once you rested your head...the pillow that held your scent for too short of a time...is to be reminded of you. To lay in the bed where we once shared the most incredible love...the most incredible touch...the most incredible passion...is to be reminded of you. To glance around the rooms of my home and notice the presents you had given me...so many gifts for such a confined and abbreviated relationship...is to be reminded of you.

Then again, even if I left this room, this house, this town, this state...I could not escape. For to fill my lungs with air is to be reminded of you. For every breath I take you are on my mind and in my heart. For you have left an impression so deep in my soul that I will never shake your memory...I will never lose this love. It will always be you.

That is unless my dreams and prayers are answered...and then it will always be us.

I miss you! I love you!

Yours Always,
Jared Christopher

July 4, 2009 – 9:41 PM

My Lovely Dawn,

Happy Fourth of July! Independence Day...a day meant to celebrate the birth of our country, and yet I'm contemplating my own independence.

I have found over the years that I am rather capable at being independent. There aren't many things I don't know or can't learn to do...on my own and for myself.

Was I born with an ability for self-reliance that then led me to find myself frequently putting it to use? Or has my personality created situations that alienated people, or distrusted them, therefore requiring me to become independent?

Either way, I have played the primary role in manifesting a situation where I currently know that I am good at being alone. But I wish that it weren't so natural, that I would find a higher need, a desperation perhaps, to force myself to depend on others. And in my need for others, I will find myself asking for, and accepting, more help. And I will display less judgment of the quantity and quality of the help I receive.

I need to change something. I am tired of being alone. And the one person I've found trust and comfort in, allowing myself to be vulnerable and in need of, is not available to me.

But oh how I wish you were. I wish you could find the kind of independence that would allow you to be with me. I wish the fireworks I saw tonight came more frequently...the result of the sparks that always occur when my lips are gifted with yours.

Happy Fourth of July.
I miss you! I love you!

Yours Always,
Jared Christopher

July 5, 2009 – 5:26 PM

My Lovely Dawn,

Today I have been downloading the photographs I took at yesterday's Fourth of July barbecue. It took place in my sister's cul-de-sac with all of my family and most of the neighbors in attendance. Days ago I had written to you of my nephews and their varied personalities... today, as I scroll through the film from yesterday, I find that I have captured an image of my nephews that pretty accurately displays each as they most often are...a still frame of their essence. I wanted to share these pictures with you.

Here is LA, always the serious one, in full concentration of the task at hand...playing Army.

Here is TJ, always the sweetheart, in company of his latest crush...or is it she that has a crush on him?

Here is NP, always the daredevil, with a fresh bump on his head and one of his classic quizzical expressions on his face.

I look at all of them and wonder, "What would our son be like if we had one?" I tend to think he would be a mix of his cousins. He would have times of quiet seriousness like LA. He would have a sweet and natural charm like TJ. He would have a bit of flair for the dramatic and love of music like NP.

And if there is any justice, he would have his mother's eyes.

Oh how I want to see those eyes again.

I miss you! I love you!

Yours Always,
Jared Christopher

July 6, 2009 – 8:14 AM

My Lovely Dawn,

Last night I dreamt of you.

I went to your house expecting to take you out on a date, but upon arrival I found your house a flurry of activity. There were your kids, your parents, your grandparents, your in-laws, and, most surprisingly, your husband. I was still invited in.

At one point we sat beside one another...you on the left, me on the right. On your left your grandfather. He seemed confused by the situation and he asked where your husband was, not realizing your husband sat to his left. Even in a dream our connection seemed to outweigh that of your husband.

The dream further unfolded...mostly in that illogical way dreams flow. Your mother quizzed me on my intentions with you...what movie was I planning on taking you to. I didn't have an answer. I was more concerned with the conversation I was overhearing between you and your husband. I didn't hear his comment but your response was loud and clear..."but that isn't what we agreed upon." You began to cry.

Was he retracting his word that he would "allow" you to go out with me? Was that one date symbolic of our real-life future? And his broken promise representing the promise he made, and will eventually break, to mutually agree t a divorce?

As your tears fell in my dream, all I wanted was to comfort you and hold you. Now, fully awake, it is still my greatest desire. Internationally, kissing and sex often get more attention...but, for me, it always comes back to the simple joy of holding you...where two bodies become one. All things begin and end with holding you. If I could choose one thing for a lifetime it would be to hold you. If I could choose an afterlife, my Heaven would be in your arms, holding you.

I long to hold you again. I promise, if given the chance, I would never let you go...you, the woman of my dreams.

I miss you! I love you!

Yours Always,
Jared Christopher

July 6, 2009 – 11:07 AM

My Lovely Dawn,

Last night I dreamt of you...today I heard from you.

A week ago I was in agony, one of the darkest days I've had since you cut me out of your life. In desperation I wrote you on Myspace. I don't know what I was thinking, why I gave in to the impulse to write you, but I did. I heard nothing for a week. I assumed you were ignoring me.

This morning you replied. Your reply is long and complicated and confusing and frightening and inspiring:

Jared,

What the hell are you doing?? You put me in a very bad situation by contacting me. You asked me to quit messing around and just rip off the "band aid". I tried to do just that. I'm trying to do just that. Don't you think it's excruciating for me not to contact you? Don't you understand how hard it is for me not to drive by your parent's a thousand times a day in hopes that I'll see your car or catch a glimpse of you? And, then, in a moment of weakness, when I do drive by your parent's and happen to see your car, don't you know that I go home and cry in my driveway?

I'm supposed to tell my husband if you try to contact me. I assured him that you wouldn't. Do you know why I assured him? Because I told him that you are an upstanding guy who would honor my request.

I have no faith that you won't go tell my sister that we've been in contact. Then she will tell others and eventually it will get out of hand. That makes me look like I'm keeping secrets...that I'm a liar. I don't know what the right and honest thing is for me to do. Why did you put me in this position? I'm trying to do things the right way...the honorable way.

I'm having a hellish time. Don't you know that I read your articles...that I want to respond and tell you how amazing you are? Do you know why I don't? Because that is unfair of me...cruel of me. Completely unfair and awful. Can't you see that I don't want to keep hurting you over and over? I need time. I've promised time...I'm sticking to my promises.

I have told the truth to my family. I've told my dad that I love you. That I don't know how I'm supposed to stop. I've told my younger sister that I'd rather be with you...

132

July 6, 2009 – 11:07 AM

Jared...please...leave me alone! I'm not strong. I hope all the time that I'll see you. I can't live the duality. So leave me alone while I sort everything out. If you contact me, then I'll contact you, and, then, the pain won't stop, the lying won't stop, nothing will be resolved.
I love you.

After reading it I got in the shower. But I couldn't stop thinking of your words. They rushed through my mind like the water rushing over my head. They so consumed me I didn't realize how long I stood under the water until I noticed my fingertips had pruned. Your words so consumed me that I began to notice that some of the water dropping off of me came from tears.
I don't know what to do.
I miss you! I love you!

Yours Always,
Jared Christopher

July 7, 2009 – 12:26 PM

My Lovely Dawn,

Today is the memorial for Michael Jackson. There are so many paying tribute to him in death. But I wonder, how many were paying tribute to him in life?

How many people pay tribute to anyone they love in life? How many share how they feel about those close to them before it's too late? I should like to address my friends and family now:

JLH...my older sister. One of the few people to have known me my whole life...I admire your intelligence, I admire your fight, I admire the mother you have become.

JA...my younger sister...my fellow Aries. It seems the fighting we did as kids caused a great distance between us as adults, but I am your big brother, I will always protect you, I will always support you.

JB...my baby brother. It is both an honor and a frustration to see you grow as a person and a man...surpassing me in categories I thought I would always be able to trump you...but you are one of my favorite competitors...you are a good man.

WB...my step-father. We are very different. But you took my sister and I on as your children, you took care of my mom...for this you have all my respect.

JP...my oldest friend. My greatest conversation partner. You have wisdom you don't realize.

LP...my friend. You have such incredible compassion and you nurture so easily. You are beautiful.

BH...my homie. Your ambition is contagious...you will find your million dollar idea.

BB...my friend. Your mind amazes me and when you find inspiration you inspire others. You are beautiful.

CBB...my neighbor and friend. For twenty years and counting you have been such an example of grace and morality...your success is well-deserved. You are beautiful.

JB...my friend. You are smart and tough, but I will always try to make you crack a smile. You are beautiful.

JE...my ex and friend. You are understanding, forgiving, smart and beautiful. And your hands...so lovely.

JC...my ex and friend. I can only be thankful for what I learned from you and thank you for your forgiveness. You are beautiful.

JB...my friend. You are easy-going as a lazy river and loyal as the day is long. I will always have a beer in the fridge for you.

MLB...my friend. So much intelligence, ambition, and wit...stop it. I need to catch up. You are beautiful.

MNB...my friend. Thank you for always asking what was going on in my life. You are beautiful.

MH, VA, TK, SM, SM, SK, KT, KM, AS, JF, KW, PVE, HF, CM, CD, NC, RB, CG, and many more I may not have mentioned...my friends. Thank you for every drink or conversation or advice you ever shared with me.

LA, TJ, and NP...my nephews. You are all so unique and special. You can always come to me for any help or advice on your way to manhood. May you be great men.

July 7, 2009 – 12:26 PM

KA...my mom. You are just the best mom. You work so hard at your
    career, and then work overtime as a mom and grandma.
    And you do it with intelligence, understanding, patience,
    and love. I love you.

Lovely Dawn...my love...my best friend. You are beauty. You are
    compassion. You are intelligence. You are elegance. You
    are the love of my life. You inspire me to be a better man.
    I will always love you.

    These are the people in my life and they mean the world
to me. I appreciate you all, and you should know this today...and
every day.
    Thank you!
    And Dawn, thank you for letting me spend one of your
letters addressing this.
    I miss you! I love you!

Yours Always,
Jared Christopher

July 8, 2009 – 8:10 PM

My Lovely Dawn,

I received my college degree in the mail today. Well the first of them. The second won't come for two more years. I've also been accepted into my major at the University of Washington. I'll register for classes soon.

I've found a few new job leads in the last couple weeks and I'm trying to be very thorough in getting them to progress to the interview stage and then, of course, getting hired. Once hired, I don't know how I will also go to school. But I will cross that bridge when I come to it.

Momentum and interest seem to be picking up in having a reunion of our teenage workplace. I've found and talked to many of our former coworkers and most seem interested in reuniting. Now we have to find a way for you and I to both be there without your husband.

This weekend I will be helping to babysit my nephews while my sister and brother-in-law travel across the state to go to the Coldplay concert I got them tickets to. I think I will take TJ to see the "Ice Age" movie. I'm sure I will be thinking of you, L, A, and J. while I'm there...wishing you all were there with us.

I miss you! I love you!

Yours Always,
Jared Christopher

July 9, 2009 – 9:43 PM

My Lovely Dawn,

I went to Green Lake today to try to do some fishing. I had absolutely no luck. I think I was more focused on the beautiful scenery. Today I wanted to be a photographer.

I was at the lake quite late in the day. The sun was nearing sunset across the water from me, reflecting a beautiful golden light on the dock where I stood. The wind blew soothingly through the willow trees along the banks.

We shared the dock with a few different groups. One of them a father with his three children...I'd guess the oldest boy was 9, the sister of 5, and a baby brother of 3. The older brother and sister sat patiently while their father put a worm on the hook at the end of their respective poles. Each pole tiny, but perfectly proportioned for their young casters. And on this day, these young casters were the best fishermen on the dock.

Almost upon the first drop of line into the shadowy water just beside the weathered old wood pier did the oldest boy get his first bite. After a mighty battle he reeled in a gorgeous, two-inch Bluegill. I did a double-take trying to determine if the fish on the line was the catch or the bait. The boy's young sister soon followed with a similarly impressive and adorable catch of her own.

This little girl was so lovely, she reminded me of A. Her fishing attire consisted of a pretty pink Cinderella dress...to match her pretty pink fishing pole. And she was so thrilled to be fishing, and even moreso to be reeling in such a funny, wiggly prize.

On this day I didn't catch a thing...and yet I couldn't have imagined a more enjoyable shutout. No, wait...I could have been shutout with you standing beside me. You would have made today perfect!

You...the most incredible of women! The kind of woman who waxes philosophically on the merging of the genders in the 21st century one moment, and in the next would be baiting her own hook without cringing. And all the while, she'd make the golden sunset seem a distant second-place finisher in a contest of beauty and grace. You...the greatest woman I have ever known!

I miss you! I love you!

Yours Always,
Jared Christopher

138

July 10, 2009 – 5:28 PM

My Lovely Dawn,

I often wonder how long I can continue writing you these letters. How long before I begin repeating myself (if I haven't repeated myself many times already)? How long before I can't even think of things to repeat? How long before a day occurs where I become so busy or distracted that I forget to spend some time writing you? How long before I simply give up?

Which would come first? I would hope, and guess, I would be forgetful before I would give up or run out of things to say.

But, then again, today I struggled to know what to write. And what I have written isn't much of a topic.

I want very much to show you at the end of this how I spent every day with you on my mind and in my heart. I want you to know my devotion. And when all 365 days are done...all 365 letters are written...I will compile them into a book...and this book will be a gift to you.

This book will be my testimony to our love. And if, in time, you decide to fulfill this love...and on, or after, that day, if your family still question your decision, I hope my written testimony to our love will be your biggest argument..."Here...this is his devotion... this is his love...this is why I need him."

And if your girls should ever question why you chose to be with me...you can show them my letters, and they can read how I love you, and they will see that you are happy, and they will accept and support this. They will say with mature and loving hearts and minds, "Mom, we only want you to be happy." And the sacrifice you tried to make for them, they will return to you.

And I will love them for it. As I love you. This is my hope.

I miss you! I love you!

Yours Always,
Jared Christopher

July 11, 2009 – 4:01 PM

My Lovely Dawn,

My sister and brother-in-law have gone to Eastern Washington for the concert I got them tickets to...so today I took my turn helping babysit one of my nephews. TJ and I decided to go see a movie.

He loves his dinosaurs so we chose "Ice Age: Dawn of the Dinosaurs". On the drive there he asked, "Uncle Kwiss, do you think you will love it?"..."I hope so," I said. Then I asked, "What kind of dinosaurs do you think we will see?" and without hesitation he answers, "A T-Rex!" It is his favorite.

This was our second attempt at seeing a movie in a theater. The first time TJ couldn't make it through the whole thing. But this time we watched from credits to credits, with only one break for the bathroom.

On the drive home T made only one comment, that he loved the movie, before he fell asleep in his car seat. When we arrived at my parents house I tried to get him out of the car without waking him, but before I could even take his seatbelt off, his eyes opened. The afternoon sun was very bright though, causing him to close them again. He spoke to me in his sweetest voice, "Uncle Kwiss, can you carry me? I'm sleepy." I lifted him out of the car and he wrapped his arms around my neck tightly. I carried him to the spare bedroom to lay him down to sleep. When I lowered him to the bed his eyes were closed tight, but I caught a smile sneak across his face. He was faking.

What a good trick. I know that trick. You know my fond memories of that trick. I'm glad to see it passed on to the next generation. I'm glad to have spent a few hours with my nephew in such a sweet mood. Days like today must be why people have children...why they can overlook the bad days and the not-so-sweet moods. Today was good.

July 11, 2009 – 4:01 PM

A few blocks away from me you are likely elbow-deep in cake frosting and wrapping paper...the shared birthday party for A, J. and their cousin T. I hope in the midst of the chaos you can find your own moments of sweetness. I hope afterwards you can find a moment to know that I'm thinking about you and the girls. I am.
I miss you! I love you!

Yours Always,
Jared Christopher

July 12, 2009 – 3:02 PM

My Lovely Dawn,

I'm thinking today of my mistakes. I'm sure most of the world would consider the relationship we shared while you were married to be a mistake. Many would think my continued secret devotion to you now to be a mistake. But these are not things I consider my mistakes. I am proud of any action I have ever made, and continue to make, in an effort to make you feel good, feel happy, feel at peace, feel content, and feel loved.

My mistakes are the mistakes of my youth. Mistakes I made with you over ten years ago, and still regret to this day. Mistakes of inexperience, ignorance, stubbornness, passivity, naiveté, and innocence. I have not forgotten those mistakes, and I am sorry for each.

I am sorry for not showing you more affection.

I am sorry for not having the confidence to tell you how I felt about you...or at least more often.

I am sorry for every time I was introverted or hard to read.

I am sorry I ever allowed my friendship with Bonnie to make you doubt my feelings for you.

I am sorry for not knowing how to better interact with your family.

I am sorry for letting my inexperience at dating intimidate me so greatly.

I am sorry for not knowing how to hear you when you spoke about God.

I am sorry for not being more tactful when I spoke about God.

I am sorry for not chasing after you when would run away.

I am sorry I ever caused our present situation to come to pass.

July 12, 2009 – 3:02 PM

I know these thoughts and apologies come late, but they also come with the belief that those qualities that once were flaws have now been changed, improved, eliminated. What once were weaknesses are now my strengths.

This is why I now have to show you such great affection and consistent vocal affirmation.

This is why I now have to communicate openly and confidently with your family.

This is why I now have to respect the way you love God and to keep strong my ever-deepening beliefs.

This is why I now have to be singularly and unquestionably devoted to you.

This is why I now can't let you run away or give up on us.

I need you in my life...if you fulfill this and come back to me, in exchange, I will be everything you need in your life. This I promise you.

I miss you! I love you!

Yours Always,
Jared Christopher

July 13, 2009 – 5:07 PM

My Lovely Dawn,

Today I am thinking of now. More specifically I am thinking of our generation, and those younger than us, who seem to be the "now" generation...and not in a hip way.

We are a generation whose idea of a great record is a compilation of hit songs from various artists collectively entitled "NOW". We are a generation of internet access and on-demand. We are a generation raised on Willy Wonka and behaving like Veruca Salt..."I want it now".

The generations before ours seemed to face greater struggles, seemed to work harder, and as a result they built America to a country rich in possibility and prosperity. But an interesting thing happens to the generation that fights for, and achieves, success...they wish for, and provide that, their children not have to go through the same struggles they faced themselves. Instead they use their success to give their children everything they need and want.

But those that are given do not seek...and those that do not seek will never find. And yet we expect all the more. And we expect with immediacy...we want it now.

When something doesn't have to be worked for, when it doesn't have to be earned, it can be taken for granted, it can be poorly planned.

We have already seen the first wave of problems of our "now" generation...the generation that spiraled into recession with credit debt and home foreclosure initiated by consumers buying things we can't afford with money we don't have in order to have it all NOW.

Our generation will likely become the first to create senior citizens with a predominance of tattoos. Tattoos that have faded and wrinkled and distorted with veracose veins. Markings of now, inconsiderate of then.

Our generation will be the first to create an era of grandmothers with sagging skin...everywhere but their breasts. Breasts that have been artificially augmented without consideration that age softens and stretches everything but silicone. Surgeries of now, inconsiderate of then.

Our generation will become the first one unable to produce a single President and First Lady candidate that don't have regrettable behavior captured by camera-phone self-portraits. Pictures that become documented forever online in Myspace and Facebook. Behaviors of now, inconsiderate of then.

How does one slow the process? How does one express to an entire generation that just because something can be had now, doesn't mean it's to be done? How do we get the world to think of "then"?

Perhaps it isn't something that is done willingly. Perhaps it must be done forcibly. Perhaps the recession will do what our generation cannot do of our own accord...and teach the children of the children of "generation now" that patience is a virtue, nothing compares to honor earned, and the spoils of a hard day's work will never spoil.

The good news is we are now doing some things for our future. Our generation is the first to truly appreciate and take action for the future of the planet and its health. Let it be the beginning of a revolution...from Mother Earth to the children of the children...and across all facet of society...let us improve and set an example for the future.

Thank you for always letting me share my dreams, and for always inspiring me to dream a little more.

I miss you! I love you!

Yours Always,
Jared Christopher

July 14, 2009 – 11:46 AM

My Lovely Dawn,

I know baseball isn't your favorite sport, but I wanted to make an observation on it.

Today is the Major League Baseball All-Star game. Last night was the exhibition Homerun Derby. Because the derby is an exhibition and not a full game, the participants generally bring their children out on the field with them. Each kid gets to wear a miniature version of the jersey their dad gets to wear, including name and number. It was a charming reminder of the innate familial nature of baseball.

Baseball, more than any other sport, seems to create such a powerful father-son bond. It begins, like "Field of Dreams", with a son asking his dad if he wants to have a catch. The dad, of course, agrees, and then something magical occurs. Somewhere in the leisure and cooling of a hot summer day...atop a lawn of freshly cut grass that seems the greenest thing you've ever seen...with the smell of some distant, delicious barbecue drifting on the breeze to mix with the scent of that old leather glove...somewhere in that place you find this special witches potion brewing, and a taste of it casting the most wonderful of spells.

Something in this potion must be why baseball, more than any other sport, finds more second and third generation players...the sons of Ken Griffey, Bob Boone, Cecil Fielder, Tony Gwynn, Bobby Bonds, Felipe Alou, Sandy Alomar, and Cal Ripken (to name a few) come to mind...all following in their father's footsteps and doing it at the highest level. What other sport can make that claim?

And baseball, unlike any other sport, is not about aggression. Football is smashmouth collisions and hitting on every snap. Hockey is not only home to checking an opponent into the boards, but also an occasional glove-dropping, dukes up, boxing match on ice. Basketball has become more and more about intimidating dunks and blocked shots, followed by primal celebration and posturing. Only baseball seems to remain the kind of sport more befitting our daughters. Whereas a football game takes place on the gridiron in a stadium, a baseball game is played on a field in a park. It's like a picnic with scoring. So much more family-friendly.

July 14, 2009 – 11:46 AM

     I'm not sure why I relate all this information. I guess I'm hoping for a time, a day, when we can take L, A, and J. to a game together...when I can expose you all to something I love... see if I can get you under the magic spell of baseball.
     I miss you! I love you!

Yours Always,
Jared Christopher

July 15, 2009 – 7:12 PM

My Lovely Dawn,

You have told me before that you feel the way we are together is like a fairy tale. You have told me it is hard for you to believe this feeling can possibly be real. You have said to me before that you feel unworthy of the way that I love you...unworthy of the letters I write you...

How can you feel unworthy? Not only are they for you, but they are from you...you inspire them as you inspire me. Never have I written as beautifully as when I write for you. You fill my heart so much that it overflows. It is only my job to take an empty page and catch the overpouring love...

I think I am not a writer...I am more a catcher, with an eye to the sky and really good hands. Hands that will catch you. Hands that will hold you. Hands that will never let you go.

For you are worthy of all this and more. For when you are able to love me, you do it with every part of your being...your mind, body, and soul. You give me support, and affection, and trust, and thought, and encouragement.

You and I are in a continuous cycle of give and take, of inspiring and inspired, of loved and loving. And a cycle is a circle...a circle the perfect form...the shape of infinity...the length of our love.

This you deserve, this I will give, this is forever. And you are worthy!

I miss you! I love you!

Yours Always,
Jared Christopher

July 16, 2009 – 3:41 PM

My Lovely Dawn,

We are in the midst of Summer...today has been a gorgeous, sunny day of 85 degrees. And yet I am noticing a subtle feeling of growth or rebirth more common to Spring.

This week has seen me registering for my first classes at the University of Washington. I am still uncertain of how I will attend the classes while working...assuming I am hired to a position soon...but I will take it quarter by quarter.

Speaking of work...this week has seen me receive phone calls from two prospective employers wanting more information on my work history and my specific skill levels. I have also been offered an interview from a third company, and that will take place tomorrow. This is in addition to a lead on a position at the hospital I worked at as a teenager, that could be quite promising.

The seeds of hope and hard work are growing, and the petals of possibility are beginning to open. Like in Spring. Plus I am twitterpated.

I am so in love with you. And for the first time in a few weeks my fear of never seeing you again is in ebb tide. I know in my heart that you still love me...I am more certain, than in some time, that this love cannot be forgotten, and will, in fact, be fulfilled.

There is work to be done...truths to be proven...dedications to be documented...and a story to be continued...

Our story. A love story.
I miss you! I love you!

Yours Always,
Jared Christopher

July 17, 2009 – 8:40 PM

My Lovely Dawn,

I am an Aries...the ram, the first sign, and the newborn infant of the zodiac.

Like an infant I am naïve, unintentionally selfish, and quick tempered. But, like an infant, I am innocent, honest, forgiving, and fearless. Many of the other Aries traits spring from me like the lines of a script, long ago written and still holding true; stubborn, blunt, affectionate, quick-witted, generous, loyal, ambitious, and a leader.

Many of these traits are why I, perhaps, dread seeking a job, seeking subserviance...instead preferring the hours spent at keyboard crafting a book or a screenplay and dreaming of self-producing and self-directing my own projects...leading a team of good men and women, all friends, to a distant goal that is pictured so clearly and completely in my own mind. A challenge that takes courage and ambition, creativity and fight.

Aries is a fire sign...capable of running too hot and leaving one burnt. But Aries is a fire sign...capable of warmth, light, creation, and the forging of the strongest of bonds. And, where astrology suggests fire signs match well with other fire signs, science suggests that fire needs oxygen...it needs air...an air sign...a Gemini.

You are a Gemini...the twins of the Zodiac. And, although you likely despise me discussing astrology, you are frequently Gemini.

You are often split in two...a flipped coin landed on its thin edge...a division of head versus (not tail, but rather:) heart...responsibilities versus fantasies. You are also intensely sociable, friendly, imaginative, curious, thirsty for knowledge, adaptable, exploratory, witty, innocent, and God-fearing.

And if Gemini has a common appearance, it must be that of divine beauty. Of long, wavy hair and sparkling blue eyes. Of heavenly curves and solar-power smiles. And lips, and fingers, and ears, and neck...and delicious perfection in each.

I know a battle rages in you...of heart and mind and selfish and selfless...but whichever side comes out the victor, please know that I love both side of you.

July 17, 2009 – 8:40 PM

No...you are not a simple, two-sided coin. You are a multi-faceted gem...like an uncut diamond. And I love every facet. And I love every flaw. I love you entirely.

And where the fire needs the air, and the 'me' needs the 'you'...perhaps the air loves the fire, and the 'twin' loves the 'ewe'? Or, in this case, the boy sheep...the ram.

I miss you! I love you!

Yours Always,
Jared Christopher

July 18, 2009 – 7:44 PM

My Lovely Dawn,

Today begins the fourth month of my notebook...the 91st consecutive day I've written you a letter. 90 days passed. 90 letters sent. 90 different thoughts and attempts at expressing how much I love you.

Each letter drops, one at a time, like grains of sand through an hour-glass...only the time lasts a year, and the grains are each pieces of my heart. I give them willingly, trustingly, faithfully, entirely.

But what happens when the last grain falls and my turn has expired? Will the hour-glass mark the end of a countdown to a new beginning for us? Or will it mark the loss of the final piece of my heart...and with it the loss of my will, and my trust, and my faith, and me...entirely?

For my life...my body, my mind, my heart...are yours. There is no one else I care to talk to...no one else I care to hold...no one else I care to care for. For no one else who compares to you.

There are a blessed few who summit the highest peaks. There are things in this world that hold a little magic. There are times in our lives we are touched by tiny miracles. Here is that peak, here is that magic, here is that miracle. Here...where you and I unite.

Here...where the empty half of the hour-glass becomes full with a simple turn of our fate.

Turn the hour-glass. Refill my heart.

I miss you! I love you!

Yours Always,
Jared Christopher

153

July 19, 2009 – 8:59 PM

My Lovely Dawn,

I'm not entirely sure who coined the phrase "lazy Sunday", but today I confirmed it.

After rising early to pick up a friend from the airport, a task I am often called to perform due to my close proximity to the airport, the summer heat drove me in-doors, into the shade and ventilation of my house. My desire to remain cool overruled my need to do chores...the clothes dryer will not be run on this day.

Instead, I quickly fell into an unproductive spell. I sat myself down in front of the television and lost myself in the joys and idiocy of cable.

First came a Seattle Mariner baseball game. The team was in Cleveland so the broadcast began quite early. It was a long, slow game, but the good guys came out the victors. Their third win in a row.

Next came a marathon of "Storm Chasers"...a program documenting a group of scientist/thrill-seekers who try to study and film tornadoes across the Midwestern United States. Every show seemed to follow a similar formula; a handful of failures, incorrect guesses, and mechanical breakdowns...before a successful storm "intercept" to conclude the episode. I find it fascinating the power and damage that is contained within wind...moving air.

Even further fascination comes to me in the thought that all four basic elements of life; earth, wind, fire, water...have, not only, the ability to power modern society (fossil fuels, hydro-electric power, wind power), but each also has the power to kill...to keep mankind reminded of who is in charge.

Throughout the day I fuel myself, snacking on junkfood. It seems I need to go to the grocery store, but, even though that would allow for some welcome air-conditioning, I am unmotivated. Instead I eat miscellaneous items from the fridge and freezer that can be prepared on the outdoor barbecue or the heat-containing microwave.

Finally, as the sun is setting, the temperature becomes more palatable, I begin to work. I sit at my computer and write the last new scene I need for my screenplay...four new pages that fill in the last gap. And then I begin a final pass at editing the whole thing. It is very near completion. I think I will somehow sneak you a copy when it is done.

July 19, 2009 – 8:59 PM

And speaking of you...
My late, but effective, creative outburst has also yielded another product...another letter for you. The streak continues. Not always deep or poetic...but faithful, consistent, and always grounded in love...like our lives together would be.
I miss you! I love you!

Yours Always,
Jared Christopher

July 20, 2009 – 8:44 PM

My Lovely Dawn,

A thought occurs to me tonight...I'm quite certain a majority of your family, and anyone in the world who may hear our story for that matter, will think I am some kind of home-wrecker...that I am the bad guy...that I am the one to blame. I only hope people can withhold judgment until the story concludes.

As I sit here today, we are not speaking. You have asked for time to see if your marriage can be repaired...if it can be something that makes you happy and fulfilled...and, although it pains me not to talk to you, I am doing my best not to interfere. And there seem to be three possible outcomes to this process...

It is possible whatever you're going through...marriage counseling, a focused attempt at "couple time", whatever it may be...may work. Your marriage may become everything you ever hoped it would be. And if I was the catalyst for this process and its resulting improvement, and if, in the end, you are happy without me...then I will take the blame.

It is also possible that the marriage counseling will do nothing. It is possible your marriage is irreconcilably damaged. You may, in the end, mutually decide to dissolve the marriage. If, after divorcing, you will have me...I will ask you to be with me. And if you allow me to give you all the love I have in my heart for you, and if you are happy and fulfilled with me...then I will take the blame.

But, finally, it is possible that you are going through this process, working on your marriage, and it is not working. It is possible you still love me and long to be with me daily...as I long to be with you. And it is possible that, regardless of these facts, you will continue your life as it is, in anxious, unconnected, tortured silence. If that is your choice, passive acceptance of status quo and "toughing it out" without me...then I will not take the blame.

Regardless of the social and moral boundaries I may have broken in the time we spent together...my only thought was of your happiness. And at the start, when you hid from me the truth of your life...the truth I now see you hide from the world...when I thought you were happy in your life...I tried to walk away from you. You asked me to come back, and I did...to make you happy. And if coming back to you made you happy...then I take the blame.

July 20, 2009 – 8:44 PM

But why I love you like I do...why you're the most incredible, sexy, intelligent woman I've ever met...why I can't imagine spending my life with anyone else...for these things...YOU are to blame. I love you with all my heart and it's all your fault.

I miss you! I love you!

Yours Always,
Jared Christopher

July 21, 2009 – 8:56 PM

My Lovely Dawn,

Tonight I am on my balcony, sitting in the twilight behind a hot summer day...sipping on whiskey and listening to the world.

Directly across from me my neighbors are struggling to ease the cries of one of their newborn twins. They succeed momentarily, but then the wails begin again. Or perhaps the twins are taking turns.

Around the corner somewhere, come sudden, synchronized cheers...perhaps a point has been scored in some adult party game. It is an odd day and time for a party. Don't they know the twins need their rest?

Further away...in the center of the valley where I live...I hear the white noise of a freeway. A simple, constant buzz that would go unnoticed if not for these big, magnificent ears..."the better to hear you with" said the wolf.

Just above I hear a pair of geese fly over. They squak intermittently like some kind of Morse code for fowl...perhaps giving directions to one another in the enclosing night.

Occasionally I can detect the squeaks of a bat as it passes. My radar even senses the buzz of a mosquito as it lands on my arm. Even after the heat and sweat of today, I still must be delicious. I will head inside before they suck me dry.

As I step in to the security of my dark, screened-in living room, I think of the things I didn't hear tonight...I didn't hear any music...I didn't hear any laughter...I didn't hear you say that you love me.

What good can these ears be if they can't hear that? Might as well be deaf.

I promise to always listen to you, and to do my best to always HEAR you...

I miss you! I love you!

Yours Always,
Jared Christopher

July 22, 2009 – 7:35 PM

My Lovely Dawn,

As the weeks and months of this recession drag on, I continue to scratch and claw and fight to find work.

My good friend BH has worked his way into a trial position at a Seattle magazine. Knowing my ability to write and general creativity, he has put me in contact with the magazine's publisher, and on Tuesday I submitted to the publisher my writing portfolio. I am told he will go over it tomorrow. I am hoping for good news.

Weeks ago I applied for a position with a nearby city and their police department. I scored high enough on their initial screening test to warrant a second written examination. I took that test today. The test was conducted in the city council hall, with many applicants tested at once. The examiner said that 48 people were called in for the test and 31, including myself, showed up today for the test. We were allowed two hours to complete the test...I was the first person to finish with a time of only 65 minutes. I think I did well. Roughly the top twelve scores will be invited back for interviews.

Although it turns out I could have dressed quite casually to take the test, I erred on the side of professionalism...dressing in slacks and dress shirt. I so much prefer my T-shirts and jeans, but with the business attire on and my beard freshly trimmed to a goatee, I must say I'm looking rather dapper.

I wish you could have seen me today. Although you always make me feel like I dress well. I love that about you. I love that you dress amazingly too. I love you in comfy hoodies and sneakers. I love you in fancy blouses and heels. And I love that when we stand together that we make a pretty pair. We'll be the envy of the world, I tell ya!

I miss you! I love you!

Yours Always,
Jared Christopher

July 23, 2009 – 8:28 PM

My Lovely Dawn,

Seasons of Love:

I sit and I dream of days now long gone
Of my love and my loss and my sweet lovely Dawn

We met as young kids and there love was new born
Innocent and pure, like a cool Summer's morn

But Summer is heat and long days of drought
And our days apart became long years without

The Fall of our love brought the fall of my hope
And each passing day became harder to cope

When you took a ring, and then you were wed
My soft heart was broken, my first tears were shed

Then came a Winter, and mine discontent
Without you to light, I found darkness, descent

Down to a cave that sheltered my heart
A place to be healed in our long time apart

But the cut was most deep and never quite healed
The love I had for you still refusing to yield

And then one dark day there came just a spark
A trail of new light that led out of the dark

The spark was a chance to find where we stood
Not sure if we could, not sure if you would

But you welcomed me back, and again we were friends
A modern-day tale showed true love never ends

July 23, 2009 – 8:28 PM

Like the sun never sets, it just hides for a while
It comes back in the morning with reason to smile

And smile we do for in time will come Spring
In time a new day and a new song to sing

With Spring comes renewal, like the birth of a fawn
Next Spring comes a new day with my sweet lovely Dawn.

I miss you! I love you!

Yours Always,
Jared Christopher

July 24, 2009 – 3:51 PM

My Lovely Dawn,

Today I saw some new pictures your sister Bonnie posted on her Myspace page. There were a couple of your daughter A. She is wearing a bright yellow dress, with her face framed by her new bobbed hairstyle, and there are flowers in the background. Just a lovely, sweet summertime moment.

Your parents may love L. best, you may favor baby J, but me...I have come to adore sweet little A.

Is it because we somehow relate because we're both second-born?

Is it because she pronounces her favorite animal "zeebwa"?

Is it because she seems drawn to guitars?

Is it because she seems quite delicate, vulnerable to accident, and in need of protection (or at least quick first aid) and I have a hero-complex?

Is it because she is so uniquely in-tune with her mother's emotions?

Or is it because, in a moment of perfect innocence and trust, she sat between me and her mother and leaned her head on my shoulder and captured my heart?

It is all of these things, but especially the last. For in that moment, whatever we were doing...whether right or inevitably wrong, my goal went from wanting us to be a couple, to wanting us to be a family.

In my life I have had a handful of these experiences...moments of clarity where the unknown becomes known, the unsure becomes sure, the undecided becomes decided. And once accepted by my head, these things become required by my heart.

In that moment, with A. so unconsciously comfortable with her head on my shoulder, the realization was not only that I want that for my life, but it felt like, for the first time, your girls might like it too. I thought, for all that I've done wrong, they might come to love me just as I was falling for them.

To this day it still stirs me to tears.

And it stirs me to action...to take any steps needed to earn their trust and respect. I would want them to know every day that I love you, their mom, more than words can express. You are an incredible woman and, in turn, they are each an incredible piece of you. I'll give them my all and I'll start by giving them each a hug. Well...maybe two for sweet little A.

We can make it work. We can make it a new kind of special.

I miss you! I miss the girls! I love you!

Yours Always,
Jared Christopher

July 25, 2009 – 8:04 PM

My Lovely Dawn,

Today I attended the wedding for two of my friends.

I turned onto a road that led into the trees. At midday on this hot summer day, the sun shone quite bright...speckling the forest floor with light and then dark...the sun and the shade flickering across my eyes as I drove.

I turned across a curve and here the trees broke. A field. And on that field a sight that was new...a game that felt of another land, another time...it's players awash in linen of white...

Before I could watch the game and it's play, my attention was taken by a building arising before me. An imposing old building of iron, glass, and brick. From it's heart a lofty tower...and atop the tower a single cross.

Beyond this ancient-looking structure another grassy field. I park my car at the top and begin walking down. I come to a large white tent sheltering a collection of tables. I shake hands and catch up with the many old friends I recognize. But something seems off. Where will the ceremony take place?

And then I notice even further down the hill the trail splits and there is a bit of a dropoff. At the head of the diverging trail the groom stands looking every bit the anxious host. As I approach to say "hello" I begin to see what sits below.

There is a small stone building...it's back and top covered in moss and showing it's age. I follow the part of the trail that leads to the right. Several old, stone steps lead me down to a clearing. In the clearing, many rows of chairs...down the center of the chairs an aisle covered in rose petals.

I have come full-around and now standing directly before me is the old, moss-covered building. Finally, I can see that the structure is a grotto, and within the grotto a matching old, stone altar. I choose one of the chairs near the back, in the shade. From here I sit and I think...

What a magical little place. With green grass under my feet and blue sky up above...majestic trees all around and yet the sun shining through...earth and stone and trees and sky and light and dark and color and breeze...I take it all in.

July 25, 2009 – 8:04 PM

I wonder...would you like it here? Would you make me complete...make me the luckiest man ever to live...and marry me...here? In this ancient, old place could we start our new lives...at a borrowed location under the bluest of skies? I wonder.

It was a beautiful day, a beautiful place, a beautiful ceremony...and in the way you always do, in my thoughts and in my heart, you were here to share it with me.

Let us do it again some day but from a standing position...your hands in mine...my eyes unable to look away from yours...my face unable to conceal the smile that you would bring me that day...and forever. I want to marry you.

I miss you! I love you!

Yours Always,
Jared Christopher

July 26, 2009 – 9:31 PM

My Lovely Dawn,

There I was in the hotel elevator...alone in a crowd...two men, two women...all strangers. The elevator door opens...we all exit. Another door, this time to the courtyard...and this time a gentle breeze...and on that breeze a hint of perfume...so faint, but so powerful...a perfume that I knew...

My sense memory fires instantly...like a life flashing before one's eyes in a moment of peril...only this moment, these memories, terrifyingly sweet...the images this scent bring to my mind are the best I've ever known...

Memories of a girl with rose-kissed lips, star-kissed eyes, and sun-kissed hair...a girl with delicate hands and strength of character...a girl with grace and beauty and love...a girl in red on a glorious day under the Seattle sun...and, oh yes, that sweet perfume...

Memories of a scent so intoxicating I'd stagger, my legs gone weak from its touch. And then sober I'd yearn for another drink...

What nectar creates this aroma? What perfect flower has this fragrance on its petals? Or is it, perhaps, the essence of dew drops? The lightest smell of the clouds themselves just before rain? Or all of these...in a perfect concentration simply entitled "Spring"?

Not only do I want the recipe...I desire to find its home. A light dusting on her clothes? A dab upon the inner wrist? What of the neck? What if her neck holds the purest, most perfect source of this scent?

Can I get close enough to find this answer? If I get close, can I leave it at that? Or will the desire for scent beget a desire for taste? To investigate that scent with lips upon neck? A kiss?

And under that kiss would pulse race...the connection electric...the electricity building to trembling. Two souls trembling like leaves on a tree touched by the wind...the wind a breeze that flows on forever...a breeze that one day carries her intoxicating perfume back to me again...

Come back to me again.

I miss you! I love you!

Yours Always,
Jared Christopher

July 27, 2009 – 5:43 PM

My Lovely Dawn,

Today both the temperature and the count of consecutive days of writing you a letter will hit 100.

One hundred degrees Fahrenheit...hot enough to put me to a decision...wear a shirt and put a barrier between myself and the artificial breeze created by the circular fan on the coffee table, or...remove my shirt and feel the breeze but feel the stick of my back to the leather couch. There is no real comfort to be had. The greatest comfort came earlier in the day...walking leisurely up and down the aisles of the local grocery store. Oh sweet AC!

One hundred letters...each its own chapter but from a common book, a common story. A story of an unending love, but with an unanswered question. Each letter I write you will hopefully give you my answer...the conclusion I seek for our story. It would be a story of love and devotion rewarded and fulfilled. This would be the only ending that would bring any real comfort. Oh sweet TD!

Until then I must withstand the heat of the Summer and the cold of your absence. Until then I must write you daily til I run out of words or hope. Like the heat, being without you is an incessant, draining, torturous test of willpower. But where the heat is sure to cool, if only by winter, being without you has no known end. I will fight through both as long as I can.

I miss you! I love you!

Yours Always,
Jared Christopher

July 28, 2009 – 9:05 PM

My Lovely Dawn,

This summer is quickly becoming the record-hottest in Seattle in over thirty years. Today the temperature, once again, broke 100 degrees.

After doing as many of my daily tasks as I could do in the cooler early-morning, I took lunch in an air conditioned restaurant. Actually it was the Dairy Queen we worked at when we met. A couple of our old managers still work there so I had some nice conversations with them. One has become the owner of the store so I took the opportunity to put a bug in his ear about eventually letting me film my movie there. It was a good talk...fingers crossed.

After lunch I headed out to my sister's in-laws' house. They live by the Cedar River and we took advantage by planning to spend the afternoon in the water. Our sizable group consisted of my sister JLH, her husband Jason, his son CH, CH's girlfriend and her younger sister, my three nephews; LA, TJ, and NP, Jason's brother TH, TH's wife LH, and TH and LH's two dogs. We all picked out a towel, slid on our flip-flops, and walked down to the river.

LH knew a spot where the low seasonal water-level revealed a river rock jetty. Here we could set up foldable chairs or lay down on towels. This spot was particularly well-crafted by Mother Nature for days and groups like this. In this spot the water of the crystal-clear river ran in two different speeds simultaneously:

There was a gentle current flowing over the lower levels of the river rock jetty...the "kiddie pool". Here one could sit in a chair just dipping one's feet in the refreshing water. It was also safe and shallow enough for TJ, and even NP when supervised, to walk in the water. There was another family on the jetty this day that had three young girls...they each had their own life-preserver on and I could overhear them making plans (in that imaginative and self-important way all kids play) for which order they would float down the river. I couldn't help but think of you and the girls.

July 28, 2009 – 9:05 PM

Closer to the farther bank of the river the water deepened and sped up producing somewhat of a natural waterslide. One could walk to the upstream side of the jetty, sit on an innertube, and be pulled into the swifter part of the current for about 100 yards. Then, as the river turned and widened, the ride would end when the water returned to a more leisurely flow. One could paddle back to the bank and ride again, or continue downstream to places unknown.

Today we didn't venture to the places unknown. We all kept near to our little riverside picnic site. I tried to show TJ how to use an old water bottle to catch the tiny fish fry that swam amongst the rocks. We also found a crawfish but he was too big to fit through the water bottle opening.

On the walk home TJ and his new little girlfriend, who had spent the whole day pretty inseparable, held hands. It was lovely. Again I thought of you. I so love to hold your hand. I feel like many men of my generation don't care for walking hand-in-hand with their wife, but I would love it. Maybe it's because I'm old-fashioned? Maybe it's because I never had the chance to hold hands with a girl in junior high...when holding hands is sort of the highest, and only, form of public affection. I don't know. I just know my increasing age hasn't "matured" me in that way...I'm still a schoolboy at heart.

I missed you on the river today...I think you would have liked it.

I miss you! I love you!

Yours Always,
Jared Christopher

July 29, 2009 – 6:49 PM

My Lovely Dawn,

Today I got a job!

I told you I was getting more and more interviews and I had one today. It went so well they hired me on the spot.

Today I got a job!

It's not as good as what I was doing before getting laid off, but it's better than most of the other jobs I've seen open lately.

Today I got a job!

On Friday I go back to fill out some paperwork, and Monday I'll begin training.

Today I got a job!

Tonight I celebrate!

I miss you! I love you!

Yours Always,
Jared Christopher

July 30, 2009 – 3:53 PM

My Lovely Dawn,

I have become a wreckless driver.

It seems wherever I go I am constantly splitting my attention between the rules of the road, and keeping an eye out for you and your car. And when I spot a car of the same make and color as yours I nearly break my neck turning to watch the car as it passes...trying to see if it is you behind the wheel.

Occasionally I will see a car that resembles yours pulling into my neighborhood. I will instantly imagine that something has gone wrong, you've had a fight with your husband, and you've come to me to be comforted.

Seems a terrible thing to think of, but the truth is I speculate the fights are happening anyways, you're just not coming to me for the comfort. No, currently you probably only share your tears with the tile in the shower, the vinyl of the steering wheel, or the linen of a pillowcase...all in moments when there are no witnesses. While a steering wheel will never judge the cause of, or reaction to, your tears, nor will it ever bring comfort, peace, or an end to your tears...or mine.

Our tears will only dry when we can be together forever. And we can only be together when you accept that there will be no fix to your marriage...that while you may expect God's will to determine your decision, you may not recognize it when it arrives...it's like this old joke:

A man named Peter falls off a boat and into the ocean and begins to swim toward shore...along comes a boat and the captain spots Peter in the water and shouts to him, "shall we throw you a line?" Peter says, "No, God will save me."

Peter swims for hours, getting more and more tired, when a second boat passes by. Again the ship's passengers offer to throw Peter a line, and again Peter refuses, insisting, "God will save me."

Moments later, the boat is out of sight and Peter is out of energy. He slips down below the water and drowns.

When Peter reaches Heaven he goes to God and asks him, "God, I believed in you so much...why didn't you save me?"

God looks down at Peter, places a hand on his shoulder and says, "Peter, my son, who do you think sent the two boats?"

171

July 30, 2009 – 3:53 PM

    So while you may be waiting for God to take action, make himself known, and to save you...don't overlook the possibility that God may have sent me to be your rescue boat...twice! Also realize that when a plane is going down, the protocol is for the parent to put a gas mask on themselves first, and then on their children. It seems counterintuitive, but it can also be true of our situation...when a mother is safe, breathing normally, and clearer-headed, THEN she has the opportunity to make sure her children will be safe too.

    Sorry to use such tragic analogies...they seemed applicable.

    I miss you! I love you!

Yours Always,
Jared Christopher

July 31, 2009 – 5:40 PM

My Lovely Dawn,

I was out on the bike trail today thinking of something you told me once...it is an awkward thing to talk about, but I feel it needs to be addressed...it is the all-too-common modern issue of women enhancing their breasts with implants.

I don't know who is more to blame for this problem; men or women. Personally, I find the the importance placed on breasts by both genders to be unfounded...the way they have become the great "icon" or indication of femininity frustrates me to no end. Some men talk too often and too loudly of large breasts, and some women don't hear it when a man insists he loves their small breasts.

I have on too many occasions heard a woman say she wants implants so that she can feel "more like a woman." First of all, there are plenty of men, in our ever-fattening American society, that have disturbingly large breasts. This does not give them one iota of femininity.

The true essence of femininity, of womanhood, can't be found in anatomy. Not even the vagina...for there are some anatomical women out there, with vagina and very large breasts, that are, in fact, quite masculine.

Because femininity is that unique combination of traits...a way of speaking, and moving, and thinking...that are a world away from the ways men behave. Whatever the recipe is, when it is put together in human form it has this incredible magic to it. It is woman.

I know men play a large role in influencing the confidence, or lack thereof, that women feel when small of chest. It'd be naïve not to. Most men seem to believe, what I think is a leftover preference of primal origins, that large breasts equate to a higher ability to feed, and therefore nurture, the children. But this is the 21st Century and the more evolved man will place less importance on breasts and their size.

As a self-professed evolved man, I find small breasts beautiful...preferable in fact. They seem to be, more often, more equally sized than larger breasts. They are less likely to sag after aging and/or breastfeeding. And they are generally just a lovelier shape. This is my opinion.

July 31, 2009 – 5:40 PM

Even if I can't win the argument that an evolved man would welcome a smaller-chested woman...at least I should be able to suggest that a small, natural breast is superior to a large, fake one. So while many men openly spout their love of large breasts, what women don't seem to realize is that this means they love large, natural breasts. This is an important distinction.

It is also important to note the distinction of what men WANT, and what they NEED. Some men may WANT a monster truck with giant, oversized wheels...but they NEED a compact car that gets good gas mileage. Furthermore, a monster truck is extremely high-maintenance and men would constantly be worried about it getting stolen. So while a man will often stop to watch a monster truck on TV or if he should see one driving down the road, he is consciously aware of its impracticality, and unconsciously aware that he lacks the confidence in his mechanical skills that would be required to maintain one.

These are sort of the secret facts of the male perspective on breasts. As for the female perspective...you have said that the reason you would consider getting them is so that you would "feel more proportioned". I, too, wish you were more proportioned. I wish your self-image or self-confidence was more proportioned to how stunningly beautiful I think you truly are. No...it's not even a matter of what I think. It's a fact! You are the most radiant, breathtakingly beautiful woman in the world!

I miss you! I love you...and this means I love you just the way you are!

Yours Always,
Jared Christopher

August 2009

∞

Lemons

August 1, 2009 – 5:45 PM

My Lovely Dawn,

Tonight I've been invited to join some friends as they spend a night out in Seattle. It occurs to me that on one of these nights...at a bar or a club or our weekly trivia night...I am going to meet a girl that will be attracted to me. Maybe it's already happened, but the feeling wasn't mutual so I didn't really notice. But eventually there may come a girl that I will notice noticing me. And maybe one day it will be mutual.

As the number of days of our separation year grow higher and higher, it will become harder and harder not to give in to temptation. How long can I go on feeling this loneliness? How long can I go on without feeling some affection? How long can I go on being devoted to someone who spends her nights in bed with another man? Even if they are passionless nights. Even if I knew of your situation before getting involved, and my envy is self-induced.

I have never been a man of expectations. I have never expected a job promotion, I have only gone about trying to earn one. And when I feel I have earned one and it goes to another, I feel wronged...that justice has not been served. The same is true of love. I feel that I have earned your love...you tell me it is true...so when I find you continuing to live with a man who doesn't hold your heart...I feel wronged. Where is my justice?

And in this righteous indignation, I fear I will lash out in bitterness or spite, and accept, if not seek out, the attention/affection of other women. You have told me that you fear this. You fear the possibility that I will find someone else who fulfills me. I don't fear this the same, for I know I have never met your equal in my first 29 years...why would I meet her in my 30th? A year when you are still so prominent in my thoughts, and there is still a lack of certainty about our future.

No, I will not find another woman this year that fulfills me. But...my fear is that I will lose the mental and emotional fortitude to spend this year without physical pleasure...I am only a man. I have so much love to give, and I give it so well, it feels so stifling not to have an outlet for this passion.

August 1, 2009 – 5:45 PM

Writing you these letters can only do so much. They are a one-way communication. They do not provide me feedback...I do not get to see you smile when reading them, I do not get to hear you laugh at the silly moments, I do not get to feel your pulse race at the intimate ones. All of these things are what fulfills me, and only with you do I write and say and feel these things with such ease...the ease of sincerity that comes only when with you...when I can simply pour out my heart and my soul.

The farther I get into this war of love, the more I realize there are battles on multiple fronts. I must continue to fight to win your heart, and I must fight my own primal, male impulses for a compromised, superficial affection in your absence. A meaningless fling is not what I want, it's not what you'd want, and it's not what some unknowing new girl would want. Or perhaps the word should be "need"?

What I want and need is to be with you...only you...and you with only me. That is the only place where I find peace, trust, and love. That is the only place where the puzzle pieces fit. Without you...life is only puzzling.

I miss you! I love you!

Yours Always,
Jared Christopher

August 2, 2009 – 4:40 PM

My Lovely Dawn,

Today was another hot summer day that began with a hot summer morning. I found myself lying in bed long after waking up. The comforter was rumpled in a pile at the foot of the bed...an electric fan pointed directly at me...a thin bedsheet and a pair of boxer-briefs the only thing standing between me and full-exposure.

I stare into the fan as it methodically pivots...first left and then right. The movement, and the breeze it creates at its most center point, soothe me and I slowly fall into an almost hypnotized state. I drift into thoughts of you.

I just want to lay in a bed with you and feel like a schoolboy. And like a schoolboy I will have the work of studying to do...my subject, for the day, will be you. I just want to search and examine and memorize every inch of your body.

I want to note that at the very inner part of your beautiful blue eyes there are actually tiny flecks of hazel.

I want to find a slight scar just under your chin I had never noticed, and another just across your nose.

I want to hold your hand in mine and trace the length of each finger until the image is locked in my mind.

I want to trace the entire shape of your body...shoulders and back, hips and thighs, collarbone and wrists...high marks in anatomy.

I want to brush the delicate tendrils of your hair away from your cheek so that I can study the entirety of your face...surely an art class...the work a masterpiece.

I want to kiss you.

I want to write my Master's thesis about your lips. Perhaps a minor on the delicate taste of your neck. A PHD in a special kind of chemistry. And then a Nobel Prize for discovering true love.

You are my favorite subject. You are the greatest teacher. I pray I am accepted to your school in time for spring quarter. I'm sure by then my tuition will be paid in full.

I miss you! I love you!

Yours Always,
Jared Christopher

August 3, 2009 – 4:49 PM

My Lovely Dawn,

I saw a movie last night called "Funny People". I was looking forward to seeing it because I knew that part of the plot involved a man reconnecting with "the girl that got away", the one woman he ever truly loved...and then when they meet up twelve years later, she has a husband and two daughters, but there are still unresolved feelings with her ex...the two of them end up having an affair. I thought I might relate to the movie for some reason.

Truthfully, I thought this movie might speak to, or perhaps even support, this romantic notion I have that love can conquer all...that love could excuse the actions that, in reality, mean she's a "cheater" and he's a "homewrecker"...the label I feel others must be silently branding on my back.

It's not that I haven't thought of these things before...or still...I'm not in denial...it's just that...

I don't know what it is.

I'm not happy. I am alone. It's been like this for a while. And then here comes this thing that gives me happiness...you...and not just happiness but optimism. And peace and joy and passion. And you tell me I make you happy too...

It was like actually reaching the end of a rainbow and being able to touch it, to taste it, to feel it living and growing inside me...building me up to something better than I was...

And then suddenly the lights are turned on and the dream is ripped away from me by the cold world of awake.

What am I supposed to do with all of this? These conflicting ideals? My instinct had been to keep fighting for us...to linger as long as possible in the optimism that I had found because of you...

And then this damn movie has to paint a picture of the aspects of this situation that I've known are hovering around us like a cloud...that may or may not drop the rain of "worst-case scenario", but that I've been able (or choosing) to see as a break in the clouds that allows for the sunlight of "best-case scenario". The truth(s) mirrored on the silver screen show me how confused and pained and guilty a woman torn between two choices can be. It shows me how hurt a young girl might feel, presented with the separation of her parents, a situation she had nothing to do with, but that causes her to feel the impact of more directly than all, and with fewer tools to deal with those emotions than her "adult" counterparts. All of these things just hit me in the head, resonate, and make me feel even deeper the guilt that I know I have already earned...if things go bad, it would be my fault.

I know I can't defend my actions, but when I think of trying to, my only reasoning is love. Every thing I've ever done was out of love for you. And I'd do almost anything out of love for your daughters. I truly would. I don't want them to hurt. And I want their mom to be happy. And I think you will be...and I think their happiness would follow.

Do you hear this L? A? J? I love your mom. I love you. Can't we make this work? I will give my all to make this work.

Dawn, I miss you! I love you!

Yours Always,
Jared Christopher

August 4, 2009 – 8:54 PM

My Lovely Dawn,

Today was my first day of in-the-field training for my new job. I notice a couple things:

1) I look great! A little over-dressed for the work perhaps...but great nonetheless. After being scarred as a child by the other kids teasing me about the clothes my mom would make me wear...followed by an adolescence of playing it safe, wearing only t-shirts...it's nice to feel I've come in to my own style-wise, to finally have confidence in my ability to put together an outfit. Although we need to think of another, more macho word for "outfit". How about "armor"?

2) Brand new work, in a brand new field, and already after day one I was doing the work with minimal supervision and even fewer mistakes. My supervisors have planned to train me for three weeks, but I feel I'll be pretty self-sufficient after one week. How long should I wait before asking for a raise?

3) It's nice to be out in the world socializing again. While out of work I really didn't do enough to meet new people. But after only a few short days interacting with my new coworkers, I've had a fantastic confidence boost. There is something extra-satisfying about making strangers and near-strangers laugh. And today I was on a roll. There were smart jokes and dumb jokes, there were impressions and puns, and there was wit...lots of quick with.

Overall, today was, "Hi, I'm Jared...and when I put forth the effort, I am stylish, smart, and hilarious." Today was a good day. I think you would have been proud of me. And I would have come home to you with a smile on my face, and a rose in my hand. I would have given you the biggest hug and kiss when I got through the door.

August 4, 2009 – 8:54 PM

Is it weird that I picture us running to hug each other? Like in the movies when they're on the beach in slow motion..only we would do it every day, coming from the kitchen and garage. I think I will always be that excited to see you again. Every day like a movie...a fairytale.

Cause you're my best friend...my angel...my muse. And you always will be.

I miss you! I love you!

Yours Always,
Jared Christopher

August 5, 2009 – 6:27 PM

My Lovely Dawn,

Him and Her Always:

Him.
He lays on the floor. Knees bent, toes curled under the couch. He's not doing his situps...At the moment his focus is above...

The texture of the ceiling, the blending of light and shadow from the last of the days' sunshine peering in from the living room window...

That too becomes unfocused. The ceiling blurs, he's no longer seeing with his eyes...His mind is showing him an image in his memory...

Her.
It's that picture of her...The picture of her in the blue dress he has saved on his cell phone. The cell phone that sits on the arm of the couch. The couch his toes are currently under...

Six.
Six feet...at most. Six feet to the picture on the phone on the couch on his toes...

But what is the distance to her heart? Her heart that is promised to another...

His heart? It is hers....She is the first and only owner...

It was hers first many years ago...they were kids...still clumsy, still learning...

Today he is an educated man. Not college, just hard knocks. He isn't finished, he'd like the PHD. His toughest course? Love. There are no letter grades, only pass or fail. He has not passed. He only needs to pass once...

Once.
Once upon a time, once upon a dream, once up on the rooftop reindeer pause...

Christmas.
Christ's birthday. It was also Christmas the day he died. The 'he' that is 'him' that has his toes curled under the couch...

The day he died he had his arms curled around her. He held on for dear life. He held on to his love. His love went away. He died...

August 5, 2009 – 6:27 PM

A year ago his love came back. She came back...
Her.
She came back first in words, in pictures, in electronic mail. Then in the flesh. In lovely, radiant, perfect flesh...
In the flesh she walked through his door, up his stairs, into his home...
In the flesh he trembled, he ached...
His heart is hers again...or still. He already knew...But what didn't he know? Her heart...
Had her heart changed? Had she taken the same courses? Had she changed her major? Or is it a "new university"?
The metaphor blurs...
Blurred like the texture of the ceiling above him and his unexercised abs... Refocus. Situps.
One.
The one.
Her.
It always comes back to her.
Always.

I miss you! I love you!

Yours Always,
Jared Christopher

August 6, 2009 – 6:38 PM

My Lovely Dawn,

Tonight I wrote my 50th article for my online column. I was rather proud of it so I thought I would also make it the bulk of my 110th letter to you...my greatest source of pride:

Modest Mouse: First and Next

I'm trying to remember the first time I ever heard Issaquah-born Modest Mouse...I think it was roughly the summer of 1997 when the songs "Summer" and "Fruit That Ate Itself" (from the EP also with the latter name) were playing in regular rotation and to frequent request on my college radio station down in Auburn.

I can still remember the station ID Modest Mouse frontman Isaac Brock recorded for the station, "This is Isaac 'drunk as a skunk' Brock and you're listening to KGRG...89.9 fm ON THE DIAL!"...his use of punctuation and word-emphasis coming across like William Shatner with Tourette's.

The band's sound was equally bizarre. Brock singing in that drunken slur he has and, with that unique way he bends his strings, making his guitar sound equally inebriated...Eric Judy's strolling basslines feeling worthy of an equally underrated bass player; Sir Paul McCartney...and drummer Jeremiah Green keeping pace for both...equally.

Later in '97, the band released the masterpiece The Lonesome Crowded West. With the heartbreaking bitter buffaloes of "Heart Cooks Brain", the rage of a cowboy scorned by the intrusion of city into his country in "Cowboy Dan", and the stunning beauty of the song about a girl who "think(s) of everything" even though she's "Trailer Trash"...Lonesome Crowded West became the moment Modest Mouse perfected the sound of overcast, wind-swept plains, indie rock.

August 6, 2009 – 6:38 PM

It would be three years between L.C.W. and the band's major-label debut, The Moon and Antarctica. In the time between records, I found myself going backwards to discover the beginnings of this wondrous band. Of course the earlier work was all a bit more rough and raw than what would follow. But occasionally, even in the early days, Modest Mouse would create something staggeringly simple...pure...and genius...like 1996's "Edit the Sad Parts" when Brock confesses that "sometimes all I really want to feel is love". To be unaffected by his words and his delivery is to be without pulse.

Unfortunately we now skip a ton of material, jumping from the band's distant-past all the way to its two-day old present...where the band has expanded in size (now including former Smith Johnny Marr and a brass section), and where a new collection of Modest Mouse B-sides and outtakes has been released (as of Tuesday). The disc is entitled No One's First and You're Next and features the song "Satellite Skin" that has been receiving some radio airplay recently, as well as seven other previously unreleased Mouse tracks.

The early entries of the release include the howling "Guilty Cocker Spaniels" (which contains classic Brock wordplay) and the quieter and sweeter "Autumn Beds" (which reminds of "Ocean Breathes Salty" but with more banjo), but it loses momentum shortly thereafter and doesn't pick it back up until "King Rat" near the end of the set. And the song is less a rock song than it is Exhibit A in the case; Isaac Brock vs. State of Insanity. The guy is certainly certifiable, but damn he makes it sound good!

I hope you liked it!
I miss you! I love you!

Yours Always,
Jared Christopher

August 7, 2009 – 10:42 AM

My Lovely Dawn,

Today I am at work...training for the fourth consecutive day, even though I had the core of the job figured out on Monday, but my current trainer won't let me do any of the work today. This has led to boredom and I've taken the opportunity to write to you. I was thinking of you anyways.

I was thinking of the way you, whether intentional or not, rarely speak definitively on something...instead speaking to both sides of an issue. I wonder if this is a woman thing? A Gemini thing? Or just your thing? But surely when it is combined with my learned behavior of looking for both sides of an issue it causes many uncertainties.

I think of a time I asked you if our separation was permanent...you didn't answer the question directly...instead deflecting by saying, "would it be easier if I said 'yes'? Jared, I'm miserable without you." First of all...no, that wouldn't make anything easier...the only way this becomes easier is if we can be together. Secondly, if the latter statement is true, that you're miserable, then why would you allow our separation to be permanent? And why would these two non-compatible thoughts be contained in the same text?

This is the hardest part of my relationship with you...reading between your lines. It is made worse by our distance and my inability to ask these clarifying questions promptly and directly. The communication between us can be spectacular, but only when it is being allowed. When I am in this current position...removed from the progress, or lack thereof, in your marriage...that is when my mind just flusters and you words become like puzzles.

And I am puzzled. There are days of tremendous faith and trust, but then there are days of fear and loathing. I don't know what sparks either...if the better of the two could be fostered and prolonged, or if it is just a cycle of my state of mind or emotion or life. All I know is that today I want to be with you...I want to marry you.

I miss you! I love you!

Yours Always,
Jared Christopher

August 8, 2009 – 6:00 PM

My Lovely Dawn,

Today I am in pain.

It's not the emotional pain that I so often think can make for these gut-wrenching letters of heartache and woe. It's a pain in my neck...literally. I must have pulled a muscle or pinched a nerve while working out this morning.

But it made me notice something about myself...when a friend, a masseuse, asked if I wanted her to try to massage the knot out of my neck I said 'no'...instinctively. It occurs to me that I am generally adverse to physical contact.

The same thought struck me last night at the baseball game I went to. While sitting in the close quarters of the stadium seats I found myself annoyed when my friends' knees and mine would make contact. It is absurd, right? I am aware that I wasn't raised in an environment that involved a lot of physical affection and that undoubtedly contributed to my present mentality. But it still occurs and it is unnecessary.

But the interesting counterpoint is that the exception to this behavior is you. I feel none of that with you. There is a safety and security that I feel with you that means I don't back away from your touch. In fact I crave it. And I desire to touch you. In fact, I can't really keep my hands off of you.

When I think of a future where you and I are together, I also think of my family and friends wondering who this new Jared is. I think they would be shocked to see me suddenly affectionate, let alone highly affectionate, when with you.

I would hold your hand walking from the car...I would pull you to me, perhaps onto my lap, when you'd pass where I was sitting...I would touch the small of your back and kiss the top of your shoulder as you helped in the kitchen.

I would just want to be as close to you as possible, as much as possible, to make you feel as good as possible. I generally believe "everything in moderation" but I would break that rule in the case of "cuddling with Dawn". THAT I could do forever and never overdose. Your touch will be the only one I will ever need.

I miss you! I love you!

Yours Always,
Jared Christopher

August 9, 2009 – 4:57 PM

My Lovely Dawn,

Today I am sobbing.

It is a Sunday afternoon...I had been doing some ironing in front of the television when I stumbled across a program...it was a story about a young girl named Alex.

Alex is four years old, has large blue eyes, and a few tufts of stringy, brown hair. Alex has the high, squeeky voice of all girls her age, but with it she expresses a unique and profound wisdom. Alex says, "When life hands you lemons, make lemonade." Alex's life has been handed some pretty bitter lemons. Alex has cancer.

No, in fact Alex *had* cancer. Alex is gone...an innocent victim of a faceless killer...taken so young.

I am so upset at this. This is injustice.

But there is more to this story. Before Alex died she asked her mom if she could have a lemonade stand. Alex wanted to make some money. Not to buy a new doll or toy of any kind. Alex wanted to raise some money to help other kids with cancer. Alex's Lemonade Stand, and the many stands created after her, in her honor, have now raised millions of dollars, with more added every day. What an incredible legacy from such an incredible vision of such a tiny, incredible, little girl.

How is it that children born with such a shortage of health, seem to be born with such an abundance of heart, of hope, of wisdom? Or is this something not born but built? Earned?

Do we, as parents, do a disservice to our children by trying to protect them from all possible dangers? Perhaps our kids' greatest strengths will be found where the breaks have healed over strong.

Is there something about a child with a powerful illness, who is constantly reminded of the illness inside them, that makes them want to do for others? To deflect the attention their illness necessitates and to give it to the less fortunate? Or the equally-unfortunate?

August 9, 2009 – 4:57 PM

Is the reason these illnesses ever befall the pure innocence of a child because it sometimes takes a great injustice to strike the heart of the jaded? Am I, with my lack of public service or charity, part of the ignorant that must be educated by the likes of little Alex?

I don't know. But I know today I am learning. Today I am wanting to buy a glass of lemonade...whatever the price. And a glass for you... my girl.

I miss you! I love you!

Yours Always,
Jared Christopher

August 10, 2009 – 12:53 PM

My Lovely Dawn,

Today was a Monday.

A day that had begun so unassumingly, under a blanket of grey, was now awash in gold and blue and green. It called out for an escape. A ride off into the sunset. A sunset that was now closer than it had been on this same ride two weeks ago.

Two weeks prior this same ride came much easier, the hill less steep, the peak less far. Perhaps it was the two week break, perhaps it was the heavy snack an hour before, but today the peak will not be summitted.

But the ride must go on. The ride will instead follow the river, for this ride this day is gestating something other. A story? A quietly brewing story?

A story of the warmth of the sun and the cool of the shade...both perfect...both arriving just as he'd had enough of the other...and then the first again.

A story of the sound of a young boy and his father...the shouts they make as they pass under a bridge...and then the giggles from the boy as his own voice echoes back to him like a tickle on the soul.

A story of the scent of wild blackberries growing along the river...they must be coming of season for the air is ripe with their sweetness...what a fragrance!

A story of the sight of the river as he rounds a bend...the sight of a lonely canoe upon that river...it's two passengers silhouettes on the quiet, flowing water...

The quiet...broken only by the click of a camera shutter and then the turn of the wheels toward home...toward home, a cool drink, a pen and paper, and a delicious brownie a la mode with fresh blackberries...

A Monday!

I miss you! I love you!

Yours Always,
Jared Christopher

August 11, 2009 – 8:35 PM

My Lovely Dawn,

It is Tuesday, but it has already been a busy week...the busiest I've had in many months. Full days of training followed by afternoons of freelance writing, workouts, errands and chores, and today an interview for another job. I am nearly spent.

Throughout these challenging last few days I have remained loyal to my goal of writing to you every day, but it has shown the beginning of the increase in challenge to continue this promise. The cracks have begun to show. The true scope of the idea is beginning to dawn on me. And it will only grow harder.

In the months to come I am tentatively planning one afternoon class a day at the UW and a three-hour film class on Thursday nights. I doubt it all can be accomplished. Something has to give. I pray it is not my letters to you.

Today is not much of a letter and I apologize. Please send me some sign that we are not over...that you are still thinking of me...that my letters are not in vain. Hear me in your heart, know me in your soul, and give me the strength to go on. This I pray.

I miss you! I love you!

Yours Always,
Jared Christopher

August 12, 2009 – 8:58 PM

My Lovely Dawn,

      Today I drove past your house. Your husband's car was in the driveway. Of course it was...but still I am wracked with envy.
      Tonight I am probably going to make a mistake.
      I miss you! I love you!

Yours Always,
Jared Christopher

August 13, 2009 – 6:57 PM

My Lovely Dawn,

Yesterday I made the mistake of driving past your house. It was a painful reminder of the reality of this situation, and envy poured through me, like fire through straw, for hours afterward.

I feel envy that it is someone else that calls you wife. Envy that it is someone else that knows the details of your life from the last ten years. Envy that it is someone else that gets to hear the laughter and dry the tears of your little girls every day. Envy that it is someone else that you have conceived those little girls with. Envy that it is someone else that shares your bed and will again on this night. Envy that it is someone else who may get to hold your hands and kiss your lips...forever.

This envy is great and it is powerful. Last night it drove me to make a mistake.

But I did not lash out and take another lover to bed. That would not be fair to her...whoever she might have been. I simply drowned my sorrows in a bottle of whiskey...internalizing all that was bothering me. It was a mistake because with every sip I was only denying that which is undeniable...that I love you. Masking the ache in my heart with vision that is blurred...and then the ache repaying me by relocating to my head and my stomach before the night was through.

So I spent my morning in the shower...my eyes closed, my head resting against the cool tiles, the hot water running over my back. I spent the day at work in poor shape...once again victim of my own actions...actions that scream, "I should have known better." But I do these things anyways. Is it stupidity or hope? A delusion that this time will be different, or that the rules of all mankind don't apply to me, or that I am special.

No...I am common.

But if I am common, why does my hurt feel so great?

August 13, 2009 – 6:57 PM

Do other people regularly survive a loss, a pain like this? If so, why do we do this to one another so much? To our fellow man and woman? To the ones we claim to love the most? Why?

And why hasn't someone invented a whiskey that has aspirin predissolved in each bottle?

I'm sorry I made this mistake. I'm sorry if I disappointed you.

I miss you! I love you!

Yours Always,
Jared Christopher

August 14, 2009 – 8:37 PM

My Lovely Dawn,

Tonight I went to write my music column as I normally do, but found myself being berated by people who didn't like a prior review. So I confronted the issue head-on in my first Op-Ed piece. Here it is:

Only An Opinion

I've just come from responding to a comment left on one of my columns by an irate reader. I didn't think the new single from his (apparent) all-time favorite band was the best thing since sliced bread and he took it personally. Actually, I should take a step back because my review wasn't even very negative. In fact, it was intentionally pretty indifferent. Indifferent with hopes of improvement. And yet something in my comments set the reader off. While I will write this editorial about the most recent incident, the following thoughts apply to any one who is taking, or has taken, offense to my critiques (or rock criticism in general).

First of all, what is that? That defensiveness. Why are the comments of a stranger…me…powerful enough for him to take such offense to them? And they're not even words about him…they're about a band who, by the way, are probably also strangers. It so frustrates me when people are offended on behalf of someone else. A similar observation can be made of the behavior at a stand-up comedy show. Let's say a white comic is doing a joke about black people…how many of the white audience members will fain shock or disgust (likely due to "white guilt"), but meanwhile glance around at the black members of the audience and they're enjoying the hell out of the joke. Can we please stop defending those that can defend themselves? Trust me…if they're offended, they will.

If a member of a band that I've reviewed (negatively) wants to contact me directly I will discuss the rationale of my review. The conversation would likely go, "Listen, I didn't dig the song, but what's the second single? Cool. Good luck with that one." But bands won't respond to my reviews. Why? Because they have better things to do! They are blessed with enough talent and/or fortitude to make a living being musicians, while I am only blessed with an opinion, a spell-checker, and the opportunity to comment on real musicians.

August 14, 2009 – 8:37 PM

Besides, it's not like I'm seeking opportunity to slam bands or songs. I would really like there to be more great songs coming out and played on the radio. Every time I go to listen to a new piece of music I'm hoping that it will be something amazing. Actually, that's not entirely true...there are times when I don't want a song to be good (the recent Chevelle track comes to mind), but generally a) those times are personal (I've met Chevelle and thought they were rude), and b) even if I hope a song won't be good I still give it a fair listen, and, if warranted, I'll give it a positive review (as I did for Chevelle). The inverse is also true... sometimes I love a band and want their new song to rule...but if it sucks, it sucks. The new Clutch is a perfect example...I love me some Clutch...have about nine of their records... the new one though bummed me out! But I try to put as much objectivity and honesty in my column as I can.

If it were possible, I'd prefer to listen to all new music Pepsi-challenge style...with no knowledge of who the band is. Then I could be completely objective. This is why my favorite songs to review are from brand new bands...bands that I can have neither high expectations nor negative prejudices. "Here is a brand new baby...who will it grow up to be? John Lennon or Uncle Bud...the singer in the 70's cover band at the hole-in-the-wall tavern in Graham?" (Now I'm gonna get letters from people in Graham. Sorry.) The point is, a new band represents a thrilling spin of the wheel, and each spin we're hoping for big money and not "bankrupt".

The last point I would like to make is a rhetorical one. Before slamming me for critiquing your favorite band...please consider whether or not you want that band to succeed in the ways my column is intended to suggest. Think about whether or not you want that band to be played on mainstream radio, perhaps even crossing over to Top-40. Think about whether or not you want ticket prices for their shows to increase in price when they step up from El Corazon to the WaMu Theatre, or beyond. Think about whether or not you want to deal with all the new fans who "don't really get it cause they weren't a fan from the beginning". Think about whether or not you want morons like me at their show. Or think about whether or not you kinda like having them all to your own...your favorite little secret. I know I, for one, like me some secrets. Take care.

**There is even a bit in there for you. Can you spot it?
I miss you! I love you!**

Yours Always,
Jared Christopher

August 15, 2009 – 5:21 PM

My Lovely Dawn,

Last night a summer storm.

At first I could hear an unknown rumbling. A car driving by? An airplane throttling up for takeoff? I mute the television to hear it more clearly. When that doesn't suffice, I slide open the glass door to the balconoy.

With the curtain for the door also now open I catch glimpse of a flash...lightning. The entire sky lights up from the power. I stand at the door waiting for another. When it finally comes it is on my right, coming from the south of my home. What had been the darkest part of the sky becomes brighter than daytime, but only for milliseconds. The bolt darts and curves, seemingly blind and unable to find a direct path to the ground.

I begin to count...one one-thousand, two one-thousand, three one-thousand, four one-thousand, five one-thousand, six one-thousand, seven one-thousand, eight one-thousand, nine one-thousand, ten...before I can finish, a clap of thunder rolls across the valley.

I walk to the wall switch and turn off the lights. The TV is next. With the sliding door and curtains still open I return to the couch...this time my head on the arm rest, my feet pointed towards the balcony.

I lie here in the dark watching and listening to Mother Nature's own little Independence Day. The pace is quite slow and in between thunder claps the rhythm of the raindrops is the only thing I hear. It lulls my eyes to close. Even when closed the awesome strength of the light from each strike can be sensed through my eyelids.

One one-thousand, two one-thousand, three one-thousand, four one-thousand, five one-thousand, six one-thousand...and the thunder rolls.

With eyes still closed I think of you. I think of the most powerful electrical strike I have ever witnessed. A bolt of lightning that must have spanned two, three centimeters...at most.

It was the evening of our first date and we were both reaching for the car stereo. I can't recall if we made contact, I only recall that we both seemed to recoil from the shock. Like two professional boxers rushing to their corners after the bell rings at the end of a round.

August 15, 2009 – 5:21 PM

And like a boxer I spent much of that night, that week, that year, in a daze. And like a boxer I am in the midst of another fight. It is terrifying and it is thrilling. It requires strategy and patience, determination and strength. It took years to train for this fight, and it is for the championship belt.

It is round three when I am hit by a powerful uppercut and I fall to my back...the flash bulbs begin popping...the referee stands over me giving me the ten-count..."One one-thousand, two one-thousand, three one-thousand"...the thunder claps and my eyes snap open.

It was just a dream.

It was just a dream and the storm, now nearly on top of me, woke me from it.

It was just a dream and yet I wake to find pain...the pain of a heart strained by too many heavy blows...the pain of living without love...of loving without you.

I will keep fighting.

I miss you! I love you!

Yours Always,
Jared Christopher

August 16, 2009 – 4:55 PM

My Lovely Dawn,

Have you ever sat and watched the wind?

The most beautiful wind is surely a summer wind. Maybe that's why Sinatra sang about it.

In summer the trees are still clinging tightly to their leaves, which means there are far more voices to sing the rustling music the wind has written.

In summer the wind reveals that, perhaps, leaves tan in the sun...the dark tops lifting up to reveal their paler underbellies.

In summer the wind reveals the weather forecast in Seattle...and it works counterintuitively, with a northern wind bringing warmth and clearer skies, and a southwestern wind bringing clouds and then rain.

In summer the wind is a blessing...pushing out the clouds when we've had our fill of grey, and bringing a cooling breath when summer heat has become too much.

Today the trees are leaning to the south... the sun is shining gloriously on me...and I sit outside and write my love her letter. And the wind...the wind is a beautiful northern summer breeze...and it makes me feel fine.

I miss you! I love you!

Yours Always,
Jared Christopher

August 17, 2009 – 9:13 PM

My Lovely Dawn,

Tonight I had a conversation with my brother and his girlfriend on some of the differences of the sexes.
On the topic of flirting:

I think women flirt knowing that it won't go anywhere. I think men flirt just in case it might go somewhere. To men, flirting is like playing the lotto...it's likely they won't win anything, but there's 100% less chance of hitting the jackpot without at least trying it. Some men play lotto out of habit and wouldn't know what to do with a winner should they manage to hit one.

This isn't the only example of a man's ignorance. To even an untrained eye it would seem men are quite poor at flirting. Oftentimes rushing an attractive woman like an overly-excited, slobbery puppy.

The truth is that man hasn't been properly trained. It is likely his prior owner (or girlfriend if we lose the metaphor) allowed his bad habits, perhaps even rewarded them, and in so doing he came to believe that all women think those behaviors are cute.

Men are a simple creature. A simple creature of habit. Chances are, if a man is doing something in the presence of a woman, in the name of flirting, it is because that same act has worked for him in the past. At the very least it hasn't been corrected or punished.

If a man wears a new cologne, and that night an attractive woman compliments him on it, chances are the next night, and every night after that, he will wear the exact same cologne...likely in overabundance...until a day comes that a new woman says she dislikes it and brings him back to reality.

This is when the male predisposition for fixing things can be taken advantage of. Tell a man something is broken...even himself...and he WILL attempt to fix it. This is another of the differences of gender.

A woman will say she is thirsty and the man will get her some water...the most obvious fix he can think of. Meanwhile, the woman is hoping for the man to sympathize with her thirst...what it is to be thirsty, and then, after sufficient conversation, she will perhaps want him to get her some water.

Actually, in all likelihood, once a woman has spoken of her thirst the man is too late to bring her water. He should have expected her impending thirst and had a glass waiting for her. When a woman speaks of her thirst today she doesn't want water today...she is actually attempting to train her man to get her water without her asking for TOMORROW.

Man cannot grasp this concept though. Not without more specific instruction. Not without proper training.

This is how men and women differ.

Except me. I often learn to anticipate the needs of others.

Just like I'm anticipating you will some day need a shoebox full of letters, written across the entirety of a year, to know the absolute certainty of my devotion to you. That this love is true. And it is good. And it is yours.

I miss you! I love you!

Yours Always,
Jared Christopher

August 18, 2009 – 8:26 PM

My Lovely Dawn,

Today I received confirmation that I will receive press credentials to attend and cover this year's Bumbershoot Festival.

A "bumbershoot" is an umbrella, so it is only fitting that Seattle's annual Labor Day music and arts festival be named after it. The name is somewhat ironic in the sense that early September is generally quite beautiful and sunny here.

In the last few months my online music column has been going so well that the editors asked me to cover the entire three-day festival. I will be given a press pass, access to exclusive entrances, backstage areas, and I will have access to some of the bands for interviews.

Some of the performers include Katy Perry, the Black Eyed Peas, All-American Rejects, Sheryl Crow, Franz Ferdinand, and my favorite...Modest Mouse.

There are still many details to iron out, but I'll have a few weeks to do it. I'm excited! It's always nice when you get to do something you love, to get some recognition for work done well, and to earn some reward for that work.

Now if only I could somehow get you to come with me...I think you would like it!

I miss you! I love you!

Yours Always,
Jared Christopher

August 19, 2009 – 8:10 PM

My Lovely Dawn,

Today I've run myself ragged.

Due to how fast I've been picking up the duties of my new job, I finished quickly and ended up only working a half day. I took the early finish as an opportunity to run a couple errands, clean the entire house, and then catch up with a couple of friends I haven't spoken to in a while.

I've also worked out, had dinner, and am shortly off to help defend my team's weekly trivia crown. We've won three weeks in a row! This week will be special...a few of my trivia teammates have a friend, Bernadette, who recently began Chemo treatment for cancer. As a sign of support and solidarity they shaved their heads bald. I don't know Bernadette and I look terrible with a shaved head, so I decided a different tribute...

Tonight our team name will be "Baldies for Bernadette". If we win I will suggest my team donate the winnings to a cancer charity in her name. I will also pass the hat, and try to ask the crowd to donate any extra cash they may have on them. That will be my contribution.

Wish us luck?

I miss you! I love you!

Yours Always,
Jared Christopher

August 20, 2009 – 9:17 PM

My Lovely Dawn,

I am so utterly exhausted today.

My eyelids are red and heavy. I need sleep. Between my late night out yesterday (we won at trivia for the fourth consecutive week), the police and the police dog outside my window making it an even later night, and an early rise for another day in the rat race...I have fought and scratched my way through the day on nothing but caffeine and will power.

But now I want to break down, and cave in, and fall asleep. I want to drift into a dream where I climb into your arms, rest my head on your chest, and enjoy every soothing stroke of your hand through my hair.

You take care of me. You know what I need. You give it without asking. You love me.

And I love you!

I love you! I love you! I love you!

Sitting here...thinking of those words...seeing them written...there comes a lump in my throat...a single tear drops from my left eye...

If my eyes weren't red before they are now.

You are my peace. You are my comfort. You are my home.

I miss you! I love you!

Yours Always,
Jared Christopher

August 21, 2009 – 8:16 PM

My Lovely Dawn,

How do people learn to parent?

It would seem, at best, someone was given a great example of parenting from their own parents. And the proper techniques for raising children were more or less absorbed by osmosis. Then, any weaknesses would be supplemented by parenting books and/or classes.

But how often does this happen? How often are a couple prepared or trained when that first pregnancy arrives? How many pregnancies are planned?

Even if planned, how many couples go into parenthood with the proper intentions? Or do they think of having a baby the same as buying a house or car...it is something to acquire, or the next thing to do, after marriage. How many people only think of it as having a baby, and not; having a toddler, a preschooler, a preteen, or a teenager?

I really have to believe that most people don't think of these things. If they did, a lot of them would likely scare themselves out of doing it.

Then comes me. I BEGAN scared of having children. For some of the reasons I've mentioned, and for my acknowledgment of the categorically tough job parenting truly is, and the respect I want to give it.

Historically, when people would ask me if I wanted to have kids, I would answer quite easily, "no". What I never quite articulated was that that was my answer at that moment. I was open to the idea that my mind could change. I really wanted to live my life on a staircase. I wanted to take the first step of being in a great relationship with a woman I truly loved before considering kids. How could I know how I would react when I was finally in that situation?

And now here I am, at 30, considering kids. I've had the experience of interacting with my nephews...I've had the experience of interacting with your daughters...I've had the experience of being in love with you...the true love I always wanted...

August 21, 2009 – 8:16 PM

   While none of these things can prepare me for the 24/7 job of being a parent...it has shown me that I want to do it. I want to be a dad. I want to be a parent with you. While this isn't enough, in some ways...in my case...it is everything. For me everything begins and builds from desire.

   I now know my desire to be a dad and I will take steps to be the best dad I can be. I will read the books. I will take the classes. And I will listen to my wife...who, I happen to think, is an amazing mom!

   But now I'm getting ahead of myself. There are a couple steps still to go...

   I miss you! I love you!

Yours Always,
Jared Christopher

August 22, 2009 – 6:44 PM

My Lovely Dawn,

I've spent much of today going over my screenplay...your screenplay...again and again.

I can't seem to make it from cover to cover without finding things that I want to change and improve. I hope they are improvements. At this point, I am so close to the material that I can't tell if it is even any good anymore. To give it to my friends to read isn't much help as none of them have experience writing or reading scripts, and know not the advice to give.

Am I crazy to think that this story...our story...of young love and young love lost...could be something that the world would care about and want to see? Is it something that the money-men of Hollywood will "get"...see as a viable concept...an interesting story with some new and unique touches...that deserves to be produced? Is this the kind of simple story that will some day find a quiet and loyal audience... like "Say Anything", "Chasing Amy", or "The Notebook"?

Or will it simply become a sweet and meaningful gift, that will find a place of honor in the home of the woman that inspired its creation? She, the only owner.

I want to share our story with the world. I want everyone to know how much I love you and how you changed my life because of the incredible person that you are. But if I never get that chance, I will still be satisfied to know that you know these things...that you know my love and devotion to you...my inspiration from you. That you know these things and choose to reward their existence, intention, and meaning by choosing to live your life, from this point forward, as my partner and wife. This would overrule the quest for any success or glory as a filmmaker.

But it would still be pretty great, very pride-worthy, for your husband to be a successful and respected filmmaker.

I miss you! I love you!

Yours Always,
Jared Christopher

August 23, 2009 – 3:22 PM

My Lovely Dawn,

In all our talks and communications prior to our "separation" (for lack of a better word) you always made it seem to me that you are doing this, not for want or hope of saving your marriage, but for want and hope of saving your children...your desire to give your daughters the best chance at a healthy and happy childhood...and that childhood coming from a household of their parents together.

Part of me doesn't believe this is the entire story. Part of me believes you are ready and willing to separate and divorce, but you want it to be by fault or cause of your husband's actions...or at least a mutual decision...than by fault of yours. I think you don't want the burden of the majority of the decision, and it's resulting guilt, to fall on you. You don't want your children blaming you for why they have two homes and won't see their parents together anymore.

But an interesting thought occurs to me...have you considered that remaining in your marriage, for a reason other than doing what is best for you alone, won't have unforeseen repercussions? Is it possible that staying in your marriage for the kids won't lead to you resenting them for your unhappiness? That you might, in time, blame THEM, even in a minute way, for your prolonged misery?

And then your good intentions backfire, which leads to a distancing between yourself and the three people you love the most...the three people you were hoping and attempting to protect in the first place.

I don't know that this would happen, but the possibility of it seems, at least, plausible. It is something I hope you will consider. And simultaneously consider that you and I together would equal a happier you...and a happier you could equal happier them. I certainly would give my all to build and maintain a happier environment for all of us. And it seems easy to do, as when I'm with you, you make me a happier me, and a happy me just wants to do for others.

I miss you! I love you!

Yours Always,
Jared Christopher

August 24, 2009 – 10:56 PM

My Lovely Dawn,

I'm sorry to be writing you so late tonight.

I've just come from dropping my mom off at home. Tonight her favorite new singer was in Seattle and I took her to see the show. First, it started late and then everything else seemed to go wrong.

Why is it that so few people seem to know any kind of concert etiquette? Drinks spilled on our shoes, people bumping into us when we're nowhere the moshpit, a couple women in heels choosing about two inches in front of me as their spot to stand and then blocking my view farther by holding their cameras up above their heads, snapping pictures through the whole show...

It was all very frustrating. And it almost made me too late to write you today. But I snuck it in anyways.

Tomorrow a special letter.

I miss you! I love you!

Yours Always,
Jared Christopher

August 25, 2009 – 7:50 PM

My Lovely Dawn,

The second chapter of our relationship began in June of 2008.

We would write each other emails, and on a handful of occasions we met in person for a few minutes at a time. We became fast friends...again. Enjoying the same taste in music and movies and more. What we didn't share, we would introduce to one another...you getting me hooked on the TV show "House", and I getting you into the music of Dustin Kensrue or Cary Brothers. It was quite fun and innocent.

Well, perhaps it wasn't that innocent on my part. I was immediately captivated by you. You were still the sweetest, loveliest woman I had ever met. No...you were lovelier.

Then one weekend you went away on a vacation with your family...your husband. I was strangely bothered a great deal by the thought.

I tried to escape that night to the distraction of the movie theater...where I could be alone in a crowd. As a good cinema patron I turned my cell phone off. After the movie, as I walked back to my car, I noted the beauty and mystique of a bright summer moon. When I arrived at my car and turned my phone back on, there was a message from you...a simple text saying "Good Night" and above it a picture of the same summer moon I had just admired, only from your vantage, above the lake where you were camping.

This simple act and the idea that it carried with it...that while I was missing and thinking of you, you were thinking of me...it sent me into tears. I knew in that moment that I was still in love with you, and I feared that my heart would be broken again.

In the days following that night I decided that I would sever ties to you...attempt to minimize the pain of losing you again. I made you a mixtape...the same mixtape I had made for you many years before...a tape you had never received featuring songs that spoke of the kind of love I have for you. I wrote you a letter...a letter that tried to articulate everything I was thinking and feeling and why I had to go. I drove to your house and gave you the presents, and, for the first time since our reunion, I hugged you goodbye. I tried to burn the feeling of that hug, your body in my arms, into my memory.

211

August 25, 2009 – 7:50 PM

And then I walked away...
As is the case with all things of sentimental value...all things that have had any connection with you...I saved a copy of that letter.
This is that letter:

August 25th 2008

Dawn,

Things that have made me cry recently:

When someone told me they thought I'd be a good dad.
When someone told me she thought my mom was beautiful.
When someone simply wished me "good night" and I realized that she made me so happy that all I wanted to do was to be where she was... every day.
And I cried again when I realized I couldn't be.
These are the reasons I must go now.
Because I love you again. I love you still. I love you always.
It's all the things you hear about love...the butterflies, the giddiness, the ache when it's gone.
But its discovery is tainted. Tainted by history, tainted by poor timing, tainted by complication, tainted by the disapproval of a jaded, unknowing public.
For this is love. A love that has stood the test of time. A love that is stronger than ever.
You've become my best friend! You check on me every day and I look forward to every email. You share your secrets and I promise to respect them all. I share my secrets and know I can trust you. You have no idea how rare that is for me... I struggle so much to give trust. But with you I've always felt safe. And I love you for it.
I love everything about you. Your mind, your heart, your beauty, your compassion, your delicacy, your exquisite femininity, your support, your fear, your hope, your lips, your hands, your laugh, your smile, your all.

August 25, 2009 – 7:50 PM

Yes! That's it...All of you. I love you, I love you, I love you.

I want so badly to marry you. I'd take such care of you, I'd work so hard to learn how to be a great step-dad to your girls. And I would have the greatest coach, the greatest partner!

The mortals would hate us for our love...how dare we love so deeply, so completely? And for all to see? But I've waited for amazing...don't hate me when amazing I find!

For you are AMAZING! And I love you! I'll always love you!!

But I know this information is inappropriate.

I promised I would always protect you...if I must protect you from me...so be it. I sacrifice myself.

But it is not a sacrifice for the greater truth is that our love is greater than time, or judgment, or life itself...and we will find each other in the end. And in the end I will hold you and never let you go!

Yours Always,
Jared Christopher

Roughly a week after that letter...a week of silence...you sent me an email that absolutely killed me. That email was two sentences long:

"Have you been gone long enough? Can you come back now?"

And we know how I reacted to those words and what came next...

I miss you! I love you!

Yours Always,
Jared Christopher

August 26, 2009 – 9:15 PM

My Lovely Dawn,

Again tonight I'm pushing myself to the end of the day to find time to write to you. I'm sorry. Continuing this promise is going to get harder and harder.

Tonight I'm at a bar and the waitress is beautiful. I become conflicted. Talk to her, try to get her number...or continue complete devotion to you?

Luckily, she has a say in the matter and would likely care less about talking to me.

And bottom line...she's not you! I'm still thinking about you! I would rather be with you!

I miss you! I love you!

Yours Always,
Jared Christopher

August 27, 2009 – 9:38 PM

My Lovely Dawn,

Oh, what a day.

Up bright and early (even though I arrived home late last night after leading my friends to a fifth consecutive win at Trivia Night) to face my increasingly busy schedule. After finishing my work early again, I drove in to the office to discuss some of my frustrations with my manager. We had a very productive meeting and I left feeling reassured.

Once home, I found the day, outside the confines of the air conditioned vacuum of offices, had warmed to quite hot. I changed clothes and jumped on my bike for exercise, fresh air, and some Vitamin D. The blackberries along the nearby river smelled so powerfully good, I could swear I still smelled them as I summitted the hill I ride...a climb of close to a mile from the valley and the slowly-flowing water.

Back at home, I felt the thickness of the air and humidity greater, once seated and still on the back patio, than I had while fighting up the hill. Sweat beaded on my brow and from the center of my chest, under my T-shirt. I had to shower before my conference call.

My conference call came at the top of the hour and it was in regards to an upcoming music festival that I will be covering. I will be one of the three featured writers, and will be given more national exposure. I think I made a good impression on the editor. I love making strangers laugh!

After the call I was excited about the project and quickly went to the computer to write a new article for it. Upon logging in to my publishing account I found that my column had been receiving a staggering amount of attention over the prior two days.

August 27, 2009 – 9:38 PM

I had written two articles the day before; a sweet, almost poetic review of a new record, and a somewhat tongue-in-cheek opinion piece about terrible song lyrics. Of the two, which received the most feedback? The negative opinion piece. I was quite proud of my lovely record review, but apparently the squeaky wheel gets the grease.

There were several other aspects of the human condition that were revealed by this accidental study, but it is becoming late...I will rest up...

Tomorrow will be another busy day...I will be finishing a present for the love of my life...and I hope you will like it...

I miss you! I love you!

Yours Always,
Jared Christopher

August 28, 2009 – 8:12 PM

My Lovely Dawn,

A long, trying week has come to a close.

Actually, I don't know if I should say "trying"...really, it was just busy. The good news is, a busy week makes the days go by faster... the year go by faster. I could use this year to go by faster.

I'm still living with this idea that you've promised your husband that you will give your marriage this year to improve. I still have this hope that your promise to him will be in vain...that your marriage is, for all intents and purposes, already over.

What I don't know, is if your husband has promised, if you remain unhappy, that he will agree to separate at the end of this year. I don't know that, even if he has made that promise, he will keep it.

What I do know?

I know that I will keep all my promises to you. I fight for us, in my own way, every day.

I know that tonight it began to rain. I opened the patio door to breathe in the smell of it.

I know that I closed my eyes and dreamt. I dreamt of grabbing your hand and pulling you out into the dark and the rain...where we stand side by side, your hand on mine as we lean over the railing, listening to each drop as it splashes down in the water below, and breathing in that fresh smell...then I whisper three words, "hey, come here", and I pull you toward me...you slide your arms between my jacket and shirt so we can share the warmth...and we kiss...every kind of kiss...you lips, your cheeks, your brow...and your lips again.

There are a lot of things I want in this life...but there may be only one that I need...and it is to have you in my life...the love of my life. This I also know.

I take another breath of the rain. This particular moment...it could go slower.

I miss you! I love you!

Yours Always,
Jared Christopher

August 29, 2009 – 6:50 PM

My Lovely Dawn,

What a day for Seattle sports fans. I hope you know what a sports fan I am. Perhaps because I have so many other pursuits, pursuits that seem to come up more often when I'm with you, my love of sports may come as a surprise to you. But it's something you should know about.

At the middle of the day the soccer team, Sounders FC, played. Although I played soccer for over ten years as a kid, and still enjoy kicking the ball around from time to time, I have never been much of a soccer spectator. I don't find it a very exciting game to watch...as today's 0-0 final score seems to attest.

A few hours later the Seattle Seahawks played one of their exhibition games. I think of conversations we have had about your love of Peyton Manning and his team the Colts. It was so surprising to me the first time we talked about football, as when we were kids it never entered our conversations. I like it though, and I look forward to a day when I can take you to a Seahawks vs. Colts game, and we can root against one another...lovingly!

It is just after 7 o'clock now and the Seattle Mariners have begun their game. Ironically, both Seattle football and baseball team are playing their counterparts from Kansas City today. You may be familiar with the term "football widow"...a woman who "loses" her husband every year when football season begins...but I think it might be worse to be a "baseball widow". You see, in football there is only one game per week, and only 16 total...in baseball season, there is a game almost every night and 10 times the number of games across the entire season. Moreso than any other sport, I am a baseball fan. While I am not fanatical about it, I will almost always watch a game if not otherwise busy.

And finally, later tonight, there is the biggest trend in sports...mixed martial arts. It falls somewhere between boxing, wrestling, and old-fashioned gladiator-style combat. Most of my peers love it...in fact many, including my brother, sister, and brother-in-law, have driven south to Portland to watch the fights live. I passed on the time and expense of going with them, and will instead watch with friends at a nearby pub. I go more for the social aspect.

August 29, 2009 – 6:50 PM

I wonder how we will mesh in terms of sporting pursuits and passions and activities. I know we will have fun with football, and I'm gonna do my best to get you to love baseball. If I can do that, then the rest I can go without. If I can get you to a couple baseball games each year, then we're gonna have such a great marriage!

I miss you! I love you!

Yours Always,
Jared Christopher

August 30, 2009 – 8:25 PM

My Lovely Dawn,

This weekend I spent some time with my nephews. My sister and brother-in-law went out of town so I helped babysit.

I first spent some time with NP. At one point we were both down on the living room carpet with his toys. I was kneeling at one end of the room and NP would be running all over. Occasionally he would turn back to me, squish up his face, and run back to me to give me a big, attack-hug. A couple times he would stop a few feet in front of me, turn around, and slowly back toward me, like a dump truck, until he reached me, at which point his legs seemed to give out, and he plopped down in my lap.

It made me wonder...is there some recognition or familiarity there that makes him comfortable enough to do that with me? Or is he that trusting and affectionate with many people?

My time with TJ began today, a warm and beautiful day, as I attempted to sit in the sun and edit my screenplay. TJ had a ton of toys to play with, but to my surprise he asked almost immediately, "Uncle Kwiss, can I sit in your lap?" I asked him if he had some sunglasses or a hat because it was awful bright in the afternoon sun. He didn't. I asked if he wanted to wear my hat instead. He said, "yes". So I take my old, Herringbone newsboy cap, a hat that fits loosely even on my adult head, and drop it down on his. The bill of the cap immediately fell down in front of his eyes. He didn't seem to mind. I pick him up and set him on my left knee, and begin to scribble changes on the script placed on my right leg.

We sat there in the sun, mostly quiet, for almost twenty minutes. He was so quiet, which is rare for him, that I had to tilt the hat back a few times to see if his eyes were closed and he had fallen asleep. He never did. He just sat there, wanting to be with his uncle, in an oversized, and adorable, newsboy cap.

A couple of sweet moments from a couple of generally sweet boys.

What did you do today?
I miss you! I love you!

Yours Always,
Jared Christopher

August 31, 2009 – 7:28 PM

My Lovely Dawn,

Today was the 31st of August, and the day and the month ended so gloriously. Today's sunset was a thing to behold.

The feathery tufts of clouds, with bodies of violet, and an underbelly of gold. Those closest to the horizon absorbing all of the light that they could, until they appear themselves to be a source of light, against the pink of the sky. It seems clouds, the very thing that can steal the light and the heat in the midst of a day, the very thing we wish would blow away, are what gives the day it's character at the end of its life...each cloud a hard-earned wrinkle on the noble countenance of an aging day.

And then there is the sun itself...the provider of life. What is the science that makes the sun seem ten times larger as it nears the horizon? And what is this color...this golden orange splendor? It is so beautiful that I must remind myself not to look too closely. I must take in this scene as the sum of its parts.

For God is in the details...and what God has done today is the most specific masterpiece.

The only thing more beautiful than the sun as it sets, is the sun as it dawns. And the only thing more beautiful than dawn of the sun, are the dreams I have of the son of lovely Dawn. And your beauty shames all these things and more...as your beauty teaches me to appreciate all of this life, inspires me to want for a newer, greater world, and invigorates me to care for and respect these things a little bit deeper.

Tonight's sunset was yours.

I miss you! I love you!

Yours Always,
Jared Christopher

September 2009

∞

Write & Song

September 1, 2009 – 6:16 PM

My Lovely Dawn,

I hate money.

I really do. I hate how much things cost, and that my taste seems to always want the things that cost more.

I don't mind working hard, in fact I like working, but I struggle to find motivation to do a job that I don't love. And I hate that the jobs I love don't pay very much...until you're at the top of those industries.

I think I read somewhere once that my astrological sign is often "pound-wise and penny-foolish," and I find it to be true for me. I'm rarely ever unable, or even late, to pay a bill...but watch me regularly and notice I probably am not a sensible shopper, certainly not a bargain-hunter, at the grocery store. I don't want to use coupons and I don't want to buy a lesser cut of meat...I want my good steaks.

And I don't want to have to be stingy with my money. I want to spend my money on my loved ones. I want to buy rounds of drinks for my friends. I want to buy great presents for my family. I want to take my girl out to beautiful dinners at the nicest restaurants. And I don't want to have to think twice about doing it.

Now, how do I get back on that path? The path to a stronger financial security. I feel like I have the creative talent to become a successful writer...of movies, or books, or even in journalism. Hopefully the movie scripts will segue into movie directing. Somewhere in all these pursuits that I have such passion for, after the hard work and a little luck, let there also be some money.

I'm already pretty sure the engagement ring that will fit my taste, will also have a heavy pricetag. But the woman I'd put it on is worth it.

I miss you! I love you!

Yours Always,
Jared Christopher

September 2, 2009 – 1:39 PM

My Lovely Dawn,

For the last three days I have driven past a picket line on my way to work. Only this line is not outside a union hall or a Boeing plant...it is outside the local high school. In fact there are teachers striking at every school in our city.

School was supposed to begin this week, but their signs seem to indicate they won't go back to work until they have a new contract. They seem to want smaller class sizes and, although I didn't see any signs mentioning it, I'm sure they would like more pay.

Although I think teachers are so important and extremely underpaid, I do not support this strike...not now. We are in the midst of a recession, unemployment levels are at all-time highs, and for someone WITH a job not to be doing it frustrates me greatly. These teachers should be taking whatever pay they previously agreed to, cashing their paychecks, and then putting that money back into the economy as consumers.

If they have been so displeased with their contract, these teachers should have negotiated a new contract over the summer, on THEIR time. Now, three days into what should be the new school year, they are on the community's time.

Kids remain at home and parents are likely scrambling to accomodate this unexpected change in plans. I rarely object to a strike, but these teachers going out on strike are causing school doors to stay closed, which robs parents of their right to go back to work, and robs this year's high school seniors of graduating on time and enjoying the entirety of their summer break post-graduation.

As for the complaint of class size...why does that feel like such a hollow, spoiled-American position? I think of the movie "Slumdog Millionaire" where the class in the Indian slum was far more crowded than any here in the States. Is the teachers' complaint that they have too many students in their class coming from a place of wanting to give each child more attention? Or do the teachers simply want to have less homework to grade? I have my doubts. Please don't let it be laziness guised as righteousness.

September 2, 2009 – 1:39 PM

I wish I could speak to you directly about this. I remember you speaking of your dislike of the American education system, and I would love to hear your thoughts now.

Thank you for allowing my opinionated ramblings.

I miss you! I love you!

Yours Always,
Jared Christopher

September 3, 2009 – 8:29 PM

My Lovely Dawn,

Oh I have such a nagging headache tonight.

I've been fortunate throughout my life to maintain good health. I rarely get colds, I don't think I've ever had the flu, I've never broken a bone...but I get me some vicious headaches. And far too often.

It seems a strange, ironic occurance that my most frequent ailment should affect one of my greatest strengths...my mind. May I joke that perhaps these headaches are a result of overuse?

The only other health problem I have ever had has been with my lungs. Which is also ironic considering I've taken pretty good care of my lungs...I've never had as much as a single puff of a cigarette.

But for some reason, beginning when I was 18, I began having lung collapses, or the clinical term, "spontaneous pneumo thorax." The first time it happened, it was a sudden, shocking, scary event. I was sitting in a car on my way out to a family dinner...you couldn't have picked a more inactive moment...and yet something felt wrong. Minutes later I had turned white as a ghost, couldn't breathe, and I was rushed to the emergency room, where I was xrayed and then intubated, because of a 25% lung collapse.

It turns out these spontaneous pneumos are a bit of a medical mystery. The doctors know that they happen when "blebs" in the lungs burst. The only other thing they seem to know is that the blebs pop most often in tall, thin males. I am a tall, thin male.

A similar experience happened a few months after my first collapse. Both times when I wasn't being particularly active physically. Both times on the left lung. After the second collapse I elected to have a surgery called a pleurectomy. It was essentially an aggravation of the inner lining of my chest cavity (the pleura), so that my lung attaches to the chest wall as it heals. This is meant to reduce the chance, or at least severity, of another collapse.

What I didn't plan for was the problem switching to the right side the next year. It was like deja vu. Two collapses followed by a pleurectomy in the fall of my 19th year.

September 3, 2009 – 8:29 PM

So now I have two lungs that are basically glued in place, and a dozen scars from the multiple intubations and surgeries. And sadly I can still feel a bleb pop every once in a while. But now when they pop, I try to trust the surgery, take a painkiller, and try to sleep it off.

It freaks my mom out, and I'm sure it would do the same to you, but I don't want to go to the hospital again. Plus I'm just that tough.

Course the same doesn't apply to headaches. Headaches turn me into a grumpy, little wuss. And right now my head is killing me.

I have to go close my eyes.

I miss you! I love you!

Yours Always,
Jared Christopher

September 4, 2009 – 6:44 PM

My Lovely Dawn,

Today...you.

My cell phone chimes the sound of an incoming email and when I look at it, it is from you. My heart, instantly, begins beating harder. Inside the email, only two sentences. It is, perhaps, the greatest compliment a woman of your caliber can give...a compliment by naming me in the same sentence as your father.

I know what these words mean to you, and so they mean all the more to me. I reply to you something modest, then appreciative, and then a little boastful.

But the more I sat and thought about it, the more it meant to me. The more it means to me.

I thought not just on the words of your email, but then on the form of your email. I realized the email address you had used to write me wasn't your usual email address. It was actually the "secret" email address I had created for you months ago, so that we could communicate privately. It was the email address you would later abandon as part of your act of marital salvage. It was the email address that I have been using to send you one letter every day for the last 139 days... unbeknownst to you.

Aha...so my "hiding spot" has been found out!

I'm not sure how I feel about this. I already had mixed emotions that you are able to read my online music column. But now to be able to read these letters that are written, specifically, for and to you...

On the one hand, it could make you miss me even more...perhaps to the point of increasing the chance and speed of our reunion.

On the other hand, it could be a daily lift...a quick hit of your want for our chemistry or my love...without your need to vacate your marriage.

And that is, ultimately, what I want...what will make me happy. And I think it's the same for you as well.

September 4, 2009 – 6:44 PM

      Should it be the dark half of the coin...that the letters are enough for you, that you won't make changes for us... bare in mind that these letters have an expiration date. They end at 365...if not sooner. And then what will you do with the deafening quiet?

      But I still have faith in the up side of the coin...that we have a destiny that doesn't end, could never end, in a hotmail account.

      I miss you! I love you!

Yours Always,
Jared Christopher

September 5, 2009 – 9:25 PM

My Lovely Dawn,

I've just left the Seattle Center where the all-day music and arts festival I am covering for my online music column is coming to a close.

My back hurts, I think I'm developing a couple blisters on my left foot, and at one point I couldn't walk due to a crazy severe cramp in my right calf...both painful and embarrassing.

But I think I captured some good pictures and better stories. The crowd was mostly happy and well-behaved. There were an incredible diversity of ages, races, and orientations represented. And the music followed suit. Or perhaps the music lead? In the course of nine hours today I saw pop music, hardcore, funk, soul, hip hop, and even some comedy. All in all it was mostly good.

And the weather even behaved itself well enough that I was only rained on for a couple minutes...which was an improvement on the forecast that called for mostly rain all day.

Let's hope for the same tomorrow? Weather and music-wise. I will be wearing different shoes and hydrating better to avoid cramping up.

We really need to do this together one year. If not this Monday...I have an extra ticket!

I miss you! I love you!

Yours Always,
Jared Christopher

September 6, 2009 – 7:20 PM

My Lovely Dawn,

I'm at day two of my concert assignment and I'm doing some people-watching. It's pretty entertaining watching the teenagers, who to my aging eyes look like twelve-year-olds. Some seem to take advantage of the freedom from their parents to sneak smokes of cigarettes...menthols by the smell of 'em. They must feel so adult, even though they way they hold their smokes reveals it is likely still the first pack they've ever had.

Other groups of kids have different, but equally obvious, forms of peer-pressure. See how many groups of young kids have almost identical forms of dress. A group of girls in lumberjack flannel shirts that seem to be all the rage now...the only identifying trait being that each has a different color of the same shirt. A group of boys all wearing the same style of hooded sweatshirt...but their uniqueness coming from a different graphic.

As they walk through the crowd you can tell which in the group is the "ringleader". Kids of that age wear their self-consciousness like their clothing, and they all smell of unsure.

I wonder if I was like them when I was that age? I never remember being that carefree. I always seemed to have had the burdens of a much older man weighing on my mind.

And I still have those burdens, only now I match them with responsibility and obligation. I am now like a mature man in a mature man's body. I think this age fits me better.

The next band is starting. I must go.

I miss you! I love you!

Yours Always,
Jared Christopher

September 7, 2009 – 6:32 PM

My Lovely Dawn,

Today is Seattle.

I am in the midst of the Seattle Center which is just north of the center of Seattle. To my left, the city's large sports and events venue Key Arena, and in the distance beyond that our active volcano Mt. Rainier...to my rear the iconic Seattle landmark, the Space Needle...to my right, a handful of theaters for drama and ballet, and just beyond that Queen Anne Hill...and in front of me, a few blocks away and down a hill, is the Puget Sound.

From where I sit, I am within walking distance of a Thai restaurant, Chinese food, an Irish pub, Indian curry, a Mexican taqueria, breakfast served all day, BBQ pork, pizza, burgers, and fondue.

From my raised position above the crowd I can watch and see that the people are bohemian, hippie, eco-friendly, yuppie, punk, skater, scruffy, shabby, chic, preppy, urban, grunge, trendy, woodsie, folksie, pirate, peasant, militant, and mod.

I am surrounded by green and grey, sun and rain. Mountain and forest and lake.

This is earth and wind, fire and water. Music and creation. Eat and drink and merriment. Life and living.

This is Seattle.

Let us always call this home?

I miss you! I love you!

Yours Always,
Jared Christopher

September 7, 2009 – 10:29 PM

My Lovely Dawn,

As I stand in the crowd of the last show of the last day of Bumbershoot (Modest Mouse), I scan through the pictures I've taken this weekend and find one I really love. I think I will send it to you. Maybe you will see what I see. I'll call it, "And Your Heart Felt Good."

As the show is coming to a close, I take one last look up at the Space Needle on my left. I notice the pristine United States of America flag flying at its top...it is blowing to the south. The wind has changed...

Tomorrow will be a better day...

I miss you! I love you!

Yours Always,
Jared Christopher

September 8, 2009 – 10:10 PM

My Lovely Dawn,

I love your name.

Do you like your name? I've never really liked my name and I always wonder if that is common...to dislike your own name. But yours...I think it is uncommon, elegant, lovely...just like you. I love the way it rolls off the tongue. There is a rhythm and a melody to it.

There are so many parents that don't seem to understand this...the music that can be found in words, in names. And the interesting thing is that the music of a name changes whether you are saying first, first and last, first and middle, or first, middle, and last.

I don't really think my first name has a good sound in, and of, itself...not in the common pronunciation. It is thick and clumsy. It could be improved if given a more French pronunciation. Say my first and middle names together and it feels unfinished. But add my last name, or better yet my mother's maiden name...which is the name I was actually born with...and it suddenly, finally feels melodic.

Your name...with your maiden surname...sounds lyrical in all of its forms. Your parents, whether they realized it or not, wrote poetry on your birth certificate.

I have a theory that all of the best girl's names end in vowel sounds. If a girl's name ends in a consonant, I'd be willing to bet it is more often abbreviated to a nickname that does end in a vowel...Jennifer to Jenny, etc. On a boy, those vowel-sound endings give a young impression (Jonnie vs Jon or Jonathon), and the consonant endings sound much more appropriate.

As for inappropriate...I sometimes say your name to myself as it would be if we were married. I can't help it. I've got to say, it's not as good as your maiden name, but it's better than...nevermind.

I miss you! I love you!

Yours Always,
Jared Christopher

September 9, 2009 – 7:24 PM

My Lovely Dawn,

It is a temperate evening, with a little bit of lingering sun. The summer will soon be over and these days harder to find. What I really want to do, is take my wife out for a walk.

We put on our walking shoes, perhaps a light coat, and head out the door. As soon as our feet first touch the sidewalk in front of our house, I hold out my hand...and you knowingly place yours in mine. I pull your hand up and kiss the back of it...I've missed you today.

I have a million questions for you, and they begin with, "How was your day?" You have a story for me about one of your sisters, then an update on the new coffee table you found online (for a bargain) and how you plan to refurbish it, and you tell me about the progress you're making on the book you're writing. It sounds amazing. I love when you write mercilessly and with your true voice.

I wonder about L's Spanish class...it turns out she's such a natural at it that she has surpassed your knowledge of it, and you're worried you won't be able to help her anymore. I try to ease your worries, suggesting it's not necessarily a bad problem to have. As they gain independence so do you...if you know what I mean.

As we walk, we pass by some neighbor kids playing basketball. The ball gets away from them and rolls to me. I ask them, "Think I can dunk it?" They shake their heads "no." I make a run at the hoop...my hands are too small to palm the ball and it slips away. But I do grab the rim...the kids are shocked. Pretty good hops from the old man.

I take the opportunity to ask if we can get J. onto a soccer team this fall. I think she'd love it...I think she'd be a great defender. You think I'm being the sports version of a stage-parent. You may be right. I do kinda want to help coach the team. I say, "I just think we should expose the girls to more sports." You remind me that A is doing her fourth year of gymnastics. I teasingly argue that gymnastics is not a sport...sports have balls. You quickly retort, "So hockey is not a sport?" Touché!

September 9, 2009 – 7:24 PM

Speaking of A...how excited am I that she figured out the E chord on the guitar? I need to get her a smaller guitar of her own, so she can use her small hands to play. I love when she sticks her head in the office door when I'm playing. Just don't ask her what songs I'm teaching her...I'm sure you'll disapprove...but only mildly. You secretly love it when you find us playing together.

Later you try to get me to commit to plans for this weekend...the girls will be with their dad and we get to have a date-night. I'm being very difficult...you think it's indecisiveness, but really I've already made us reservations at a special restaurant, and I'm going to surprise you. And the surprise will continue the next morning when I cook you breakfast...waffles with strawberries...your favorite! But for now I'm being difficult...shoulda been an actor and gotten nominated for "Best Performance by a Husband With Secret Romantic Plans."

We've made our loop of the neighborhood, and walk back to our front door. You open it to head inside, but I pull you back...I place my hands on either of your cheeks and kiss you. I just love to kiss you on porches and in doorways...it has become our little tradition...

Mmm...I drift further into daydreaming...

I miss you! I miss our walks! I love you!

Yours Always,
Jared Christopher

236

September 10, 2009 – 9:42 PM

My Lovely Dawn,

In my life there have been two loves...you and music.

Music has become my profession, indirectly, as I've moved in and out of the industry as a radio DJ and programmer, and today as a music journalist. From my early days in college radio I have discovered I have this incredible ear for music...what songs have a long future ahead of them, what bands have the talent to breakthrough, and where the musical trends will go. I hear these things before the world...and my predictions hold true.

In addition to picking music for the masses, I have found I can design a musical experience for an individual that is one-of-a-kind...a mixtape. And nothing pleases me more than to combine my two loves...and to make a mixtape for the greatest woman I know...a woman that allows the music and the melodies and the words to pour over her, touch her, fill her, consume her.

I miss, so very much, being able to share music with you on a daily basis...to find a song that is beautiful that I know you would love, and to immediately send it to you in an email. I miss that.

So I keep these lists in my head..."songs for Dawn". Eventually the list becomes a mixtape. Eventually the mixtape will find your ears.

This is one of those lists.

These are the songs that bridge us from Summer to Fall of 2009. These are the songs that are the soundtrack to some of my letters. These are the songs that I love. These are the songs that are sweet and thoughtful and beautiful. These are the songs that remind me of you and how much I love you:

September 10, 2009 – 9:42 PM

Owl City "Fireflies"
Matisyahu "On Nature"
Imogen Heap "Bad Body Double"
Placebo "Bright Lights"
Ingrid Michaelson "Soldiers"
Michael Franti "Nobody Right, Nobody Wrong"
Stars of Track and Field "End of All Time"
Mat Kearney "On and On"
Great Northern "Fingers"
Our Lady Peace "Signs of Life"
Ben Harper "Faithfully Remain"

May you hear them...really HEAR them...and love them too.
I miss you! I love you!

Yours Always,
Jared Christopher

September 11, 2009 – 7:37 PM

My Lovely Dawn,

I'm sitting in the backyard shade as the sun is setting on a beautiful day.

You are likely only blocks away, but it is too far. You could be at the other side of this patio, and it would be too far. I would be happy to always have you within arm's length of me...just close enough so that I can reach out and rub your back, close enough to touch your hand, close enough to move a tendril of hair that has fallen in front of your eyes, close enough to hear you laugh.

Close enough that you can rest your hand on my thigh, close enough that you can touch the skin through the hole in the knee of my jeans, close enough that you can graze my stomach in that unconscious way that you do when you walk past, close enough that you can see me mouth, "I love you"...our secret little moment. I would be happy to always be within arms length of you.

There is a kind of magic that occurs when we are together. We both can tend toward the introverted, but together I feel like we will grow our social muscle, perhaps even becoming the life of the party. And we will do so because there is this overwhelming trust between us, and an ever-present knowledge that we will support one another in everything. And in this place together we grow, we learn, and we try new things...at arm's length, and closer, to love.

I know this is true for us.

I miss you! I love you!

Yours Always,
Jared Christopher

September 12, 2009 – 8:55 PM

My Lovely Dawn,

Do you ever wonder how you would be as a mother to sons? If there are innate qualities about you that lend better to parenting a boy, rather than a girl.

I think there really are some people that don't know how to parent one gender. Generally, it is men not knowing how to parent daughters, and women not knowing how to parent sons. But there are occasions of same-sex difficulties. I guess that would mean it is less about gender and more about personality.

I don't know how I would be as a parent of any child...boy or girl...but I remember when you told me you thought I'd be a good dad. That statement meant the world to me.

I think I would be a good parent to both genders. With boys I would share my love of sports. I could help with math and science homework. I think I could be an example of strength without needing to be macho or chauvinistic.

With girls I could share my love of music and language. I could write stories of fantasy for them to dream on. I think I could be an example of a quiet sensitivity and consistent affirmation.

And with both I would try to be entirely affectionate. As I grew up I never knew much affection...either from lack of its presence or my inability to accept it. I want to insure that does not become a pattern. I will not allow my kids to struggle with physical contact the way that I did. Certainly I hope to have you for my partner, and where we are together an example of an open affection is sure to follow.

As will thoughtful conversation, and concern for one's fellow man (or siblings), and passion for life. These are things I think we could teach beautifully together.

I miss you! I love you!

Yours Always,
Jared Christopher

September 13, 2009 – 10:22 PM

My Lovely Dawn,

I have spent the weekend in frequent observance of addiction. Observation, not participation in...for I prefer to observe and learn, comment then teach.

This weekend I have seen those that are addicted to alcohol, marijuana, cocaine, caffeine, food, attention, sex, or uncountable others.

I wonder if everyone has at least one vice. Does each and every one of us have something that they can't live without, that they can't cease? Seen or unseen. If not a personal vice, how many of us are codependent and enablers of another's addictions?

I wonder how often the codependent are women. I wonder if a woman, more often, is not addicted to a substance, but rather to the experience of sharing it with someone she cares for. Change the loved one, and find the experience she is addicted to sharing changes as well.

I wonder if there are those that escape addiction. Am I, having never done any illegal drugs and rarely partaking of alcohol or sex (or food), free of addiction? Or is my addiction simply to control my temptations? Am I a control addict?

At what point does it become considered an addiction? At what point do the rebellious, experimentations of youth become the inappropriate, irresponsible actions of the adults that should know better? At what point should people have moved beyond the immature desires to "get high"? At what point do we, should we, learn our lesson?

I wonder what is your vice? Can you be addicted to seeking the approval of others? Or is it not approval, but a desire not to disappoint? I wonder if, then when, can I convince you to become addicted to only my love? A renewable resource that refreshes every time you smile.

September 13, 2009 – 10:22 PM

     As I have talked and thought my way through this topic I find that, no, I am not without addiction...I am an addict. I am addicted to your smile...I am addicted to your spirit...I am addicted to your love.

     And I am in massive withdrawal.

     I miss you! I love you!

Yours Always,
Jared Christopher

September 14, 2009 – 10:22 PM

My Lovely Dawn,

I've just spent this evening writing you a letter. A letter that began late last night after waking from a dream. I began the letter in the dark, and finished almost 24 hours later by candlelight. This is not that letter.

I realized after I finished writing it, that it felt quite special. It was not merely the letter of the day. It needed to be saved for a special occasion.

Then I noticed...today marks the 149th consecutive day I've written you a letter. Tomorrow will be 150.

150 letters.

150 thoughts I've been wanting to share with you.

150 ways in which I'm trying to show how I love you.

150 days that would have been better spent beside you.

150 submissions to the courtroom of public opinion, as evidence of a true and just love.

My love. Your love. Our love.

For all those that may question how or why we belong together...exhibit 150 arrives tomorrow...and it is from my heart to yours...

And more will follow...
I miss you! I love you!

Yours Always,
Jared Christopher

September 15, 2009 – 5:44 AM

My Lovely Dawn,

I think of our love, the love we would have, and the life we would build around it, and it makes me smile.

It would be this outwardly complex love, with the simplest of explanations. It would be a love that is constantly growing, but never quite changing. It would be persistently climbing to find these great heights, because those are the best places to jump from.

We jump hand-in-hand and take wing then to flight...some jumps we both sprout wings and soar with such might...some jumps only one of us has the strength to fly, and we lean on the stronger and upon a breeze glide gently back down to earth. And then we do it all over again...hiking, jumping, flying. Each part having it's own unique troubles and treasures. What is not beautiful of its own, is beautiful for the lesson it teaches and the pride of overcoming that lights in its wake.

Our life together would be spent constantly wandering seemlessly from acts bearing the silliness of youth, to the moments sparked of wisdom far beyond our years...and in the midst of maturity we find time to giggle again. From acts of sublimely lazy relaxation, to staggering triumphs of ambition-fueled hard work. From the heart of the right, to the mind of the left. From the exhilaration of life's most inexplicable peaks, to the pain and injustice of life's unexpected tragedy. From the dark, to the light. This is how we would travel to and fro.

In so moving from one of life's aspects, to its equal but opposite counterpoint, we find that most of our time will be lived in-between, where we see every side and consider every shade. As we shift from the black to the white, we find that we live in the grey. And when we look back on our lives grown here in Seattle, perhaps we find that the grey lives in us.

September 15, 2009 – 5:44 AM

You see, all of life comes together, overlaps, intersects, and merges to grey...and in the end, we rejoin at the start...a simple love story, so hard to explain.

I explain it like this...you are the woman of my dreams and the love of my life.

I miss you so much! I love you to death!

I am...

Yours Always,
Jared Christopher

September 16, 2009 – 5:09 PM

My Lovely Dawn,

While our economy is in recession we cut expenses. When I cut expenses I cut my supply of Rogaine.

Yes, I am losing my hair. I have been for years now, and I feel pretty lucky to have held on to as much of it as I have. Although, since I've stopped using Rogaine I feel the loss has sped up. And I don't like the way I look bald. Ironically, I never liked my hair when I had it...never knew how to wear it...and soon it won't really matter.

I notice something about balding: men who are balding have facial hair about 80% of the time. Beards, mustaches, goatees. I feel like it is either some kind of overcompensation for the lack of hair on their heads, or, perhaps, men who are balding have some kind of elevated testosterone level that makes them want to wear a rough and rugged beard.

The second point I just mentioned is actually an interesting one...baldness as a result of higher testosterone levels. Firstly, it's easy to observe that baldness rarely occurs in women. But a more telling sign may be if one were to research women that are undergoing gender reassignment to become men. How many, when taking testosterone injections or supplements, grow facial hair and begin male-pattern balding? If this ever becomes studied, see how quickly science engineers the next hair regrowth formula to include some kind of genetically altered estrogen.

Balding is probably the single biggest source of my own self-consciousness and low self-image. It is at its worst when I am around a male, older than myself, who has a much thicker head of hair. And I am utterly powerless against it. I have no control over it. It truly frustrates.

My only options at this point are; 1) use the Rogaine, which seems to slow the loss, but not regrow new hair. 2) hair transplant or toupee, which are both so obvious and gross. 3) wear a hat, which I do as much as possible, but that is getting old. 4) shave my head completely, which, combined with my thin build and light skin, makes me look sickly. 5) Just deal.

Well, there may be an option 6. Find a good woman who loves me in spite and irregardless of my hairline, and then do option 5, which will become so much easier. You have been this kind of woman to me.

September 16, 2009 – 5:09 PM

I remember so vividly the day I revealed that I wear a hat because I'm losing my hair...you told me you thought my honesty was sweet and that you loved me regardless. The next time I saw you, and every time after that, I didn't have to wear a hat. In fact, you told me you thought it was alluring when I'd take my hat off in front of you. Not only does your support give me the confidence to push through my fears, you actually turn it in to a positive...a turn on. I can't tell you how much that means to me. And how much I want that back. I want you back. Your love, your acceptance, your trust and support. And your beautiful curly hair.

I miss you! I love you!

Yours Always,
Jared Christopher

September 17, 2009 – 5:15 PM

My Lovely Dawn,

Last night I worked feverishly into the night to finish my screenplay, so that today I could bring it to you. I wanted you to be the first to read it.

I drove to your house, walked to your door, and took a deep breath. Which turned out to be a good thing. You see, as soon as you opened that door, you took my next breath away.

There you stood, in an outfit that would be quite ordinary on most women...blue jeans and a grey tank top...and yet I was floored by your beauty. I've never seen you look lovelier. Your hair, a lighter shade than I remember. Your skin, tan and soft and almost aglow. Your eyes, bright and blue and mesmerizing. You are every bit a beautiful summer day. You are every bit the most radiantly stunning woman I have ever laid eyes on.

My nerves hit me hard and instantly. My throat went dry. My legs began to shake. I didn't know what to say. I don't know that I could have voiced the words had my mind slowed enough to choose a sentence.

To my relief, I didn't need many words as I found us embracing. I don't know who initiated it. I only know I wanted it, I needed it. Then it was interrupted by L. We pushed back from each other, exchanged some small-talk, and when the coast was clear...we held each other some more.

Your words meant a lot to me. But alas they were cut short by the matters of reality that came intruding down around us in the form of daughters, and neighbors, and jobs. It took everything I had to walk away from that door, but I knew this was not our day, not our moment.

As I drove away I was hit by the scent of you that lingered faintly on my shirt. I shouldn't have been driving...I was surely intoxicated. I was so tempted to pull over, take my shirt off, and bury my face in it...to imagine it was the nape of your neck and I was taking in every taste of your scent. It conjures such lovely dreams.

I want to live on your shoulder. From there I would be a whisper away from your ear, within a gentle lean from your lips and other kissable features, and I'd have a front-porch view of so many of your perfect features. Yes, I think I could call that home.

September 17, 2009 – 5:15 PM

Home is where the heart is...which surely means that I am homeless, and will be until we can be together. And when we can be together, our home will be a mansion, to match the overflowing fullness of our hearts. That will be our day, that will be our moment.

Thank you for opening your door to me today. You are a vision and an angel. I hope you read the script. I hope you like it.

I miss you! I love you!

Yours Always,
Jared Christopher

September 18, 2009 – 10:46 PM

My Lovely Dawn,

A thought reoccurs to me recently...it really bothers me the way many Americans speak of immigrants to the United States.

This was an issue that was prevalent during last year's presidential election, and many elections prior. It has come up again as one of the objections to Obama's health care bill. I hear these conversations where people discuss how much they object to illegal immigration, but there are so many things they forget to consider.

They object to Mexicans sneaking across the border into Texas, but have they ever considered the time they, themselves, snuck across the border into Canada when they were 18 so that they could smuggle beer back to their underage friends?

They object to Mexicans coming here for fear they will "take jobs away from Americans," but have they ever considered how many Americans take jobs away from Americans when they outsource jobs to cheaper-labor countries like India and China?

Can these people tell the difference between a Mexican-American, living here legally, and a Mexican, living here illegally, or have they considered that they just don't like ALL Mexicans living here? Have they considered that there may be Canadians, Brits, Aussies living here illegally that they don't object to? Have they considered that their objections may be a result of Mexicans having a different skin tone and/or speaking a different language? Have they considered that this doesn't make them a patriot, it makes them a racist bigot?

Have they considered that they have a rather selective memory? For, as their American education should have taught them, the U.S. is a country formed of and by immigrants. And while there was little or less government, at earlier stages of the countries' growth, to determine and regulate who could legally enter, members of all Native American tribes might suggest every single one of us is descendant of illegal immigrants...but them.

September 18, 2009 – 10:46 PM

    We can't be a society that fights so hard to knock down the doors that lead to the houses of opportunity, a society that is so admired for having so many doors, only to build brick walls where all the doors had been once we are inside. It is not right to disallow the priviledges we enjoy to those that follow.

    And it is not right to have such cruel thoughts for a people that are so lovely, and hardworking, and caring, and humble.

    I miss you! I love you!

Yours Always,
Jared Christopher

September 19, 2009 – 9:14 PM

My Lovely Dawn,

I cannot shake the image of you answering your door in that tanktop the other day. Oh, how I wanted us to steal off to a bathroom somewhere, lock the door and begin to undress each other.

You looked sensationally sexy to me. But was it sexy? Or was it distinctly normal? Plain? And only elevated to such heights in my mind because I am so utterly in love with you?

There is the saying that love, whatever the cause and symptom, is blind. In my experience, personal and observational, there is a lot of truth to this. This is why, during build-up and courtship, people speak so highly of their partner...but once things have gone south, people generally hate the other person. All the characteristics that were once tolerable quirks become obnoxious, glaring flaws. Has the ex really made some huge transformation? No. We are just seeing them through a different filter. Love may be blind, but it is trumped by the 20/20 vision of hindsight.

So how will I see you in hindsight? There was a time, after you were married, that I looked back on you and, outwardly, claimed I hated you. That's what I said to people. But really, I was actually hating the pain I felt from losing you. When I was alone with my thoughts, I still loved you...and, unbeknownst to most of the world, I never stopped thinking about you. I couldn't...I was writing a movie about you, for you. Even in hindsight I saw the best in you, I saw loveliness.

Back in the present...I wonder if this love I have for you stems more from your incredible physical beauty, or your mind and spirit. I wanted to make some analogy that I've known beautiful women who weren't as smart as you, and smart women who weren't as beautiful as you...but as I thought about it, I've never known a single woman who was more beautiful. Nor have I ever known a single woman who I found more intellectually incredible than you.

This, of course, means I have never known a single woman who is BOTH as sexy and smart as you. So it's not really possible to isolate a single variable. But it still serves to show that I love everything about you. Your predominant characteristics are unmatched by all other women. They are only matched by the description of a woman that I find perfect for me.

September 19, 2009 – 9:14 PM

I'm suddenly realizing that I began this letter talking about how sexy you are. Isn't it funny that I felt I needed to defend that by adding how much I also love your mind? Is that a result of how society teaches us to feel guilty or ashamed about sex? For the record, I have never wanted a woman more. And the best part is that I want you for my wife...

The honeymoon...I don't know the location, but I'm picturing slowly lifting off your tanktop...because I am so utterly in love with you AND because you are the sexiest woman ever. You are the kind of sexy that is effortless. The kind of sexy that makes plain, ordinary tanktops the stuff of my most vivid fantasy.

I miss you! I love you!

Yours Always,
Jared Christopher

September 20, 2009 – 6:40 PM

My Lovely Dawn,

Tonight are the Emmy Awards. I am a sucker for award shows.

I love seeing the actors and actresses out of character and all dressed up. I love predicting who will win. I love the spontaneity and emotion of the acceptance speeches. I love planning my own acceptance speech.

Is that wrong? I can't help myself. I know I only finished my first script days ago, I have no idea if/when the movie will be produced, but I try to plan ahead. Actually, I shouldn't say "plan" because that implies, to me, a definitive schedule of events, and obviously I know there is nothing definitive about what I want to do. But it is my nature to always think of, to question, what would be next. And to set the goals that would make it so.

And to that end, I think of my movie filmed, released, and a success. What would be next? An Academy Award ceremony, an undetermined number of years into the future, where I am fortunate enough to be attending as a nominee. The category is "Best Original Screenplay" and, since this is a fantasy, let's add on "Best Director."

I arrive on the red carpet, like many writers and directors, with many days growth of beard and an incredible case of nerves. Walking beside me, this incredible vision of a woman...with long tendrils of wavy, brown hair...a dress of midnight blue showing off lovely arms and a lovelier decolletage...and these eyes, lit by the afternoon sun, that sparkle like sapphires. The media along the carpet will wonder, "Who is this stunning creature, and what movie is she in?" To help calm my nerves you'll hold my hand and whisper to me, "Don't worry, no one will ever see this." It makes me smile because years before, as we both stood nervously before a camera, in tux and gown, I whispered the same line to you as we posed for a high school prom picture.

And what would be next? A win of course. Likely for the writing nomination, because the directing award will go to some hack named Tarantino. I begin my acceptance speech, as all good speeches should, with a joke. I have the joke already written, but I'll save it for the night of. After the joke, my acceptance will take a more serious turn. That, I will also save.

September 20, 2009 – 6:40 PM

And what will be next? People will be so charmed by my speech, on top of the acclaim for my film, that I will be given numerous offers to write and direct other new projects. But the studio that I will work with will be the one that comes to me and says, "What do YOU want to do next?" And I will say, "I have this idea...a story of star-crossed lovers...a year apart...and every day a letter."

That's what would be next. But first, I've got to get the girl in the blue dress to marry me.

I miss you! I love you!

Yours Always,
Jared Christopher

September 21, 2009 – 12:26 PM

My Lovely Dawn,

Follow my brain on this ride...

I'm sitting in a restaurant, under a ceiling fan, which is right next to an air-conditioning vent. I'm basically freezing. Outside it is beautiful and about 75 degrees.

I begin to wonder why the restaurant staff, who all appear to be women, have it so cold...I thought women love when it's warmer and try to take advantage whenever they can because they are almost always cold on their own...unless they're going through menopause, at which point they get the infamous hot-flashes. So I think to myself, if the hot-flashes occur upon the end of menstruation, and women are always cold in the years while ovulating, perhaps they are all tied together.

While on her period, a woman is losing blood, therefore losing rate of circulation, and therefore colder. After years of this cycle, perhaps the body makes some adjustment to anticipate the impending lowered body temperature. Then when menopause arrives, the body is still making the adjustment to raise body temperature, but with no loss of blood, it is now overcompensating and it overheats...hot flash.

Does this sound at all logical? Obviously, I don't know enough about this personally, but it seemed to make sense when it hit me. Maybe this is common knowledge for women, I just don't know it because I generally try to avoid discussions of womanly issues. But I am working on being more mature about it. I have a feeling it could be an adjustment that could save me some time down the road.

Today's letter is a strange one. Perhaps I will write again later. Perhaps you will come over to watch "House" with me? Although we both know how that would end...in which case you should definitely come over.

A guy can dream, can't he?

I miss you! I love you!

Yours Always,
Jared Christopher

September 21, 2009 – 9:15 PM

My Lovely Dawn,

Sometimes life just puts a lump in my throat and a tear in my eye.

There are these moments in life when I can't bare how much beauty there is in the world. It just consumes me. And I bathe in it. I linger under its light. Please, just a moment more. Let me stay?

The beauty is there when we look for it...when we accept it...when we appreciate it...when we nurture it...when we believe in it...

The beauty is in a thoughtful gesture...the beauty is in the melody of a song...the beauty is in the laughter of a stranger...the beauty is in the fluttering of a flag...the beauty is in the simplicity of a sandwich...the beauty is in the grace of a gentle touch...the beauty is in the fight for a worthy cause...the beauty is in needing someone very, very much...the beauty is in the way a mother holds her child...the beauty is in the truth of the tears that now cloud my eyes...

You are beauty.

I miss you! I love you!

Yours Always,
Jared Christopher

September 22, 2009 – 5:43 PM

My Lovely Dawn,

There are so many things we are missing from each other's lives when we are not together.

We didn't get to celebrate our birthdays, together.

We didn't get to go to church on Easter, together.

We didn't get to celebrate when we both got 4.0 grades in our college courses, together.

We didn't get to celebrate my first college degree, together.

We didn't get to go see Candlebox or Pearl Jam in concert, together.

We didn't get to see movies like "The Brothers Bloom" and "Away We Go," together.

We didn't get to wish the girls a happy birthday, together.

We didn't get to go to my nephews' soccer jamborees, together.

We didn't get to see L. off for her first day of first grade, together.

We didn't get to watch NP furiously playing the drums, together.

We didn't get to watch the season premiere of "The Office" and "House" this week, together.

We didn't get to watch the Hawks on Sunday and the Colts on Monday, together.

We didn't get to ride along the river today, together.

We didn't get to sit on the back patio tonight, in the cool of the shade on the last perfect day of summer, together.

We won't find the cool of the sheets and the warmth of each other's skin in bed tonight, together.

Will we ever be, together?

I miss you! I love you!

Yours Always,
Jared Christopher

September 23, 2009 – 7:12 PM

My Lovely Dawn,

There are some things about both genders that I don't understand.

I don't understand why women will call someone on the phone, male or female, and immediately open with, "What are you doing?" First of all, it sounds accusatory, and that puts someone (primarily men) on the defensive. And if you're calling during work hours, chances are I'm working. Why not ask, "How's work going?" or, better yet, "Do you have time to talk?" then proceed from there.

I don't understand why men are generally so romantically challenged. It's understandable if you can't articulate your feelings very well, but there has to be a greeting card or a song that would encapsulate it pretty well. Look for one. When in doubt, keep three expressions at the ready at all times; 1) "You make me want to be a better man." 2) "You look beautiful tonight." 3) "I love you so much." That's it. It doesn't have to get all flowery or poetic. Just those three expressions, given sincerely, on a regular rotation, and you'll be in good shape.

I don't understand when women are upset, and their man finally notices and asks if she's okay, she says she is alright. And yet she keeps a secret, mental notebook of his transgression(s) which she will use against him later. Let him know when he is in the wrong. Help train him.

I don't understand why men are so indecisive. Stop worrying if she will be okay with your choice, and make a decision. Girls love when you are assertive. Yes, sometimes she will argue, but that is only because she is testing you. And because women do like to argue from time to time. Let her argue.

I don't understand why women seem to want to complain without needing resolution or improvement to the offensive situation. Fortunately I am learning to empathize.

I don't understand why men wear clothes that have worn down to holey rags. Fortunately not all of my traits fall in line with the average man.

September 23, 2009 – 7:12 PM

     I don't understand why women complain about the toilet seat. If you're worried about falling in, don't back blindly into a toilet. You shouldn't be doing that anyways because sometimes the seat and the lid are both down. When you do find a toilet with a seat up, don't complain...it takes a drop of your hand to fix the problem...gravity does the rest. Complaining about this makes you seem unobservant, lazy, and whiny.

     I don't understand why men leave the toilet seat up. Just imagine the toilet seat is the same as changing the oil in your car. You get very frustrated when your wife/girlfriend/daughter runs her oil pan dry...well putting the toilet seat back down when you're done is just preventative maintenance. Don't give your wife reason to overheat.

     I don't understand what you're going through. But I want to. It would be easier if I could talk to you. I learn so much better when my questions are asked to a person and not a place-holding, unresponsive email account.

     I don't understand how I came to be so lucky to know you, to love you, to have you love me back...but I am. You make me a better man. You, undoubtedly, look beautiful tonight. I love you so much!

     I miss you! I love you!

Yours Always,
Jared Christopher

September 24, 2009 – 9:18 PM

My Lovely Dawn,

There are many things I'm hoping for in the midst of all of this...but one of them is my hope that you will write.

I feel like there is so much inside of you...dark side and light...history and hope...terrors and triumphs...and these things must be shared in your writing.

I love when you write! Especially when you open up and reveal something true. Truths can be painful, but what else is painful? Growing? But at the root of growing pain is growth. I will always stand by you in your growth, even if it comes in the form of something painful to me, as standing by you unconditionally will grow the heights and depths of us. And, speaking of depths, when you write things of a deep and dark nature, and do it unmercifully and without fear, your writing elevates and becomes riveting. I've seen it many times.

There are other times I've found your writing to be too precious. Intentional or not, I don't think that is your voice. I think you sometimes write with consideration that your family will read it and judge it, judge you, for any truth behind it. So you preemptively censor yourself. With all the reasons, and ways, writing can be judged, why not give yourself the best chance to be judged as "good"? And you are GOOD at writing suspense.

You can make an airplane ride intense for reasons outside of a fear of flying. You can make a dorm inspection a pulse-racing, sweat-inducing nightmare. You can make a stop sign seem the most difficult decision a life will ever have to make. You can write suspense!

Believe in yourself. Let go of your inhibitions. Trust that your family will always be family...or, at least, that memories will be short. And write!

If you still can't write for the world, for public consumption, then write for me. I will be consumed by the way your writing consumes me, and savor every savory word. Feed my soul at every meal and write.

It is in you. And it is good. It is incredible!

I miss you! I love you!

Yours Always,
Jared Christopher

September 25, 2009 – 4:55 PM

My Lovely Dawn,

   I am hating this. I am removed from the conversation. I am removed from your life. I think you still love me, so I feel my banishment is unjustified. This silence hurts me. It really does. In my righteous indignation I want to lash out.

   I consider showing you that I have other options...there are other women who want to be with me...and maybe I should start spending some time fulfilling their wishes instead of continuing in my quest to show you a new kind of faith and devotion. You may not even care what I'm trying to do for you. If you do care, if it is not a strong enough emotion to become actionable, it's sort of irrelevant...actions speak louder than words. Maybe if the tables become turned, if you are presented with the fear of losing ME, you will wake up to what you're doing, what you're missing, and hasten the process and take action.

   I hate the patronizing sound of what I'm about to say, but...I wonder if I need to show you that you need to start being a more active participant in your own life. You give me the impression that you consistently give in to the wishes of other people. What percentage of your life decisions are yours? When we were kids you wouldn't date me because you thought your parents would object, if not flat-out order you not to. Now, you are continuing in a marriage, that has never been a loving marriage, because of pressure from your husband. Or his request for more time. Deny your marriage is, and has always been, troubled if you wish, but that would mean you're either lying to me now, or you lied when you revealed things about your marriage to me in the past.

   If not your husband, maybe you'll deflect making the decision I want you to make, and I believe you want to make, under the guise of protecting your children. First of all, I really dislike this assumption. If we're going with assumption, let me share mine...I assume, if you continue in a marriage that your heart is not in, there will come a day when your daughters have matured to young women, when they can better think and speak for themselves, and they will say to you, "Mom we just want you to be happy. Don't stay together for us." I've spoken to grown children of divorce, and they have never spoken of a wish that their parents had stayed together.

September 25, 2009 – 4:55 PM

The question is, do you want to continue the status quo, or do you want to break the cycle? The cycle of living in a loveless marriage "for the kids". The cycle of not living for yourself. And yes, I realize the irony of me wanting you to make your own decision and for that decision to be the one I'm suggesting. But at the heart of my suggestion is the belief that you love me and want to find a way to us. My suggestion is that you not look for a way to us, but CREATE a way to us.

I know there are many questions about the future...fears if you do, fears if you don't...but we can't answer ANY of those...therefore they cancel each other out. We must move forward with the things we do know. So...do you know if you love me?

I know I love you. I know I will marry you if you'll have me. I know I will adore L, A, and J. I know I will work. I know I will learn. I know I will be a good dad. I know I will be a good husband.

I know I miss you! I love you!

Yours Temporarily,
Jared Christopher

September 26, 2009 – 8:41 PM

My Lovely Dawn,

It's a Saturday night...I am watching reruns of The Office and scrolling through the address book of my phone. I want to call someone. I want to go out. I want to enjoy my weekend. I don't want to be alone. But none of these names will get a call tonight.

Is it because the number is for a married friend who won't want me to be the third wheel? Is it because the number is for a friend that has kids now and can't find a babysitter short-notice? Is it because the number is for a friend that has moved far away and couldn't go out in Seattle if they wanted to? Is it because the number isn't actually for a friend, but rather the Chinese restaurant that I order take-out from? Is it because the number is for a friend that never calls me and may not be much of a friend after all?

Yes and no.

Yes, it is all of these things. No, it is because, even if none of these conditions were applicable, the truth is I only want to call one of these numbers...yours...my best friend.

With you beside me, I would no longer be a third wheel because I would be on a double date. With you beside me, no one would have to find a babysitter because we would have family dinners and playdates with our friends and their kids. With you beside me, my long-distance friends would be an excuse for us to travel together. With you beside me, we would simply order larger portions of Chinese takeout. With you beside me, I would never need my phone to ring again. With you beside me I would have all that I would ever need. With you beside me all other things would be possible, all other things would be better.

The Office is over now and I should probably eat something...especially if I start drinking tonight, like I think I will. Where did the number for that Chinese restaurant go?

I miss you! I love you!

Yours Today,
Jared Christopher

September 27, 2009 – 5:44 PM

My Lovely Dawn,

I remember when you told me how smart you thought I was. It meant a lot to me because of how smart I think you are. It meant a lot to me because I think so much is possible through the power of deep thought, and I want to be someone who thinks deeply and accomplishes great things.

But, today, I'm not so sure you're right.

How smart can I be when I got fired from a career that I truly loved...twice? How smart can I be when I've wasted so much time NOT furthering my education and increasing my pay-scale with higher degrees? How smart can I be when I'm doing the ridiculous job I'm doing now, and struggling to pay my bills?

How smart can I be when I seem to alienate all the people around me? How smart can I be when I've ruined relationships with women that are doctors and bikini models, accountants and ballet dancers, PHD candidates and massage therapists? How smart can I be when I've devoted myself to a woman that has broken my heart...twice?

How smart can I be when this is my life?

How smart can I be?

I miss you! I love you!

Yours Today,
Jared Christopher

September 28, 2009 – 8:11 PM

My Lovely Dawn,

      I am living a life that no one knows.
      I want to have kids and no one knows.
      I am a specifically gifted, hard-working employee and no one knows.
      I keep a very clean house and no one knows.
      I do my own interior design and no one knows.
      I make a pretty good waffle and no one knows.
      I can dunk a basketball and no one knows.
      I can juggle a soccerball with my feet and no one knows.
      I've worked my body to a chiseled specimen and no one knows.
      I write words of poetry and no one knows.
      I take beautiful photographs and no one knows.
      I play songs on the guitar and no one knows.
      I write you a letter every day and no one knows.
      I am extremely loyal and no one knows.
      I am thoughtful and no one knows.
      I am naïve and no one knows.
      I am sensitive and no one knows.
      I am confused and no one knows.
      I am idealistic and no one knows.
      I care so deeply and no one knows.
      I am alone and no one knows.
      You still love me and no one knows.
      I could disappear tonight and no one would know.
      I am a man that no one knows.

      I miss you! I love you!

Yours,
Jared Christopher

September 29, 2009 – 9:21 PM

My Lovely Dawn,

It's been a rough day. After staring at a computer screen all day, I came home to a house renovation project. I'm installing a new fan in the ceiling. Between the dust and bits of drywall falling in my eyes, I also managed to beat up one of my shins, both knees, and both hands.

I left the project unfinished so that I could get an article written before the next deadline. Looking at another computer screen only worsened the burning in my eyes. I think I could use some tears to wash away the dry sting I am now feeling. I think I will listen to our wedding song...that always seems to get my eyes to well up. And then sleep.

We hope for better tomorrow.

I miss you! I love you!

Yours,
Jared Christopher

September 30, 2009 – 7:36 PM

My Lovely Dawn,

      This is not my week. Today I am all thumbs. I nearly broke a printer at work. When I got home I dropped a piece of my new ceiling fan squarely on my nose. There's a bit of a cut on the bridge. I've taken an Advil and I'm trying to prevent any bruising by icing it down with a bag of frozen green beans. What a sight this must be.

      I'm contemplating telling my new coworkers that I am a member of an underground fight club. "I am Jack's clumsy left feet." That is a movie reference you probably don't get.

      I miss you! I love you!

Yours,
Jared Christopher

October 2009

∞

Falling

October 1, 2009 – 7:19 PM

My Lovely Dawn,

I've had a bad week. No question. My body has felt beat up, my spirit broken down. But today, as I sat at a red light, my soul left me for a second and I regained sight of the bigger picture.

This is my test. This is my trial. This is my suffering. This is my passion.

I will continue in my dedication to this symbol of my love, because I continue to love you. Even in your absence, this love continues. Have faith in this. See me fight the pain of your absence...see me pay my penance and carry the cross that is mine to bear...see our love resurrected when our trial ends next Easter.

This is my gift to you.

Your gift to me? Recognition and acceptance. Recognize what I'm attempting to do for you, and accept that it is real...it is true. Recognize that the unconditional love you once thought could only come from heaven, can exist here on Earth. Accept that this is how I love you...unconditionally. Recognize that you have hurt me...you have gone against what I hoped for us, but accept my word that I love you still. Recognize what your heart tells you about me, and accept that it is there with reason...that that feeling is okay...it is good...it will be amazing. Recognize how incredibly special our relationship is...how I adore you...how you complete me, and accept my hand in marriage.

That will be your second gift to me.

I miss you! I love you!

Yours Always,
Jared Christopher

October 2, 2009 – 11:32 PM

My Lovely Dawn,

Friday. A difficult week is coming to a close. And it ends on a curious note of coincidence or fate.

It is not really in my personality to speak of my personal life...my romantic relationships, my dates, my...whatever. Or perhaps it isn't about personality, but rather my one-sided history that generally had little to speak of. Regardless, my shy, private nature includes discussions about you.

I do not speak of our relationship, nor our current lack thereof. Not to friends or family. No one knows the status of "us" right now. I should say, "no one knew the status of us."

Today, under completely independent, isolated acts, two people in my life asked me about you. It has been months since I have spoken to anyone about you, so it struck me as quite odd for it to happen twice today.

This did point out a couple things to me...when people don't ask me about you, I don't tell. When they do ask about you, I tell... everything. Well, not everything. But plenty. Ask me the right question and I won't shut up. It also demonstrated to me that you are loved in ways you don't realize, by people you didn't know would care.

Today showed me that, while you may worry about the way your circle of family and friends may shatter and change should you divorce, you have a new support structure ready and waiting and excited to see you, should you decide to change course.

You have so many people who will love and adore you, because you are so completely love- and adore-able. My friends and family are rooting for us.

I wanted you to know that.

Those that aren't pulling for us already will jump on the bandwagon when they see us together. They'll be lucky not to overdose on our collective charm. We will win over all cynics. In no short time, they will come to us to discover the secrets of a healthy, trusting, passionate, thoughtful marriage. They will wonder how we do it...

October 2, 2009 – 11:32 PM

And we will tell them "compete". When you compete, compete at "who can love the deepest"...when you win, win your lovers heart...when you lose, lose yourself in their eyes...when you fight, fight for love to never falter...fight for every day to be spent in the moment...fight for every moment to be with your lover.

I am fighting. And in my corner...friends and family that showed me today they support you...and us.

I miss you! I love you!

Yours Always,
Jared Christopher

October 3, 2009 – 9:51 PM

My Lovely Dawn,

What do you think about when you go out on your walks?
Is every walk the same? Or do you vary your route?
When is your favorite time for a walk? Early morning with a dew on the lawn and a crispness in the air? Perhaps at dusk when the light is all golden and the day begins to cool but is still warm enough?

What season is best? Spring, when life is renewing and birds sing the loudest? Summer, when the air fills the senses with smells of cut grass and charcoal barbecues? Fall, when the leaves become a hundred different shades and then crunch under foot? Winter, when there is the magic of stillness and a hope for snow to fall?

Where do you go? Are there houses you pass that inspire new decor or a better way to landscape? Are there places you seek where you'll see and hear children at play? Is there a spot that you've found that brings a peace to your soul?

Are your walks a time for exercise? Or is it a time for quiet? Time away from your kids? Or time away from your husband? Is it time when you plan the events of your life? Or is it time for escape?

Do you escape to memories of the past? Do you escape to dreams or goals for the future? Do you contemplate your ever-present?

Are your walks for your body, or more for your mind?
Are your walks just for you, or may I tag along?
If I am invited, may I hold your hand?
I miss you! I love you!

Yours Always,
Jared Christopher

October 4, 2009 – 8:50 PM

My Lovely Dawn,

Oh it's a marvelous night for a moondance, with the stars up above in your eyes.
A fantabulous night to make romance, 'neath the cover of October skies.
And all the leaves on the trees are falling, to the sound of the breezes that blow.
And I'm trying to please to the calling, of your heartstrings that play soft and low.

Of course, these are not my words...but the words of the great Van Morrison. And as I drove home this evening...a chill in the air, not a cloud in the sky, stars abounding, and the fullest, clearest moon you could ever hope to see...these are the words that ring in my ears.

It is a wonder to me that the greatest pieces of art are the ones that simply hold a mirror up to life. A song that captures the senses and feelings of a season. A painting that holds the essence and mystery behind the smile of a woman. An actor that is so invested in his role that we feel his pain and share his heartbreak.

It amazes me this human capacity for empathy. That, when we live with an open mind and an open heart, the art of another can affect us, can stir our emotions. Music seems to be the strongest conveyor of this. Film would be second, because within film it's director can manipulate emotion WITH music.

When we listen with our heart, music can consume us. It can take a bad day and make it better. It can make us feel less alone. It can make our experiences seem relatable when shared by others. For every emotion and experience, we can find a piece of art that matches it.

And when there isn't a piece of art that captures what we're feeling, WE can become the artist. And somewhere down the road our fellow man will turn to our piece of art as THEIR touching stone. And the cycle will continue.

I miss you! I love you!

Yours Always,
Jared Christopher

October 5, 2009 – 8:35 PM

My Lovely Dawn,

You are, without a doubt, the most exquisitely beautiful woman I have ever seen.

I've just been on Facebook where I discovered your sisters have some pictures of you. In one of them you are wearing a black bikini. My jaw must have hit the floor. Look at your shoulders, your collarbones, your breasts, your stomach. Look at that stomach! This is a woman that has carried and birthed three babies!! And look at that stomach! I know the picture quality is lacking, but do I detect some serious ab definition? Have you increased your workouts? You look amazing! And I know the picture is recent because your second-youngest sister is pregnant in the picture.

I scroll through some more pictures to find one where you hold your young niece on your hip. Your hair has grown so long. You haven't straightened it. Good. Never straighten your glorious curls. It looks lovely. Your skin is tan and luminous. Oh, how I love this woman. How I love you!

But this series of pictures reveals something else. It reveals a lack. These pictures all lack your smile. What is the woman, who was blessed with the most perfect smile ever, doing without even the hint of a grin in all of these photographs?

Some people, perhaps even you, will downplay it as coincidence...a toss of the dice as a result of the candid nature of the shots. But I see it differently. I see a woman who may not have reason to smile. I see a woman who is not happy.

This is unacceptable.

In all of these pictures you are surrounded by family...do none of them notice what is going on? Do none of them care? Or is every single one of them more comfortable with the idea that a little blood in the mouth is better than a little blood on the ground?

This is unacceptable.

The last thing I notice is...no, it's not something I notice...it is something I fear. I fear, if we can end up together, that I will never fit in with your family. This has always been my fear. Your family is beautiful. Your family is sunshine. Me...I am more like a shadow. I am dark and deep and complicated...

October 5, 2009 – 8:35 PM

    I am feeling self-conscious tonight. I should keep in mind that once upon a time you thought I looked hot and that you thought you might need plastic surgery to keep pace with me (so to speak...and don't you dare)...that you once said you felt unworthy of my love...that you once said you envied MY family in many ways. So, we both have some insecurities. But when put into words, it really goes to show that we are two sides of the same coin. We can balance each other out. You can give me the confidence and support to relax around your family, and I can give you reason to smile!
    And we can work on our six-packs together!
    I miss you! I love you!

Yours Always,
Jared Christopher

October 6, 2009 – 8:38 PM

My Lovely Dawn,

I awoke this morning from a dream...a dream of writing a letter...a letter to your father to explain all that has gone on and all that I hope is yet to come. These thoughts wake me an hour before my alarm clock would have. I spend that hour tossing and turning, trying to return to sleep but failing. Words are pouring through me.

Words of apology. Words of explanation. Words of bitterness. Words of envy. Words of fear. Words of gratitude. Words of thanks. Words of respect. Words of honor.

All these words and so many of them don't belong together. How does one explain the past, the present, and the future while encapsulating the nuance of all these powerful words...these powerful emotions?

With one word...with one emotion...the most powerful of both... love!

Love is my explanation for everything.

Mr. B...I am in love with your daughter. I am in love with Dawn I loved her then, I love her now, I will love her always. I won't apologize for the way I love her...so truly, so deeply, so madly, so blindly. I am bitter for the loss of so many years without her, but I can look past it because I love her and a minute in her arms can heal a year's worth of pain. I love her so much that I envy those in her life where I wish to be. I love her so much I fear a life without her. I love her so much I am grateful to you for raising her the way that you have. I am so thankful to have had even a moment in time to love her. In the future I will respect you better and love her in a way that you will be proud of. I give you my word of honor that I will always take care of her, cherish her, believe in her, and love her. Thank you Mr. B.

This is what I would like to tell your father.
I miss you! I love you!

Yours Always,
Jared Christopher

October 7, 2009 – 8:01 PM

My Lovely Dawn,

I stumbled onto something fascinating and frustrating today.

There is an office I go to for work where ninety percent of the employees are female. And I'm venturing a guess that of those women, 75 percent are lesbian. A couple of the men that work there may also be gay. I am drawing the inference that someone in the position to hire new employees is gay.

This seems inappropriate in a way. Not because they may or may not be gay, but because it seems to be a double-standard. If a white, heterosexual man was in the practice of hiring an overwhelming majority of other white, heterosexual men, he would be completely chastised for it...accused of racism, chauvinism, and more.

Is it not possible that a good portion of the long history of what has been called racism, was never about the white man trying to keep the black man down (or women, or Jews, or gays, etc.), but rather just a desire, or a comfort, that all people share, to be around people that are similar to us? Birds of a feather...

The best way to test this theory is to study how a member of these other groups handle themselves, and their company, when they earn a position of power. Let's take one of the most powerful people in America...who is a woman...who is black...who is Oprah Winfrey. For whatever reason, I noticed an episode of her show that profiled a behind-the-scenes look at her company, Harpo. You know what I noticed? It seemed to me that there was an underlying pecking order for hiring. Black women were at the top. Then women in general. Then black men. It seemed the only white man I noticed in the show was gay. I don't think I saw a single straight, white guy. Why the lack of men like me?

October 7, 2009 – 8:01 PM

I sort of understand that people would want to "make up for lost time"...give other people the opportunities they never had. But I think that ignores the fact that those opportunities did come. Someone gave Oprah the opportunity to anchor the news. Someone gave Jackie Robinson the opportunity to play in the major leagues. A lot of someones fought to give women the right to vote and, literally, fought to free slaves. And of course in all those cases the opportunities were deserved. History proves that. But trace the line back through generations and you find that a lot of the someones giving the opportunities were straight, white men.

Straight, white men who knew the equality of all races and genders, and knew they had to correct the injustices of their fathers. But this gets forgotten, because it is bad form to take credit for correcting something that should never have occurred in the first place. And some day a lot of straight, white men will stand beside all the gay men and women of the world in correcting the injustice of their exclusion from marriage.

The point of this is not, "oh poor me...just another struggling white dude." The point of this is that we all like to hang out and work with our friends, people we have the most in common with. The point is; don't forget that your parents fought to give you the right to be included. After you have gained inclusion, in time, you will gain power. Once you have power, don't use that power to be exclusive. When you gain the power of the Jedi, do not join the darkside...do not become that which your parents fought against.

Let us all be included because we are all the same. We are not wo-man, we are not black-man, we are not gay-man, we are not man. We are all HUMAN.

I miss you! I love you!

Yours Always,
Jared Christopher

October 8, 2009 – 10:38 PM

My Lovely Dawn,

One year ago today I was laid off from my job of four years...a job that I loved in a field that I had been working in since high school. There were two people I had to talk to immediately...my mother and you.

As I drove home from Seattle with my box of shame...the contents of which came from my hastily emptied work locker...I didn't want to go home. I asked if I could come see you. I needed to come see you.

You opened your front door and wrapped your arms around me. You invited me in. This was the first time I had ventured more then two steps into your house. We ended up at the dining room table...you on the end near the kitchen and I at the opposite side.

We proceeded to talk for a couple hours. I don't remember all the topics we must have covered, but there were many. I remember two moments very specifically though...

I remember finding myself, in the midst of what had been a pretty terrible day, sitting far beyond arm's reach of you and simply talking...feeling relaxed by your words and your company. Sometimes a lot can be expressed through a simple sentence, so when I looked at you and said only three words, "This is nice," you knew what I meant.

The other thing I remember, is seeing you holding J. on your lap, mustering every ounce of energy, every remnant from the nonstop work of fulltime motherhood, and using that energy to make J. giggle. As she took refuge from the tickling, trying to hide in the crook of your arm, I raised my hands to form an imaginary camera...and fired off a single frame. The picture of a mom. The picture of a woman. The picture of the love of my life in the very presence of the love of her life...her child.

October 8, 2009 – 10:38 PM

To this day I carry that picture with me...an imaginary photograph of the realest moment of the truest love I have ever witnessed. I keep it on my heart. I will always cherish it.

I will always cherish the way you talked with me that day...the way you love your children...the person you are. I will always love you.

Always.

I miss you! I love you!

Yours Always,
Jared Christopher

October 9, 2009 – 8:59 PM

My Lovely Dawn,

People are missing so much great music!

Of course there are many people who would take offense at that, because they consider themselves very ahead-of-the-curve musically…very musically inquisitive and exploratory…the kind of person that lives by the slogan, "My favorite band hasn't even been born yet."

For most people though, the people that depend on media to draw attention to new music, there is a lot they are missing out on. And the problem is not theirs, but rather the music industry's. Record labels and radio stations, and most of their respective employees, are predominantly clueless about music (and about the jobs of their counterparts at the label/station).

One of my biggest frustrations is the way that record labels have been taken over by douchebags with marketing degrees, rather than folks that purely love music and may have dropped out of college. I'm not bagging on all label employees…there are still many talented, passionate people working for labels. But the people in charge, the "decision-makers," are basically suits with a pulse. In fact, the less money you're making working for a record label, the more equipped you probably are to know what bands and what songs should be promoted to the masses…where the trends are. By the time you've achieved any kind of success in the industry, you have basically aged yourself out of being in the demographics for your own products. The whole system is backwards. Rock music, much like the Wu-tang Clan, is for the babies… so the music industry should be run by the young, and idealistic youth.

But that point, generally, only applies to discovering new talent. The music industry also screws up delivering (and redelivering) known talent/artists to the masses. That half of the blame falls on radio and radio programmers. Radio programmers have two fatal flaws: 1) they only have a short-term memory, and 2) they are bigger chickens than Marty McFly.

The first trait becomes a flaw because programmers are constantly relying on a band's previous single as a barometer, rather than judging each and every song on its own merit. If a single is a hit, that band's follow-up will get an instant "add" to radio station playlists, even if the song kinda sucks, simply because, in the program director's short-term memory, the band is currently golden. The inverse is also true...when that second single tanks, programmers will feel betrayed and never even consider playing the third single (or the followup record, etc.).

Let's take a real life example...Marcy Playground. Marcy Playground put out "Sex and Candy" and it goes HUGE! To this day, you know that song. So, of course, most radio programmers played the follow-up track, "Saint Joe on the School Bus." You may remember hearing it, or you might recognize it if someone played it for you today. But... "Saint Joe" flopped! Chances are pretty slim that you have any recollection of what the third single from that album was... because all the PD's jumped off the Marcy Playground bandwagon and never played it. Short-term memory. Marcy Playground proceeded to release their sophomore and junior albums (both excellent) to no notoriety or recognition. Find those albums today on the web and discover that songs like "Our Generation" and "Brand New Day" (and others) are excellent, radio-worthy songs. The same could be said of bands like Nada Surf, Blues Traveler, Stabbing Westward, the Verve Pipe, and artists like Poe, Richard Ashcroft, and Mike Doughty. I mean, have you heard Nada Surf's "Inside of Love"??? It's one of the most beautiful songs EVER, but it forever lives (and died), commercially, in the shadow of "Popular," and under the label of "one-hit wonder". It reeks of injustice.

That's where the second flaw of radio programmers comes into play. Even when enough time has passed that the statute of limitations on negative short-term memory is up, programmers are too scared to lead out on a track. Which is also why they are slow to pick up on new bands. If you had been unemployed and looking for a job recently, you could relate to what a new band goes through. Every employer wants you to have "two years of experience" in that field, but how can you ever get the experience if someone doesn't give you the first chance when you

have NO experience? Same for bands dealing with radio stations…
programmers won't play a song until it has sold enough records or
received enough airplay so that they'll know they aren't the only one
playing it…that they will have to do all the legwork. Heaven forbid
they should try to lead other programmers, and then listeners, to
something great. Or it could be that they need a statistic to clue
them in to the fact that something is good, since they can't hear it
for themselves.

That is far more common than it should be. I have seen it
in action. I have been in conference room performances of bands,
seen a programmer ask a record rep what the band's second single
will be, and then walk up to the band and ask them to play that
song…as if he had listened to the record and knew it well enough to
"predict" the second single. Sleazy, right? So maybe there are four
flaws in radio programmers; short-term memory, lack of courage,
sleaziness, and the hearing ability of Helen Keller.

I wonder how often this is the case in other fields? People
having nowhere near the proper skillset to execute a job that they
are hired for. Perhaps the greatest flaw in many businesses is the
all-too-common inability for managers to interview and hire to
positions of power…and then the inability rolls downhill. And we
end up with a cycle of employees with pretty resumes but no actual,
intangible skills…a set of employees whose only real skill is writing
a resume and interviewing for a job.

Or perhaps I'm just bitter…upset that I have all the
intangibles EXCEPT the skill to give a good interview, and envious
of those that have more to list on that resume. Maybe I just wish
people would listen to and trust me more. I'll take care of them. I'll
point them toward the best new music.

I miss you! I love you!

Yours Always,
Jared Christopher

October 10, 2009 – 2:17 PM

My Lovely Dawn,

I had some friends over on Thursday to watch "The Office" wedding episode. It was fun to watch in a group, but I also recorded it so I could watch it on my own. There were some moments I really wanted to be able to have to myself. Today I watched it again...alone.

There is something very special about that show. Of course there are the funny moments, but the true mark of a great show is how often they can touch your heart...and to be both funny and touching in the same show, like this episode, is an even higher mark of excellence. I have shed a few tears from watching "The Office" over the years. My emotions generally seem to stir from the storyline of Jim and his relationship with Pam. The two of them have always reminded me of the two of us.

They began as coworkers, and then became such great friends. Jim had already fallen for Pam, but she was betrothed to be married. Then one night, when the date of Pam's marriage was speeding closer, Jim found a moment alone with her, he kissed her and told her how he loved her. Pam deflected his declaration...Jim was heartbroken...and I hurt too, as I recognized the scene from my own failed, last-ditch attempt to derail your engagement. Later in the episode, Pam seemed confused and conflicted as she spoke to her mom on the phone...the same conflicted confusion your sister once told me you secretly felt after our moment together.

Then came this week's episode...an episode where Jim and Pam make the very same "mental photograph" gesture that I made at your kitchen table exactly one year, to the day, prior.

And then there is Jim...ever a man of wit, but also thoughtful with a romantic turn of phrase...he stands to give a speech at the rehearsal dinner, and his words hit me in my gut..."years ago I was just a guy who had a crush on a girl who had a boyfriend, and I had to do the hardest thing that I have ever had to do which was just to wait. For a really long time that's all I had. I just had little moments with a girl who saw me as a friend. And a lot of people told me I was crazy to wait this long for a date with a girl who I worked with, but I think, even then, I knew...that I was waiting for my wife."

October 10, 2009 – 2:17 PM

Do you know that this is how I feel? This is what I am doing. I am waiting for my wife. That is the only reason for any of this. This isn't some sort of cheap thrill from trying to seduce a married woman. This is about fighting for the only woman that has ever really seen me, that has ever made me feel complete, that is the only woman I have ever truly loved. I am waiting for my wife.

Jim closes the episode with more special thoughts...getting married to Pam on the boat at Niagara Falls wasn't his first choice...plan A was to marry her a long, long time ago...pretty much the day he met her.

It wasn't my plan to have an affair with you after you married someone else...plan A was to marry you a long, long time ago...pretty much the day I met you.

I don't know if we're on plan B or plan C at this point...it doesn't matter...plan D is to marry you...plan E is to marry you...no matter when it happens, my plan is to marry you...as soon as you'll have me. It's just a question of how long you want to wait.

I miss you! I love you!

Yours Always,
Jared Christopher

October 11, 2009 – 9:02 PM

My Lovely Dawn,

Do you ever wonder if you're doing things right? Big things, little things, any things? "Is this how everyone else does it?"

I wonder that, for myself, a lot. I've often felt behind the curve of my peers on so many things. There are some things I've never learned to do. I've never learned to drive a stick-shift. I'm not entirely sure I know how to swim, since I've almost always avoided lakes and pools since I fell through a hole in a pier when I was a kid. I've never really been in a serious relationship. The last point is the one that concerns me the most.

I wonder how I will be when I finally do have a relationship. I wonder about the big things; how will I interact and mesh with her friends and family? How will I be as a partner in life? Can I put away some of my need to always be right...to have the last word? How will I be as a parent? How will I be as a lover? How will she react to seeing me fully nude for the first time? Am I an intolerable bastard first thing in the morning?

I wonder about the little things; how will she react to how restless I am when I try to sleep? How will she react to the fact that I drool in my sleep? Are my dietary habits and pickiness something that I can overcome, and if not can she tolerate them?

Are there things that I'm not worried about because I've never been in a relationship and never been taught to worry about them? Things that I'm not even aware of?

Then, on top of these worries, there are the worries of "doing it right." Am I kissing the right way? Am I communicating the right way? Am I dressing the right way? Am I remodeling the kitchen the right way? Am I parenting the right way? Am I progressing through life the right way?

October 11, 2009 – 9:02 PM

A part of me knows there probably is no "right way". Another part of me thinks I am doing things the right way and anyone who differs is doing things the wrong way. But probably the biggest part of me thinks, however I'm doing things, I'm doing things the right way for you. And the way you do things is right for me. And whatever isn't right, neither of us seem to be too proud to change and make it right for the other person. We just seem to synchronize, simplify, harmonize, and then everything works when we're together. You always seem to know just what I need, when I need it. Everything works in your arms.

But does this mean the inverse would also be true...nothing works, nothing is right without you?

It feels that way.

I'd really like to get back to right soon...

I miss you! I love you!

Yours Always,
Jared Christopher

October 12, 2009 – 7:53 PM

My Lovely Dawn,

I officially hate insurance.

The entire concept and process of insurance bothers me. Home insurance, health insurance, flood insurance, auto insurance...all gross. It is all paranoia, speculation, and negative thinking at its worst.

I've just come from a homeowners' association meeting where the main topic of conversation was the suspected impending flood of the river and valley where I live. Apparently it has been decided to purchase flood insurance policies for the entire condo complex at a cost of $55 per month in increased homeowners' dues. This does not take into account cost-of-living expense increases that will be voted on in November. This is a guaranteed 30% increase in dues...if not more. Are they crazy?

There are already 11 condos in various stages of sale, foreclosure, or bankruptcy. All of the empty units aren't paying dues and therefore increasing the deficit of the association reserve. And, oh by the way, who is going to buy a condo with hyper-inflated homeowners' dues during a recession and in the dead center of a FLOOD ZONE?!?

Hear that siphoning sound? That is the sound of the downward spiral speeding up.

And it all begins with the paranoia of a natural disaster that may never come.

Why do we all put so much weight into these "what-if" scenarios? And why don't I have more of an objection to all of these payments I am making for my love insurance? My "what-if you get divorced" policy? I guess I don't think you can put too high of a premium on hope and love. For that I will pay any amount of dues.

I wish you were here to talk me through some of this. I could use your mind right now.

I miss you! I love you!

Yours Always,
Jared Christopher

October 13, 2009 – 9:19 PM

My Lovely Dawn,

I've noticed something about women...and perhaps, indirectly, men.

I feel like women make snap-judgments in most situations. Men are a little more methodical in their decision-making. But the interesting thing is that women are quite capable of reassessing and changing their mind after that initial judgment. Whereas men, once they have chosen a side or an opinion, seem to lock in to that view and don't bend from it easily, if ever.

Let's use the example of dating:

There is a common belief that a woman, when meeting a man for the first time, decides within seconds whether or not she will sleep with him. What is less commonly discussed is the fact that many women are eventually won over, then marry, a man who failed on initial impression. Women, like men, WANT a man they have great sexual chemistry with. But they NEED a man of great resilience, character, and stability, and with underlying mental and emotional chemistry. And they seem to recognize or realize those qualities can be missed without deeper study.

Men, on the other hand, act on two levels at most times... simultaneously seeking women who could be either attractive sexual partners OR possible marriage material. These two acts have two very different speeds, but this is because these two different types of women have very different speeds. Once a man recognizes which category a woman falls into ("the one" or "the one-night-stand") she becomes locked in that category indefinitely. Try to talk a man out of being in love with the woman he loves...or try to talk a man into loving you after he's decided you are better in bed than you are in the head...and find both to be impossible.

Men lock in...like a hunter with prey in his sights. Women pick and choose...like a gatherer (and regatherer) who discovers the sweetest fruit is sometimes the ripe piece that found a bruise or two on its way to the ground.

October 13, 2009 – 9:19 PM

    It seems, even with all the bells and whistles of technology, gene-mapping, and psychoanalysis, humanity still comes down to: men hunt, women gather.
    Now if only I could win you over, change your mind...I've already decided you're "the one". Of course, I contradict my own theory...you see, I made a snap-judgment...I knew within seconds that I would want to marry you...
    I miss you! I love you!

Yours Always,
Jared Christopher

October 14, 2009 – 8:13 PM

My Lovely Dawn,

I asked you the other day if you ever worry if you're doing things right...

I guess it was mostly rhetorical, as I know that you do worry. Your biggest worry, I'm sure, is if you're raising your kids right.

You wonder which is right: home-schooling or sending them to public school. You wonder if it would be wrong to go back to work, and if it would be okay...then when. You wonder if it's best to raise your kids in a home with their father, where your heart may be missing...or whether they could accept your desire to start a new life, with the idea that your improved daily happiness will be a benefit to them in the long run.

You know how I would vote. And it's not just so I can be with you. I truly want to be a part of their lives. I miss them in a way that I don't really understand. The emotion that stirs while thinking of them these last six months has taken me by surprise. It is a powerful thing.

I am coming to understand, more and more, the love an adoptive parent can find for a child with no blood-relation. It's not about blood. It's about finding a perfect, innocent new soul and doing everything in your power to nurture and protect that soul. I do want to protect them. And I've come to believe they would be safe under my wing.

The answer to all of this may be that there is no right way to parent. I think of the movie, "The Breakfast Club"...five students that all came from different backgrounds with different parents who used vastly different parenting methods...and yet their kids all ended up with detention that day. There are a million different ways to parent, and none of them are promised to work. That's the negative. The positive? In the crazy, magical way of things...kids will inevitably love their parents. In part, because kids will generally come to realize that they weren't always the best kids or the most willing to be parented. All people are, in a sense, self-centered in that way.

October 14, 2009 – 8:13 PM

We've spoken before about the different ways you and I were raised...and how each set of our parents were deficient in this, or overbearing on that. But we turned out okay. We turned out better than okay.

When it comes to parenting, let us always remember...just breathe.

Let us fill our cup with love and watch the overflow pour down upon those around us.

I miss you! I love you!

Yours Always,
Jared Christopher

October 15, 2009 – 4:39 PM

My Lovely Dawn,

      It's been a rough day so far. Everything seemed to go wrong. Work was terrible and my managers all seemed to be AWOL. I did something to my left shoulder that feels pretty bad. My right middle finger has a cut on it that I keep reopening. I'm starting to think I need eyeglasses. I wasn't able to sit down to lunch til after 3:00. The Honeycrisp apple I snapped into then was the best part of the lunch AND the day. The only saving grace is the knowledge that tonight I begin my first filmmaking class in Seattle. It will be a new beginning of sorts. Another step in the direction of a dream.

      I so very much want to learn as much about filmmaking as I can, as quickly as I can. I want to turn the screenplay I wrote for you into the movie I produced for you. I want the film to find it's way through the politics of Hollywood and onto the silverscreen and into the hearts of the world. I want to to be self-employed, a financial success, and able to write and produce my own books and films for years to come. I want to provide you and the girls a comfortable living. I want to make commercial art.

      But first...class at 7:00.

      I miss you! I love you!

Yours Always,
Jared Christopher

October 16, 2009 – 8:51 PM

My Lovely Dawn,

You have told me before how smart and talented you think I am...I can't tell you how much I appreciate that...how much I need that...

But I hope that will never be an intimidation to you...not in an actionable way. I mean, I am intimidated by your beauty, but not in a way that can't be overcome for sake of the greater benefit that would come from being with you.

The bottom line is, there are times when I need you to be smarter than me...to know that there are so many ways that you ARE smarter than me. And I need you to always remember that, practice that, use that. Keep me in check.

Remember the day we went to your college to get information for you to go back to school? On the drive home I made a wrong turn and you corrected me on it. Later you worried that you came across bitchy...no you didn't. You came across as right. While I was embarassed at my mistake, I prefer that you correct me when you need to, because a small mistake is far better than a bigger, prolonged one. I am a firm believer in the saying, "If you're gonna fail, fail quickly."

For me, this means always searching and striving for truth. Not MY truth, but a bigger truth...an empirical truth. And that means not being too proud or stubborn to fight for a cause I've recognized to be flawed or wrong. For you, this means trusting in your incredible mind, having pride in that mind, and then trusting that I believe in you and will always listen.

In my life I have found that I am at my best when I am being challenged. For that reason, I think I have, subconsciously, surrounded myself with people that challenge me. My friends...we argue, we debate, we pontificate, we laugh, we hug, we move on. And there is no grudge to be had.

I can recognize in myself the desire to always be right...but I also recognize that that desire dwarfs in comparison to my desire to be with you. All other desires are meaningless without you in my life. I can be right all day, every day if I want to...it's quite easy to win every argument when you're alone. I don't want to be alone. I want to be in a partnership. I want to be in a marriage. I want to be with you.

So if you've ever wondered why we don't argue much...it is, firstly, because we seem to naturally agree on most things. Then when we do start to argue, a couple things happen...I recognize things are escalating (either by your use of my full name or perhaps a curse word), then I'll become more selective, more tactful with my words (to try to get my point across without emotion), and, if that is still not working, then I will simply stop abruptly and remind myself (and you) that I love you. I may even get you to laugh. I think you know this is true. You've wondered aloud how it is that we do that. I think you may be the only person I've ever been that way with. You make me a better man. You really do.

I truly believe we will never be a couple that goes to bed mad at one another. It's just not worth it. I love to win...but I want to win WITH you, not AGAINST you. Plus there's a pretty significant fear that if you're willing to keep fighting for an idea, then you're probably right.

Now if you could just refocus some of that fight towards fighting for US...

I miss you! I love you!

Yours Always,
Jared Christopher

October 17, 2009 – 8:55 PM

My Lovely Dawn,

This is continually becoming the toughest year-plus time period of my life. I have taken on the greatest challenges I've ever had to face...in career, in family, in home, in love...

It began when I was laid off from my job...a job that I loved and was proud of my accomplishments in...a job lost for reasons unrelated to the performance I had given in that position.

Then came the sickness and death of my grandmother...the grandparent that I was the closest to and loved the most...the first time I have ever been witness to someone dying.

Through last winter and into the spring came the roller coaster of emotions and eventual loss of my relationship with you...the closest I've ever come to a real relationship, with a woman I loved and was proud to show off to the world...a loss that didn't come from lack of love.

And now comes a new autumn and with it the speculation of widespread flooding...a flood that could cause me to lose my home...a home that I've worked hard to mold into a place that I love and am proud to show off to my friends...and a loss for reasons unrelated to anything that I have caused or incurred.

What more can be thrown at me? What more will I have to overcome? Will I overcome it all? Or will I finally break?

I worry about all these things when I sit in the deafening quiet of my solitary life. Through all of my trials there have been very few constants. But one constant has been my devotion to spend a little time each night to pray. Most nights I pray just to say 'thanks'. But lately I've been needing to ask for help...to ask for strength...to ask for hope...

I hope I'm worthy of being heard. I'm trying to be good, to be exemplary, to be righteous. I'm trying.

I miss you! I need you! I love you!

Yours Always,
Jared Christopher

October 18, 2009 – 3:37 PM

My Lovely Dawn,

Today is the 183rd consecutive day I have written you a letter. 182 letters down, 182 letters still to go. When I have finished and sent this letter, I will have officially more letters completed than days still remaining in my quest. We are entering the homestretch.

I want so badly for it to be less than 182 days though. I want you to grow so frustrated of living without me that you initiate a break-up...regardless of whether the "blame" will fall on you or not. I want you to admit that you don't have a connection with your husband, that whatever you began with is gone, or whatever you hoped would build never did. I want you to admit that you still feel this incredible love for me, and a void in your life without me there to fulfill that love. I just want you back. I want to spend the rest of my life with you and I want the rest of my life to start as soon as possible.

I'm not looking forward to spending the holidays without you. The holidays always seem to make the fact that I am the only single member of my family more pronounced. And I think you feel the pressures of the holidays differently than I do, and I will be sorry that I won't be there to calm your nerves. I'm going to miss exchanging gifts with you. I'm going to miss spending New Year's Eve with you, as last year's New Year spent with you was the best of my life. I'm going to miss spending Valentine's Day with you, and showering you with presents and affection.

And I'm going to miss every other day. All the days that represent an anniversary of a special moment specific to our lives, and all the days that the special moment was simply getting to see you. Every time I see you it is special to me. Every time I see you I discover anew the stunning beauty that you are. Every time I see you my heart races and my hands shake. Every time I see you I just want you to know that I love you.

I am ready to see you again. I am ready to be with you forever. And the countdown starts at T-minus 183 days...and counting...

I miss you! I love you!

Yours Always,
Jared Christopher

October 19, 2009 – 8:58 PM

My Lovely Dawn,

It seems the strangest thing...the time of the day when I most often sit down to write to you, would be the time of the day that I picture we would have our best talks and moments if we were together.

The way I imagine it, it's generally the late evening...after we've worked separately on our daily routines, you making dinner and me helping the girls with their homework...after we've had dinner as a family, you take the girls upstairs to give them their baths and I clear the table and wash the dishes (cause whoever cooks doesn't have to do dishes)... after we nestle the girls into their beds, you reading a book to J, me playing A. to sleep with a song on guitar, and L. finding more independence and reading a book to herself...after all this is done, THEN we find each other.

Some nights we join together on the couch for a favorite TV show. Some nights we do more work together...perhaps making the girls their sack lunches for the following day...while catching each other up on the things we miss while apart at work. Some nights we collapse into bed early with only enough energy to whisper of all our hopes and dreams and plans and schemes together. Some nights we find bed early but with more active intentions...to hug and to kiss and to touch and make love together.

But every night we end up together. Every night we go to sleep peaceful and content. Every night we know tomorrow will hold struggles and conflict, but we're okay with that...because we know that is life, and we know at the end of tomorrow is another perfect moment like this...when, again, five become two, and two become one.

And when the one is us, we'll never want or need for anything more. You and I...in the stillness of night...with the stillness of mind that births from the peaceful at heart.

And we sleep together.

I miss you! I love you!

Yours Always,
Jared Christopher

October 20, 2009 – 10:20 PM

My Lovely Dawn,

Occasionally a thought will creep into mind that I wish would go away..."what if, in our time apart, something major happens?" It scares me.

I often worry, "What if you get pregnant?" With two of your sisters having babies this year, I worry that you will want to have another as well. Even if you don't, I worry that either your family or your in-laws will pressure you into doing it. Even if they don't, I worry that you could get pregnant by accident. Then, if you did, would there ever be a chance you could leave your husband?

That fear strikes me fairly often. But the other day I realized a new one...what if I got some other girl pregnant? It's not something I want to happen, it's not something that has come close to happening, but if I got frustrated enough, lonely enough, I know it could happen. Would you ever look at me the same? What if there was no baby, but only me having sex with some other woman? How would you react to that? What are the rules of these rhetorical nightmares?

The other major recurring fear is, "What if one of us should be in an accident?" I'm not sure I could go on living if I knew that you weren't here anymore. At least in the situation we're currently in, I feel like we will be together eventually...even if it means waiting till we're old and grey...there will come a time, either by natural occurance or by you finally having a change of heart after the girls have grown up and moved out, where we will be together. As long as I have a pulse there will be a heart that beats for you. But there are things that are out of our control. That's why I wish you would take control of the situation, be true to your heart, and come back to me.

We are not promised tomorrow. When you find something that you love, like the love we share, you have to grab it up. You have to demand the things in your life that you truly want. You can't wait for them to come to you, you can't wait for them to be given, you just can't wait.

October 20, 2009 – 10:20 PM

     Stop with simply tolerating a situation and start with creating a better situation. Don't put off till tomorrow that which may be gone by the end of today. And by doing it today, change the entire course of tomorrow. It is the only way.

     I need you today. And, if I'm still here, I'll need you tomorrow. Let us not waste another day.

     I miss you! I love you!

Yours Always,
Jared Christopher

October 21, 2009 – 7:11 PM

My Lovely Dawn,

As I mentioned before, I've begun my first filmmaking class. To my surprise, the first assignment called on an unexpected talent. We were asked to draw storyboards.

A storyboard is basically extremely simplified animation. You draw one cell for each shot you expect to later shoot on film. In this case, we are working backwards. We need to draw 15 shots of an existing film. I chose the wonderful, little, neo-film-noir of "Brick".

To be perfectly honest, I chose the film, and the specific scene, for mostly the wrong reasons. There were a couple shots that were very simple (a street sign, a cigarette)...there were very few shots that required camera movement (which can be more difficult to represent)...and the scene seemed to have a beginning, a middle, and an end...with a little bit of suspense thrown in. Essentially I was trying to find a scene that would be easy to draw.

But then I started drawing...and the simple frames started gaining more and more detail and shading. Instead of merely drawing passable representations of the images, I began to create my own little graphic novel (which was ironic because before "Brick" was a film it was a graphic novel...novel begets film begets novel). The more I drew, the more I noticed, "hey, these sketches aren't bad."

One frame...a simple closeup shot of a payphone sitting on its cradle...has become like this great still-life drawing. Another...of our hero on that same phone handset he has just answered...has the most incredible shading. The detail of his face gives us the feeling of his ominous concern. I wish I had drawn them bigger so that I could frame them after they are graded.

October 21, 2009 – 7:11 PM

I'm not sure why I bring this up. I guess I'm a little proud of myself tonight. It has long been a goal of mine to help reinvigorate the idea of the Renaissance man. To first become a man of the arts, of the sciences, and of the athletics. And then to somehow inspire other men to do the same.

Tonight, I feel closer to that goal. Closer to my distant brethren, and fellow Aries, da Vinci and van Gogh. I will save these sketches so that I may someday share them with you.

I miss you! I love you!

Yours Always,
Jared Christopher

October 22, 2009 – 4:22 PM

My Lovely Dawn,

There was a time when I was embarassed of my inexperience with women. I would hide it as much as I could behind big talk and false bravado. But the more I've grown and matured the more I'm thankful, and proud, that I took things as slowly and carefully as I did.

Every time I met a new girl, I would consistently feel the fear of being found out for the novice that I was. I would always require their patience and their guidance. I know that it wasn't easy. I know that it was neither smooth nor swift. But, I hope they know, I WAS learning. I learned from every kiss and every touch.

More importantly, however, in the mix of my ability to judge and select patient partners and the way I would eventually open up and be candid about my history, all of these women made an incredible transformation to me.

What would begin as a quest or a challenge, whether noble or proud, would then reveal an unfortunate reality...a lack of chemistry, a simple mismatch, a dishonest moment can not be an artifice I can carry. I cannot fake my way through life and certainly not through love. And this truth would cause panic, and the panic would lead to poor choices...hurtful choices. I've never been a guy who claimed to get things right the first time, but I do claim to be a guy who recognizes his own failures and proactively seeks to improve those problems. So I see when I make mistakes, and these mistakes become a new quest, a new challenge...how can I make this relationship better...how can I maintain the truth of my heart, while being a better man to this woman today and tomorrow?

The answer is not easy...it is a humility for me and a forgiveness for them. It is regretting a hundred little things, but not regretting the greater outcome...the result of an inevitable truth. It is a 'thank you' for time and patience and learning, and a 'please' for forgiveness and friendship. It is a grey area, but I ask for it, and in my life I've generally been granted it.

October 22, 2009 – 4:22 PM

And if there comes a day when I can call you mine forever, I hope these women, that I now proudly call 'friend', will look upon you and I together and see two things: 1) that, even in failure, I was indeed learning from them and always respecting them. 2) that they can never take any fault or blame for that failure, for they should know that my heart has always been with you. In fact, they should take credit, for they helped me become the man I am today...the man who won your heart.

A man who now knows how to give, and to always give his all. A man who knows when to be assertive, and when you need to be taken. A man with strength AND sensitivity...in both my character and the way I touch a woman. A man that falls like snowflakes and roars like thunder. A man of integrity, humility, sincerity, and truth. A man of exquisite passion, thought, and heart. And love.

Love is really the key that unlocks all the doors. The missing ingredient that completes the recipe. The switch that turns me on to be a guiding light for any who may benefit. Love does this.

And I love you! And I miss you!

Yours Always,
Jared Christopher

October 23, 2009 – 5:05 PM

My Lovely Dawn,

If it is true what they say, that Nature is our Mother, than oaks and maples and firs and spruce are her many daughters. In the fall all these lovely ladies transform...they change to radiant blondes and reds and every shade between. Their hair blows in the wind, and then they sing and dance.

It is an elegant burlesque where day by day they shed layer after layer. The number is choreographed in waves to prolong the dance and lenthen our admiration.

Or perhaps it isn't a dance, but a fight. A fight to hold on to their crowning glory. To protect their pride and hide their fragility. For these women are delicate. But these women, even stripped of their superficial covering, are beautiful and special creatures.

Forever bending but never breaking. They can be shelter, they can be support, they can be a playground. They give their all, they give their life. They give us a home, they give us nourishment, they give us the very air that we breathe.

All we must do is let them set down their roots and give them room to stand in the light. And they return the gifts they receive, but in numbers tenfold.

Strength, beauty, inspiration, life...yes, the tree is divinely feminine. And oh, how they sing and dance.

I miss you! I love you!

Yours Always,
Jared Christopher

October 24, 2009 – 7:15 PM

My Lovely Dawn,

You know that I started watching "House" because I knew that you liked it and I wanted to be able to share that with you. And it didn't take long for me to become hooked. And now I watch every week and the show speaks to me...I find odd and eerily specific parallels to my life in it. I love this show now.

Over five months ago I reviewed a new album by Ben Harper and the Relentless 7...this is part of what I wrote:

"We close the record with 'Faithfully Remain'. There is an art to tracking a CD and I am particularly fond of those who close on a hushed, thoughtful plateau. It's the stunning view you get at the peak of the hike. It's a quiet moment away from the world where you are closest to your thoughts. "Faithfully Remain" is that kind of moment. A chord progression reminiscent of Van Morrison's "Old Old Woodstock" and a vocal where Harper's voice breaks in all the right places, and our hearts break right along with it."

A few weeks ago I made a CD mixtape of songs that currently mean a lot to me. I wanted to give the CD to you. But I've been hesitating because I don't know if you would listen to it. The last song on the CD is Ben Harper's "Faithfully Remain". This week's episode of "House" closed with Ben Harper's "Faithfully Remain".

I hope you've been reading my articles, I hope you've been finding the bits I write for you...like Morse code for only you to understand. I hope you watched "House" this week and heard the song there too, I hope you felt the same chill of finding a fated moment that I did. There are things that are meant to be...

I miss you! I love you!

Yours Always,
Jared Christopher

October 25, 2009 – 6:57 PM

My Lovely Dawn,

Today was a woefully unproductive day...until about five o'clock.

Then I folded the laundry that had been sitting in the dryer for a day and a half, I read all of my homework reading, I began a script for my first filmmaking project, I checked all of my email accounts and filled out the expense report for work, and then I burnt you a new version of the CD I made for you weeks ago with a couple new songs added on.

I haven't completely verified it yet, but I have this feeling that each song on the CD may correspond to a letter I have written you in the past. I didn't set out to do that, but as I've been listening to these songs the last few weeks I find myself finding little connections between song and letter. I don't know if I heard the song and it stuck in my subconscious and later came back out in my writing...or if I wrote you the letter and then heard a song that matched it beautifully and added it to my mental playlist. It's probably both, at different times.

So now I have this CD that begs for you to hear it. I will bring it to you soon. And when you hear it, there will be a game...a game of trying to match each song to the corresponding letter that sits in your email in-box. And long after the game has been completed, this CD will be a peaceful place for you to go. Every time you find yourself in times of trouble, put this CD on and I will be with you. I will wrap my arms around you, we will transcend all that life is not, become together as one...and dance. A lovely, peaceful slow-dance. And I will hold you tighter and you will hear me say, "I Love You," and know there is nothing truer.

I miss you! I love you!

Yours Always,
Jared Christopher

October 26, 2009 – 8:06 PM

My Lovely Dawn,

I mentioned before that my film class had required that we do some drawing for the first assignment...I was so proud of the job that I had done, and the drawings got such a good reception from my classmates, that I decided to draw something else.

One of our anniversaries is in a couple days, so I decided to draw something that is very dear to both of our hearts. I think this new drawing will make a nice present to go with the CD I've made for you. I do so love to give you presents.

And I love the presents that you give me. I think I still have all of the presents you've ever given me, save for the ones that were edible. I have the first birthday card you ever gave me with Ziggy on it. I have the shirt you gave me the time you took me out to dinner at the restaurant on top of that hotel. I was pretty overwhelmed by nerves that night. There have been other presents...books, appliances, clothes...but the best thing you ever gave me never came in a box or with a ribbon. The best present I have ever received...from anyone...is your love. I still can remember the first time I heard you say you loved me.

When you go as long as I had gone without love you start to wonder what you're doing wrong. But it was never what I was doing that was wrong...it was simply that I never found that someone right. Well, I found the right girl but at the wrong time, and I never could match the feeling I had with you. Having seen you again with the eyes of maturity and experience, I now know all those failed attempts at love that followed you, weren't examples of my shortcomings, but simply examples of mismatches. It wasn't my fault, it wasn't their fault, it just wasn't meant to be.

What IS meant to be is you and I. I am more convinced of that today than ever. And I am meant to shower you with love and affection...and gifts! I hope to see you soon...and if I don't see you, the drawing is from me.

I miss you! I love you!

Yours Always,
Jared Christopher

October 27, 2009 – 8:06 PM

My Lovely Dawn,

Last night I went to bed at a reasonable hour...and like I do every night, I took that time, with my head on the pillow, to speak to God. But on this night, as He sometimes does, God spoke back to me. He speaks in ideas and inspirations, but only there and then.

What is that place? That time? Between wake and sleep...when we can hear and see things we can't find when fully awake, but they still have a logic and a reality...a logic and reality that seem to dilute the deeper we fall into sleep. It is those moments, those few seconds, when the setting sun touches the horizon...and in that time, if you are open and if you are true, you can hear God...and because he is a generous God, He takes those moments and gives...He gives the wonders of inspiration and creation.

Last night God gave me the gift of a short film. No, the gift had already been given...God merely shined a light on it. For the first time in my fledgling film career I will not be taking a writing credit. This time the author is you.

It hit me like a bolt last night...one of your stories, one of your beautiful little pieces of heart-suspense-magic, should be a film. It is elegant in it's simplicity...with imagery so evocative I can make the film without dialogue. It is deep with emotion, conflict, and humanity. These qualities make it so relatable...so in need of being filmed.

And you wrote it. You opened your heart, you spoke your truth...a conflicted truth, but truth...and it became amazing and it touched me. I can only hope that I can do it justice when I transfer your story to the screen.

As I lay in bed I directed the whole story. I placed all the cameras, I made all the edits, and I pulled a touching, tragic, and brave performance from my lead actress. The film is completed...in my head. As you know, all I need is to be able to see it, even if only in my head, and I can achieve it. And I see it...

October 27, 2009 – 8:06 PM

       This little, perfect creation from this little, perfect inspiration from this little, perfect window of dialogue with that which is greater than all of us...He that brought me to you...sweet little, perfect you.

       You should know, though, that your inspiration kept me awake for hours last night. So can you do me a favor? Next time you want to keep me awake for hours past bedtime...just be in bed beside me?

       I miss you! I love you!

Yours Always,
Jared Christopher

October 28, 2009 – 6:08 PM

My Lovely Dawn,

You are such an incredible sister.

Today I learned that you were not only present when one of your sisters gave birth to her daughter, but you actually caught her as she emerged from the womb. What an incredible thing to share with a sister and a niece. How many people can ever say that they have done such a thing? What an honor and mark of trust.

And I have already seen how much you take care of your sisters and help them with their daycare whenever you can. You dote on your nieces and nephews so beautifully. I wonder, of all your nieces and nephews, how many are you godmother to? How many of your sisters would ask you to be their children's guardian should it ever become necessary?

I remember when we were younger, your sisters were very much younger...only kids, and we all went out sledding in the snow. To see you interact with your sisters in that way...one part instigator and one part protector...just touched me and has always stuck with me. And you were so alive in that moment. That image is always with me.

The way you have led your life, with so much internal pressure to be a good example to your sisters, has had such an impact on them. But I wonder how much they recognize who you are and the successes you have had, and whether that inspires them to follow in your footsteps or to throw their hands up in defeat and admission that they, "could never live up to T's example." The point is debatable but also not really the point. The point is really that you created that example and you were available all along the way to help with their success should they want it.

October 28, 2009 – 6:08 PM

But I sometimes wish you would stop applying that pressure to yourself. Recognize that your sisters are walking their own paths...they have not always followed your lead when you lived righteously, stop thinking they would follow your lead should you falter or make a mistake. And start knowing that you don't always have to be the rock for others to lean on...your sisters are there for you should you need someone to lean on...I believe this. They are all good people.

I think you are a wonderful sister.

I miss you! I love you!

Yours Always,
Jared Christopher

October 29, 2009 – 4:44 PM

My Lovely Dawn,

I don't know if it comes from my time playing poker or if it has been with me longer, but I think I have a special talent for reading people.

There are facial features that reveal a person's tendencies to bluff or lie...ways to recognize when someone commonly suppresses emotions...

And when I see recent pictures of you, I see a tension in your face that I take to mean there is a tension in your life. The twinkle in your eyes is missing. You don't look happy.

This bothers me beyond words. Are there no others that see this about you? Are there no others that care? Who is looking out for you? Defending you? Protecting you?

You know that is what I would do. Every day we worked together at Dairy Queen as kids, I was looking out for you. The first time we went into the pit at a rock concert, I was protecting you. Any time anyone says a negative or cynical word about you now, I am defending you.

You are my love. I am your man. You are my light. I am your rock. You are the air that I breathe. I am that breath given a voice, to say the words that you can not. We only work together, in synchronicity.

I miss you! I love you!

Yours Always,
Jared Christopher

October 30, 2009 – 10:24 PM

My Lovely Dawn,

I had a rough day at work. This weekend is Halloween. I miss you like crazy. I am drinking too much. I am sorry.

Poetry does not spring willingly from the mind of the inebriated. You deserve better. Grant me a pass? Let me be better tomorrow?

I miss you! I love you!

Yours Always,
Jared Christopher

October 31, 2009 – 8:03 PM

My Lovely Dawn,

There have been seemingly more and more female temptations recently. Women that are longtime friends, women that I used to work with, women I currently work with, women that I've met socially...

Last night alone, for various reasons and happenstance, I was tempted and honored by women from most of those categories. And in my lonely frame of mind I wanted so badly to connect with any one of them. By the end of the evening I had met a women and we delved into conversation. As one partygoer after another filtered out of the Halloween party, fewer and fewer remained, and she and I continued to talk. We eventually made our way to a diner where we spoke over breakfast and into the morning. It was an impressively effortless conversation. Never any awkward silences. It was the kind of conversation that I rarely find, but that thrills me so. It was the kind of conversation that is the norm for you and I.

I enjoy the way that women communicate and the way it differs from men. I enjoy the things that women need from conversation and social interaction. I enjoy learning how to excel at giving them the things they need from communication. And I enjoy the things they give in return. While I miss, and want, physical contact and affection, I NEED the mental and emotional connection that I only get from a woman.

As the minutes and hours ticked by, and the sun began to rise this morning, my body was beginning to fail from exhaustion, but my mind was so alive. Thrilled just to have this someone to talk to in this moment. I didn't want to go home...back to the silence.

I am a good man. I love and respect women. I love and respect you most of all. I want you to be my partner in the conversations that last till morning.

But in the meantime I am occupying myself spending time with the smartest, most beautiful women I can find...the women that are goodly enough to spend their time with me.

I miss you! I love you!

Yours Always,
Jared Christopher

November 2009

∞

Focus

November 1, 2009 – 8:30 PM

My Lovely Dawn,

After a long week and a longer weekend...filled with some high "highs" and low "lows"...I awoke this morning to the wind blowing from the North and a day of blue skies and sunshine.

I took the opportunity to pack up my rented camera, a reel of film and a tripod, to begin shooting my first film. After a series of difficulties finding any friends that were willing or able to act for me, I made the executive decision to make my film a documentary.

The story will begin peacefully, tranquilly with shots of the beauty of this Autumn day...the sun shining through the canopy of trees, leaves rustling and falling, Canadian Geese landing gracefully on the pond by the flock-full, the wind blowing gently across the tall grass near the river...and then...

One sweeping pan-shot...from the grass, across the river, under the sun, to a seemingly infinite wall of huge, black sandbags snaking into the distance. You see, this is the Green River...the river whose dam is failing...the river that may flood when the rains come...the river that is only yards from my home.

Just on the other side of the river, up the hill that I ride my bike on for exercise, there is an excavation site. Backhoes and bulldozers...dirt piles and dumptrucks...and beside them all, layer upon layer, a makeshift pyramid, of earth-filled, giant sandbags. It is at once impressive and frightening. Just across the road from this site there is a view of the entire valley below, and down in the valley, at least a mile away...the unmistakable site of the neverending wall of sandbags.

The film begins with nature...then the lengths and efforts man goes to to contain it...and it will end back on scenes of nature...the wind blowing harder through the trees...clouds in the sky...a closeup of the flowing river...a single leaf, dropped from its tree and drifting in the current...and then...

The tiny splash and ripple of raindrops landing upon the water...so it begins...

My first film.

I miss you! I love you!

Yours Always,
Jared Christopher

November 2, 2009 – 3:56 PM

My Lovely Dawn,

It has been a low self-confidence day.

I wonder if most men have these days. It certainly isn't something men talk about amongst themselves. If they do talk about it, it would be my guess that they only talk about it to their wives or girlfriends. At the same time, I feel like if I had a wife or girlfriend, she would be an instant self-confidence booster all the time. Someone I could always turn to and trust that she loved me for who I am and how I look and everything else. Someone that validates me and encourages my quirks. Maybe with someone like that, it would never get to the point of conversation. Maybe that's how it is for most men...they never have to express when they feel unsure of themselves. Maybe they weren't that self-aware to begin with.

All I know is lately I have heard more things hurtful to my ego than helpful. Whether spoken in malice or carelessness, in jest or in sincere truth, there have been comments that have stung. So I guess the other day when I hoped to see you, and I wanted to hear what you thought about some new clothes I wore, you astutely asked if I wanted feedback or compliments. At the time I wanted feedback because I would rather correct something that is bad. But, in hindsight, I really could have used the compliment.

I'm trying so hard. I work on all the things that are in my power to fix. I just feel like there are so many things that are out of my control. I don't like that feeling. I never have. And when those times occur, I could use your calming hand to tell me not everything can, or should, be controlled, and that I'm doing okay. That even if no one else sees my efforts, you do. And that you love me for it.

If you can give me that, my low points will be exponentially briefer, and I will bounce back with all the love you could ever want and then a whole lot more. I promise.

I miss you! I need you! I love you!

Yours Always,
Jared Christopher

November 3, 2009 – 5:25 PM

My Lovely Dawn,

Do you ever sit in rush hour traffic and lose yourself in thought? Silly thoughts? Like thinking of the type of person various species of bird most closely resemble.

Canadian Geese, with their clean uniforms and precision flying formation, are airforce pilots. Seagulls, with their clumsy landings and obnoxious squawking, a drunken tugboat captain. The bald eagle, with it's noble presence and white wig, a high court judge in the British Parliament. An owl, with its wide eyes, nighttime hours, and paranoid cries of "who...who", a fiending crack addict. And there are so many more.

Then there is the bird that spawned this absurd line of thinking...the common crow. I believe the crow as man would be a biker. The bird is often found off to itself and always dressed in black. Then, every day as the sun is setting, all the crows find each other and fly playfully, in careless formation...an impressive, intimidating gang (or "murder")...swarming across the highway of sky to settle in upon their favorite reststop for dinner and boisterous conversation. The analogy holds up too, when we consider the crows' penchant for mischief, or for pilfering and nicking the occasional item that doesn't belong to them. Or notice when the bald eagle, the "law", comes across the crow territory, a few of the birds will take flight to chase the eagle away.

It is silly. I know. But there is something there. It may someday be a story for the girls.

Hmm...we'll see.

I miss you! I love you!

Yours Always,
Jared Christopher

November 4, 2009 – 5:39 PM

My Lovely Dawn,

Today marks the 200th consecutive day and 200th letter I have written you. It is the cherry on top of this sundae that has been my great day.

Today is the reason we fight...we push through the down times and bad days and fears...because there is light ahead. We never concede defeat, we never stop believing, we try and try and try-again. There is justice for the true and reward for the patient. There is today.

And what better testament to true love than my fight to be with you. What better preparation for the vows of marriage, "in good times and in bad," than to need to turn to you when I am losing confidence in myself like two days ago, AND to want to celebrate with you, thank you, hold you, when I gain my confidence back and am in joy with the world like today? It can never be one without the other.

This is how I need you...my savior and my saved...my protector and my protected...my lion and my lamb...my question and my answer...my love and my lover. Life is always two...always twins. Life is finding, at once, the woman that lights up my life AND the woman who is with me everywhere I go, moving as I move, the equal shadow of my heart. Always two.

I wondered today, should we ever get pregnant, would fate see to it that we had twins? A boy and a girl. Would that be written for us? The boy to be the son you are yet to have, the girl to be the granddaughter my mom is missing for now. And both equal and opposite lessons in life and love for me. Would it be?

But first thing's first...Day 201...as we fight on tomorrow...
I miss you! I love you!

Yours Always,
Jared Christopher

324

November 5, 2009 – 10:53 PM

My Lovely Dawn,

     Occasionally my body will tell me that it needs to be taken care of better. It will tell me that a night of over-drinking or days of terrible eating habits are depriving it of what it needs. It will lower my immune system and I will get very sick.

     I woke up today knowing this has just happened to me. My head was throbbing, my throat was sore, and I could barely breathe.

     I hate being sick. I also hate taking medicines. If I didn't have to go to work I wouldn't take any medicine. I would power through the sickness by mind over matter. But I must be presentable at work, so I take some psuedophedrine and cross my fingers. Inevitably the drugs mask the symptoms, but also put my mind in a fog. I walk through the day without a sharp wit, without a clear mind, at a diminished capacity.

     Some people reccommend various cures for what ails me, but I just don't have the resources or energy to try to make them. I just want someone to take care of me...to tell me to slow down and get some rest. Instead, I find myself getting home from class and finally slipping into bed at almost midnight...exhausted and still foggy. I almost forgot to write to you today.

     It will probably happen. And I will feel such embarassment when I do forget. All this work gone to waste for a slip-up, a sick-day, or an overload of activities.

     I almost forgot to write you tonight...in my drug-induced haze I almost forgot. You know what made me remember? God. I lay my head down and began to pray...my common prayer of thanks and appreciation for the blessings of my life...a prayer that always includes you...just to be thankful to have ever known and loved you. I began it tonight and remembered to write.

     I'll return to this prayer shortly, and tonight I'll be thankful for little reminders of the hugely important. And maybe a little prayer that the fog will burn off before Dawn.

     I miss you! I love you!

Yours Always,
Jared Christopher

November 6, 2009 – 7:42 PM

My Lovely Dawn,

     I saw the raw footage of my first student film last night. It's very rough, occasionally poorly executed, but man is it beautiful! There are a few shots I didn't get to do and may go back to at a later time. This weekend I will begin to edit the shots I do have together, to try to form the storyline as I am imagining it. I will try to find the perfect song to act as the soundtrack. That will help dictate the pace and placement of the cuts. It could also inform the second round of shooting...to fill in any gaps I may find.

     Last night's class was primarily about editing...first a lecture on editing theory and then a demonstration on the editing computer program. I must have seemed two different people...almost bored to sleep during the theory portion, and then I think I caught myself sitting on the edge of my seat with excitement while learning the software.

     You see, I don't want to learn the "art" of editing. Because I don't think art of any sort can be taught. Art comes from within. Art is a series of stubborn decisions born of the gut and instinct of artists. If a thing can be taught, it implies it can be repeated, and if a thing can be repeated it is not art...it is science. And science is not emotion. If you ask me why one director/editor or another made a cut here or there, my answer would always be the same..."that is where the edit felt right." Always.

     So spare me the lie that there is an "art" of editing, and teach me the science of editing. Give me the tools and technique. But leave the art of editing unknown...a discovery only found when I get that light in my eye and that burning in my belly that means a thing is good and right. The proverbial "spidey-sense".

     As it was once depicted of Mozart, his art never had too many, or too few, notes...it always had just as many notes as he felt were required. And he was right. And that wasn't something he was taught. He was an artist.

     I miss you! I love you!

Yours Always,
Jared Christopher

November 7, 2009 – 5:56 PM

My Lovely Dawn,

Today there are a million little things I want to share with you. I've become so busy that the days are blurring and I lose focus on all that I want to say and do...for you and in life.

I had a nightmare. Not a traditional nightmare, but something frightening for me personally. Quite possibly the worst fear I have right now. Oh, the hint of reality in the dream haunts me long after waking.

Today I found the music I will use for my first student film. It gives me visions of how great the finished product can be. It is quite perfect actually. It will elevate the film footage in a magical way. Now it is up to me to execute it.

Tonight my brother-in-law's birthday. I will be so close to your house, so tempted to walk around the corner in hopes of catching a glance of you. So wishing I could be there with you and the girls...to turn off all the lights and be entertained by the thunderstorm that is surrounding us this night. If not to be with you, I'd wish you could be with me. To cheer me on as I attempt to win at the poker game that is planned for the party. I so wish to see you interact with my sisters. At the same time, I question and I worry.

There was a moment...I forget when, but it has been since you and I reunited last year...that my sisters told me that I was forbidden from dating a woman that was prettier than they are. This was said almost like a throw-away joke, but my thought was, "many a truth is spoken in jest." Why would they think, and say, such a thing? My thoughts, for all my siblings, has always been one of protection of them and a wish that they find the best partner they can. Why would they want me limited or held-back in any way?

November 7, 2009 – 5:56 PM

It must be insecurity, but is it direct or indirect? Are they directly insecure in the presence of a woman they find more beautiful than they are? Or is it, perhaps, that they worry a woman more beautiful than they are could cause their husband or boyfriend's eye to wander? Either way, my response to them was, "I'm sorry but I'm going to try." Little did they know then that I had already found the woman I want to marry, and she is the most beautiful woman in the world.

I believe my sisters will come to be at peace with my choice when they learn that she also has the most beautiful soul in the world. And they will become friends.

I must change for the party.

I miss you! I love you!

Yours Always,
Jared Christopher

November 8, 2009 – 8:08 PM

My Lovely Dawn,

I have never understood peer-pressure...the idea that people are so insecure in a behavior they are partaking in that they need someone else, or many others, to do it as well, so as to deflect the guilt or the consequence?

After all, if a thing is a good thing, we need not pressure our peers to do it. They will find it on their own and participate quite willingly. If a thing is a bad thing and we knowingly pressure our peers to do it, it is, as I have suggested, a want or a need to have accomplices in wrong-doing. To better allow us to suffer less consequence as we hide in a crowd of the guilty. Or is it a desire to eliminate the possibility that a peer may have superiority over us? "You can't judge what I'm doing if you're doing it too."

As a teen, I can remember two distinctly different forms of peer-pressure...friends that wished me to join them in underage drinking and drugging, and friends that wished me to join them in religious activity or study. I could never embrace either completely, as both seemed to be ways of hiding different forms of sadness. One seemed to be a chemical mask and the other a spiritual one. I could also never embrace either, as both seemed to judge the other, and I was not willing to stand in judgment and choose sides amongst my friends...amongst good people.

I have theorized on why people pressure friends to join them in debauchery, but why the peer-pressure for me to join in religious activity? In part, because one of the long-standing tennants of most religions is that of fellowship...to expand the popularity of that religion. This is likely a remnant of a long history of Holy wars...a belief initiated to increase populations of one religion that would go to war with the population of another religion. Whoever has the most followers prepared to die for their God, wins...and therefore gets control.

But perhaps a truer, more subconscious, reason the religious segment of the world pressure their peers to join in religious dedication, is because they know, deep down, they are the same as the kids that are drinking and drugging and having sex. They know they are tempted by sins, but perhaps, if they are weak, they can find greater strength in numbers. They, much like the "sinners," can hide in numbers. Perhaps they can be a lamb if they dress as a lamb and stand shrouded by the rest of the flock. What no one ever acknowledges is that the entire flock are really just wolves in sheep's clothing.

Perhaps this is why you were always trying to get me to become friends with your friends, and they would then try to recruit me to church? Perhaps when you were around me you had desires unbecoming a child of Christ...and the best way to manage those feelings, without abandoning our relationship or giving in to desire, was to get me to be your strength. Perhaps that is why you began dating your husband...it was easier for you to be strong against lust with a man who you desired so little?

I don't know. All I know is that I don't like to be pressured and I don't like to pressure others. I would never pressure you to do anything but to believe in yourself as much as I believe in you. We've had conversations where I hate to make an argument in favor of us being together, to pressure you into choosing me. I would much rather you be free to decide on your own. I only argue for me because I know there are others arguing against me.

You are an amazing woman, good to your very core, and when you decide to ignore peer-pressure and listen to your heart, you make the right decisions. I want to move beyond this so badly so that I can show you again how much I believe in you, and to always give you the support that belief deserves.

I miss you! I love you!

Yours Always,
Jared Christopher

November 9, 2009 – 9:44 PM

My Lovely Dawn,

Tonight I am a filmmaker!

After a full day at work, I rushed home to make myself a passable steak dinner, before driving up to Seattle to attempt to edit my footage. I had never used the editing software program before, and I was only given a brief overview last week. I certainly wasn't shown how to add music or sound. But I think in terms of music, so I had to teach myself how to score my film...if you will. I already had the music chosen.

Less than three hours after I began, I emerged from the editing room with a film I am satisfied with for this first project. Admittedly, the total runtime of the first version is about 60 seconds long. But I was only given three minutes of film to shoot with. I think my film has a beginning, a suspenseful build-up, and a cliff-hanger ending. It could pass for a teaser trailer for an actual Hollywood movie.

I may try to smooth some things out with it before the next class Thursday. For tonight though, I am satisfied...I am a filmmaker. I am rewarding myself with a bowl of cereal before heading off to sleep. Maybe there I will find an idea for a future project? This is a job I can do...a job I want to do...a job I would love!

I miss you! I love you!

Yours Always,
Jared Christopher

November 10, 2009 – 5:16 PM

My Lovely Dawn,

Today there was a news report on the decrease of circumcision in America. It frustrated me for some reason. Or many reasons.

First of all...it is a trend. And what a gross thing to be done (or not done) so as to keep up with the Joneses.

Then there is the argument that men were born with a foreskin for a reason. Of course they were...because men once lived in a world of dirt and filth and complete lack of sanitation, and foreskin was a layer of protection from infection and disease. Know what else performed a similar function? The appendix. And, like the male foreskin, the appendix is now pretty unnecessary.

Others will argue that cutting the foreskin deprives a boy of a lot of sensitive nerve-endings. A) Am I the only one who finds it a little creepy to think of a parent so concerned about their child's (eventual) sex-life? B) Know what else has a lot of sensitive nerve endings? The entire rest of the penis. Do they really want to allow boys to receive more pleasure from their penises? Do they really want to open that door? You open that door and another will close...the door to the bathroom where their son will be locking himself inside every other hour so as to enjoy those extra nerve-endings. And am I mistaken to think that more men have a problem being premature in sex than those that last too long? Wouldn't more nerve-endings magnify that problem?

Speaking of women...women need to stop commenting on circumcusion altogether. If ever there was a time that a man's opinion holds complete sway, it would be at times like this. This may be the only time. Just as a father should not try to speak on his maturing daughter's choice of gynecologist. Know what you know, and yield the floor to the most expert on the given subject. I am circumcised therefore I can speak on this more expertly than any woman. And I say, I have no recollection of the procedure nor any pain in recovery. I have never felt lack of sensation. And I've never once felt I was mutilated...in fact, I think I would feel I looked more mutilated uncircumcised, with the unaesthetic quality of the foreskin.

November 10, 2009 – 5:16 PM

My last complaint came when the news report featured a writer who had tremendous difficulty deciding whether or not to circumcise his son...stop sniveling and decide. It's a nice gesture to want your son to be able to decide for himself, but you created your own little dictatorship when you decided to procreate, and it will remain that way for at least a few years...during which time you will make far more lasting, impactful decisions than "tip or clip". If you decide to circumcise your son, the conversation pretty much ends there. Whereas when you decide what religion to raise your children in, for example, the decision ripples into many facets of their lives and their later decisions. If you can't decide on circumcision you probably shouldn't have become a parent in the first place.

Oh world...how you manage to complicate every little thing. Does what I'm saying not seem simple? I know you'll understand.

I miss you! I love you!

Yours Always,
Jared Christopher

November 11, 2009 – 5:46 PM

My Lovely Dawn,

As I drove to work today, the early morning rainclouds had gone and the sun came out. Little pockets of fog formed where the sun was evaporating the rain from the streets. It lingered there, seemingly knowing its time was short, yet wishing to stay in that place-between as long as it could. As the sun shone through the trees and fog it created these tangible beams of light that were so beautiful. I wished it to stay as long as possible too.

It gave me a calm...a peace...that has been harder and harder to find lately...when the days have grown shorter yet seem to drag on. I take these precious moments...these visions of beauty...these replenishing breaths...and I try to dwell in them and appreciate them for everything they are.

It is the same with every second I spend with you. You bring me peace...you are the air that I breathe...your radiant beauty is like a tangible light...you fill my heart and replenish my soul...and I appreciate you every day and wish to linger near you as long as I can.

Today the sun broke through the clouds and the beauty it created broke through my heart in the most perfect way. In that moment of this morning I was happy. This was a lovely dawn.

I miss you! I love you!

Yours Always,
Jared Christopher

November 12, 2009 – 10:40 PM

My Lovely Dawn,

Language...

I love language. I love words. Language is so gloriously fluid and maleable...like water. And like water, words can be inspiration and beauty. Or a poorly placed verbal storm can bring disaster or destruction.

The best of language can become frozen in time like the arctic permafreeze. But more often it falls to the ground in a common puddle only to evaporate and be forgotten the very same day. Language ebbs and flows across the land and ages, occasionally turning back on itself in a whirlpool of contradiction, slang, and irony. What was old becomes new. To those that learn it best, language can be harnessed and turned into power. It can be manipulated and bent to one's best purposes...to any purposes.

In my years in radio I learned that "brevity is the soul of wit"...how a person can say much with little. A tremendous skill to have. But the constrictions of radio can also breed a creative rebellion...how can one say that which society deems inappropriate without committing an actual violation. In that process, I discover that society has created a hypocrisy...a double standard...and a hundred contradictions. Society has invented a taboo against words...the words deemed profane. But is it the word or its meaning that is profane?

Words are merely a collection of letters...letters and spellings that vary as one crosses the borders of language and dialect. In Thailand there is a place called Phuket...when an American says its name it is often followed by giggling or a double-take because it sounds like an American obscenity.

Words also have multiple meanings and synonyms and spellings. For example, "ass" was once thought to be another name for donkey or mule, and we can still use it in that context without objection. The word pronounced "hol" can be spelled as either "hole" or "whole" and will have different meanings for the respective spellings. If one were to have a donkey or "ass" costume, where one person wears the head half, and another person wears the half with rear legs and tail, one could say that there were two ass halves. Now if we were to have both people join together to complete the costume, couldn't it be said that they created an ass whole? Logically, of course. I've referenced neither a part of anatomy nor any type of opening. But, said over the radio, "ass whole" would elicit fines or suspension.

One could also cite the example of "dam" vs "damn". They sound the same, but add "God" to the front of one and you have a problem because you're taking the Lord's name in vain...add it to the other and you're a sweetheart for dedicating a structure blocking a river to the Almighty.

So the objection is meaning? No, not always. Society has deemed "damn" inappropriate but "darn" as an acceptable alternative for the church-going fans of "Gilmore Girls". How is the changing of one letter the difference between broadcast television acceptability and profanity? They both mean the same. Both are used in the same ways and contexts. If they are both used with the same intentions, in the same ways, with the same meaning, why is "damn" the evil twin? Why can't "darn" be more profane? Because the letter "M" is worse than the letter "R"?? How arbitrary.

The truth is, a word is only as powerful as we decide it is. A word only means what we want it to mean. And the best way to take the power out of a word isn't to lock it away in a box. It is to use it...freely and openly. And then, when it is being used regularly, it will begin to evolve, change, and find new meaning.

And maybe that new meaning will be a better one. Then again, I don't even know what the frick I'm talking about. I'm talking about the power of words. The meaning we give to words. And what more powerful, meaningful words can exist than...

I miss you! I love you!

I Am Yours Always,
Jared Christopher

November 13, 2009 – 8:57 PM

My Lovely Dawn,

Today is Friday the 13th and ironically it comes at the end of a week in which I've had some pretty good luck. Perhaps calling it "luck" is a disservice to myself.

Saturday night last I won the poker tournament at my brother-in-law's birthday party, and a modest cash prize. Wednesday night I led my friends to another win at the trivia night...our 13th win...and a modest cash prize. Thursday night I premiered my short film in class and was greeted with very favorable comments.

"Suspenseful."
"Foreboding."
"Good use of music and broad implications."
"I really liked how we had no idea where it was going until the end."
"I liked the ominous music and that last shot - grainy and cool."
"Great visuals...music plays beautiful role."
"Great mood and soundtrack."
"This was one of my top 3."
"Nice photography...subtle yet powerful."

...but no cash prize...yet!

The true prize of the week was simply seeing this little thing that I had conceived, carried to term, and delivered...projected onto a huge screen in a darkened room...feeling incredible personal nervousness just before my film received its turn, and then a tension quite thick across the whole room as the frames rolled by. And the quiet...the quiet was incredible! The film is so brief but, as such, it would be no exaggeration to say that the audience held their breath for its entirety. I think I held them captivated.

In that moment...in the dark and quiet...a chill went over my body. This is my destiny! And this destiny will join me back to you, as I will someday soon tell our story!

I miss you! I love you!

Yours Always,
Jared Christopher

November 14, 2009 – 4:45 PM

My Lovely Dawn,

This week marked Veteran's Day. I think about the kind of men (and women) who sign up to fight for our country...who risk their lives...my grandfather, my uncles, my cousins, my friends.

Then I think about the kind of men that negotiate with these lives...that send these men off to war and unknown fate. I think about that and grow so frustrated.

If a country is anything like an individual (and I think it is), and if there is a man that can live his life without ever raising arms in anger, while simultaneously always reaching his goals and being able to express his ideals...can't it be that countries and continents and the world as a whole can live this way? That all men can live this way?

When do we learn that an election, run with the intention of finding the best "commander-in-chief" is not something to strive for or to be proud of? When do we learn that no war is ever won? Wars are only fuel for a fire that will burn on eternally with grudge and resentment as its most hidden, yet heated, embers.

For you see wars kill...they kill implicitly, but not completely. Kill one man and the fight becomes his brother's...kill a generation of men and the fight becomes their sons'...kill enough of anything and the fight becomes a fight to save our humanity. A humanity that would be found better with the diplomat-in-chief...the scholar-in-chief...the humanitarian-in-chief.

There is no grudge held or revenged against a man that sought peace through communication. There is no movie in which a character says, "my name is Indigo Montoya...you debated and compromised with my father...prepare to die." No one of sound mind anyways.

I understand this holiday meant to recognize our officers...I just wish there was, instead, a worldwide day to recognize our gentlemen. I wish there was less association that kindness equals weakness...less belief that "muscle" equals strength.

November 14, 2009 – 4:45 PM

I have lived my life forever the skinny kid...but I challenge you to find one man any stronger than me. Find one that has come from where I've come from, in the body I was given, with the verbosity and mouth that I have, that has ever physically fought or been picked on less. Find one man who sets higher goals and then reaches out and accomplishes them as thoroughly as I have and will.

If one man can live this way, an entire country can do it too...the entire world if it wanted to. Only then do we evolve and the fires of war exhaust and die. I hope for better and try to live as an example.

I miss you! I love you!

Yours Always,
Jared Christopher

November 15, 2009 – 6:22 PM

My Lovely Dawn,

    I don't know if it was the way I was raised or if there is some innate quality about me, but I've never been a physically affectionate person. I've generally been unsure how to give affection and, what's worse, I've never known how to receive it. I've had to learn it.

    I think this problem was a huge barrier for us when we were kids. Although I didn't realize to what extent. I knew that I always wanted to hold you and to kiss you...but I didn't know how. I didn't know the mechanics of a kiss, but, more importantly, I didn't know the emotions of a kiss...the way a kiss can make a woman feel...the way a kiss shows a woman who you are as a man...the way a kiss reveals to a woman, in ways that words can not, that a man loves her and wants to make that love physical. I also underestimated the timing of a kiss...the way women seem to have a limited window of opportunity that a man will be allowed, if not expected, to take that first kiss. And it almost always must be taken.

    Perhaps it is an experience shared by women raised under strong religious beliefs, perhaps it is an experience of all women raised under the lingering Puritanical beliefs that sex is wrong, perhaps it is an experience of all women before they have any "experience"...but my years on this Earth have shown me that women need a man to make the first move. This is especially true of women before that first kiss or that first sexual encounter.

    I don't know the exact statistic...I doubt whatever statistic exists is close to accurate...but I would be willing to wager that a majority of women have their first sexual encounter forced upon them. This sort of experience generally has one of two vastly different repercussions...either a woman retreats into fear and avoidance of sex entirely, or she becomes an active seeker of further and frequent sexual encounters, as either a predator seeking inexperienced boys, or as a repeated victim subject to be continually preyed upon by evil men.

November 15, 2009 – 6:22 PM

I've never wanted to be one of those men. I've never wanted to force a woman into a physical relationship before she was ready. As such, I have found I missed out on a few windows of opportunity. I think this is part of the reason I lost my patience and kissed you when I did...while you were a married woman. I didn't know how much longer I would be able to see you, and if I were to lose you again, I wanted you to make that decision knowing my love for you had an amazing physical passion...that our kiss would be electric...that our emotional chemistry has an equal when we touch. I wanted you to know I have learned affection and learned a great deal. And if my actions failed and it didn't spark something within you, then you would have all the information you needed and no decision to make. You could walk out my door and not need to look back. I just didn't want to miss a window of opportunity for a dream to come true.

Is this an excuse...no. I won't excuse what I've done nor expect it to be understood or forgiven. I just didn't want you to walk out that door, to walk out of my life, and to risk living the rest of my life having never kissed the only woman that ever really mattered...the only woman I've ever truly loved. For that experience to come true I will take any responsibility or blame. I needed you to know.

I miss you! I love you!

Yours Always,
Jared Christopher

November 16, 2009 – 7:05 PM

My Lovely Dawn,

Today marks the one-year anniversary of my Grandmother's death. In memoriam of her, my letter tonight will be the words I wrote the day we drove from Seattle to southern Oregon when we found out she had taken ill and would not likely recover:

We got to the hospital late last night. My uncle DK greeted us in the hall outside Mimi's room. He is a big, tough, bear of a man but he looked completely depleted. I've never seen him that way. He warns us that Mimi is a "little loopy".

We enter the hospital room, Mimi's bed angled with the foot pointed toward the door. There's a cool wash cloth on her forehead to help combat fever. Her eyes can barely open, her vision almost gone, as is her hearing. We all take turns walking to her side, kissing her cheek, holding her hand...both wrists seemingly shackled by a collection of hospital identifying bracelets...an IV in either arm.

JA tries to hug her and accidentally puts too much pressure on her stomach...Mimi grimaces in pain..."Do you want more medicine?" we ask..."Just a twinge (more)" she says in a scratchy whisper, revealing the tough old broad she still is.

Her thoughts come in waves of logic and senility. At one point asking for balloons at her birthday party and then an admission she is ready to "lay down with father".

Some in the room make small-talk...some frustrate me by talking about Mimi as though she is not in the room, like she's already gone.

I just stand silent...not really able to take my eyes away from her. I watch the pillow on her chest rise and fall...every breath is labored. Her lips thin and chapped...her skin, once softened by age, now growing thin, pale, and tight from dehydration...her chin more prominent than I had ever noticed.

At one point the room empties and I find myself alone with my Mimi. She can't see me and feels abandoned in the sudden silence. I move to the chair by her side, take her hand, "I'm still here". She smiles, "I love you". "I love you too." I cry.

November 16, 2009 – 7:05 PM

A period of silence...I see her begin to speak...she struggles to get the words from her throat past her lips. When it comes it is a quite coherent thought..."do you remember all those good foot massages you used to give me?""I do. And you paid me with cheese-eggs and sticky-buns...pretty good deal."

Another memory comes to me..."Do you remember the summer we drove from Oregon to Tennessee for the family reunion?" "You were such a good navigator," she says. I was ten years old and it was one of the best summers of my life.

Then more silence. We remain alone for what feels like 20 minutes. I cover her hand with mine and secretly pray...asking God to take her...to end her pain. I cry.

It doesn't come this night. I hope when it does come she isn't alone. No one should ever die alone.

I cry.

I miss her. I miss my Mimi!
I miss you too! I love you as I loved her!

Yours Always,
Jared Christopher

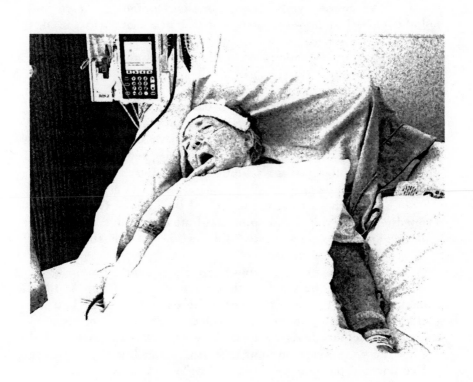

November 17, 2009 – 1:39 PM

My Lovely Dawn,

Where is the wind and from what is it born? How does wind build and when will it end? Does it blow on forever, twisting and winding its way round the world? Or does it wither and die like it's cousin the cloud? Never has nature bequeathed us such a mystery as the invisible winds that now blow.

As gentle, lyrical breeze or, like tonight, a fierce and spiteful gale. But how stagnant and dull the clouds in the sky, without a steady pace on the zephyr to fly. How placid and stifled the oceans would be, without a forceful gust raising frothy waves on the sea.

In spring wind is matchmaker, putting hand-in-hand destined lovers; petal and pollen. In summer breeze is composer, and the arrangement a lullabye; tall grass and wind-chime soothing us to rest. Come fall blustery days are a maid, and the earth to be swept; stripping down natures old bedding and washing them clean. A cold winter gust is a sculpter at heart; freshly fallen snow as the clay in its hands.

Or perhaps wind is the art and the artist is God...dealing in mediums of textures and sounds...of movement and touch...soft and then loud...cooling and then cold...swiftly and then still...

Yes...and then still.

The wind outside is quiet now. I listen and dream.

You are the wind...with a force strong enough to fill a million ships' sails, and yet never to be caught or held. You are gentle and warm. You are music and sculpture. A mystery of impossible depths. Invisible to all...but one. Will you wither and die...or meet me again on your next trip round the world? I have solved not this question. I only know I will love you then still.

Yes...and then still.

I miss you! I love you!

Yours Always,
Jared Christopher

November 18, 2009 – 5:52 PM

My Lovely Dawn,

 Tonight I want to get lost in music.

 I want a mixtape of all the wonderful songs so much of the world in general has no idea about...Nada Surf "Inside of Love," Rocky Votolato "White Daisy Passing," The Velvet Teen "Prize Fighter," Rhett Miller "Come Around," Brad "The Day Brings," Blues Traveler "Pretty Angry," Richard Ashcroft "Sound of Silence," Morphine "The Night," Alkaline Trio "Queen of Pain," Ben Harper "Amen Omen," Jimmy Eat World "Hear You Me," Corrosion of Conformity "Stare Too Long," Dustin Kensrue "Consider the Ravens," Poe "Haunted," Van Morrison "Warm Love"...each its own kind of masterpiece...each sending chills over my body from the beauty within.

 I want to lay in bed with my eyes closed, but not sleeping, and listen to every nuance of note and perfect placement of phrase. I want to hear every lyric and know the truth that exists in their meaning, and admire the courage the singer of those words has to reveal such honest confessions. I want to cry at the way those truths, so completely personal to that artist, are so completely universal, as I realize when and where that same prose could have been written by me of a true story from my life.

 Did I say I want to get lost in music? Then why do I suddenly feel so found? Is it only music that can do this? Or is it beauty? Or is it truth? Or is it love?

 If it is all...beauty and truth and love...it would explain why, when I'm with you, I feel found...I feel home. Home with my beautiful true love.

 I miss you! I love you!

Yours Always,
Jared Christopher

November 19, 2009 – 10:20 PM

My Lovely Dawn,

Another late class and another late-late dinner from a drive-thru windo...this can't be healthy.

Outside the rain is pouring down. Every time I drive past the river I note how much the water level has risen. I fear the worst of it will come later, when the snow in the mountains begins to melt.

Inside the house is entirely too messy. I haven't had the time or motivation to keep it as clean as I would like...as clean as I normally do. Is there a correlation between the shortening amount of daylight and the idea that there will be more dark or shadow that will hide the dirty floors?

My body is losing it's definition. As the days grow colder, my morning workouts have all but disappeared. It's so much nicer to wake up and jump into a hot shower. My only hope is to get home from work and immediately lift some weights.

I miss you more and more. There are days I fantasize about you so vividly. There are days I realize I can't remember how you smell. There are days I hear your voice...sometimes A's too. There are days I forget how you laugh.

I must keep myself busy. I give myself special little occurances to mark each day of the week...things to look forward to tomorrow. Sunday is a day to write my music column and often a dinner with my parents. Monday is "House" on television. Tuesday I have lunch with my mom. Wednesday is my weekly trivia night at the bar with friends. Thursday is film class. Friday...Friday and Saturday are hard. They are the nights that are the most wide open, and yet always seem the most empty. I go to sleep early too often those nights.

I wish tonight was one of those nights...early to bed. Tomorrow will be a struggle. Tomorrow will be a Friday.

I miss you! I love you!

Yours Always,
Jared Christopher

November 20, 2009 – 9:05 PM

My Lovely Dawn,

I thought today was going to be different.

After writing you a letter the same way, every day for the last 215, or so, days...I thought today would be something new. I thought tonight I would write your letter from my new BlackBerry instead of my old one.

Initially I wanted so badly to write every letter from the same phone...just to say that I had. But I have quite literally worn this phone out. Some of the keys stick, some produce duplicate letters when you only push the key once, and it all adds up to taking entirely longer than it should to write a letter...a process that has already been complicated by my necessity to write the letters as emails from the undersized keyboard of a "smartphone"...my only consistent means of email.

But alas the new BlackBerry I purchased yesterday will take a little longer to set up, as I need some new computer software to transfer all of my saved emails and files from old phone to the new.

In addition to being able to write better, and more fluidly, I'm excited for the new phone because it has a Texas Hold Em poker game on it. I can already see how much time I will waste playing that. Oh simple pleasures.

In the meantime, I will take whatever means are necessary to continue to make sure you know a little of what goes on in my mind, in my heart, and in my life, every day of our time apart. Every day you will know that I'm thinking of you. Every day you will know that...

I miss you! I love you!

Yours Always,
Jared Christopher

November 21, 2009 – 4:56 PM

My Lovely Dawn,

Forgive me.

Forgive me for my silence when all you needed were my words.
Forgive me for my words when they were spoken without thought.

Forgive me for my blunt nature when you needed delicate touch.
Forgive me for my patience when you needed a forceful hand.

Forgive me for my earnest nature when you needed a joyful laugh.
Forgive me for my wisecracks when the moment called for tender words.

Forgive me for my stubborn ways when you needed to see me bend.
Forgive me for my compromise when you needed to see me strong.

Forgive me for my speechlessness when I was stunned by your beauty.
Forgive me for loving your beauty when you wanted to be loved for your incredible mind.

Forgive me for my leisurely pace when you needed to see quick progression.
Forgive me for my eager hands when your body arose my passion.

Forgive me for my hesitancy when you needed bold declaration.
Forgive me for my bold declaration when you were betrothed to another.

Forgive me for my timing.

　　　But I will not ask forgiveness for my effort, my intention, or my love. They are constant and they are true.
　　　I miss you! I love you!

Yours Always,
Jared Christopher

November 22, 2009 – 9:00 PM

My Lovely Dawn,

Today I drove to Seattle in search of a church. I am scouting locations for my next film project.

I wonder how often I drive past churches without even noticing. Today, while I was seeking them out, not only was I surprised at how many I found, but I fell in love with how beautiful they can be.

There was a lovely, old wood church...apparently the oldest wood church in Seattle...that would have been perfectly placed in "Little House on the Prairie." It was every bit the most quaint and charming church I have ever seen. At its front a narrow stair that led to the door, and above the door a beautiful steeple. This church was shoebox-sized when compared to its more modern counterparts, but oh how it compensated with its simple elegance. It felt somewhat out of place here...a daisy through concrete.

A few blocks away I found a massive compound of a church, with glass and brick and multiple floors. Being from America, a country young by international standards, we do not have castles or colosseums or any of the ancient architecture. Our churches are the only buildings we have deemed worthy to protect and maintain across the centuries. They are, at once, the museum and the artwork it displays.

And I feel so ignorant to the meanings of their design. What is the origin of the steeple? When did stained-glass become a pallette of the Catholic church? Are there design elements unique to certain denominations? How have churches always seemed to be able to afford such lavish design? Is it, perhaps, nearing hypocrisy for an institution that preaches the valor of modesty to often reside in such garish homes? Or is there something to be said for utterly simple, yet stunning, shoeboxes of a church?

I found beauty today...in a place I had never looked. And it made me think of you.

I miss you! I love you!

Yours Always,
Jared Christopher

November 23, 2009 – 9:37 PM

My Lovely Dawn,

Someone asked me this week what I was thinking...I ran off quite a laundry list of the things that ran through my mind, in the oddly sequitor way my mind works, right then. I saved the message because I thought it important:

> *"My next film project will be magical.*
> *It will be about the love that I lost.*
> *Is there something wrong with me that makes me so terrible at love?*
> *Is my inability at love a result of my elevated ability at thought?*
> *Am I a genius?*
> *Is there really bliss in ignorance?*
> *Where can I find me some dumb?"*

I think many of those things more than I care to admit.

How can I turn this off? How can I learn to be okay with less-than? If I can't be with the one I love, how can I love the one I'm with? Isn't that how the song goes? Isn't that what people do? Then how do I?

Tonight, "House," as it often does, echoed my life back to me. A child prodigy...a genius...has taken sick because he has been poisoning his body in an attempt to poison, and kill, his mind...or at least to stifle it in a chemical fog. The reason? So that he can be blissful in ignorance, and, in ignorance, be satisfied with his simple wife.

The timing of this episode, days after I wrote those words, is haunting.

November 23, 2009 – 9:37 PM

      Fortunately I don't think I would ever risk losing my gift, nor would I ever marry a simple woman. The truth is, I want a greater bliss than that of the ignorant I so often envy. I want to find an incandescent happiness at a level unprecedented before, with a woman of unparalleled beauty and impeccable thought. And I want to be consciously, intellectually aware of every miraculous moment.

      I want it all.

      I want you.

      I miss you! I love you!

Yours Always,
Jared Christopher

November 24, 2009 – 10:02 PM

My Lovely Dawn,

I've been staring at my phone for almost an hour...not sure what to write. I try so hard to be creative, to be original, not to repeat myself. But it's getting harder and harder.

As I was out for a drive earlier tonight, there was a lovely fog coming in...it was coming up from the asphalt like a smoldering fire...from the sides like incoming waves...and above like the softest moonlight. But I've written so much of wind and rain and heat and lightning. There must be something else...don't write about this tonight.

I could write of my life and the things that occurred today...still not entirely original. Although today stands out because there was correspondence from multiple women...initiated by them...almost as if choreographed...like temptation en masse. One of them asked me to come by because she thought "it would be good to see (me)." Another said, "I'm glad to have you in my life, Chris" A third girl had been having a bad day and when I checked to see how she was holding up she said, "well aren't you sweet." Each comment made me feel good. Each comment was only words on a page. Each woman remaining untouched and unseen. But how do I tell you these things without scaring you. How do I reassure you that every interaction I have with every other woman is practice? That they are a job I am doing to pay my emotional bills until I can live my dreams...direct my movies...and marry you.

I suddenly feel I am living two lives. Or at least I am recognizing it in a conscious way. My "todays" are not 24 hours...they are 8-10 at best. The rest of the time, and even some of the today-time I will borrow, is for tomorrow. Always two masters...always multi-tasking...always looking for ways to economize. While my feet walk a yard pulling the plow, my eyes scan the horizon for the rain clouds that will end the drought.

But now, here I am talking about weather, even though I said I would not.

Perhaps I should have stared at my phone a little longer...

I miss you! I love you!

Yours Always,
Jared Christopher

November 25, 2009 – 6:20 PM

My Lovely Dawn,

The fog of last night had burned off by this morning and revealed the sun. As I drove east toward work I had to put on sunglasses and lower the visor to block out some of the light. Somewhere along the way I began getting lost in thought...silently dictating a letter in my head. A car pulled in front of me for no apparent reason and began braking...I think to myself, "moron! Did you miss your turn?" I check my mirrors and the blind spot over my right shoulder...all clear...I signal and merge to the right lane to pass.

I turn forward from glancing at my blind spot...OH SHIT!!!! A car is crossing directly in front of me! I slam on the brakes and the wheels lock up and screech across the wet pavement...all I can hear is that sound, that horrible screeching sound...time slows and I slide toward the broadside of the other car. My mind races, "Tires please catch...please catch...please catch." And then a miracle...my car slows enough or the other car rolls beyond the path I'm on...there is no crunching metal, there is no breaking glass, there is no contact of any kind.

I sit in my motionless car...I flip the visor back to its resting place against the ceiling...I glance directly above me at the ominous eye of a red light. I ran the red light. I nearly wrecked my car and could have killed an innocent person.

I didn't know what to do. I rolled through the rest of the intersection, looked in my rear-view mirror, saw everyone was okay, and continued on my way. I got to work, sat at my desk, said a prayer, and trembled for the next 45 minutes.

I don't know how it happened...the sun, the visor, the blindspot, the daydreaming...or all...but today, more than ever, I shall hope to never repeat this letter again. On this Thanksgiving Eve, I am thankful to be unharmed and thankful that I didn't harm another.

I miss you! I love you!

Yours Always,
Jared Christopher

November 26, 2009 – 6:55 PM

My Lovely Dawn,

      Happy Thanksgiving.
      Today I am thankful.
For family and friends.
For nephews that give unexpected and perfect neck-hugs.
For keeping my head above water...figuratively and literally.
For film school and forward progress.
For compliments and rewards.
For forgiveness and second chance.
For knowing a true love.
For three little girls that will teach me so much.
For a woman that inspires my heart, my soul, my ambition, my art.
For the chance to correct a regret and to know your kiss.
For who you are and who you're building to be.
For the days you let me know.
For the possibility of tomorrow.
For the days that fly by and the moments we hope will last forever.
For the first dance and the song I'm waiting to sing to you.
      I am so thankful.
      I miss you! I love you!

Yours Always,
Jared Christopher

November 27, 2009 – 8:08 PM

My Lovely Dawn,

I'm getting nervous.

I woke up today feeling sick for the second day in a row. It's this lingering, dull headache and a horrible body chill. Do you ever get that? Where your skin feels hyper sensitive to touch and temperature. And the timing is terrible as I am supposed to film most, if not all, of my second film project in two days.

In addition, I haven't felt up to finishing drawing all of the story boards even though I had the day off yesterday and got home early today. I'm also nervous about using an untested actor and being, myself, an untested director. Will I know how to pull a performance from him? Do I have any sort of directing instincts that will kick in?

How do I get what is in my head onto the page, into the actors performance, and then capture and edit it in a compelling way? This is the part that can't be taught. This is the part when we find out if I am an artist...or just a dreamer.

I miss you! I miss your ginger root cure for a cold! I love you!

Yours Always,
Jared Christopher

November 28, 2009 – 9:26 PM

My Lovely Dawn,

I am thinking of the night two of my oldest friends stopped by my house after a night out...two of the friends that you also know from our time working at the same restaurant when we met...I don't see them often anymore because they are often busy with their young families...we had had a couple drinks and, for some reason, I got it in my head that we should have an impromptu larger reunion, and I invited you to come down too.

To my surprise, I get the reply, "I'm on my way!" I was THRILLED! Two of my greatest friends AND the person I love most in the world in my little condo in Kent!

Then the reality dawned on me...what if they're offended that I'm hanging out with a married woman...what if you're offended by us boys being boys...what if...what if...

"Stop thinking and let life happen!" I have to remind myself of that, to get better at it until it comes without thinking. I need to get out of my head and into the world.

Cause what happens when I do that? I make people laugh...I make people think...I make new friends...I have a great time with my buddies and my girl, talking about soup recipes and families and reminiscing...and when one of the guys drops a four-letter word I cringe, but you don't seem to react..."It's okay!" I think to myself, "you're a big girl."

I was so proud of you, of me, of us that night. It was the "us" I can so clearly see we would be. We would be this amazing couple that the world would love to be around. And I need to remember that night when fears arise that you wouldn't get along with people in my life.

Do most of my friends, or family, have the same morality as you...no. I think your morals are generally of the highest caliber. I also know that most of my friends and family don't have the same morals as me. And we get along fine most of the time. We have the option to meet them on their terms. We have the option to try to bring them to our terms. We have the option not to judge those that are different than us and to just coexist when we cross paths.

November 28, 2009 – 9:26 PM

     The night you came to the mini-DQ reunion you gave me great hope and deepened my belief that there is something magical that happens when we are together. I loved that night!
     I miss you! I love you!

Yours Always,
Jared Christopher

November 29, 2009 – 8:10 PM

My Lovely Dawn,

I woke up early this Sunday morning...even before my alarm clock blared. This came after last night, when thoughts kept coming to me, reminding me of things to prepare for today, and keeping me awake past my intended bed time. I was excited and nervous for today's film shoot.

I won't say much about the shoot itself, I don't know how much I could say...it turns out we have become spoiled by the wonders of digital technology and its instantaneous results...and when working with these delicate, old film cameras there really is no knowledge of what you actually have captured until days later, after the film has been processed and can be viewed.

I feel like we got some great shots. I know there is one shot I would like another take on...something I rushed through in the urgency of filming on the streets of Seattle. There is one shot, if I didn't run out of film, could be the best moment of the entire film...a happy little accident that made me smile behind my viewfinder. I hope it's there.

Now it is off to the editing room...to try to put it all together with the music I have picked out. Having done this once already now, I am anticipating growing calloused to the effect of the shots when I watch them endlessly while editing. But I will also anticipate the possibility of a wonderful reception from my classmates and peers, even if I become doubtful of my results from the repetitious viewing. There will be a little bit of "hope for the best, and plan for the worst."

Good or bad, I can't wait to have a finished project. Good or bad, I can't wait to see it projected on that big old screen, in that dark, dark room. I will watch it and think of you.

I miss you! I love you!

Yours Always,
Jared Christopher

November 30, 2009 – 8:52 PM

My Lovely Dawn,

I don't think I'm as proud of my Saturday and Sunday letters as I am of my Monday through Friday. To know that I spend eight-plus hours working a job that I can't stand, come home to a workout or to handle any of the plethora of chores that all fall on me, and then find a good chunk of time to sit and talk to you...well, I'm writing you, but if I do it at all like I think I can, hopefully when you read each letter you can feel me there with you, and we're just talking...to know I can do this without you gives me faith that I can do it with you.

I want to always find time each day to be alone with you, just to talk. I hope that I will be a great and grateful listener. If I am not, force me to be. I think that I will be a thoughtful and open communicator. If I am not, force me to be. I know you have it in you to call me on my BS. And I know I have it in me to be humbled by your thoughts.

Moreso than with any person I've ever known, with you I am patient and understanding and tactful. Is it because you so often earn my respect with the way you give to others and to me? Is it because I am so afraid to lose you that I learn my mistakes much quicker around you? Or is it because we just fit? Like the perfect dance partners or those infamous puzzle pieces...and we'll never stray too far from this peaceful center...never leave a room in anger...never hold on to a stubborn point of view at cost of that which we hold most dear...this love.

None of these really seem enough of an answer. Perhaps no words could ever suffice. But let me give words a try...every day...in quiet conversations for just you and I. In the morning, in bed before you head to the girls' rooms to wake them with that gentle nudge...in the middle of the day's greatest chaos and frustration, as I pull you into a bathroom for three words and a hug...at night, when we stand side-by-side in the kitchen, giving each other the abridged highlights of that day, while one washes dishes and the other loads the dishwasher.

November 30, 2009 – 8:52 PM

     And it will be this way Monday through Friday. Saturday and Sunday...well that depends...are the girls with their dad? I'm sure we could find something fun to do...
     I miss you! I love you!

Yours Always,
Jared Christopher

December 2009

∞

Death

December 1, 2009 – 10:00 PM

My Lovely Dawn,

Did you ever notice, or think it funny, how often we would dress similarly? Especially our shoes.

I remember the first time you came to my place...it was summer and we both had on flip flops and our clothes were both some shade of blue. Or the time you asked me out for a walk...I didn't know you would do that, and yet, that day, I had worn my running shoes...which were oddly similar to yours. We also both wear some form of a Converse Chuck Taylor, and often on the same day. It makes me smile.

I remember the last time I saw you...you in a grey tank top, and me in grey pants. A complete coincidence...but then again, as often as we have those coincidences, it makes you wonder. I didn't notice your shoes that day...perhaps you didn't have any on yet...I only noticed you were the most stunning vision I had ever seen. We stood on the front porch, which left the sun blocked by your house, and yet you seemed to shine as if standing in direct light. At least that is how I remember it.

I remember a time we didn't wear the same shoes...it was the night we met at the movies last year...and it was because you were wearing heels. I loved to see you glammed up that night as we walked from the theatre under the stars. Everything seemed heightened...scent and temperature and touch. I tried to remember the last time I saw you wear heels before then...it must have been the night we went to my homecoming dance. I remember before we went to that dance you were concerned that you would be taller than me if you wore heels. I was concerned that you thought I was short. I'm not short. I couldn't figure where that came from.

December 1, 2009 – 10:00 PM

Thinking about that dance now made me look just to my right...at the nightstand beside my bed...on it stands the picture of us we took at that homecoming. It's still there. One of the few pictures I have of us. I still look at it and think of you. I know that night I could have been better. But you were my first...first of everything...and I couldn't learn all the lessons fast enough. I was still taking babysteps.

Babysteps in shoes I couldn't yet fill...

The shoes are now filled. All they need is a matching pair to walk with.

I miss you! I love you!

Yours Always,
Jared Christopher

December 2, 2009 – 7:49 PM

My Lovely Dawn,

     Today a beautiful late-Autumn day. A perfectly clear sky with a biting chill in the air. The days are growing quite short, leaving me to drive home from work into the marvelous vanilla twilight. These days the dusk seems to last longer than the day itself. I won't complain as I love the night. I love the quiet of it...the slower pace. I love that at night there is a better reason for the fact that I go so unnoticed.

     Unnoticed...until I choose to be seen. Let it be on my terms. Let it be for exceptional reasons. Tonight, let it be for a joke or a nod, a thought or a smile. Let it be for an attempt and a success at excellence in something, in anything, in all things.

     Tonight your letter is brief...abbreviated like the daylight on this picture-perfect day. Short...but hopefully sweet.

     I miss you! I love you!

Yours Always,
Jared Christopher

December 3, 2009 – 4:16 PM

My Lovely Dawn,

I don't feel right. For over a week now I have had this feeling. It is partly a cold, but it is also just an overall malaise. I don't feel sharp. My mind is foggy. I have been forgetful and distracted and clumsy. I don't like it.

Is this a seasonal malady? Physical or mental? Are the stresses of work and school and bills and living without you racking my body and weakening my immune system? Attack my body, but leave my mind.

I don't know what to do. I've tried to take medicine, but it seems to make the feeling worse. I feel like the medicine kills a part of me. I also fear the drinking I have been doing more frequently lately is damaging me. I fear I am killing my gift.

I wonder if others have noticed. Or am I, even in a fog, a passable intellectual? Do I need to stop speaking of myself and my "intellect"? I worry about that too.

I have to find my way out of this though. I need to break through to some kind of clarity. I need to breathe-deep clean air again. I need you...my oxygen.

Dawn I am getting lost.

I miss you! I love you!

Yours Always,
Jared Christopher

December 4, 2009 – 10:06 PM

My Lovely Dawn,

I sometimes get the feeling that people have no clue who I really am. Not only do they not know who I am, they think I am someone so far removed from who I really am. How does that happen?

I have a feeling some people think I am some kind of stoner. I assume this is because I often have these red, irritated eyes. I don't know why...my best guess is because I don't generally sleep well. Even now, as I write tonight, my eyes are burning and I don't know why. For all I know people may think I do harder drugs because of my thin build and pale complexion. But the truth is I've never even smoked a cigarette. I'm too big of a control-freak to let a drug make me lose control.

Some people think I am this intimidating, unfriendly person. I most often find this observation from people that I've worked with. I've never understood it. I have learned there can be a condition that causes a person's face to a have an angry or upset appearance when it is, in fact, in a relaxed state...and I wonder if that occurs with me. I don't seem to get that response when I smile. People like my smile and want me to smile more, but I can't really walk around smiling all day...that would look crazy. Wouldn't it?

Some people think I am this incredible ladies man. They see one picture of me with a group of female friends, or a series of pics of me with various female friends, or perhaps they see the way I interact with women in-person, and they assume I am sleeping around...to a significant degree. The truth is I haven't done anything with anyone since I was with you. I haven't slept with anyone. I haven't kissed anyone. I may have hugged a couple girls, but if a hug meant much at all I wouldn't hug my sisters or nephews.

December 4, 2009 – 10:06 PM

No the truth is, I am a straight-laced, clean and sober guy, who longs to be liked by all, and loved by only one...you. The reality is I am lying in bed alone, after spending an entire Friday night alone, having consumed no harder drug than, perhaps, the MSG in my takeout Chinese food.

I am a good boy who is trying to be a better man.

When will they see this? When will they see me? When will they see me like you do? When will I see you?

I miss you! I love you!

Yours Always,
Jared Christopher

December 5, 2009 – 8:52 PM

My Lovely Dawn,

I have just come from the film editing room. I hadn't seen the raw footage until today, and unfortunately there were some camera mistakes and problems...some footage that is unusable. I spent eight hours today building the first cut. I made solid progress but there is still so much to do. In addition to film editing I am simultaneously building opening and closing credits, and doing the audio editing. The music I am using has far more vocals than I need, and not nearly enough instrumental for what I want. I am making it work though.

While driving home from the studio in Seattle I was quite tired. The car heater was turned on "high" so as to guard me from the current cold snap that is plaguing the city. The stereo was cranked even higher so as to overpower the sounds of the heater blower and hum of the wheels barreling down the freeway.

The song on the cd was a song we have talked about before...powerful and vulnerable...drenched in intellectualism and sexuality. I got lost in the beauty of it. I fantasized of making love to you surrounded by this soundtrack. Feeling the heat from your body touching mine...getting lost in the rhythm of our movements...becoming one with you...one in vulnerability and security and thought and spirit...

You make weak...you make me strong...you make me think...you make me feel...and it feels amazing!

I miss you! I love you!

Yours Always,
Jared Christopher

December 6, 2009 – 3:35 PM

My Lovely Dawn,

I love creativity. I love trying to find something new or building an improvement on something existing. I love the way creativity can have a life of its own and simultaneously pinball around topics with a similar rooting, while also snowballing...increasing in momentum and scope.

As you know, I'm finishing my second film project. Unlike the first project, this film has been an idea that has been with me for a long time. If the result is at all what I think it can be, I will be quite proud. I will want to show off my work and my progress to my friends and family. In that spirit, I have begun thinking about a premiere for my little film. There won't be a red carpet...no flashbulbs or Hollywood stars. Just a nice evening of sharing cocktails and conversation with any that are curious about what I've been working on, capped off with a viewing of the completed effort.

That idea gave way to the idea that a special night deserves a special drink or two. And if the night is for movies...what better cocktail than one inspired by everyone's favorite movie theatre snacks? How about a redvine-infused vodka? Or somehow suggesting buttered popcorn in a drink using a butterscotch liqueur? I called a friend of mine who is currently in a bartending course to gain his insights and advice. We proceeded to come up with a handful of pretty solid ideas for the party including a drink using chocolate, coconut, and Amaretto flavors that we could call the Almond Joy.

December 6, 2009 – 3:35 PM

        After I got off the phone with him, the creativity was still pinballing around in my head. What if these drinks weren't just for a special occasion or a private party? What if this were something made available to the public? All of these adult beverages, that have inspirations from movie theatre foods...but then take it further, to include existing drinks inspired by foods outside the theatre, like the Chocolate Cake or the Jolly Rancher, but that all still fall under a similar theme...then think of a clever, or at least punny, name that could encapsulate the whole theme...and what do you get??? The Snack Bar. A bar that specializes in mixed drinks inspired by all of our guilty-pleasure snack foods. And perhaps, eventually, our own micro-brew beers...like the licorice lager. I, literally, just made that up as I was typing.
        Oh creativity...you are my second favorite high.
        My favorite is...the love of a beautiful woman. Best high ever!
        I miss you! I love you!

Yours Always,
Jared Christopher

December 7, 2009 – 10:20 PM

My Lovely Dawn,

Awake since six o'clock...eight-plus hours of work...a break for lunch and dinner...then four hours in the editing room...I've got knives in my eyes...my words will be brief.

You know what I think is sort of miraculous? We met when we were kids...and when I think of it now, we were every bit the part...children. So incomplete...so unrefined. And yet we were smart enough to recognize in each other some kind of brilliant raw material...the carbon that would become a diamond, over time and under pressure. We felt the spark that would ignite a powerful blaze...the fire that is this love that burns on and on.

You didn't know that my tastes would grow and mature like fine wine...becoming a resource for music and film and maybe even some fashion. I didn't know that you would develop this incredible sex appeal...with ways of moving and touching that I hadn't even dreamt you could have. We couldn't have known that all the years we spent growing apart in distance, we were growing so much closer in personality. I found a deeper spirituality and you found a greater understanding. You became all-the-more the woman of my dreams. I continue to sculpt myself into the man of yours.

It is a beautiful intersection of life- and love-lines.

I miss you! I love you!

Yours Always,
Jared Christopher

December 8, 2009 – 5:06 PM

My Lovely Dawn,

Tonight a memorial...three men, one woman...all in blue...four fallen police officers.

Not fallen, but slain. Murdered in cold blood as they, likely, sat enjoying coffee and each other's company before the beginning of a long day's work protecting the public. Taken unnecessarily, unmercifully at the hands of a man who had given up...a man who wanted only to inflict damage and pain on his way to his certain hell.

How can we do more to prevent this kind of tragedy?

We must fix the bureaucracy...the flaws in the legal system that allowed a sick individual to be roaming the streets when, again and again, it was shown that he was not well. We must provide better resources to law enforcement...for investigation, for recruitment, for prosecution. We must lessen plea-bargains in the court system and force more criminals to face the full sentence of their convicted crimes.

Most importantly, we must fix the societal fascination with guns. If we cannot convince our country that they should no longer have the right to bear arms, let us convince more and more of them that they do not have the NEED to bear arms. We must redirect the focus from blowing the world up as fast as we can arrange it, to finding more ways to BUILD the world up as strong and righteous as we can arrange it. Building confidence...building infrastructure...building opportunity... building brotherhood and community. Building faith...faith that when we are in time of danger, those that are in law enforcement, trained to operate a firearm, will protect us.

I will be one to set an example...I pledge to never own a gun...to never bring a gun into my home, where it could fall into the wrong hands...an innocent and untrained child, nor a violent and ill-intentioned criminal. I will never again seek out, nor accept, an occasion to raise or a deploy a firearm...not in aggression, not in self-defense, not in recreation. The buckshot stops here.

December 8, 2009 – 5:06 PM

I will promise that my legal transgressions will include no more than speeding...for while I can live without ever using lead bullets, I can't seem to stifle the use of my own lead foot.

Tonight I am sorry for the families of the officers we lost. And I pray for safe travels for those that will suit up from here on and always.

And I pray for, and promise, the safety of you and your girls.

I miss you! I love you!

Yours Always,
Jared Christopher

December 9, 2009 – 9:04 PM

My Lovely Dawn,

How has this year seen both the hottest day Seattle has ever seen, and now, this week, it has seen the coldest day in its history? And is this a really bad omen?

Tomorrow is the last filmmaking class of the quarter...I still don't have my film completed. I need to mix the sound and create closing credits. I'll have to leave straight from work, and edit all the way up until class begins. The progress has been good. I hope for a good reaction from the class.

I'm sorry I don't have much to write tonight. I need to go to sleep early, to wake up early, to finish work early, to get to Seattle early, to finish the film on time.

I miss you! I love you!

Yours Always,
Jared Christopher

December 10, 2009 – 10:53 PM

My Lovely Dawn,

Today was the world on a pinhead...a lifetime in a second...the good and the bad...the beauty and the beast...the hurt and the heal.

It begins with the world frozen over. Driving to work with the sun shining down and twinkling across the morn's early frost that blankets the ground. It creeps up to rooftops and meets and mixes with smoke and steam there, billowing from chimney tops. Across the roads, steam from exhaust pipes lingers behind cars only long enough to be sliced through by the next one to pass. No geese on the pond today as it has frozen solid. There is a stillness. There is a peace.

At work there are new clients. New faces. New names to forget. New routines to learn and improve. The adjustment to "new" puts me behind schedule. It begins my chaos.

After lunch there is a moment out on the road...it is a clear day and you can see for miles. I find a place in the valley where you can see the skyline of Seattle. As the mile markers pass and the foothills lift and plunge, there comes a point where the distant mountains thunder into view. High and jagged, and capped in snow and drowned in sun. Standing before our city like a guardian gate...to protect our emerald jewel from danger and harm. It is security. It is peace.

I work late into the day...behind schedule from the start and never to catch up. I need to finish early but they just won't let me do that. Work stacks up higher and higher around me. Standing before me like a wall...this wall is not to keep harm out, but to lock me in. I chip away hour after hour. The struggle and the shrapnel left in its wake...nothing more than chaos.

December 10, 2009 – 10:53 PM

I climb out...I escape. Out to the world I flee...only to find the chaos of a traffic jam. But this traffic jam runs parallel to a vision of the golds and crimsons and blues of this day's sunset...as the sun nestles behind those same jagged mountains, that stand behind the evergreen foothills, that sit atop the silvery lake that, at this moment, give frozen reflection to all...mirroring the beauty...doubling the peace.

The world is such chaos...but when you see chaos it allows you to see, and appreciate, that which gives you peace. Today I saw it all.

Today I close with these words for you...the words that I hope will give you some peace in the midst of any chaos.

You are my peace.

Yours Always,
Jared Christopher

December 11, 2009 – 9:46 PM

My Lovely Dawn,

A long and strenuous, yet rewarding, week is coming to a close. My Blackberry buzzes to life with a flurry of invitations to go out. Part of me thinks I should save my money, avoid the temptations, and just stay home. Part of me thinks I should go...because the socializing, the joking around, the camaraderie, is good for my spirits. Part of me thinks I can face the temptation head-on and walk away. Part of me wants to give in to the temptations.

I am not obligated to be faithful. Not today...not as we currently stand. I certainly am not afraid I will fall in love with another woman. I am only afraid of offending you...damaging what I hope, but have no guarantee, will come for us. Do you have expectations that I will be celibate now? Or are you okay with whatever happens as long as I will be yours if and when you decide to change? Are you understanding that my time alone is mine alone, as it is yours alone, and that no judgment should pass?

I don't know. I just know the farther I get from your touch the more I long for any kind of affection.

I must go now. Temptation awaits. Wish me luck. Or perhaps wish me strength.

I miss you! I love you!

Yours Always,
Jared Christopher

December 12, 2009 – 10:56 PM

My Lovely Dawn,

Everyone has heard of I.Q. as it relates to "intelligence quotient"...but no one ever seems to think of an intimacy quotient. And like a high traditional I.Q. a high intimacy quotient seems rare.

People don't even seem to understand what intimacy is anymore. The common definition has come to be one of a sexual nature, when true intimacy is meant to refer to a mental and emotional connection of a private and personal nature. The world has come to fear true intimacy...primarily for the vulnerablility that it generally brings.

People have come to prefer a night out with an activity that almost always interferes with intimacy...a movie theatre where the courtesy expected prevents most communication...a night at a bar or club where music blares over the sound system drowning out conversation, or people take turns throwing darts or shooting pool...even sitting down to a dinner, with people pausing conversation to politely chew their food, minimizes an intimate moment.

Even when a situation allows for an intimate moment, most people will avoid it because in that moment they could be asked to truly be honest about who they are. This might entail recognizing their own flaws. If you recognize your flaws, you have one of two reactions...continue as you are, therefore marking yourself as lazy or cruel...or try to change, which entails humility and hard work. In fact, it seems most people will only reveal their most intimate selves when they lay on a couch and pay hundreds of dollars an hour to speak with a psychiatrist. What they don't realize is, they would never need a psychiatrist if they would open up their lives to those around them and be intimate.

I, on the other hand, love intimacy. I crave it. I love sitting across a table from someone and knowing who they are...how they think. And I can't help but share who I am with others. All they have to do is ask the right question and I open up and pour myself out like rain clouds. I have no secrets. As I write those words, "I have no secrets" I wonder if that might be the secret...to life.

December 12, 2009 – 10:56 PM

       I mean, here I am...writing all the thoughts I have, all the things most people never say...sharing them with you and willing to share them with the world...my most intimate pains and pleasures, my fears and my hopes...and the release of them is like choosing my freedom.
       I love every moment of intimacy we have ever shared...there is no one else who has ever made me more confident to be me...to strive for a higher I.Q.
       I miss you! I love you!

Yours Always,
Jared Christopher

December 13, 2009 – 9:59 PM

My Lovely Dawn,

I want to learn all of your favorite things...I want to learn them and learn how to give them to you.

I want to learn if waffles are your favorite breakfast...and bring them to you in bed with whipped cream and strawberries.

I want to learn what your favorite dinner is...and learn to make that, and to do so on a day when you feel too spent to cook.

I want to learn your favorite way to take your coffee...if it is a soy caramel latte...and I want to make you think I left early for work, when in fact I went to your favorite coffee shop and am coming back to spend the morning with you.

I want to learn if your favorite adult beverage is a pomegranate mojito...and I want to take you out to this quiet little bar in Seattle that makes the best one you've ever tasted.

I want to learn your all-time favorite movie...and create a private viewing at a drive-in theatre I'll create in the backyard.

I want to learn your all-time favorite song...and then learn it on the guitar to play for you and you alone.

I want to learn your favorite place in the world...and I want to take you there once every year on our anniversary.

I want to learn your favorite place to be kissed...well, the most PG place...and I want to kiss you there in public, completely oblivious and inconsiderate of the world, and only focused on you.

I want to learn your favorite time of day...and I want to pull you aside, or call you on the phone, every day at that time, and tell you I love you.

Cause I do. Cause you're my favorite everything.

I miss you! I love you!

Yours Always,
Jared Christopher

December 14, 2009 – 9:25 PM

My Lovely Dawn,

I'm thinking tonight of the girls.

I just don't know how they would react if their parents got divorced, if their mom dated and married someone new.

I know how important a father is to his daughters. I know this.

I don't know what kind of father your husband is. I don't know what kind of father I would be.

I know that a marriage without love is a house divided, and a house divided is not a good example for any child. I know that children feel the tension and, if not corrected, will repeat it in their future relationships and families.

I don't know if, or when, the girls will learn our story...that I loved you long before they arrived. I don't know if they will allow me to love you, and be with you, now when they are here.

I know that I am committed to being a great man, a great example for them. I know that I want to show them strength and sensitivity, thoughtfulness and affection, humor and patience.

I don't know how to co-parent and balance time for the girls with multiple families. I don't know how you and the legal system would manage a divorce nor custody.

I know that if the girls want to see their dad or their grandma, we should do our best to help them. I know that, for me to complain of having to carpool the girls across town to see their dad, would be bad form...considering the situation would result from me having the woman of my dreams.

I don't know if the girls could come to respect me. I don't know if they could come to love me.

I know that I can come to love the girls. I know that I'm crying right now. I know that I love them already.

Will you let them know?

I miss you! I love you!

Yours Always,
Jared Christopher

December 15, 2009 – 10:02 PM

My Lovely Dawn,

Do you remember the time you wanted to move away? When you wanted to move closer to your sister in Eastern Washington? You said you wanted to live in a small house, go to a small church, and live a small life...and get a dog. Can't forget about the dog.

I immediately thought you were running away. My first, and self-centered, thought was that you were running from me...from the feelings that had already begun stirring between us. It wouldn't have been the first time you ran from me.

I later realized, from your explanation that you would move there while your husband worked his way through college, that it was him you were wanting to run from. I wonder how long you have had those feelings. If I am to trust the words you share with me, which I do, then my assessment is that you have always had them. No, perhaps not the feeling of desire to run, but always a feeling of void. And the void is a deficit of love.

You always justify it somehow...before marriage: "the love will grow in time"...at the beginning of your marriage while living abroad, "the love will come when we return home to a less foreign environment"...after children, "the stresses of raising kids distracts from being able to focus on love and pushes us apart"...while in the midst of an affair, "how can I fall in love with my husband when I'm in love with someone else." They are all just excuses. You say your husband wants, and has been granted, the right to "win back your heart"...but how can he? You cannot recreate that which has yet to be created.

You claim you have a good life, a comfortable life and you feel guilty to complain about it. But what is a home that isn't built on a foundation of love? Aren't there examples in the world, of households whose ONLY resource is love, who are far richer than those with full cupboards? We are in the midst of the Christmas season...wasn't Tiny Tim's humble little family so much happier than that rich old Ebenezer Scrooge?

Why do you think that love is a luxury and not a necessity? A requirement? Let's be broke and madly in love if we have to. I would make that trade any day of the year.

December 15, 2009 – 10:02 PM

     A house can go unheated when you love to hold close the warm body beside you. Cable for the television can be cancelled if you love the entertainment of endless conversation with your partner. The gas tank can go empty if you truly love your life, and love your spouse, and stop running away.

     But it starts with love.

     Who do you love?

     I love you! And I miss you!

Yours Always,
Jared Christopher

December 16, 2009 – 8:41 PM

My Lovely Dawn,

Technology is amazing!

Technology allowed me to reconnect with you last year when I found your profile on Myspace and messaged you.

Technology allows me to burn you cd's of all those songs I want you to hear.

Technology allows me to take digital photographs and then transfer them to the internet seconds later, where they can be viewed by the world.

Technology allows me to take digitally transferred film footage and edit it on my home computer.

Technology allows me to take my finished mini-films and burn them to a DVD, which can then be shown to all of my friends and family at their leisure, in the comfort of their own home.

Technology allows me to create an email address for you, where I can send you a letter every day, and it documents it with a date-stamp.

Technology allows me to write and email each letter I write from anywhere, anytime on my BlackBerry cell phone...so I never go a day without tell you, in some way, that I love you!

I miss you! I love you!

Yours Always,
Jared Christopher

December 17, 2009 – 8:00 PM

My Lovely Dawn,

I am so horribly uncultured. I have been to no foreign countries. I have no taste for foreign cuisine...in fact, I rather fear it. Come to think of it, I'm rather useless with many American cuisines. And I don't know how to fix it. I certainly can't, or won't, fix it while a bachelor, living alone and cooking for one.

Please tell me that if we can get married that you will train me better to be braver with foods? Cook things for me that I don't want to try, and then make me try them...baby-steps or baby-bites at a time if need be.

I want to be better. I don't want to have obstacles or short-comings in this life. I want to learn to fly a plane to conquer my fear of heights. I want to conquer my fear of drowning. I want to conquer my fear of new or unkonw social situations.

It all can be done. I just need opportunity. Or I need to create my opportunity. Add in a dash of your wonderful support and constructive advice and I can do it. You are also the best motivator. You make me want to be the best possible man I can be. Every time I feel myself, in the moment, being negative, to someone else or myself, I wonder if I would do that if you were with me. I don't think I would. Not only do you make me want to be a better man, you make it true. Cause all I need is the desire...I have the work ethic...I have the ability.

I just need you.

I miss you! I love you!

Yours Always,
Jared Christopher

December 18, 2009 – 8:34 PM

My Lovely Dawn,

I overheard a conversation today about the stereotype that men get into relationships for the sex, women get into relationships for the love, and they both barter one for the other...often faking it along the way.

There is some truth to this. Men get the worse of the two labels, as it is far more unseemly to feign love to get sex, than it is to feign enjoying sex to get love. But it is mostly a bad idea to feign anything, as karma dictates that you will get what you have given, and, often, in an unchosen or unexpected form.

I wondered today...could we put a number on the ratios of love to sex? And wouldn't the male and female ratios be closer to the middle, and each other, than initially suspected?

Not all men are faking love to get sex...certainly not all the time. Some men truly love "love" and the fact that sex comes along with it is just an added bonus. Sometimes men, raised to be macho and hide their emotions, downplay their desire to be loved...when, in fact, they do want that.

The inverse is true for women. There are a great number of women that have grown to love sex...while in-love and sometimes when they simply want sex. Sometimes, as I've previously discussed, women fear true intimacy and prefer the superficial high that comes from sex. Sometimes women want sex simply as a way to mask another feeling, such as stress or sadness.

So what are the numbers? If simply considering love and sex...taken out of 100 points...how many points would men and women give, respectively, to love...to sex? I think most people would guess men would give the advantage to sex by an 80-20 margin. Women would give sex like a 10 compared to the 90 for love. I don't think either is right.

My guesses are; men, if speaking truthfully, rate sex at 60 percent of the pie, love at 40 percent...women would truthfully rate love at 60, sex at 40.

December 18, 2009 – 8:34 PM

The reason most people's estimates differ so greatly is because most people haven't found, and don't know how to find, a true love. The majority of people do not have the patience to find a true love, and because they have settled for a "good enough" love, in time, men lose interest and disconnect from the emotions of the relationship, and women lose interest and disconnect from the physicality of the relationship. This is why you always hear that couples sex-lives take a nose-dive after they marry.

When a true love is found two things happen simultaneously; men become less preoccupied with wanting or seeking sex and can learn to find more pleasure in pleasing their partner's heart and mind because they are getting tremendous support and confidence from the love and desire shown by their wife; and women, having a man heap love, support, affection, and effort upon them will fall deeper in love, and deeper in-love they will be more aroused and want, and give, sex more frequently.

Sex is better in love...love is better with sex. It's the yin and yang of the 60/40 rule. At least in theory...

In reality...I love you 100 percent of the time...I want you 100 percent of the time.

I miss you! I want you! I love you!

Yours Always,
Jared Christopher

December 19, 2009 – 3:27 PM

My Lovely Dawn,

I went to a birthday party this week...there was sushi but I don't eat sushi...there was dancing but I don't dance...there was a photographer but I don't pose for pictures...but there was conversation and I conversed my ass off.

There was a guy that loved football and we talked about the Seahawks for twenty minutes...whether or not they can bring Mike Holmgren back as their General Manager and why the new coach won't let their young running back Forsett get more carries. There was a woman that loved fashion and we talked for a while...about theories that men with designer jeans must have a girlfriend and she must be the one that picks out his pants. There was a married couple that work in the local film industry...we talked for some time about cameras and film schools and good resources for finding work in the area to help build a resume.

Every moment of the evening, if you found the primary activity for that moment...the food, the dancing, the playful photo-taking...you wouldn't find me. But as I looked over some of the photographs from the evening, and as I looked beyond the focus of the shot, I would see me in the background...sitting in a corner with one or two people and having these wonderful still moments of sharing life through conversation.

I don't know how to be flashy or cultured or fleet-footed...I don't know if I care to be any of those. I care about people. I care about finding common ground with them. I care about respecting their thoughts and beliefs. I care about sincerity, and humor, and intelligence. I care about moments. I care about intimacy. I care.

It's not always apparent...it's not always standard...but it's this well of compassion and interest in humanity that is living beneath the surface. And maybe I don't want to give it in large doses...maybe I can't...maybe if I gave these moments in higher quantity, the quality would suffer...maybe my well would run dry.

December 19, 2009 – 3:27 PM

I must give my full self only in doses...until the moment comes when the stage and the spotlight are big enough that I can reach all the world at once...and when that moment comes I will exhaust my heart and soul when I give them something pure and true. I will give them the story of my one and only love and the fight I fought just to be by her side...to stand beside her and fade, hand-in-hand, into the intimate unfocus...

I miss you! I love you!

Yours Always,
Jared Christopher

December 20, 2009 – 8:40 PM

My Lovely Dawn,

If my count is right, and I sometimes wonder if I've kept correct count all the way, then this is my 246th letter. We have begun the final third, the final four months, the final 120 days of this year...our year of challenge, our year of penance, our year of misery, our year apart. This is the hardest thing I have ever done.

I have gone through physical pains including an appendectomy at four years old, and a series of lung problems and surgeries in my teens. I have gone through emotional pains including dealing with the fact that I was raised under the lie of who my father truly is, and then the pain that came when I found out why I have never met my real father. I have dealt with all the mental pains that come as a result of all the problems I have mentioned, as well as all the many everyday problems that become exaggerated in my never-resting brain. But none of these things hurt as much as losing you...again.

When I first lost you all those years ago it didn't hurt as much as it does now. Back then there was this naivete and ignorance in me. As much as I thought you loved me...as much as I tried to get you to confess that you loved me...even when I gave you the opportunity to say that you didn't love me...you gave me only silence. And in that silence I could assume that you didn't love me. That was strangely comforting.

I never wanted to be with someone that didn't love me. I didn't want to force you to be with me or to love me. I wanted to be with you cause I had never known a woman like you, who gave me the feeling I got around you, who made me feel loved the way I felt around you. It felt like we were so special together...with a chemistry and a camaraderie like I had never known. I wanted so badly to give in to that feeling. I wanted you to have that feeling and give in to it too.

But you never did. You never admitted to having that feeling. So maybe you didn't love me. That is how I began to justify losing you...you didn't love me. That I could accept. Love is all that matters, if you didn't love me I couldn't expect that you would be with me. Now, however, I cannot accept it.

December 20, 2009 – 8:40 PM

You have told me that you love me and I believe it to my core. I love you as well. Therefore I can not accept you continuing in a life that deprives both of us of this miraculous love. Knowing this consciously...that I am here alone, missing my love, and hurting...that you are there with a husband you do not love, missing your true love, and hurting...it is the greatest collective pain that I have ever known. I hurt for me, I hurt for you, I hurt for innocent young girls with a complicated future, I hurt for family members in disappointment, I hurt for family members that wish me happiness but know that I'm not, I hurt in mind, I hurt in body, I hurt in soul.

My consolation, though, is thus: I have hope, I have knowledge, I have obligation and fortitude. I have hope that there is a future together for us. I have knowledge that I can accept and overcome the trials we have faced, and will face, to become one. I have an obligation to prove myself worthy of you to all that may be hurt or disappointed by my actions, and I have the fortitude to work tirelessly to gain their understanding and forgiveness.

But first I need you. But first...119 more days...

I miss you! I love you!

Yours Always,
Jared Christopher

December 21, 2009 – 9:49 PM

My Lovely Dawn,

Here is the beginning of a new movie that came to me tonight:

Int. Movie Producer Office - Day

> **Producer 1**
> *We also have to make some changes with the girl. The audience will have no sympathy for her if she goes through with the wedding. Plus it's not very realistic.*
>
> **Jason**
> *Not very realistic? The divorce rate in this country is 50%! I'd say there's a pretty good chance some of those marriages began even though the bride knew she shouldn't go through with it.*
>
> **Producer 2**
> *Before we even talk about rewrites, there's a huge problem with this soundtrack wishlist you gave us. Do you have any idea how much it costs to secure the rights to these bands? Seriously?*
>
> **Jason**
> *No. I don't.*
>
> **Producer 2**
> *The rights to these songs...Pearl Jam, The Who, Red Hot Chili Peppers...these bands will cost a fortune.*
>
> **Jason**
> *Well can we take it out of my cut? I need to have those songs in there. I'll shoot quickly, I'll bring it in under budget...I'll make everyone I know work on it for free...*
>
> **Producer 1**
> *Kid, you're dreaming.*
>
> **Jason**
> *Yeah, I am. But that's what makes it important.*

The group sits in silence for a time. Producer 1 flips through a screenplay on his desk.

Producer 1
I really don't like this ending. Who goes that far only to turn around and walk away.

Jason
Let me say two things...1) this is based on a true story. And 2)...

Jason takes the script away from the Producers, stows them away in his messenger bag, and walks out of the meeting.

Jason is standing at the reception counter of the production office.

Jason (to the receptionist)
Can you get me the number for a cab?

Receptionist
Of course.

Jason feels a tap on the shoulder and turns.

Producer 2
Jason?

Jason
Mr. Weinstein, I'm really sorry about that. This is new to me, and I just can't...

Producer 2
Can you do it with $3 million?

Jason
What?

Producer 2
$3 million. You'll get paid for the script, you direct it for nothing, but you get to keep your ending.

December 21, 2009 – 9:49 PM

Jason (he grabs his hand and shakes it)
What...yes! Sir, I won't disappoint you! I'm gonna make
you all your money back and then some. I'll be the best...

Producer 2
It's okay kid. Breathe. I believe in you.

Jason (breathes in)
Thank you.

Producer 2
Come on back upstairs.

Jason
Can I ask you something?

Producer 2
Sure.

Jason
What made you change your mind?

Producer 2
I'm a sucker for a true story. Now let me ask you
something. Whatever happened to the girl?

(Roll Opening Credits)

Yes, whatever did happen with the girl?
I miss you! I love you!

Yours Always,
Jared Christopher

December 22, 2009 – 11:07 PM

My Lovely Dawn,

I think women are their own worst enemy. I can't count the number of times I have seen or sensed a woman building something up in their minds...they construct a fantasy of a situation based on some small little detail. Maybe the fantasy is more of a dream, and dreams should be fulfilled. But how many women actively attempt to fulfill their dreams? Or do they, instead, tear down their dreams before they have even articulated what said dream would be?

Isn't it true that at some point in our teenage friendship you thought of a relationship between us. I didn't know that until months or years later. At which time you had already torn down the idea of us being together...because of an insecurity that I was dating other girls (which never happened), or because you assumed your family wouldn't welcome me in as your boyfriend due to my religious differences. Didn't you fantasize the downfall of our relationship before I even knew there was a relationship to be had? Before I had a chance to prove the dream could be realized?

Does this happen often? Do women "crap on the dream" when something feels too good, or does it happen long before they feel any real connection? Do they assume the good feeling they begin with would create an equal but opposite pain if they lost the dream after committing themselves to it fully? Do they, instead, preemptively take themselves out of the game?

Do these same principles also apply to career or any other ambitions that end up going unfulfilled? How many women live a life of "safe" choices, of a chosen unfulfillment, rather than risk the life of a dream lost...a fall from on high that comes unexpectedly? Do they more often prefer a manageable mediocrity than something amazing but vulnerable?

December 22, 2009 – 11:07 PM

    I, for one, will take amazing and vulnerable. And you are the most amazing woman I have ever known, and you make me completely vulnerable. With you I am entirely exposed because you see me entirely. You know who I am and you take care of me so beautifully. There is no risk too great for the reward of holding you in my arms. I will choose the dream for it is not a dream...it is the truth of a love this real and lasting. I will choose it, and I will nurture and build it up to a love even greater than one could dream.
    I miss you! I love you!

Yours Always,
Jared Christopher

December 23, 2009 –

December 24, 2009 –

December 25, 2009 – 2:50 PM

"No. That's not okay."
And a "Merry Christmas" to me...
Two days ago I sent a text message to your cell phone. I hadn't sent you a message on that number in almost two months. The last time, it was actually a response to a text that you had initiated. Out of the blue one day you sent me a picture of your sister, her husband, and their brand new baby girl. You had helped deliver her into the world, and I could sense the pride in your sister and yourself and the experience. The next day happened to be the anniversary of our first kiss. I had been wanting to give you a present...I had it all ready to go...but I wasn't sure how, or if, you would accept it. I took your inclusion of me, distantly, in the birth of your niece, as a sign that you weren't over me. At the very least, you hadn't deleted my number from your phone.

I drove to your house and rang your doorbell...no answer. I left the package on your porch and sent a text asking you to look there for it. Eventually you responded and we proceeded to exchange texts back and forth, catching up on the happenings of our respective families. You told me you loved the present. The last thing I wrote, in regard to your brand new baby niece, "Just think how you and she will always share a special bond from that." You didn't reply. That was the last I heard from you.

Until two days ago.

Christmas was days away and I had another present for you. I sent you a text to ask if it was okay for me to bring the present to you. Your response, "No. That's not okay." Nothing more. I tried to illicit a reason from you, but there was nothing more. "Would there be a better time at some point next week?" but nothing more. I asked if you were over me, but got nothing more.

My stomach dropped, my heart and mind began to race. Could I have picked a terrible time to text you, and in my bad timing was my question intercepted by your husband? Were those words actually his? Or is your answer incomplete, with the more elaborate response including some explanation that this is a bad time for me to come over as you have extended family staying with you for the holidays? Is it not okay because you don't want me to see you because, in our time apart, you have become pregnant...something I have had nightmares about? This truly scares me. Or is it because you have simply lost your love for me? No, more likely, you still love me but have come to find enough resolve to fight the urge to see me. This scares me even more.

As a result of those words, and the lack of clarification for them, I became quite depressed. I went on a bit of a bender. I stayed out very late and drank very much...wishing that something in the glass could somehow kill the brain cells that hold your memory. Alas, it only blocked the memory that I have an obligation to write you a letter every day. Or at least I had that obligation. In my binge I lost the sense to write you. No. Before I even began drinking I lost my inspiration to write you. That little flicker of hope that has kept me alive and fighting was extinguished. Snuffed out by four cold, little words.

The day following my lapse I spent thinking... contemplating what I should do. For some time I have been wondering if there is something in these letters that could be useful to the world at large...if there could be a book here worth publishing. Today, with my confidence shattered, I begin to doubt it. I know I can never complete my goal as I had intended. What's worse...I don't know that I will ever see you again.

And I die.

December 26, 2009 –

December 27, 2009 –

December 28, 2009 –

December 29, 2009 –

December 30, 2009 –

December 31, 2009 –

January 2010

∞

Silence

January 1, 2010 –

January 2, 2010 –

January 3, 2010 –

January 4, 2010 –

January 5, 2010 –

January 6, 2010 –

January 7, 2010 –

January 8, 2010 –

January 9, 2010 –

January 10, 2010 –

January 11, 2010 –

January 12, 2010 –

January 13, 2010 –

January 14, 2010 –

January 15, 2010 –

January 16, 2010 –

January 17, 2010 –

January 18, 2010 –

January 19, 2010 –

January 20, 2010 –

January 21, 2010 –

January 22, 2010 –

January 23, 2010 – 9:24 PM

D,

I miss you so much.

I miss the feeling that these letters had a home they were going to where they would be read, cherished, and loved. I miss the hope that if I loved you passionately, elegantly, powerfully enough, regardless of distance and obstacle, that we could be together in time. I don't have that now.

What I have now are regrets. They are not regrets for the times we spent together. They are not regrets for all the time I have spent, and still spend, pining for and trying to win your heart. They are regrets for the lies I have told, and will tell, every other woman I will meet from this day forward.

Lies from my lips that will never kiss with the passion that I kissed you. Lies from my hands that will never hold on as tight as I held you. Lies from my eyes that will close and still picture only you. Lies that I will tell in the hopes that being with someone without truth will feel better than being honest and alone.

It has already begun.

Somewhere in the mix of emotions...sadness, loneliness, bitterness, betrayal...I have in the wake of your denial of my visit to see you, I have sought out distraction and some form of relief in the company of other women. It has been a colossal failure. There have been two occasions in the last thirty days I have let women into my home...both times I had intentions of convincing them to sleep with me...but both times I found myself having to convince myself to sleep with them...both times wishing the women would stop talking...both times wishing I could be aroused...both times finding my body couldn't do what my heart wasn't in. These lies do not come willingly to me. Not like they seem to come to you.

I don't believe what you are doing now is true. I never will. I believe what we shared was the truth. I believe a truth THAT powerful does not die. A truth THAT powerful is a mighty river...and rivers can be dammed...they can be troughed and redirected...they can be manipulated by man who is then lulled into thinking that the river is controlled...but dams can break, levees can be breached, and rivers can show the world their true strength. The more you try to contain our love, the more it will wear you down, until one day your wall will fall and chaos will ensue from the resulting flood of emotions.

January 23, 2010 – 9:24 PM

I don't want this to happen. I don't want to live without you, lying to every woman I meet. I don't want you lying to your family and being worn down by the effort it takes to maintain such a facade. I want you to return to peace. I want you to return to passion. I want you to return to true love. I want to love only you.
I love you so much!

Yours Always,
Jared Christopher

January 24, 2010 – 8:43 PM

D,

I was thinking about you today. It's the Sunday of the NFL conference championships...New Orleans Saints versus the Minnesota Vikings, and the New York Jets versus the Indianapolis Colts. I think of the conversations we had last year about your fondness for the Colts and their quarterback, Peyton Manning. We had never talked about sports much when we were teens, and to find you excited and knowledgeable about the NFL was a wonderful discovery for me.

And as I generally do, often without thinking about it, I began to do a little research about Peyton Manning. I like to know about the things that my girl likes. It can make conversations more interesting and it can give me ideas for future projects. In my research about Peyton there was one fact that stood out to me...he and I share the same astrological sign; Aries.

I hope that this means that he and I share some of the common traits of an Aries; leadership, loyalty, stubbornness, fearlessness. I remember telling you about this fact and your comment was something to the effect of, "I guess I'm just destined to be attracted to Aries." Oh, how I wish you would be. Especially if that Aries is me.

Back in the present, Peyton and the Colts played brilliantly and won 30-17. At one point, after a big play, the TV broadcast cut to a shot of Eli Manning up in one of the luxury suites animatedly cheering for his big brother. I enjoyed that image very much.

The other game, as I predicted, was the best of the playoffs so far. The aged warrior that is Brett Favre taking on the Saints, in the city that has seen such trials over the years, and especially in the time since Hurricane Katrina. Whichever team would win would provide a fantastic storyline for the Super Bowl. The game teetered back and forth, ending regulation dead-locked at 28-28, before a Saints field goal sent New Orleans to their first Super Bowl ever!

January 24, 2010 – 8:43 PM

    I think if we were together now, we might have to cheer for opposing sides come the big game. I will root for the Saints...I know your heart lies with the Colts...but it will be a playful competition. I will have no problem seeing the Colts win. They are a classy organization with a tremendous leader...an Aries! I will mostly be hoping for another great game.

    And that, at some point, we will spend the Super Bowl together.

    I miss you! I love you!

Yours Always,
J

January 25, 2010 – 8:14 PM

D,

Were you always sincere when I recommended a song or a movie to you and you would rave about it after seeing or hearing it? I always thought you were sincere. I only ask tonight because it dawns on me how often our tastes seemed so in line with one another, and how completely uncommon that is in life...miraculous even. It has never happened for me, and I suspect it rarely happens for anyone else...ever.

On the few occasions I have given-in to the urge to peek at your Facebook page I notice things like your favorite TV shows; "House," "The Office," "30 Rock"...are also favorites of mine. Your favorite music; "Graham Colton," "Cary Brothers," "Matt Nathanson"...happen to be singers I think I introduced you to. And although it wasn't listed on your page, I'll always remember the way you described the visceral reaction you had when I let you borrow my copy of the movie "Brick".

What does this mean? I guess it means that I love the idea that we would never fight over the remote control, we would never argue about what movie to see on date night, we could easily agree on what radio stations to set on our car stereo pre-sets. In addition, what we didn't immediately agree on would never be an issue as I would be open to the things you felt strongly about...I would trust that you have excellent taste and wouldn't lead me toward something that didn't have a level of quality...I would recognize that your passion for something could indicate that maybe I was being close-minded. And I think you would do the same for me.

I want that more than I can express. A partner who I can share everything in life with...and to share it openly and effortlessly. This is further reason why I want to be with you. The trials I am enduring now will be justified by the ease of our communication and love once we are together. You are the effortless inhale after a peaceful sigh. When I am with you, you are my instant peace of mind. You are what I need before I know I'm needing. And you are so worth this fight.

I miss you! I love you!

Yours Always,
J

January 26, 2010 – 10:03 PM

D,

My legs are so sore. Although I haven't been considering it a "New Years resolution" I have been working out at a gym for the last four weeks...which coincides with the new year. I'm going three nights each week to lift weights. At home I am making a greater effort to eat more as well. I very much want to put on about 20-25 pounds of muscle. I want to look amazing so that if and when we are reunited your jaw will drop when you seem me shirtless for the first time. I want to be as sexy to you as you are to me.

Ironically, I think you see it the other way...you are compelled to workout more to keep pace with me. That is absurd...you are the sexiest mother of three I have ever known. You don't even look like you've had three babies. I want so very much to be your husband and to be allowed to cherish and admire your body. I have seen in our brief times together that our emotional connection relaxes me, and in that relaxed state I become this wonderfully affectionate man. I've never known that about myself before. I've never been that before.

And in return...I will be the best male physical specimen I can be for you. At whatever weight I can reach.

Like so many things in my life...it is a work in progress.

I miss you! I love you!

Yours Always,
J

January 27, 2010 – 10:21 PM

D,

This morning you came to me in my dreams. Oh what it was to touch you again. To hold you...to kiss you...to bury myself in your arms and drown in your scent. We talked like friends and touched like lovers. But as I looked closer I saw pain in your eyes. The pain of days wasted and lies told. The lies you tell husband and family and friends and self. You are lying to the world. And only in my arms do you find and reveal truth. Only in your arms do I find peace and completion.

This life has much to be unfolded, but the one thing I am quite certain of...I will never give all of my heart and myself to another woman...I don't have a heart to give as it still belongs to you. It is still yours and I wait for you to claim it. And while I wait I'll look for you in my dreams...

You are the woman of my dreams!
I miss you! I love you!

Yours Always,
J

January 28, 2010 – 9:36 PM

D,

Today I was wrathful.

I made a public observation of something in my life...something I had commented on months ago that now seems to be coming true. I was, in essence, saying, "I told you so" to this event. A woman I know questioned my observation for a completely parallel point. I began rather gently...trying to show her that she doesn't know the context of which I was speaking. She pushed the issue, seemingly arrogant in her ignorance, and I began to anger. I finally get her to understand my original point wasn't spoken in error or ignorance on my part. She, now realizing her mistake, didn't react with humility or contrition...but rather she put the blame on me for having not explained the situation clearly. My anger built.

I don't appreciate being questioned on most things. I feel I have a track record of impeccable logic, memory, and decision-making abilities. I feel I have earned the right to be trusted on most issues, and at the very least to be given the benefit of the doubt. I certainly do not appreciate someone questioning me further immediately following my proving myself entirely correct on an issue. The correct response for my debate opponent, in such a situation, is to fail quickly...recognize your error, possibly apologize, and retreat swiftly, tail between your legs, into silence.

She did not react that way...she pushed the issue further, insisting on having the last word, and my anger boiled over. I layed into her with a verbal assault that would be found harsh if directed at one's greatest enemy...let alone a friendly associate. I was very near merciless. I wanted to shame her into submission.

January 28, 2010 – 9:36 PM

      This isn't the first time this week I have felt this way. Last night I was disturbed by the reaction of many colleagues, family, and friends to President Obama's State of the Union Address. I found the speech to be incredible...thoughtful, strong, funny, touching, human. It is the way I want my President to speak, and I want his words to find execution. But some found objection to his speech. They didn't appreciate his comments on the recent actions of the Supreme Court. They cite the lack of previous Presidents addressing the Justices as an indication that Obama was in the wrong. I say, just because a thing has never been done doesn't mean it isn't a good and just thing to do. Perhaps Obama is the first person to get it right. It certainly strikes me as righteous, as the United States government was established in the three-tier form so as to maintain checks and balances. I find no objection in the President checking the Court. Besides, at worst, it was only his opinion. And the President has been elected with the understanding that he has impeccable logic, memory, and decision-making. We should give him the benefit of the doubt.

      I pray things begin going better for him and the country so as to establish him a positive track-record and earn him the benefit of the doubt.

      In the meantime I will work on my wrath. I hope others will work on their trusting me and their humility in defeat.

      I miss you! I love you!

Yours Always,

J

January 29, 2010 –

January 30, 2010 – 9:41 PM

D,

I didn't write you a letter yesterday. I worked my usual eight-hour shift and immediately after work I went out with my coworkers to a nearby bar to celebrate a birthday.

The evening began very slowly. I am one of the only men that works in my office...I was also one of the few people there under 35...and I'm probably the newest employee out of the group that was there...so I felt pretty out of place from the start. I sat isolated at one end of the table, not having much to contribute to the conversations that were surrounding me. I quickly ordered a drink, knowing that I could find liquid social in each sip of that whiskey.

As the night progressed, in the mix of a younger crowd of my coworkers filtering in, the older crowd filtering out, the conversations wandering into topics I was more versed in, and the whiskey doing its job...it became quite a night. I took quiet satisfaction in making, what I felt was, a great impression on a handful of coworkers I had previously not known very well. I was proud as a peacock in that moment.

Before I even realized it, we had been at the bar for many hours, drank far more than I normally drink, made some new friends, but missed my midnight deadline for writing you a letter. I went to bed feeling quite sad and disappointed in myself.

Today, in an act of God's ceaseless sense of karmic balance, I was humbled by the quiet and loneliness of a day when calls and emails went unanswered. How can I go from making such great strides in socializing and networking, with people I hardly know, on Friday night, and wake up to find a cold, uninterested welcome from the friends I've had for months and years longer?

Where is the loyalty? Where is the loyalty?

I'm so frustrated. And I don't have you...the real you...to tell this story to. To get your feedback and likely support. You may not realize it...many women may not realize it...but one of the things a man needs most is just to know that someone has their back. Someone that sees their man's point of view, regardless of whether it's right or wrong, and finds a way to support it.

January 30, 2010 – 9:41 PM

This is something that I need. I don't need someone to play devil's advocate...I can generally think of all possible scenarios. I just need someone to say, "what you're saying makes sense." That's so important.

And I need someone to write me back.

I miss you! I love you!

Yours Always,
J

January 31, 2010 – 8:43 PM

D,

In a couple days the Oscar nominations will be announced and I think I have a fairly strong idea of who will be nominated. I consider myself a student of film...and have since long-before I became a student of film-making...so I think I speak with some credibility when I say the following, This year's nominees for Best Picture will likely be:

Precious (haven't seen it, but we need something indie and gut-wrenching)

Avatar (biggest movie ever...but it's more of an amusement park ride than the best pic)

Up In The Air (I found it disappointing...it doesn't have that one perfect scene that would put it over the top)

Inglourious Basterds (Tarantino continues to be one of my fave filmmakers...but it will not win)

Invictus (haven't seen it, but we need a biopic)

The Hurt Locker (I expected something more intense and revelatory from this, but didn't get it)

Nine (haven't seen it, but we need a musical)

An Education (haven't seen it, but we need something British)

The Blind Side (haven't seen it, but we need a commercial/sentimental hit)

Up (haven't seen it, but we need an animated flick)

January 31, 2010 – 8:43 PM

At this point I don't like any of the movies I've seen for Best Pic. I have "Inglourious Basterds" at the top of the list of my personal enjoyment...of the films I've seen, I would predict "Up In The Air" gets the actual vote. But I need to see some more of the nominees before I decide for sure. Overall, I feel disappointed by this year at the movies. I would have chosen many of the films that lost the Oscar in the last two years as superior to any of the films I have seen this year. Films like "The Reader", "Michael Clayton", or "There Will Be Blood".

The other categories seem to be more predictable...Best Actor/Actress should go to Jeff Bridges and Sandra Bullock...Supporting awards for MoNique and Christoph Waltz...Best Director may again go to James Cameron for revolutionizing moviemaking...and the screenplay awards should go to "Up In The Air" and "Inglourious Basterds".

I don't know if it is because I consider myself first a writer, or if it is because writing is the where the most creation takes place, but I generally find the winners of the writing awards to be the best films. Movies like "Good Will Hunting", "Sling Blade", "Lost In Translation", and "Juno". This year will likely follow that pattern. I love the well-written word.

One day we'll have our moment to celebrate words, and films, and inspirations, and love. And if you're not there beside me, I will dedicate the night to you regardless.

I miss you! I love you!

Yours Always,
J

February 2010

∞

Man/Woman

February 1, 2010 – 8:39 PM

D,

Sometimes I wonder why you did this to me. How much were you conscious of what you were doing? Was any of it manipulation? What was the bigger-picture goal for you?

For me, within months of reuniting with you as friends, I became conscious that I still loved you...I didn't have expectations then that you could love me, or that you could cheat on your husband, that we could begin down a path that would lead to us being together...the things that I immediately wanted. I became conscious of these desires and I tried to do the "right" thing...I tried to walk away. But when I did try to walk away, you begged me to come back.

Did you want me to come back and give you all my words and all my praise, but think that I would not want something in return? That I wouldn't want our relationship to ever progress? And then when it did progress, and our love became wonderful physical affection, and you discovered that you loved our secret meetings and rendezvous...did you expect that that would be enough? Did you expect it would be enough for me, or enough for you? Who came to want those meetings more?

What were you getting out of our relationship at that level? Why did your words to me suggest that you wanted to build to a higher level...an eventual marriage...but your actions suggested that you never had that intention? My intention was to marry you. That has been my intention since I can remember. It is my intention still.

Was I correct in my belief in our special moments, that you did want to marry me, but you can't find the way to do that? I always felt that when I was with you those were the true moments. That was when you were your truest you, and I was my truest me. I always believed in us. But actions speak louder than words. And your actions have left me alone and heartbroken. I want you to be held accountable for that. The same way I want your family to be held accountable for not giving you an environment in which a divorce, that would lead you to a greater happiness, can be an okay choice. I want your family to be held accountable for raising you to

February 1, 2010 – 8:39 PM

think so black and white...that a boy raised without religion couldn't be a good and just man...that a boy raised without God couldn't be the man that finds God in marvelous ways...that a girl raised with God couldn't be a beautiful and wondrous teacher for that boy. All these things.

I will be held accountable too. I will stand behind every decision I have ever made if that decision put me in your thoughts...in your presence...in your arms. I can proudly say to parents, daughters, friends that I will dedicate my life to enriching your life and theirs, as you are the only riches my life will ever need. I believe in the spiraling of positivity that will begin with you and I, and touch all those that we can contact. I have made the conscious decision to share my life with you and I want to know and love all those that love you. And, in time, I want to become a touchstone for them as well. All this I want and will do.

Now if only they would have me. If only you would tell them that I am who you want. Or allow me to stand beside you and we can tell all the world together. I am at your beckon call...but you must dial that phone. Trust in us and I will do the rest.

I miss you! I love you!

Yours Always,
J

February 2, 2010 – 8:54 PM

D,

The way you are currently treating me, and the way I have reacted toward other women as a result, makes me wonder...

Men are often cited as being emotionally lacking...emotionally reserved...certainly moreso than women...but what if the emotional withholding is not the action, but the reaction?

I think I have shown in this last year that I am a sensitive, emotional, passionate man. Let's assume that most men have some of whatever I have. I also know that in the last month I have shown that I can be selfish, inconsiderate, and cold. It is already commonly believed that most men have some of that.

But tonight, while articulating my current state of mind to a friend, I realized something...I am not seeking out opportunities to hurt or deceive women by depriving them of an emotional connection...I am sheltering my own heart so as not to risk my own hurt at the hand of a woman who shuns my genuine emotion. And that cautiousness is a reaction to having been burnt by losing the only woman I have ever loved...again. Perhaps this is a more accurate depiction of what and why most men behave they way they do...it is a reaction to a past trauma that leads to a present, and sometimes future, of aggressive romantic passiveness. Perhaps every insensitive man is merely a hurt young boy with the protective mask of indifference.

The stereotype of man as insensitive lothario is made worse by man's predilection toward covering the heart scars of love with the physical bliss of sex. If the choice is between wallowing in pain and feeling something enjoyable, however superficial, men will almost always choose the latter. And yes, this sometimes creates the hurt anew in the heart of an unknowing woman. The buck is passed.

450

February 2, 2010 – 8:54 PM

And perhaps, in smaller ways with more frequent occurrence, women lessen a man's desire to be sensitive by their lack of discretion and tact while in a relationship, and when presented with a man's vulnerable moments. Even a lack of appreciation for the attempt, could be a deterrent to a man's future attempts at romance. For most men, romance is like a game of football...and when a man finds a play that gets him into the endzone, he will note it and return to that play until he finds it doesn't get him there anymore.

Now, stereotypically, it is believed that men feel that sex is the "endzone"...it is "scoring"...but perhaps that is the opinion because that is the "appreciation" women most often give. Perhaps women don't know how to give appropriate, vulnerable, verbal feedback to their man for his attempt at romance. If a man be like the dog...isn't a pat on the head and a "good boy" sometimes as good a reward as a bone? Don't both earn love and devotion? Train a man to be sensitive and sensitively trained he will be.

Ultimately, don't we all need to learn how to be more honest? To express our true feelings and give our fellow humanity the chance to be sensitive to our delicacies, strong for our weakness, and brief in their offensiveness. The shortest distance between two points is truth.

The shortest distance to your true happiness is to be with a man you truly love. And I truly love you.

I miss you! I love you!

Yours Always,
J

February 3, 2010 – 6:52 PM

D,

I miss creating for you. Or I miss your immediate feedback after I've created something for you. You always found the most beautiful way to compliment my writing or my photography. You would find some little detail that most others would miss. That would always let me know that you really took in what I was trying to say.

Today, the day after the groundhog saw his shadow and foretold of more winter...I want to say this...

In winter I live in darkness, in grey...
But into this grey, new life comes today...

Tiny angels in white, from the heavens they fall...
Dancing and drifting, on branches they stall...

The land disappears, under a winter snow storm...
We know it is cold, but our hearts feel quite warm...

It wraps all around us, our faces aglow...
We find a new meaning, in "blanket of snow"...

A blanket of snow, that covers the earth...
Covers life's scars, covers the hurt...

All that was wrong, now becomes pure...
The winter that ails us, now has a cure...

And newly I see, this winter of grey...
The grey mixes with white, making silver today...

The silver a mirror, that doubles the light...
It lights up my soul, and turns dark winter to bright.

I miss you! I love you!

Yours Always,
J

February 4, 2010 – 9:41 PM

D,

There is an interesting phenomenon I notice...it may apply to all people, but my observation has been primarily of women...and the behavior is that of a sort of selective honesty. It seems women will only share things, or share things in the way, that will most benefit themselves.

In most circumstances this comes across as a kind of pandering: A woman, we'll call her Jill, will have two friends...Betty and Veronica. Betty and Veronica do not get along. How often do we find Jill, when alone with Betty, prone to make fun of Veronica for, let's say, how much she eats or weighs? Jill does this because Betty does it, and Jill wants to feel included when with Betty. She wants to entertain her. But then, when alone with Veronica, Jill would never think of teasing Veronica about her weight. In fact, she will probably judge Betty for some flaw that Veronica perceives Betty has.

There is also an issue of women consistently telling people what they think they want to hear. The example of this is a woman I work with contemplating divorce. This woman has been married for unknown years...in that time she has rarely, if ever, heard dissenting opinion of her husband or marriage. Now, when she comes closer and closer to choosing divorce, she becomes more and more open and honest about said thought...all of her friends suddenly come out of the woodwork saying things like, "I could have told you he was no good." Yeah, you could have...so why didn't you? It seems to me, this woman's friends couldn't have been sincere about supporting her choice of husband before she married him, and also be sincere about their degradation of him now as the relationship deteriorates. If there is sincerity at both times, than there is also an ignorance or an inability to judge situations. If there is an inability to judge a situation in the past, then it is still there and one should not trust that person's poor judgment in the present. No, more likely, this woman's friends were once being insincere in the attempt to be supportive...but are now freed to be sincere now that their true opinion will not contradict hers.

It seems to me, when an individual is asked for an opinion, we have five options...

We can waffle and be indecisive. This leads to no real harm, but never yields any help either.

454

February 4, 2010 – 9:41 PM

We can be insincerely pessimistic. This rarely happens as the pessimism is distasteful in the present and the insincerity will likely be found out in the future yielding no benefit.

We can be sincerely pessimistic. This can cause short-term distaste if disagreed with, or it can lead to helping someone from making a mistake if followed and correct. I think I am often this way.

We can be sincerely optimistic. This is generally a good thing...unless it is supportive of an issue that proves wrong.

We can be insincerely optimistic. This is meant to be supportive, but it almost always catches up with someone in the end, and the person you were trying to support will find they have wasted so much time that could have been saved had those close to them given their honest opinion. I think your family is often this way.

The point of this is not to bash your family. The point is to show that, even if your family has been insincerely optimistic about your marriage, there is still a possibility that they will also be the types to be supportive when you change your mind. When they see that you are seeing more clearly something they had suspected all along but didn't have the convictions to express.

We have to learn to scrutinize the subtle difference between someone supporting our ideas and actions, and someone supporting us. Do Moms think their child is beautiful because the child is beautiful, or because the child is theirs? At some point we, as a humanity, need to be honest with ourselves and each other. If we don't, tone-deaf singers will continue to show up on American Idol clueless of the fact they can't sing, and women will continue to end up in marriages that most of their family and friends always secretly thought were bad ideas.

The shortest distance between two points is truth.

I miss you! I love you!

Yours Always,
J

February 5, 2010 – 10:05 PM

D,

I find more and more recently that I am attracted to women that have had babies and, more specifically, I am fascinated by women in the midst of pregnancy.

There are physical attributes of a pregnant woman that are incredible. Many men enjoy the idea of the engorged breasts, but I prefer the thickening of the bottom and the widening of the hips. Somewhere in the evolution of the physical female form in the last 60-70 years, women began losing some of their curves. I don't understand the reason for it, but the modern women is slighter of hip and broader of shoulder than the images I've seen of the women of eras gone by. I don't care for this change. Maybe it's something in the water. Maybe it's how wearing tight jeans has become the norm for women, and this is literally stifling their hips the way bound feet once created Chinese women with tiny shoes. I prefer a woman look like a woman...not this emasculated form that I see these days. I want hips and waist and butt and legs.

The other thing I suspect about my attraction to mothers and pregnant women is the fact that they are at an elevated intelligence and maturity level. This, of course, is relative to their starting level. But taking care of the life of another will inevitably cause one to grow. And I like that. Having a child seems to put a woman more in touch with her body and her sexuality. And I like that. Raising a child makes a woman less precious about getting her hands dirty and less concerned with superficiality. And I like that. Having a child makes a girl a woman. And I love that.

We've spoken some about your past experience being pregnant. It never sounded like you enjoyed it. I think deeply sometimes on why that would be. I have my theory. I won't dwell on that theory here. I will only tell you that I love you with all my heart, and when we became intertwined in our short-lived affair, for the first time ever I felt the desire to have a child. You told me you believed I would be a good dad. You told me how you would daydream of a baby boy we would have. You inspired me to be the man worthy of having a baby, having a family. But I can only see these things if I am with you.

February 5, 2010 – 10:05 PM

I want to experience the moments when you finish feeding our baby, you pass him to me, and for those few seconds the three of us are all touching...all one...and you kiss him tenderly on his head...and then a kiss for me. It may be the kind of thing most would overlook, but I would relish in it. I would soak in every second, every micron. I would burn it into my memory. I would cherish it.

And one day I would share with our son the words I wrote of those moments...the photographs I took. I would show him the way to be a strong and sensitive man. I would show him how beautiful his mother was when she held him still in her tummy. I would love him. And if it be a daughter...with her mother's sparkling eyes and delicate grace... well then I would love her even more.

D, I miss you! I love you!

Yours Always,
J

February 6, 2010 – 5:05 PM

D,

Tonight I am studying film. I am educating myself with "The Graduate". I had always imagined that Zach Braff's "Garden State" had been influenced by it and tonight it is confirmed. But I don't begrudge the filmmakers that wear their influences on their sleeve...the people that pay homage to those that came before with a wink and a nod, a borrowed line here, a replicated shot there, and a touch of the nose to tell us that the sting is on.

In my own screenplay I have sprinkled in these very kinds of moments. Some are quite opaque, some are more cerebral. Some are specific and intended, some come from the unknown divinity...the serendipitous fate of life's written story. But there they are in layers of hints and allusions and gestures and praise.

They are there for those that love the movies. They are there for those that helped me come to love movies. They are there because my film is my life, my life includes film...and art imitates life imitating art and so on forever in beautiful echoes and ripples.

My film will also hold all the people in my life. They are there in the words and the names and the music and the laughs. They are there because my film is my life, and my life is my family, my friends, and my greatest inspiration...the one true love of mine...

My sweet lovely Dawn...

She once was a true love of mine...

I miss you! I love you!

Yours Always,

J

February 7, 2010 – 8:42 PM

D,

The Super Bowl is now a few hours past finishing and I'm happy with the conclusion. But moreso, I'm happy with the way the game was played. I am glad the game was played without many turnovers, without many penalties, and with a lot of heart...from both teams. Here, we had the two best teams, with the two best records, and the two best quarterback, lining up and giving it their all.

And there was Drew Brees...the man responsible for my two favorite moments of the day. The first moment came before the coin was even tossed... Brees stood in the center of a throng of his teammates and led them through an impassioned, call-and-response rally cry. It is the same cheer I have seen him lead his team through each pre-game all season. I saw it and thought to myself, "THIS is a leader".

The second moment that will stay with me, came minutes after the final seconds had ticked away on the game clock: the center of the field had became a convoluted mass of players and officials, media members and family members...and once again, there in the middle, stood Drew Brees. In his arms a tremendous trophy. This trophy was not sterling silver and labeled "Lombardi". This trophy was a young baby boy...ear muffs covering his ears and protecting him from the roar of the crowd...a noise he could not yet understand wasn't of anger but of appreciation. And this baby boy wasn't frightened. He was in the arms of his daddy and he was safe. And there in his daddy's eyes...tears!

February 7, 2010 – 8:42 PM

Drew Brees had taken the hopes and dreams of his teammates, his city, and the people of that city who had seen and conquered so much adversity...he had now brought such a joy to that city...all of this could be enough to touch the heart of anyone...but the thing that brought him to tears, was getting to stand in the midst of a dream come true and share it with his own baby boy. As Brees stood in all that chaos and noise, his eyes locked on his son, and he spoke to him in a whisper. The words we'll never know, but the gesture we'll never forget. And in that moment I thought to myself, "THIS is a man". From fiery, emboldened leader of many, to open and sensitive father of one...today I found reminder of the man I am trying to be.

I miss you! I love you!

Yours Always,
J

February 8, 2010 – 9:27 PM

D,

The winter in the Northwest is long and grey and isolating. I feel the brunt of the isolation daily. I don't have a wife or girlfriend, I don't have any kids, I don't have a roommate, not even a pet. And I am at an age where all my friends have these things. I cannot call on someone to come and keep me company knowing it would take them away from their spouse or kids. So I don't even try. I accept that this is my sentence now.

And when those days come when a friend calls me up and invites me out for a drink, I say 'yes'. I say 'yes' and we go out and I give my all...I give my wittiest jokes, I give my deepest thoughts, and I give every truth that I know. And the grey begins to fade and I bask in the warmth of friendship...companionship. I know when those moments are happening and I dwell there as long as I can.

Today the warmth was the light of the sun on a winter's day. As the day progressed, I sat at my desk and did so little work. I watched the sun cross the sky until it hit me flush on the face. It was nearly blinding but I didn't want to close my eyes or look away. I didn't want to look away. I once knew a light that beautiful...but it is now gone.

How does one live this life? Do I so admire the beauty of this sunset, knowing full well that clouds will return tomorrow or the next day? Do I underappreciate today, expecting that there will be other pretty sunsets? How do I reconcile my true heart's belief that I will never love another, with the fear that you will never be strong enough to choose to be with me? How do I process the idea that the only woman that has ever loved me won't love me? How do I accept a life with no more sunshine?

Today I bathed in the light...and because of now knowing such warmth, I will feel more stingingly the cold of the grey when it comes tomorrow.

This is my sentence.
I miss you! I love you!

Yours Always,
J

February 9, 2010 – 9:09 PM

D,

As I go through my days I listen to the world. It speaks in riddles and winds, in dreams and melodies. It tells me things. It tells me answers to questions yet to be asked. It tells me when there is trouble on the horizon.

Today I listened to the world and I heard your cries for help. There is something wrong in your life. The voices tell me that you are running yourself ragged...that all you are trying to do is failing...and there is no one you can turn to for comfort or support. Somehow all of this travail has escalated this week. I feel that your soul is troubled.

Please know that I am still here. I am still waiting. I am still in love with you. All can be forgiven if we can be together. It is all I need. We can join together, help the girls to adjust in every way we can, and push forward without looking back. I have never been a history major...I prefer to be present in the present and building to a brighter future. Standing beside you I will have the brightest future I could ever hope for.

If only I knew where you were in the present...where you want to be in the future...why today the world told me of your tears...

I miss you! I love you!

Yours Always,
J

February 10, 2010 – 8:04 PM

D,

I have decided that women are incredible at keeping a secret. But not necessarily in the obvious way. I don't know that women often make the choice to keep a secret shared with them by a friend. But a woman can, and often does, take her own secrets to the grave. In my life, I have found most of the women I have been closest to have kept some rather large secrets.

The biggest, of course, was the secret my mother kept for many years...that the man I was raised believing was my father, was not. Actually, I had figured out the secret years before my mother would eventually tell me. There were too many physical differences between my younger brother and sister, and my older sister and me. So I learned on my own that I didn't know my father, but it would take my older sister discovering her original birth certificate when marrying and changing her surname for my mother to reveal the secret of why I didn't know my father. It's the kind of secret you wish would remain secret. It still hurts and confuses and angers me.

There are many other women I know that keep a secret of sex. Sometimes they hide a secret sexual affair from their boyfriend, sometimes they hide from their parents the truth of when they lost their virginity, sometimes they hide a pregnancy or a pregnancy lost or aborted, sometimes they hide a lesbian experimentation or even a complete gay orientation...

I know firsthand the reality of the female ability to hide an infidelity. Long before you, I had experienced, taken part, in women cheating on their partners. I've experienced it a couple times since you as well. While the cheating was never consummated, the definition is still unavoidably cheating. And to this day, only two people know of each indiscretion.

February 10, 2010 – 8:04 PM

     The only affair that has ever become known...is ours. It was made public, by me (regrettably), because it was the first affair that I took part in for love. And I didn't care, and still don't, if the world knows the "when" or "how" we came to be together...because I am so proud of the "why" we came together. I love you. I wanted to be with you. When you told me you loved me too, I thought there would be a future of us together, and therefore the end would justify the means. Yes, we began in sin, but I could see that the sin would become justified. That is why, unlike any other woman's secret in which I participated, I returned to the indiscretion with you. Only with you did I repeat the act. Only with you did I not feel any guilt. Only with you was the chemistry indescribably perfect. It always comes back to that electric storm between us. It is powerful, and beautiful, and completely unavoidable. We cannot turn back the lightning strike.
     We cannot keep the storm a secret.
     I miss you! I love you!

Yours Always,
J

February 11, 2010 – 9:40 PM

D,

Tonight I am exhausted. Of all the artistic endeavors I have taken on over this year, none has been as tiring as my attempt at sculpture. I am taking the hammer and chisel, and molding my body into a work of art.

For approximately six weeks I have elevated my efforts, been more consistent with my training days, and pushed my body harder and higher. The change is already noticeable. My body weight is up and every part of my body is firm. My thighs are thickening. My arms are popping with definition. My abs becoming a washboard. My glutes like a rock.

Clothes fit tighter. It feels different when I move. My confidence is improved.

If you should soon decide to see me again, you will be finding a new man. Modified, intensified, and revolutionized. And it is all for you.

I miss you! I love you!

Yours Always,
J

February 12, 2010 – 10:21 PM

D,

I'm thinking of pictures of you...

There is the picture of you at your sister's wedding. You are standing there in your navy blue bridesmaid dress...your hair, long, dark and pulled back, revealing the entirety of your gorgeous face. Your cheek bones...incredible. Your lips...soft and pink. Your eyes...beaming with pride as you look upon your oldest daughter, and her excitement at being a flower girl.

There is the picture of you on top of a mountain...the peak of a hike you had taken with your father. Your hair, long and curly and brushed by the wind. Your expression is blank. It could be from physical exhaustion...the result of the climb. Or it could be an emotional exhaustion...the result of who you were at that time...living two lives...a public persona of the happy homemaker, but then the silent disconnection from that life and the intensifying dreams of another man.

There is the picture of you with three of your sisters. You wear a yellow blouse with your hair in a ponytail. Your smile is bright and wonderful, but look closer...your eyes bear the look of pain and sadness. Look closer still, and I see a small tennis bracelet on your right hand. Could it be the bracelet I had given you for Christmas all those years ago?

There is the picture of you at some kind of summertime family gathering. You hold one of your nieces on your hip. You wear a white tank-top revealing beautiful, tan skin. Your hair lightened from the sun and showing it's natural curl...I love your hair that way. But again, look closer...there is no light in your eye, your lips turned down with not a hint of smile. Your entire countenance heavy with the weight of something great.

And then there is the picture of you in the black dress. Your hair...blonde and raised in a bun. Your cheeks...pink from blushing. Your smile...wide and magnificent. Your eyes...bright and blue and twinkling. Your date...awkward and skinny and undeserving, but filled with the joy of holding the only woman he has ever loved. This is the picture of you and I at my homecoming. It is one of the few I have of us. And it still resides on the nightstand beside my bed. There it will stay.

February 12, 2010 – 10:21 PM

Maybe I am biased and unable to see things objectively, but to my eye there is a distinct difference to all of these pictures. When you are with me there is a light about you. It could be argued that even the picture taken at your sister's wedding bears some of my influence. It was, after all, taken only a day or two after I had come to see you, to give you some music for the wedding, and we had shared a nice moment. But every picture I have seen of you since you stopped seeing me has such a darkness to it...a sadness.

Dawn, I don't want that. You deserve to be the bright, shining woman I see in the photo of you and I together. You deserve to turn that hue of pink again when you become my blushing bride. You deserve that every day should be a wondrous blessing...a gift of growth and creation and communication and passion...not the heavy burden that now is so visibly dragging you down. It is not right. It is not fair. Why won't anyone else open their eyes and their hearts and see this?

I miss you! I love you!

Yours Always,
J

February 13, 2010 –

February 14, 2010 – 1:14 AM

D,

      I've spent all day locked inside my house. Accomplishing little but giving myself cabin fever. So when friends invite me out to play bingo on the indian reservation, I accept the offer even though I've never played before and I have my doubts that it will be any kind of enjoyable. And it isn't. What is worse is that my Blackberry is getting no reception here and by the time I return to an area where I can send you this email the clock will have crossed over to the next day. I didn't send you a letter for Saturday February 13th. This makes me sad. It was a disappointing night.

      I miss you! I love you!

Yours Always,
J

February 14, 2010 – 2:53 PM

D,

Happy Valentine's Day.

Last year, a few days prior to this holiday, your husband was out of town on business and you invited me over to your house to spend some time together. I had presents to give. The traditional: a vase of roses and lilies. The untraditional: a very personal art piece that I had designed for you, incorporating your daughter's names and your love for them.

We sat on the couch and talked. There was tension between us because you were torn about continuing our relationship. Then we were interrupted by a phone call from your sister. In the middle of the phone call you leaned over and kissed me. It was the kind of gesture that felt so sweet and reassuring in the moment, but now, in hindsight, seems so misleading.

Those feelings continued a few days later when you made a point to break away from your family and husband, and to come to my house to wish me a Happy Valentine's Day. The emotions were high, varied, and worn on our sleeves. We've never been able to hide our emotions when we're together. The kisses so passionate...the tears so free-flowing. You had brought me a present...a card you had made personally. It was further personalized by the inscription inside. I keep the card close to my bed and today I opened it to revisit your words:

> *"Jared,*
>
> *You are an amazing, brilliant, strong, handsome man. And you have captured my heart.*
> *I love you.*
> *Happy Valentine's Day*
>
> *~T"*

It is the only true valentine I have ever been given. And it is perfect. There is no more that I could ever want from my love than her belief and support of me...her love.

470

February 14, 2010 – 2:53 PM

So today, when I have none of these things, my heart is heavy.

Please know...please feel...please sense...across the distance between us...over the barriers dividing us...and all the unknown before us...that my heart still loves you with all that is left of it. And I always will.

I love you lovely Dawn. I love you!

Yours Always,
J

February 15, 2010 – 5:58 AM

D,

Where do dreams come from and what do they mean?

Last night, only a couple hours after falling asleep, I was dreaming. I dreamt I was riding a bicycle towards your house. I wore a ballcap pulled down low thinking that could hide my identity. Everything moved in slow-motion. As I approached your house the door opened. From inside came your husband holding a baby. He walked with the baby along the sidewalk. We passed each other rather closely. He didn't seem to recognize me.

The door opened again and this time you emerged. Your clothes and hair were unlike you would normally wear...almost tribal-African in style. You walked to the trunk of a car and we made eye contact. You recognized me. You smiled in a way that seemed to progress from joy to uncomfortable realization as your eyes darted back and forth from me and your husband, and the baby that you must have been keeping secret from me. You knew this would hurt me.

I bolted awake, a cold sweat enveloping me, my heart thumping rapidly against the bed mattress. Is God speaking to me? Warning me again to stay away from your home in an attempt to protect me from a sight that could hurt me deeply. Or is this merely my subconscious mind dramatizing something that is a frequent visitor in my conscious thought?

Why does this thought scare me so? You have three children with that man, why would the fourth be different? Because the first three were created before I came back into the picture, before you told me you loved me. For you to have participated so actively in my seduction, and then to abandon me and to have the child we discussed having together, but with another man...even if the man is your husband...seems such a stinging betrayal.

February 15, 2010 – 5:58 AM

   Even if this imagined pregnancy weren't created intentionally, the act of creation would have been. And what is worse, is that a new child brought into the drama of our adult decisions and mistakes, would surely only motivate you further to remain in a relationship that is not, and never has been, healthy or true. If your words to me have been true, you are staying in your marriage for your kids. Adding another child would add another heart not to break, increasing your burden and guilt exponentially. Decreasing my hope of ever being able to hold you again and completing the breakage of MY heart.
   I can only hope now this has only been a dream...a nightmare. And upon first light there will be hope anew that there is a destiny for us. That all my love has not been in vain. That love will return again to this bed.
   I miss you! I love you!

Yours Always,
J

February 16, 2010 – 9:48 PM

D,

I feel like man and woman are evolving in a way that scares me. I've written before of the changes I notice in women, but there are changes in men too. I feel like men are, more and more frequently, asked, and/or choose, to be more and more feminine.

For years women have been attracted to male musicians with long, flowing hair. The image is further forwarded by the female fascination with male falsetto. Is there a safety, a non-threatening vibe that women get from these men? A vibe that is supported by the apparent sensitivity those singers can have in their lyrics?

In more modern examples we find the term "metrosexual"...a term that refers to a man who spends a lot of time and effort on grooming and fashion. The current trend is against a man having a beard or facial hair. That has been escalated to a point where a man can't have body hair either.

Is this man's natural progression or is this something pushed on him by women? Do women want this out of their natural taste, or is it some kind of subconscious revenge-wish for the years of shaving and waxing that women have had to endure to please men?

Don't these changes lead to problems? The blurring of the borders between straight men with higher learned sensibility, and gay men (the men that have always been the natural front-runners in style and taste)? And doesn't that blurring lead to women unable to distinguish the two, and therefore dating gay men? Are women okay with this? Or are there still women who want their man to be a man? Or has the definition of a man become one of an unkempt, clumsy, insensitive oaf, and therefore these groomed, communicative, sensitive men become attractive...regardless of orientation?

Do these two types have to be mutually exclusive? Or can we learn to be, and seek, a man with the body of a man, the heart of a woman, and the mind of an artist/scientist/dreamer/doer? We must somehow find a better middle-ground.

I miss you! I love you!

Yours Always,
J

474

February 17, 2010 – 7:09 PM

D,

   The sun was glorious today. And it has given way to a crystal clear evening. The air is crisp, the Orion constellation stands above, and the faintest sliver of a moon appears in the western sky. Tonight I cooked a wonderful meal and I will soon meet up with friends for our weekly drink. Do you know I have a present for you? I do. I always do. And if I don't, there is a present I'm searching for, creating from scratch, or saving up to buy. There is always one foot in the present and the other striding for the future.
   What is your present and what is your future?
   I miss you! I love you!

Yours Always,
J

February 18, 2010 – 8:59 PM

D,

I'm watching the Winter Olympics taking place only a few hours North of here, in Vancouver, Canada, and it occurs to me...how is it that the United States has come to be so good at so many things?

How does this relatively young country seem to find its way to near the top, if not absolute apex, of so many fields...industry, charity, innovation, performing arts, athletics? And how do we do it with such an admittedly flawed educational system? Does our lax system fail us in general education, allowing the average student to skate by with underwhelming abilities in math, science, English, but at the same time being broad enough to allow so many people to find greater single ability in a smaller niche?

Why does the United States do so well at all of these endeavors? Is it because of it's relative youth? A country young and brash by international standards, and too naïve to know that which all the others may fear to try. Is it because the United States is the rare example of a place founded and grounded in concept...the pursuit of dream...of possibility and hope? Is it because this is not the "American Dream", but the dream of all mankind? And as a result the United States has been, and always will be, the great melting pot...welcoming Russian and Chinese, Saudi and Italian, Vietnamese and Mexican...any race and all that are unwilling to accept status quo, to risk and fight for a greater tomorrow, in a land far away and unknown.

Is it because these are not just the United States of America, but, more importantly, the American States of Unity?

And isn't that the beauty of the Olympics? A uniting of all the world with one true goal...not to compete against one another, but to compete WITH one another...and to push us all to increase and improve and invent and inspire as a single humanity. One.

I miss you! I love you!

Yours Always,
J

February 19, 2010 – 7:38 PM

D,

I spoke to a woman at work today...she is a wife and mother of two...for some reason she felt the need, and simultaneously the safety, to reveal something of herself to me...she and her husband are in marriage counseling. At some point in the process she has had a moment of clarity...she realizes that she has not been in love with her husband for eight years. That's what she said to me..."eight years"!! Of course the realization isn't that she doesn't love her husband...she has known that for eight years, otherwise how could she pinpoint such a number? The realization is that she has wasted all those years and must now make a change.

She tells me he accuses her of putting up a wall. I think I know the wall of which she speaks. It is the wall a woman puts up to distance herself from her husband. It is meant to deprive him of her...her true self. Because her true self isn't in love with that man. But her true self is weak and ashamed and confused and ridden with guilt...

The guilt she feels because she thinks she would be the one giving up on the marriage and causing pain to her children. The confusion is the blurring of wanting something so deeply but hating what it would cause. The shame is twofold...public shame from wanting a change, an untraditional change that would alter her family and friend's impression of her, and personal shame from not being able to do it anyways. That is the weakness...she is too weak to make the choice, risk the shame, bear the guilt, and fight for forgiveness and change. She is too weak to demand something greater than a tolerable familiarity.

Well, she was too weak. And it only took eight years to build that muscle.

Dawn, please don't be like her. Please be strong...be brave...be true. And then be mine?

I miss you! I love you!

Yours Always,

J

February 20, 2010 – 1:00 PM

D,

There is another reason women put a wall up between themselves and their husband...the hope is that he will become so frustrated by the lack of support, the lack of affection, that he will be the one to take action to end the marriage. He will either take the responsible route and choose to legitimately end the marriage, or he will act out and seek the support and affection from someone outside of the marriage and his cheating will become grounds for his wife to end things. Women, although often first to leave a marriage emotionally, seem to insist that the final end of the marriage be the fault, the blame, the choice of the husband. The rest is a battle of wills.

Can she tolerate living a lie, faking presence and interest, long enough, from the safety behind her wall, that she can drive him away or, better yet, drive him to cheat? Then she can leave the marriage without guilt.

But isn't the truth every failed marriage is a failure of two people? If one spouse is guilty of cheating, isn't the other guilty of the ignorance that didn't recognize they might be marrying a cheater and/or the negligence that drove a partner to cheat? For every partner living in an emotional bubble, isn't there also a partner without the acuity to recognize and burst said bubble? If one person is a bad spouse, isn't the other a bad spouse-picker?

In this modern world of increasing opportunity and choice, every day we are complicit in two actions: the actions we make and the actions we allow made upon us. When we can't immediately control an action, we can control how we react to that action. We can be passive, complacent, a victim...or we can be aggressive, ambitious, resilient, and triumphant.

We can live our lives behind walls or we can tear them down. We can marry men that we wish to be walled away from, or we can marry a man that has the key to our heart and who no wall could ever keep out.

There is a knock at your door...

I miss you! I love you!

Yours Always,

J

478

February 21, 2010 – 7:10 PM

D,

I opened the "shoebox" today.

It was actually an email inbox where I have saved most of your words to me. I just sat there reading email after email. My eyes began to strain and my stomach began to rumble. But I just kept reading. I must have been there for hours. There are so many incredible memories...so many thoughtful conversations...so many sweet sentiments. But there is so much heartache.

I am the kind of person that will always wonder if there was something I could have done better. A joke that misfired that I could take back. A passionate moment where I should have gone further. A way I could have better known and matched your emotion that would have compelled you to choose to be with me.

That's all I was ever trying to do...to inspire you to be with me. I wanted you to know with me you would always find laughter and passion and thought and generosity. And surprise. I wanted you to always wonder which of my facets would show up and when. But to love them all.

To my surprise...you did. You always seemed to laugh when I was joking. To tremble at my touch. To hear the truth I was seeking in my thoughts. And to appreciate and reciprocate the generosity I always gave.

These emails are such a perfect exhibit of the love and incredible communication we shared. Whereas the conversation in most relationships play out like a professional volleyball game...where there are rarely more than two touches before someone tries to spike home a point with a "kill"...our conversation more closely resembles volleyball the way children play it with a simple oxygen-filled balloon. The idea is only to keep the ball in the air and the conversation going. And oh the rallies we shared.

February 21, 2010 – 7:10 PM

The news was not always good. The truths sometimes hard to hear. But they were truths and they were shared. We always came back to open communication. So why this? Why silence? What is going on now that you cannot communicate to me? Is your silence for your protection or mine? Without your answers I am left with only questions. I am left with nothing in my inbox.

I miss you! I love you!

Yours Always,
J

February 22, 2010 – 9:30 PM

D,

I have a wicked tongue. It can be a weapon in everyday situations, but even moreso in the heat of battle when it sharpens its aim to find the vital organs for the kill shot. Whereas my brevity can be the soul of my wit when seeking to entertain, that same precision can do unforeseen damage when wielded carelessly or in anger.

In these waning days of winter...or perhaps because of the ever-widening gap between our love and my loss...I find my fuse is short and my patience little. I have no time to be questioned or doubted. When I am unsure they will know and I will ask for guidance. I am not always right but I am more right than wrong. And when wrong, the goal immediately becomes, "what is the fastest way back to right?" This can be admission, concession, apology...to ease the hurt or harm done by my error. And it will be followed by investigation, education, and memorization...to ensure that the same mistake is never repeated.

I want to be someone respected and admired not only for his wisdom and his words, but his tact and taste in when, where, and how to offer said words. Perhaps this is already why I am so often quiet...pensive even. I want to choose my words and choose the spots when the things I say will be best heard and most understood. Otherwise it is inefficient use of time and energy...theirs and mine.

Plus, to take time to express one's thoughts is to know when to be light as a feather to cushion a fall, and when to be sharp as a tack to drive home a point. But let the latter never be done recklessly.

And always have a voice of reason, a trusted friend and confidante, beside you to support you when righteous in thought, and correct you when mistaken in judgment. You are my reason...the reason I write even when I'm writing of reason.

I miss you! I love you!

Yours Always,

J

February 23, 2010 – 9:41 PM

D,

A longtime friend of a friend of mine has cancer. She has become so weak they have had to cease her chemo treatments. She has asked for, and been granted, release from the hospital. It's just a matter of time...her remaining days will be few. And all she wants to do is to sleep in her own bed with her beloved husband and to make one more trip into the beautiful, snow-capped mountains.

I don't even know her. All I know of her are a few pictures I've seen...thin and pale...her head completely bald from the potency of the chemo treatments...posing for pictures hugging all of her many loved ones. As the cancer sucks every ounce of her energy it can get, she tries to replenish, sucking every ounce of life and love she can get from her family. But it breaks my heart.

What is cancer? What is the feeling? It must be pain, but does it come in waves or is it ever-present? Is the pain localized or does it spread to every tip of our body? Is the greater pain when our mind realizes it cannot escape from the anchor our body is to the physical pain? Is the greatest pain our heart breaking from seeing our loved ones suffering a sympathetic pain of their own?

What is that moment when the power of hope and will become suffocated by the reality of science and medicine? The reality that medicine cannot fix us...the reality that God has chosen a shorter path for us...the reality that we are dying and it may be tomorrow. Is that moment defeat or relief? Is it fear-inducing or freedom? A death sentence or a life sentence? It depends how we choose to punctuate our sentence.

Some will go out with an exclamation...living out dreams from their personal bucket list. Some will end with a question...wondering what they could have done differently, or what they'll miss. Some will simply end. Then there are those that will...

I miss you! I love you!

Yours Always,

J

February 24, 2010 – 10:21 PM

D,

There is a certain challenge and thrill I get from listening to new musicians. The challenge is judging the star quality from those that are merely excellent. The thrill is being right, as I generally am.

An interesting test of this skill is watching "American Idol". Skip past the initial, cattle-call auditions where inevitably a plethora of clinically deluded individuals show up and butcher their chosen song. Stack up a slate of 24 great singers...and they all will be...but now, how do we determine the best of the best? I let my arms do the talking.

More specifically, I look to my arms to see when they get goosebumps. When I get that "chill" over my body I know I am hearing something special. What makes the little hairs on your body stand on end though? That is harder to explain.

It must be a combination of things. A tone in the voice, the way a singer attacks a note, a certain amount of vibrato...these all speak to us in ways we do not know. I have come to believe that the human ear likes to hear a voice pushed to the point of strain without breaking. Our ears instinctively perk up for voices at the extreme high and extreme low of the human range. And there are choices...the way one singer will make instinctive choices of how to wrap their voice around and through a melody...bending and sliding from one note to the next...spinning pop into jazz, and then, if done just right, it is back to pop again.

And then there is the ever-necessary charisma...stage-presence...the "it" factor. Surely it is God-given. How else do we explain why some must jump about a stage, creating a spectacle of themselves, and others can simply sit on a stool, strum their guitar, and be utterly captivating...riveting to the point of not wanting to blink and miss a single moment?

I love those moments...I love watching those kinds of performers. The people that exude complete confidence in themselves and their art, but that simultaneously make that art inclusive for their fans. Art where the fans fuel the performer and the performer accepts their love and energy and puts it immediately back into the performance and back into the hearts of the audience.

February 24, 2010 – 10:21 PM

And this happens instantaneously. It is completely cohesive, codependent, and coexistant.

It is much like the way we were when we were together. You...my one and only "it-girl".

I miss you! I love you!

Yours Always,
J

February 25, 2010 – 9:41 PM

D,

I have my days where I wish we could wash away some of the things we've done and we could go back to being friends. Just friends. Just to be able to talk to you again. Cause even before our relationship ever became physical, I was so enamored of who you are...the things you say, the way you think, the way you listen, the way you give such endless support...and do it all without being asked. It always made me so happy.

I ran into a friend I hadn't seen in a while this morning. We haven't talked in some time either. The reason? I had come to the realization that our friendship was completely driven by me...completely one-sided. And I don't want those kind of relationships. I want balance and equality. To test my theory of how lacking their participation is in our friendship, I decided to stop initiating contact. If we are truly friends, at some point they will contact me. It never happened. This isn't the first time I've experienced this either. In fact, it's disturbingly common.

But you never did that to me. With you there was never any worry that I was the only person invested in our relationship. There was never a time I felt I was initiating every conversation. In fact, we probably rarely went back-to-back days with the same person starting the talk. And we rarely went more than a day without talking.

We would talk about everything...sports and religion and gender and music and politics and children. It was divine. I sometimes wondered if we really honestly shared the same views on as many of the topics as we agreed on...or if there was some level of pandering going on so as to please the other. I don't think that was the case. I think we truly have grown into two people with so much in common.

Plus, we developed this incredible mutual level of respect and trust that allowed for open communication. I never wanted to judge anything you said because I never wanted to risk losing the chance to hear your next thought. And you...you had such an incredible way of making me feel my thoughts were not only valid but really smart...wise even. You always "got" me and what I was trying to say. If you didn't, I always somehow knew to clarify until you did understand.

February 25, 2010 – 9:41 PM

     I miss that so much. I like to think I would be happy for the chance at just corresponding with you again. But in truth, we're both now fully aware of how things start and how they build between us. The only way our love can be denied is by active avoidance...complete denial.

     I, for one, do not wish to deny this. I want your words, I want your body, I want all of you. I want my best friend back.

     I miss you! I love you!

Yours Always,
J

February 26, 2010 – 11:11 PM

D,

     Tonight was another night spent wasting away in the bottom of a bottle. There were laughs but no loves. No love.
     There is only one love.
     I miss you! I love you!

Yours Always,
J

February 27, 2010 – 2:30 PM

D,

Do you remember how I once said, "God didn't give me muscles, he gave me strength"? Sometimes I wonder if all this working out, to give me some muscles, will also detract from my inner strength.

I already notice an increase in vanity. I often find myself posing and flexing in the mirror. It is in part to see how I'm doing, in part because I'm proud of the improvement, but it is also something I do too much.

I also wonder if there is something inside me that is changing. Could this increase in exercise, increase my physique AND simultaneously increase levels of testosterone? Could an increase in testosterone cause changes in my behaviors and moods?

These are not things I want to see happen. I want to improve my body so as to improve myself. That is all. I want to improve myself so as to be more worthy of a woman as incredible as you. You are my greatest inspiration in all things.

I miss you! I love you!

Yours Always,
J

February 28, 2010 – 9:00 PM

D,

I need a lighthearted day...a moment of levity...a safe place to be the silly boy that I know I can be. I don't want to be this serious all the time. I want to entertain people. I want to make you laugh. I want to hear your laugh again...
I miss you! I love you!

Yours Always,
J

March 2010

∞

Mind/Body/Soul

March 1, 2010 – 8:43 PM

D,

I am running out of words. Running out of ways to say 'I Love You'. Running out of hope that we will be together. Running out of thoughts with any remnant of originality. Running out of patience for living this solitary life. Running down. Running ragged. Running on empty.

And you...you're simply running. Running from the difficulty of transition. Running from the label of failure or cheater or "bad guy". Running from the vulnerability of true love. Running, and running, and running.

You've always been a runner. Unfortunately your recent course has been running away emotionally which, unlike literal running, isn't great for your heart. Actually, that isn't fair of me to say. The truth is that you're probably trying not to run away. To change your usual way of doing things and to learn and grow. Trying not to run away from your marriage, from the hardships you've found within it. I just wish I believed in that lesson. I don't. I believe you would have been right to be a runaway bride. I don't believe you ever loved your husband. I believe you are lying.

I also believe saying this about you will hurt you. I don't like to hurt you. But I can not, will not, lie to you. I would rather tell you the truth of my heart...as painful as it may be...than to ever tell you a pretty lie. If I always tell you the hard truths than you can always have complete faith in the beautiful truths.

And the truth is I love you. Still. Always. Pasts and choices can be forgiven. All I need is to hear that you still love me and that you will choose to be with me. I can even forgive a little running if it be you picking up the pace on your way down the aisle to marry me.

I miss you! I love you!

Yours Always,
J

March 2, 2010 – 9:14 PM

D,

Is there anything more wonderful than the way spring comes to visit?

It begins with a call...the birds awaken from silent winter to sing of hope and announce of what is to come.

Then a knock...the tapping of April showers upon windows and doors.

Then a changing of wardrobe...the greens and greys of winter get splashed in daffodil yellow and soft cherry blossom pink.

And last we wait for the warmth...we wait for the sun...so that we may take exodus and walk amongst the birdsong and blossoms.

Can we promise each other that in our perfect future that we will plant a grove of trees for our children? Should we have a son...let him have a fine strong oak...with deep roots and arms fit enough for tire swings or tree houses...so that in spring there will play. For your girls and ours...let them each have a cherry tree...so that every spring we may rise in the morning to find those beautiful, perfect, pink petals and be reminded of the delicacy of woman...reminded to take care of our girls for soon they will be women and gone away to grow their own gardens...

And every spring we will be thankful for rains for refreshing our souls and giving birth to new...

Oh spring, come to visit soon?

I miss you! I love you!

Yours Always,
J

March 3, 2010 – 9:57 PM

D,

Who can I talk to to allow you to return? Whose favor must I earn? What nerves or apprehensions must I calm? What grace could allow us to be together...finally...forever? Who do I ask?

Is it your family? Your father? I will do it. I will tell him how unfathomably deep my love is for you. I will tell him of our past: the road not taken...our present:a love found and denied...and our future: unknown, but with a promise of love if allowed. I will state my case and include exhibit 1 thru 365...all the letters I have written, and will write, to show this love to you.

Is it your husband? His family? I will beg and plead that they try to see that where you are now is not love, and only when love is found and accepted and allowed will L, A, J, and Dawn find a greater peace. I will promise them that I will strive to nurture them as a second male role model and never attempt to replace their father.

Is it God? He and I are already speaking. I ask Him daily to be your strength and guidance and protection. I ask Him daily to let me love you. I do. I promise Him my love is true. He already knows. But He is not who holds my answers.

It is you. Only you can answer all of this. Only you can tell your family, your father, your husband, your daughters, that the love we have is pure and good and what you truly want. Only you can tell me why you have gone. Only you can tell me that you don't love me anymore. Only you can break my heart. Only you can make me whole again.

Perhaps this is why you choose silence.

I miss you! I love you!

Yours Always,
J

493

March 4, 2010 – 9:24 PM

D,

I've had a rough couple weeks in the realm of friendship. There have been moments where conflicts have arisen from what I feel, rather objectively, are caused by lack of chemistry. There is something in my stubborn, intelligent, and blunt ways that have not been mixing well with the carefree, unaccountable, simpler ways of some friends and acquaintances. I feel my strengths are of higher value because they are the more rare. I feel these strengths are going unappreciated. And I don't have patience for them to catch up.

So it was with great relief that a different friend gave me a tremendous compliment last night. The support was so needed. The belief in my art was like a shot in the arm. Not only was it a compliment of what I wrote, but it was a push to pursue it more actively. A push to stop wasting time in menial work and go do, go be something brilliant. It was, at once, a reality check and a dream check. "Why can't my dream be my reality?" It can. "How?" Aha...that is the question.

In the course of my discussion with my friend, while she was questioning why I wasn't using my talent, I was defending myself, and creative-types throughout time, with the idea that when God creates an artist, He gives them an extra helping of talent, but, simultaneously, He makes them deficient in business-savvy. It was true of Mozart who died broke and was buried in an unmarked, communal grave. It was true of Van Gogh who rarely, if ever, sold a painting while living and died broke, heartbroke, and one-eared.

While I can't compare myself to those masters, I certainly can relate to not having, or even caring much for, money. I don't want to negotiate and haggle and beg and plead. I want to write and direct and score and create. This is why artists must have agents and managers. So maybe this is my next step. Maybe this is my answer to "how?"

March 4, 2010 – 9:24 PM

     In the meantime, I continue to try and create every day. And I dwell in the moments of support and recognition for as long as I can. The kind of praise you would always give so freely and sincerely.
     I miss you! I love you!

Yours Always,
J

March 5, 2010 – 9:06 PM

D,

I saw a couple tonight having a fight. Actually I'm not even sure it was a fight...that might have just been how they talk...but it seemed horrible to me. The girl wanted to watch a silly reality TV show...the guy instantly became quite short with her, demanding she turn it off. There were so many issues I had with that moment.

If you can't tolerate something that your partner enjoys, or at least ask them in a respectful manner not to partake in it around you, then you probably shouldn't be dating them.

If you can't respect your partner enough to learn the things that they don't like, and attempt to minimize your participation in them on their behalf, then you probably shouldn't be dating them.

If you don't have a predominance of common attributes and interests, then you probably shouldn't be dating.

Relationships can work in one of two ways: Yin and Yang, or the shadow principle.

Yin and Yang is, of course, the idea that two beings are essentially equal but opposite forms. Where one is weak the other is strong and vice versa. It is a great way to be...in theory...but in reality it generally ends up being more like S & M. One person is domineering and one person is submissive. Where one person's greatest attribute is stating what to do, and the other person's greatest attribute is allowing themself to be told what to do. The word "greatest" becomes a measure of quantity and not quality. A relationship formed like that is a ticking timebomb. One day one half will grow weary of always being dominated and told what to do, or perhaps it will be the dominant half growing tired of always having to take the lead and make the decisions. Either way it would be a combustible situation.

March 5, 2010 – 9:06 PM

      The shadow principle is commonly thought to be purely speculative. It is the idea that two are so closely linked that they do not move as dancers, with the lead's right step forward equaling the partner's left step back, but rather right matches to right and both move forward together. It is a phenomenon so rare that it has never been photographed. It is this rare because it requires that both partners not only have traits equal to that of their partner, but also that each partner contain a certain balance individually. Neither partner can have a great flaw as then their opposite would have to overcompensate in that area, and the concept would contradict it's core principle and implode.

      What do you think we would be? I fully believe we would be a true and functioning Yin and Yang, but I also have high hopes we could prove the elusive shadow principle.

      Either way...I so miss dancing with you.

      I miss you! I love you!

Yours Always,

J

March 6, 2010 – 9:03 PM

D,

I went to a party last night. I didn't know most of the people there, and the two I did know I only know very passively. In such a situation my mind began to wander.

How would you fit in at this party? Would you come with me? Would I ask? How would you react to this group, in their skinny jeans, with their indie music, as they break out a hookah pipe and speak as though they are high-culture? Of course they are not high-culture. Those of high-culture would have less "culture" growing in their bathrooms.

The answer is that you wouldn't fit in there. The truth is that I don't fit in there. The truth is that I was only there because I don't have a beautiful wife to stay home with. I don't have wonderful children around that need my guidance and provide my entertainment. And I don't have many friends that are also this lacking of "responsibilities". So my options become isolation...staying home again to silently contemplate this life, or to accept invitations to activities outside of my comfort zone, with people that I don't share closeness, but with whom I can experiment and learn.

The lesson, so far, is generally one of who I am not. I am not a cool, indie kid up on the hottest tech trends who smokes flavored tobaccos and drinks Rainier tall-boys. I am not a hippy, earth-child wearing hand-knit clothing and eating natural vegan foods. I am not a gun-toting, blue-collar guy who spends every Sunday drinking heavily, watching football, and degrading our current government administration. I am not a card-carrying member of the church of any-of-the-above who spends the predominance of his free time reading a good book and donating time to church or charity.

Who are these people I describe? They are my friends. Each and every one. And I love to spend time in their company, but it is never more than a visit. I never feel at home there. I barely feel at home with my parents and siblings. I don't think I ever felt a true and peaceful and easy space until I found myself in your arms. Only there did I find all the little pieces of my family and friends, the little pieces that all live in me and make my whole, reflected in a single place, a single person. Only with you did I find my home.

March 6, 2010 – 9:03 PM

    And once you find a home like that, you no longer need a night out with friends. Well, except for those nights we go out together and our home becomes mobile. We'll be the greatest trailer-parkers ever! We'll be the first to drink champagne-in-a-box...cause we're high-cultured like that!
    I miss you! I love you!

Yours Always,
J

March 7, 2010 – 9:43 PM

D,

I have just come from watching The Academy Award telecast. There weren't many surprise winners. I found myself thinking more of the acceptance speech that I would give if I won than enjoying the actual speeches of tonight's winners.

I want so badly to put it down to paper...to construct and edit it until it is just right...until it is poetry. But there are some things that shouldn't be prepared. There are some things that should be a surprise. Better yet, there are some things that should pour forth from the heart when lost in a magic moment. That is the true poetry.

All I can say now is that I would like to speak of inspiration should I ever be blessed to have that dream come true.

I miss you! I love you!

Yours Always,
J

March 8, 2010 – 9:51 PM

D,

I get so frustrated at people's misuse of language. Words like "socialism" and "chauvinism" take on the negative connotation of their best-known, but worst examples. And it's just not right.

Socialism...yes, we know it from the National Socialist party...the Nazis. But that isn't the full picture of socialism. Shouldn't we put the emphasis on the fact the Nazis were brutal, murderous, genocidal maniacs that happened to call themselves socialists...traits that, by the way, all contradict the core principle of socialism, thereby making them hypocrites and liars and not socialists at all...rather than hear "socialist" and think "Nazi"? Isn't the wonderfully tranquil, beautiful, docile country of Sweden socialist? Can't we redefine the common understanding of the term so that our first thought when hearing the word "socialism" is of a country with statuesque blonde people that love dance-pop music and particulated furniture? That's not exactly accurate either.

So what is socialism? Isn't it the idea that we should protect the entirety of a society and every member in it...to give reward for the work and not the wardrobe...to promote a lesser sense of "me" and a greater sense of "we"? Didn't the framers of our country and our constitution plant the seed of socialism when they defined that "all men are created equal"? Why do we take such pride in those words and yet seek every opportunity to display any form of supremacy we can have over our fellow man? Is "creation" where equal ends, or should we water that plant and grow our country a forest?

Chauvinism...it has come to mean men that show undue favoritism for their own gender. But in truth this is actually "male chauvinism". The truth is that many feminists are actually chauvinists...female chauvinists. But, because men have long held more power in society historically, the term has come to be known by its most well-known, most common example. It is also overlooked that chauvinism could be the way that Hitler was blindly loyal to Germans of Aryan bloodlines, or the way the economic elite try to keep their clubs exclusive, or the way almost everyone you'll ever meet roots for their college alma mater till the day they die. These are all chauvinists.

March 8, 2010 – 9:51 PM

   Before labeling something, and judging it based on said label, we have to know what we're saying. And once we know what we're saying, perhaps we can make better decisions as a society, for the society. I say this to help my fellow man learn and elevate, so that we can have a greater equality. I think that's my contribution to socialism.
   I miss you! I love you!

Yours Always,
J

March 9, 2010 – 9:47 PM

D,

You asked me once if I was prepared for the changes having kids would bring...I answered that I wasn't. I don't think one is ever prepared for kids. I won't know the entirety of the requirements until I am given the job...IF I am given the job. But what I AM prepared for is the exchange.

I am prepared to give up fast food, because I know you are an amazing cook.

I am prepared to give up Friday night drinking, because I know I will get bi-weekly date night dinners out.

I am prepared to give up staying up late Saturday, because I know I will get to make you all waffles Sunday morning.

I am prepared to give up games of no-limit poker, because I know I will get games of Candyland and Memory.

I am prepared to give up watching so much TV, because I know I will be entertained by the funny things the girls will say.

I am prepared to give up my pride and vanity, because I know letting the girls give me a makeover will bring them to laughter.

I am prepared to give up all of my wisdom, because I know they will teach me so much more.

I am prepared to give up time with my friends, because I know most have given me up already.

I am prepared to give up time to myself, because I know I will get to stop being alone.

I am prepared to give up peace and quiet, because I know I will get peace of mind.

I am prepared to give up my bachelor pad, because I know I will get a home.

I am prepared to give up my money, because I know that it doesn't buy me love.

I am prepared to give up belongings, because I know that with you I belong.

I am prepared to give up everything I have, because I know I will have everything I need. I will have you.

March 9, 2010 – 9:47 PM

Maybe I am prepared after all.

The more that I think about it...the only thing I'm not prepared for, is giving up on us.

I miss you! I love you!

Yours Always,
J

March 10, 2010 – 10:18 PM

D,

Even without you in my life, you are my single greatest distraction every day. I can not count the times each day that I become lost in thought and memory and daydream of you. There is fantasy of your body, there is nightmare of your decisions, there is reality of unknown.

Ultimately you are currently silent...I am currently respecting this silence...and I am left to live in my mind. To play out the tragedy of my tragedy...to cling by my fingertips to hope of true love...to walk the walk of step by step and day by day toward the goals that live in my soul.

Writing, directing, scoring, creating, fighting, crying, loving, dreaming.

I miss you! I love you!

Yours Always,
J

March 11, 2010 – 10:24 PM

D,

Tomorrow my family will celebrate my stepdad's 60th birthday. Although he is leary of this occasion, although he and I rarely see eye-to-eye, I can say rather sincerely that he looks very good for his age. Somewhere in the dozens of pill bottles and the refrigerator full of elixirs and oils he has found a recipe for a relative youthfulness. But still he grimaces. I try to console him with the expression, "60 is the new 45." My mother agrees. And this isn't just in our house.

People are living longer than ever these days. Is it healthier diets? Better medicine? Higher technology that enables more passive living and less wear-and-tear on our bodies? Is it a good thing that we're living longer? I'm not sure that it is.

Of course, my primary point of reference is the experience I had with my grandmother in her advancing years. I can't shake the image. Body ravaged by broken hips and major surgeries. Teeth fallen out and decimating her once lovely smile. Slowly withering away, tethered to life by tubes and wires. Knowing, perhaps wanting, that the end will come soon. I don't know that this is the way things should happen.

I don't want to go that way. I have never been one to "wither" and I shouldn't like to ever start. But I also like to win a hard-fought battle. Let me fight those battles though when I am young enough to accomplish further dreams after they're won. And then, in the end, let me go suddenly. Maybe it's the artist in me, but as I sit here tonight, I wouldn't mind leaving this world in the midst of a

I miss you! I love you!

Yours Always,

J

506

March 12, 2010 – 9:08 PM

D,

How do I write you my heart when I'm in the midst of what I'm in the midst of? I somehow know family gatherings are incredibly different from your family to mine. Here there are '60's costumes, fondue, and classic karaoke. Your family...I have no idea. But if you can come with me to a few of these, I would be honored to go to any of yours.

I miss you! I love you!

Yours Always,
J

March 13, 2010 – 6:22 PM

D,

Do you remember the night we went to the movie? Afterwards we walked to a restaurant, sat in the bar, and had a drink together. Part of me simply wanted to extend that wonderful evening as long as I could. I know, had the situation been different, we could have sat in that bar or walked around that parking lot until morning and had the most incredible time, the loveliest conversation.

But we couldn't. We didn't. I walked you to your car...a minivan...a car you seem embarrassed of...a car that reminded us both of the reality of your motherhood and marriage. You drove me back to my car. I still couldn't say goodbye, and then, with alcohol in my system, my inhibition was lowered...slightly. As we hugged goodnight, my heart was bursting. I knew better than to do what I wanted to do. I fought that urge. But I still had to feel you. I took your hand in mine...examining it's perfect form...kissing the back ever so gently...holding it up to my cheek...a beautiful poetry of movement and touch. There is so much to love of you. And I love it all. The core of your being to the tips of your fingers.

When you think of that night, do you still feel the power in those simple touches? In my thirty years of life, I have had a few occasions of physical intimacy with other women. There have been a few sexual encounters...even more experiences of deep kissing...but, to that point in my life, I had never experienced something as profoundly powerful, intimate, and passionate as that night, with your hand to my cheek. Nothing more. Your simple touch means more to me than any degree of relation I've ever had with every woman I've ever known...combined. This isn't an attempt at a poetic sentiment. This is just a truth. Just a touch of your fingertip and a moment of your time fill me beyond bursting.

This is how I know I love you. One of the million acts and reasons and signs that define something I've never before known or replicated...before and since...that are beyond my understanding but so clearly understood. It is you. And only you.

I miss you! I love you!

Yours Always,

J

March 14, 2010 – 10:41 PM

D,

I have had discussions recently of the impression I give to people, the way I treat them, the way I am understood and perceived. I am frustrated by the common thread.

People find me to be arrogant. I know what they mean, but I find this to be an unfair conclusion, an incomplete portrait.

I believe in a concept called situational dynamics. It is an idea that different parts of our personalities emerge in different situations. Our reactions vary according to action, and allowance, and construct.

In practice this means that in situations in which I excel I will take charge...where I am weak I will humbly follow. If surrounded by extroverts, I will be the introvert. If the group is quiet, I will become more boisterous. If an occupation allows leniency, I will be indulgent. If a job is high-pressure, I become hyper-focused and excel.

And all of these things are shrouded in self-awareness. It is equally important to recognize our strengths and weaknesses so that we may know when and where to apply ourselves and when to have humility and seek guidance. Self-awareness is also the first step to self-improvement. To know my weaknesses is to choose my next project. The idea is to eliminate as many flaws as possible. What can't be eliminated can still be polished and improved. This takes hard work but I do the work.

For as long as I can remember I have been the skinny, nerdy kid. I have sought to counter the "nerd" image by diversifying the application of my intellect. I have never understood why people of highest intelligence are so often lowest of social competence. Take that intellect and find an academic way to apply it to things like girls, and fashion, and athletics. Study these things just as you would physics or string theory or the writings of Tolkien. Find the frontrunners of the "social sciences" and learn their methods.

I have also, more recently, been very proactive in eliminating my skinny stature. I am working on a new diet and schedule of eating and I go to a gym to lift weights at least three times a week. And when I go to the gym, I am not arrogant. I put myself in the hands of a trainer and I do as he tells me. And when there is some trash-talking, I take the brunt of it as I know I am low-man on the totem pole.

Sometimes I wonder if my quest for self-improvement isn't perceived as its own form of arrogance. I wonder if people don't see my efforts and think, "who does he think he is? Is he trying to be better than us?" The answer is "no". I don't care about being better than other people. I care about things being done to a high standard. If you can do the job better than me, than I will follow your lead or cheer you on, and congratulate you upon conclusion. And I care about being a better me. Without comparison to anyone else. I only compare myself to who I was yesterday.

And even yesterday I wasn't too arrogant to set up the karaoke equipment, dj the night so everyone could have a good time, help clean up the equipment after most had left to go to a bar, and wash the dishes for my mom who had cooked. I work really hard so that people who can't, or won't, or shouldn't have to, do what I do, don't have to. I learn to cook, not so I can be better at it than you, but so you won't always have to cook. In the end, all that I'm trying to do will have direct benefit for those around me as much as, if not more than, for me.

If I think I can do something, and I have the skill or do the work, and I get the desired result...how can that really be considered arrogance? Isn't that more accurately just a truth? An occasionally blunt, yet prophetic, truth? Is there not valor in that?

I miss you! I love you!

Yours Always,
J

March 15, 2010 – 10:56 PM

D,

I don't, for the life of me, understand daylight savings time.

First of all, it is a misnomer. Daylight is never saved, or lost, by the setting of a clock. We had as much daylight today as we did before the time-switch two nights ago, save for the few-minute increase in day-length that occurs every year in this season irregardless. The only thing changing our clocks does is change where the daylight hours are located. Well, it also causes some confusion to our bodies and our social calendars when we lose an hour of sleep, forcefully and unnaturally alter our internal meal schedule, and scratch our heads at the lack of logic in late-night businesses closing an hour earlier when the literal time-change is meant to take place after they would normally close.

Why do we still partake in this seemingly unnecessary practice? Why did it ever begin in the first place? If there is a job that is dependent upon daylight, let them adjust individually. This would not be a difficult adjustment to make for, as I just mentioned, daylight changes in a nice, gradual manner on its own.

But the truth is, in this modern society, there are so few jobs that depend on natural daylight. Technology and electricity now enable us to do most any job and any recreation at any time of the day. Go for a jog on a treadmill at a gym open 24 hours. Get a tan in the middle of winter under the light of a tanning bed. Play a round of golf digitally, on your home entertainment system and gaming console whenever you want. Of course, all of these things are most greatly enjoyed under a blue sky with a golden sun, but they CAN all now be simulated otherwise.

Isn't this really some sort of manmade, ego-driven power grab against Mother Nature? "Oh, Mother Nature wants to change when sunrise and sunset are...well we'll see about that! We're gonna take this hour and move it over there. Take that!" But it's all an illusion. Yes, as a result of the clock-change on Sunday there was more daylight remaining after I finished work today. And I made specific note that a larger number of people were taking advantage of the light, out and about for dog-walks and bike rides, today. But this was also helped by the seasonal change in weather to a warmer, less overcast day. Even without a manufactured time change, Mother Nature would still gradually expand to give the people of the Seattle-area daylight until roughly 8:00 PM by the summer solstice. And no amount of time-tinkering can ever convince Mother Nature to give us enough light to enable us to drive to and fro work without use of headlights in the depths of our winter.

Or think of it in terms of the most extreme...think of cities and countries at highest global latitudes...places where winter can mean 23 hours of darkness (or more). Shall we adjust our clocks so that the one hour of light fall during our preferred late-evening stroll...or should we take our stroll during whichever hour has light? The answer is the latter, because either way the walk takes place at dusk, but only the second option doesn't require us to run around the house and try to remember how to adjust all of our clocks.

At the end of the day...pun intended...we still have to accept what we are given and adjust accordingly. Our bodies and minds and careers can accept the lack in winter...therefore it is safe to assume we can accept the slow growth to full as, and when, nature intends it.

Stop fighting the natural. Let it be.
I miss you! I love you!

Yours Always,
J

March 16, 2010 – 10:50 PM

D,

Tis the season...for baseball. Spring training. And I love it.

This is a sport without bias. There is no bias of race. Its players come from every continent of the world...Asia, South America, Australia. There is no bias of age. The elite players, like Ken Griffey Jr. make it to the big leagues while still in their teenage years, and can maintain that playing career well into their 40's, like 47-year-old Jamie Moyer. There is no bias of size. From the 5'6" of David Eckstein to the 6'10" of Randy Johnson, from 130 pounds soaking weight to upwards of 300 pounds-plus.

The only requirement is that you be able to hit a baseball. Scientists will tell you that hitting a baseball is one of the hardest things to do in sport. Football's greatest challenge is simply surviving the toll exerted on the players' bodies. Basketball shots can be made by random fans pulled from the crowd of a game in a half-court contest. Golf may have a smaller ball to target, but it is stationary. Tennis balls may reach greater velocity, but they are hit with a racket with greater surface area. Baseball, however, requires a player to contact a 3-inch diameter ball with a 3-inch diameter piece of wood while it is traveling in excess of 90 miles per hour. Did I mention that the ball is also curving or sliding or sinking...or quite possibly coming directly at your head. Even if you can make contact, what are the chances you can make contact so squarely that you can hit the ball 400 feet?

The chances are minuscule. Take the top 1% of all baseball players in the entire world and you will still only find them successful at their job once every three tries. Those are the BEST players. There must be a reason for that.

Plus baseball is a sport with such romance...played in a park, on the most perfect grass you'll ever see, under the glorious sunshine of summer, with the smells of hotdogs and popcorn and leather gloves and hot roasted peanuts. While the invention of baseball can never really be pinpointed, as it took years to evolve and perfect...it seems to be openly accepted to be all American.

March 16, 2010 – 10:50 PM

    It is my favorite way to spend a Sunday afternoon...it is my pastime and my pastime is nearly here. And when you don't have time or access to a game, there will always be time for a father and son to have a catch.

    I miss you! I love you!

Yours Always,

J

March 17, 2010 – 10:24 PM

D,

I'm not sure how or when it happened, but at some point the concept of "quitting" became entirely too one-dimensional, with such a negative connotation. But the truth is persistence, stubbornness, the constant fight against quitting is only a noble virtue when the fight is for a true and noble cause. I, for one, would like to begin promoting quitting.

I want people to learn how to quit their bad habits...from the simple of nail-biting to the hardcore of drug use.

I want people to learn how to quit the job that they don't love...for whenever I go to their place of business and have to deal with them in whatever disgruntled mood they are in, that negativity seeps out and passes on to everyone it touches.

I want people to learn how to quit arguments that they have lost, or even to quit arguments they recognize will have no winner, or even to quit conversations they realize have become arguments.

I want people to quit marriages that aren't created from, saturated in, and example of...love...for anything less than is shortchanging their friends, their family, their children, themselves.

I want people to quit thinking "quitting" is such a terrible thing...why not see it as the recognition of a flaw or something lived-with but undesirable, and then the first proactive step to cease the flaw and step toward self-improvement?

Quit it.

Quit it so you can begin.

March 17, 2010 – 10:24 PM

Begin living healthily and untethered to bad habit.

Begin loving your station in life and sharing positivity that will breed.

Begin hearing one another speak and realizing all thoughts have valid and powerful origin.

Begin seeing that a loveless marriage is damaging to all.

Begin seeing that a true and powerful love can be your reality.

Begin seeing that truth and love are the greater virtues to insincere resiliency.

Begin a new life with me.

I miss you! I love you!

And that I will never quit.

Yours Always,

J

March 18, 2010 – 9:42 PM

D,

Just when I think I'm making tremendous strides at something, life comes and knocks me down. I have been pushing myself so hard at the gym that I think I may have caused a stress fracture in my arm. And wouldn't you know it, I don't have health insurance. Why can't the government make greater strides at passing a new healthcare bill? But that is another issue altogether.

For now, I am left wondering what is causing this pain when I bend my arm certain ways or lift something incorrectly. In 30 years of life I have never broken a bone before. This certainly isn't a compound fracture. And, strangely, the pain isn't that bad. I can tolerate it pretty well. I am more panicking mentally, worrying that, if not treated, I could easily make the break worse.

As with most things in my life, everything starts and ends in my mind. And when something is unknown by my mind, it begins to whirl. I wonder if I had become too proud of how my body was beginning to look, and if this is God or karma putting a halt to it. Was it too much vanity? Or is this not an issue of exterior, but rather a problem of interior...of diet? Is this a warning that something is wrong with my diet and I need to do research and take strides to fix myself?

Irregardless, how do I go about life for the next few months if this is indeed a fracture that I am feeling? I can't have an x-ray. I can't get my arm cast. Even if I could, how do I continue my work with a cast on my arm, when my work requires so much of my arms? Oh, this is not good.

This is one of the times, one of the issues, when men so need a woman. In part, for their nurturing nature...their ability to kiss a wound and make it better. But also, in part, because in a situation like this the sensible thing to do is to go to a doctor and have things checked correctly, and women always bring this kind of no-nonsense sensibility.

I need your nurturing. I need your sensibility. I need you. I miss you! I love you!

Yours Always,
J

March 19, 2010 – 10:52 PM

D,

It likely doesn't take much guesswork to figure my inspirations for these letters I write you...the content inspired by you, the concept inspired by "The Notebook". It is a story that knows where I come from, and depicts with such grace where I want to go.

It is a story of virtues. The virtues of confidence and patience. The virtues of hard work and promises kept. The virtues of resilience and truth. The virtues of innocent youth and adult communication. The virtues of passion, commitment, and an endless love divine. Oh such love.

There is love as passion...when Noah tells Allie, "it wasn't over...it still isn't over" and bursts forward to grab her and kiss her and have her.

There is love as devotion...when Noah spends his every remaining day, in sickness and in health, taking care of his girl, even when she is no longer aware and able to return such a promise.

There is love as unity...when two souls join in perfect harmony...and when a young woman with innocence and fantasy wishes to be a bird, her young man has trust enough to let her be a bird...and then he has love and wisdom enough that when she asks him to be a bird too he says so touchingly, so sincerely, so matter-of-factly, "if you're a bird, I'm a bird". It is the perfect moment of the story.

That is what love should be and is. That whatever and however we choose our partner, we choose that they be who they are, and we choose that we will be whatever they are, whoever they are, wherever they are too, and we will choose this forever.

Let a love be strange to all of those outside the partnership...let friends roll their eyes when two dorks in love speak of World of Warcraft and elfen kissing...let people shrug their shoulders at the couple drunken wrestling beside the bonfire...let a gathering scratch their respective head at the serendipitous fortune that one would have to find a partner so in sync with all the quirks that are otherwise deal-breakers for both halves of the pair, and to finally find those "flaws" are not flaws but rather screening markers...or let families bite their tongues at the beautiful girl from the church who finds common ground with the skinny boy from without. And let all live in confusion who don't know what it's like to find their bird...to be a bird...to truly, truly love.

My beautiful Dawn, if you're a bird, I'm a bird. I love you so much.

I miss you! I love you!

Yours Always,

J

March 20, 2010 – 9:04 PM

D,

Today I've spent all day and into tonight working on a film set. It is my first set outside of film school, and my role is a small one, as a PA, but just to be around this creative environment, with so many like-minded creative personalities is fulfilling and inspiring. I know that I can do this. I can lead a crew of hard-working, giving people to create something beautiful and funny and thoughtful...something that will stand the test of time and touch the lives of others. If I am given the reigns I will lead with vision and patience, decisiveness and tact, efficiency and strength.

This is what I want to do. This is what I am called to do.

And the stories I tell...they will be ours.

Because I miss you! And I love you!

Yours Always,

J

March 21, 2010 – 9:39 PM

D,

An interesting thought occurs to me tonight. I have long-known that I am very much a control freak...I like to control my intake, or lack thereof, of drugs and alcohol...I prefer jobs of a creative nature where I have the most possible control over content and execution...I simply love to have that power and responsibility of control. And I think, when allowed it, I use any control I have with efficiency, morality, and an uncommon thoughtfulness.

And yet, on many occasions, I found that I tended to follow your lead on most issues we became presented with. From the choice of movie to see, to following your directions driving around the city, to wanting so badly to take you and make love to you but instead waiting for you to decide when you were ready...when we were ready. In fact, I've so often relinquished control to you that I begin to wonder if it doesn't come across as weak or indecisive. That, perhaps, you wouldn't like me to take more control when we're together. But I think I am still epitomizing decisiveness...I have decided to fulfill as many of your wishes and desires as I can because I have already decided that you are my one true love. Well the second part may not have been a decision but rather an undeniable fact.

And one of the ways I recognize the fact of this love is the ease with which I can give up control to you. There is so much trust I have for you...in your thoughts, in your concerns, in your tastes...that I don't feel I need to try to control everything. In fact I don't need to control anything. And history suggests that our thinking falls so closely in line with one another on most issues that decision-making becomes more about speed, with credit going to whomever voices the idea first, with agreement soon-to-follow from whichever of us is second. Control becomes an irrelevant concept. We can share everything. Nothing would make me happier.

March 21, 2010 – 9:39 PM

    And if there is ever thought or question as to why I won't seek a greater voice in any decision-making process with you, please know that I am preferring to make the decision to be united with my best friend and true love, the one biggest decision any man will ever make, than to try to control all the hundreds or thousands of little decisions a couple will face together. My line of thinking is that, if I am sitting beside you, we can make any choice of movie into a great night. So I won't sweat the small stuff.
    I miss you! I love you!

Yours Always,
J

March 22, 2010 – 9:55 PM

D,

Last night the Healthcare Bill was passed by Congress. Today I have spent a fair amount of time hearing and reading reaction to what the bill will bring. It doesn't seem to be adding up.

On the one hand, the left, I hear friends talk about the idea that everyone will now be covered, with special attention going to the unemployed, those with pre-existing conditions, the elderly, and twenty-somethings still needing to remain on their parents insurance, and can receive health care...this all sounds incredible. Friends on the right keep objecting to the idea that we will now be forced to purchase health insurance...this seems incredulous. Firstly, if the idea is to help those that can't afford health insurance, how can we mandate that all adults purchase a plan? Secondly, even if all Americans had the means to afford health insurance, I would never agree that we should all be required to purchase it.

One of my long-standing favorite aspects of being an American and living in the United States is the simple concept of choice. From the simple choice of what foreign cuisine to have for dinner, to the complex choice allowed by the freedom of religion, our country is always at its best when we are tolerant of multiple choices.

Here we should have the right to bear arms. This doesn't mean we should take guns away from those that have them, nor should we ever force those to use them that wish not to, by means of a military draft...let it be a choice. I will choose not to own a gun and I have lived my life so as to never require one.

Here we should have the right to an abortion. This doesn't mean we should take the procedure away from those that want one, nor should we ever force any woman to have an abortion even if they are unfit to parent...let it be a choice. I will choose not to ever choose abortion and I have lived my life so as to never require one.

That is actually an important point...let our government give us choice and let us choose well. Let us make all the simple, righteous choices that mean we will never have to make the hard choices.

March 22, 2010 – 9:55 PM

Let us choose to live a sensible, healthy life that means we will rarely have to choose to need health insurance. But let it be a choice. This means allowing all Americans who wish to have health insurance, regardless of pre-existing condition, to choose a provider, pay the premiums, and have their coverage...and for their provider to do their job and insure our health. This also means allowing those that choose not to purchase health insurance, to take healthcare in to their homes or kitchens through healthier living or dieting, or to simply push their luck living dangerously, and being refused healthcare should their luck fail.

But let it be choice.

I miss you! I love you!

Yours Always,

J

March 23, 2010 – 10:08 PM

D,

I was driving to my parents' house today. The entrance to your neighborhood is literally one block before theirs. There is a stoplight at that intersection. Today the car in front of me ran that red light. The light was fully red as he entered the intersection and his brake lights never lit as he drove through full-speed.

In my mind, I immediately envisioned the accident that could have occurred. It felt so frighteningly real: an innocent driver, and any passengers, broadsided as they attempted to use their right-of-way to make a left turn. I imagined a maroon Chevy Suburban. It was your car. You at the wheel. Your beautiful daughters in the seats behind. It all flashed before my eyes.

The vision continued...

I jump from my car barely remembering to put it in park. I fumble for the cell phone in my pocket as I run toward the wreckage. I reach the door and tears begin stinging my face...no, no, no...please God, not her, not Dawn I scream in such horror the operator can barely discern what has happened.

I have often thought I perform so well under pressure...but this would not be cramming for a test or rushing to meet some deadline. This is the life or death of the only thing in my life I would give my life for. This is the only thing that matters. This is the meaning of my life. To love and cherish and sacrifice for the great love of the greatest woman I have ever known. And to give all the same to her children, her blood, the greatest love of her life.

I know I have no reason to, no right to...but as I passed through that same intersection on the trip back home, under cover of night, this vision returned to me, and the thought of you and those girls feeling any ounce of that kind of pain shook me to my core...terrified me...and brought me to tears.

March 23, 2010 – 10:08 PM

     So as I sit and I snivel and hover over this phone, trying to recount what has not been an enjoyable moment, please hear my words and know that I know, I may have never shared their conception, their birth, their life of this many years...but I can share with them my love. From any point that we should meet again...from this day forward...I will love them. And I do. These tears are the same as any man's who is fortunate enough to be called "dad" or "stepdad". The title will be different, but the effort, the intent, the meaning will all be the same. Their joy will be my joy...their pain will be my pain.

     And I feel pain...the pain of not being able to see them, hear them, know them...the pain of not knowing how each of them is becoming a new version of you.

     Please let us create a new vision. A vision of you and I and a family of love.

     Please be safe...I pray and I pray you please be safe...

     I miss you! I love you!

Yours Always,

J

March 24, 2010 – 11:00 PM

D,

Tonight, the wonders of technology; a Blackberry smartphone browsing the internet...and the beauty of glorious music; streaming forth from a personalized Pandora radio station on said phone. I lay in bed, the phone resting squarely in the center of my chest, and I listen with quiet anticipation for what unknown wonders will bless me next.

I choose a station with a twangy, spiritual, breathiness and am rewarded with song after song of liquid peace. Each song of earthy parts but from the heavens. Each song sparse in construction...the singer's voice open and exposed, but rich in content and meaning...the singer's soul completely exposed with his words speaking only truth.

There is the Velvet Underground...Lou Reed singing of "Pale Blue Eyes"...a woman he knew personally, the story I know personally.

We then have Radiohead's underappreciated study of a suburban life, begging for a quiet, carbon monoxide-poisoned existence with no alarms and "No Surprises". Or is that mundane, common existence even worth considering a life, or does it deserve its poison?

My life has regrets...some of non-participation or bystanding...some of tardiness. Tonight I am reminded of all the years I wasted not ingesting the music of Ben Harper. Ben now sings of "Another Lonely Day"...a song I don't know, but know so well. This bite is late but better late than never.

And finally "Hallelujah"...Jeff Buckley singing Leonard Cohen's tale of the secret chord. But it is more than a secret chord...it is a heavenly melody...it builds and swells, inspires and breaks, breaking my heart in one fell swoop. A chill begins at the phone speaker above my heart, and I feel every ripple of a wave that eminates down and out across the whole of my body. It is a moment of music so haunting and powerful that I am overcome. My eyes fill and burst.

March 24, 2010 – 11:00 PM

It will never receive the attention or respect of the religions of the world, but here...in dark, in stillness, in peace, in love with the miracle of song...I am at church. The best of this church are heaven-sent, divinely inspired, and blessed by God...truly. Tonight my church finds the broken hallelujah to be healing. And I say 'Thank You'. I say 'Hallelujah'.

I miss you! I love you!

Yours Always,
J

March 25, 2010 – 9:49 PM

D,

I'm feeling very self-conscious lately.

Bald...pale...skinny...old...and a hundred other little problems. Part of me knows this is just the low-tide of the cycle...it happens all the time and I rebound from it. But in the midst of it, it feels so terrible...

Do you have these waves? These ebbs and flows of confidence and mood? Promise me that you'll let me know when you're low. Promise me that, because I will have a hundred little ways to bring you back up. A hundred little reasons why I think you're the sexiest woman I've ever known. A hundred little reasons why I love the heart and mind within you. And one big reason why you can just speed-walk out of any down times...I just love every single thing about you. You make me know bliss. And, if there is a breath to be breathed within me, that bliss will be shared tenfold.

That is the other promise I will ask of you...promise that you will let me know when you are happy. Joyfully, gleefully, incandescantly happy. That those wonderful afternoons when the light is just right, the girls are being so sweet, and we are just getting lost in conversation...promise that we will take a moment to recognize and articulate such a thing...that I will interrupt you, but only to tell you how beautiful you look today...that you will look across the table to me and just say, "this is nice," and I will simply nod in knowing agreement. Just a moment to realize that we're on a peak and to appreciate the view.

I promise you that. You will always know where I'm at. When my hand is out to lead and when my hand is out to be led. Need or needed. Valleys and peaks. High tide and low.

I miss you! I love you!

Yours Always,
J

March 26, 2010 – 8:44 PM

D,

    Tonight I shaved my head. I have been keeping my hair progressively shorter the last few years, but tonight I pretty much got rid of it all. I don't really care for the result, but I didn't really care for what I had before. In fact, I don't know that I've ever liked a hairstyle I've had. So maybe this is karma.

    Do you remember all of the hairstyles you have had in the years we've known each other? I remember most. I remember last year when you cut your hair shorter, with bangs. I thought, at the time, you cut it like that for me. Can I just tell you, now and forever, that I truly adore your hair long and with its natural curl. I don't remember ever liking, or even noticing, curly hair before you, but I can't help but notice and be drawn to it since falling for you.

    You don't ever have to do anything to it. The same goes for your makeup. You don't even need any. You are a naturally stunning woman. Your eyes are glorious. Your cheek bones incredible. Your lips simply my favorite lips ever. And your ears...well, we'll talk about that another time.

    Unfortunately, the evening is now calling. More specifically it is shouting at me. I can't be articulate and passionate in this setting.

    But I miss you still! I love you forever!

Yours Always,
J

March 27, 2010 – 11:59 PM

D,

It came to me in dream...

We live in conflict, we live in strife
We live in question of how best to live a life
To follow our heart, to follow our mind
To choose incorrectly is to follow the blind

We were raised by parents whose intentions were good
They made their mistakes, but did the best that they could
Some give their kids freedom, and choices to make
Choices can go wrong, it's a risk that they take

Some parents work in structure, enforcing many rules
But without the chance to choose, do their kids learn all the tools
For in time we all must make choices our parents can't decide
The choices of adulthood have bigger consequences to abide

Choice of career and choice when to wed
Choice of how young to take a lover to bed
These are the choices we all eventually face
But why do so many feel the choice is a race

The law of the land says choice can begin at eighteen
But shouldn't such choices be delayed till more of life has been
seen
Patience is a virtue and in time it breeds clearer thought
Waiting for all things breeds the better choices that we've sought

You were once a little girl with a big faith in your heart
But as you've grown and lived, faith and heart are farther apart
Where once there was read the righteous word
Now there is internal conflict and morals are blurred

While morals may have blurred, my motive is quite clear
I have only sought to show how much I love and hold you dear
You are my one and only, I love you more and more
I would marry you in rich times, I would marry you in poor

March 27, 2010 – 11:59 PM

In my time without you, you are always on my mind
There is no woman who compares to you, none that I can find
So I bide my time and anxiously wait for you and only you
And pray my own patience will be rewarded, a most deserved
virtue

I pray that life has shown you that choice is not just black and
white
Choices have their nuance, and are more than wrong and right
I pray that you still love me and will return to me some day
And I hope you see the meaning in the daily choice I make to pray

I miss you! I love you!

Yours Always,
J

March 28, 2010 – 9:22 PM

D,

A friend asked how I was today...I told her, "bored". She asked what I would rather be doing and I answered without thinking, "living". And there it was...meant to be a joke but, as is often the case, many a truth is spoken in jest.

This isn't my life. Not the one I want. Not the one I have planned. Not the one I am building toward. This is merely the pastime, the renovation, until my life's grand re-opening.

I can be an epic success. A creator of thoughtful, meaningful art that may come to outlive me. An artist working across the mediums of word and image and music. An intermediary of life...bridging the gap between observed reality and dramatized commentary...discovering life's truths and then inventing them.

I can have an epic love story. A tale of devotion so pure that it's truth will be doubted, but whose story is living and breathing within me...within you...within us. A story of unfathomably impeccable communication. A story of glorious physical attraction and affection. A story of trust and belief, and effort and action. A story that rises and falls with romance and suspense...and an ending yet to be written.

My friend questioned me further tonight on why I didn't feel I was "living" and I spoke of passion. I am a passionate man and I have never been able to sellout to things I am not passionate about. And I pray I will never be able to accept less than my true passions. When will you join me? Join me in our true passion for each other. Join me in writing an epic happy ending.

I miss you! I love you!

Yours Always,
J

March 29, 2010 – 10:22 PM

D,

There are only days remaining in this year-long sentence...a sentence growing short on words and longer on punctuation, on question marks. Tonight I haven't spent my time writing TO you, but I have spent my time writing OF you. A friend, who has moved across the whole of the country, and I have spent the night catching up. I can' t help but speak of you...even to strangers who know nothing of our tale.

This is a transcription of that conversation:

R: Other than that, how've you been lately?

J: I miss creating. I miss being funny...professionally. I miss many friends. I miss a girl. THE girl.

R: What's holding you back from creating and being funny? Who is the girl?

J: I create, but it's being constantly interrupted by work. I would rather combine the two. The girl is the love of my life. My muse forever.

R: I think all people who create strive to make creation and work one in the same, but struggle with it. Does this girl know how you feel about her?

J: Yeah. For a time she felt the same way. Then she remembered she's married. So I wait. And write her a letter every day. To a mailbox she can't open.

R: That really sucks. You deserve someone amazing who is able to love you as much as you love her though.

J: Deserve is a terrible word. I don't know what I "deserve". But I want her. I need her. Everything else is the settle.

March 29, 2010 – 10:22 PM

> *R: I'm not saying she can't provide that. I'm just saying you should have that. As long as you're following your heart, I don't think you can go wrong.*

> *J: Wanna read a letter?*

(I send her one of your letters, and minutes later...)

> *R: Jared, that's a beautiful letter. I wish I had a better reply than that. I'm touched that you shared that with me. I hope this someday works out.*

And so it goes...this is how I speak of you when you're not around. And this is how my family and friends react...with support and understanding. And hope.

It will be okay. All you have to do is choose it.

I miss you! I love you!

Yours Always,

J

March 30, 2010 – 10:32 PM

D,

Tonight I watched a woman hold back her emotion and I was offended and disappointed and confused by it. This kind of scene is all too familiar. I know you do it. You've told me you have a breathing technique you go through to keep yourself from crying.

I don't understand this. One of the greatest differences between men and women is a woman's heightened sense of emotion. That delicate sensitivity you find when someone wears their heart on their sleeve. Why do women hide this? Is it because men are so uncomfortable in their own emotion that they have teased or stifled women into feeling the need to hide theirs? Those men are morons. I am so offended by them and how they have jaded the women I so adore into disguising their true selves. For men of true wisdom realize that to support a woman in her time of sadness, an act as simple as giving a hug and an open ear, is to get a hug and further strengthen the foundation of a relationship.

When will people realize the actions of today don't have to be about today? Today's giving can beget tomorrow's receiving. Today's humility can beget tomorrow's arrogance forgiven. Today's support of a woman can beget her support of you tomorrow. Today's emptying the garbage can beget tomorrow's fooling around. Today's selflessness can beget tomorrow's personal reward. Life is a chess match and it, literally, cannot be won in a single move, it cannot be won by a single piece.

In this modern society it seems, more and more, the attitude is "me, me, me". We spoke many years ago on the question of the existence of a perfectly selfless act...I don't know that I've ever been convinced that everything we do in life isn't for our own selfish desires. Be it direct or indirect...pleasing to us or pleasing to us because it pleases those we care for...I honestly believe all people at all times are trying to gain favor or benefit for themselves.

March 30, 2010 – 10:32 PM

Having said that, it would still be beneficial to all of society if we could just take that "me, me, me" and change it to "you". It doesn't have to be "you, you, you"...it could just be a "you, you, me". And if enough people followed this ideal there would be competition, but the competition would be of courtesy...who can let the other person go first the fastest or the most. What a charming contest that would be. Maybe we could add to that a contest of who could cry first...the man or the woman? How much would you wager that the second-to-cry wouldn't be very far behind to cross the line?

Emotions are an incredible thing. They are what bind us. So we must let our true emotions out, and give our loved ones' emotions safe-haven. That is why the day you came to me to end our affair, and we sat on the couch holding each other and crying, I knew the pain and love and fear and regret that fell with each tear. There was truth in those tears. And after you left that day you wrote to me...you thanked me for "letting you blubber all over me"...although I didn't say it to you at the time, my thought was, "thank you for blubbering all over me." It was my honor. It always will be. To know your true emotion...your true self. My shoulder is always yours for the crying. My arms yours for the holding. My love yours for the rest of my life.

I miss you! I love you!

Yours Always,
J

March 31, 2010 – 10:49 PM

D,

I was out with another woman tonight. I don't know that it would qualify as a date. We went to the film premiere for the film I worked on a couple weeks ago. One of her friends acted in the film. It was a good intersection of friendships and business relationships. It was good company. She is very beautiful. I will try to see her again.

But the only reason tonight happened, the only reason I would see her again, is because I don't have you. Tonight is the best alternative I've found to loneliness. This is something I could give up in a heartbeat to be with you. This merely the best me I can be with the dynamics of our current situation.

Make me change. Give me the opportunity to show you that I will.

I miss you! I love you!

Yours Always,
J

April 2010

∞

Question

April 1, 2010 – 9:09 PM

D,

I am just so tired.

I am tired from staying out late last night and waking up early this morning and not sleeping soundly the whole night through.

I am tired from pushing my body to make gains and progressions against what I am in my natural state.

I am tired from cooking and cleaning and laundry and shopping and accounting and barbering and styling and maintenance and thinking and doing it all by myself.

I am tired of a world that doesn't recognize the beauty around it...that prefers building walls that divide and tears down our self-confidence, rather than building up another's confidence and tearing walls down.

I am tired of squinting at this tiny cellphone keypad to write something that I am hoping and attempting will be bigger than us all.

I am tired of lies and denial and settling and passivity and status quo.

I am tired of trying to think of new and special ways to say I love you to a ghost.

I am tired of not hearing you love me too.

I am tired of missing you.

But I do. I miss you. Everyday.

I miss you! I love you!

Yours Always,
J

April 2, 2010 – 8:04 PM

D,

Do you realize how many of my "firsts" are held by you?

I met you at work in my first job...the Dairy Queen on Benson.

You are the first girl I ever went out with...we went to the Red Hot Chili Peppers concert at the Key Arena in Seattle.

You are the first girl I ever fell in love with...the exact moment I knew I loved you was at that Chili Peppers concert...you were gorgeous and smart and kind and you liked cool music...you were my perfect match.

You are the first girl I ever slow-danced with...it was at your sister's birthday...the one where we all got dressed up and went to the Four Seasons Hotel...we danced to Billy Joel's "Just The Way You Are"...we couldn't have had a more fitting song.

You are the first girl I ever went to meet her parents and family...a fact that was probably pretty apparent by my nerves and poor social interaction...I never quite overcame that.

You are the first girl I ever asked to marry me...the timing was terrible and the proposal wasn't what I would want it to be...it was my last-ditch plea that you not marry the man you had just become engaged to, the man I didn't believe you truly loved, and to instead marry me...it wasn't very romantic, I didn't have your father's permission, but it was every bit the most sincere moment of my life.

You are the first woman that broke my heart.

And after that broken heart came so many "firsts" that I didn't get to share with you...

First kiss.
First marriage.
First lover.
First born child.
First anniversary.
First house.

April 2, 2010 – 8:04 PM

All of those "firsts" being missed are huge regrets in my life. My only consolation is the knowledge that there is something that trumps "first"...and that is "only".

To this day you are the only woman I want to marry. You are the only woman I want to have a baby with. You are the only woman I have ever loved. But it only means anything if you make the choice, take the action, and fulfill my heart and make us one again. First and only.

I miss you! I love you!

Yours Always,
J

April 3, 2010 – 9:49 PM

D,

Last night I was telling a coworker some of our story and she called me a "homewrecker". She said it in jest, but it still really stung. I'm sure it is not the first time it's been thought. I'm sure it won't be the last. This is my new reality. This is how the world will see me. But I beg to differ. I beg to clarify. I beg for rebuttal.

This is not merely a story of a lonely, lifelong bachelor and an unfulfilled, unhappy housewife finding each other and meeting in secret to partake of simple pleasures of the flesh. In fact, the physical part of our affair was the least of importance for me.

For me, ours is a story fifteen years in the making. It involves the night I asked you to marry me and not the man who was your fiancé at the time. You refused. More recently you revealed to me how much you wish we had run away that night. More specifically, I think you said you wished I had kidnapped you that night. So that the decision wouldn't have been yours. You have never liked making decisions. In turn, that would have meant you wouldn't have had to face the guilt of disappointing the various parties who this change would have affected. Instead you went through with the marriage...thrilling your family, your future in-laws, and your fiancé...but simultaneously sentencing yourself to a silent torment for all the years since...sentencing me to a broken heart and a life without love.

Until two years ago I served that sentence begrudgingly but respectfully. And then one day I was compelled to find you, to know you again. I found you. I came to know you. The more I learned of this more mature version of you, the more I discovered you were still the incredible woman I had fallen in love with as a kid. Still the same, but different...lovelier, more thoughtful, more complex, more of a woman. Your life experience had honed many of your most delightful traits and yet relaxed others in equally wonderful ways. And the more I discovered this new you, the more I knew I had made a grave mistake. I was still in love with you. And when I realized openly the nature of my feelings for you, I knew these feelings were inappropriate and could never be returned, I came to you to say goodbye. I sought to end our relationship and minimize my heartbreak.

April 3, 2010 – 9:49 PM

But then you asked me to come back. You asked me to come back. All I ever wanted was for you to be happy, so if my returning would make you happy, even though it would undoubtedly cause me want and desire and pain, then I would return and do my best to ease your sadness. For months after that I gave you everything I was. My thoughts, my praise, my support, my love. For months it went unreturned. And then one day you loved me. You said the words. I remember the exact place and time when it happened.

When it became about love, I couldn't sit idly by and not will it to become fulfilled...for both of us. I immediately recognized I wanted you to divorce and for you and I to marry. It was never even a question. Divorce has existed for hundreds of years...both sets of my grandparents are divorced...all of my aunts and uncles have had at least one divorce...many of my cousins are divorced...to judge divorce negatively is to judge almost everyone in my life. And if you were to be a divorcee I would judge you least of any. I would hope our love was part of the reason for your divorce.

But then I realized our love, and my part in it, makes us guilty...guilty of conspiring to change the lives of three innocent girls...guilty of a divorce brought on not simply by the failure of a marriage, but by the suggestion of something better...it would make me guilty of being a "homewrecker". You know all of this. Maybe that is why you asked for this year apart? So that you can prove to all that your divorce would be about a lack in your marriage...without outside interference or influence. I am doing my best to comply. You asked me to give you time and I am giving you time. Perhaps, in some incredible foreplanning, you are doing this to distance us from the labels of "cheater" and "homewrecker".

While part of me doesn't care...not about the label...I only care that we are together...the other part of me sees that you can't end things that way. You are entirely concerned with appearances. I, on the other hand, am entirely concerned with truth. And I believe the truth is you never loved your husband...the truth is the only commonality you and he share is a fondness for pretty lies...the truth is your home has never not been wrecked. And an even bigger

544

April 3, 2010 – 9:49 PM

truth is that this happens all the time. All over this country right now there are marriages continuing to exist because of convenience and fear and deception. None of those people should cast a stone if they, themselves, live in a glass house. A home is where the heart is...if your heart is with me, then you merely have a house...and a "housewrecker" I feel no shame in being. That label I will bear. Especially if a beautiful home will rise up from those ashes.

I miss you! I love you!

Yours Always,
J

April 4, 2010 – 8:34 PM

D,

Happy Easter.

We've talked many times before about religion. You know how little of it I knew growing up. I still know very little, and sort of prefer it that way. Anytime I am around deeper discussion of religion, my analytical nature takes over and I want to point out the illogical nature of this point or that...or religion as a whole. It is completely illogical. But, it's okay that way. It is not logical...it is emotion. It is not knowledge...it is belief.

It took me many years to wrap my mind around it, to find a way of considering it that made sense to me, and I came to three conclusions: 1) there is a greater power behind all of this and He has a greater purpose, 2) it's okay if we don't put a name or a face or a label on our belief, 3) the greater purpose behind any and all religions should be that it gives us hope, strength, and direction toward being the greatest person our body and soul can become...for ourselves and for all of humanity.

I don't know if I can, or will, ever call myself a Christian. But in my heart I hope and strive to live as Jesus lived. Many of His followers put highest emphasis on His death for our sins. But what about His life? Didn't He live so beautifully? Let me be a man of wisdom and grace and charity and faith like He was. Let me bear the burden, the pain, of those who cannot. Let me learn to forgive and to teach, to lead and to love. It is one thing to be thankful that He is our savior, but is another to not take that fact for granted and to live a life less in need of a rescue. Let us spend less time mourning and more time learning, improving, and striving toward higher consciousness and behavior.

What I want, what I pray on, more than anything else in life, is just that I may be a good man. That would be a label I could welcome and cherish.

I miss you! I love you!

Yours Always,
J

April 5, 2010 – 9:26 PM

D,

I went to see our friends JP and LSP tonight. It was the first time I had seen LSP since she had her second baby. And the first time I met little Harper...although he wasn't that little. At one point in the evening I noticed that older brother Jonas, with long reddish locks, and Harper, with a perfectly bald little baby head, looked a little like Larry and Curly from the Three Stooges.

This evening came on the heels of an Easter dinner yesterday with my nephews. TJ continues to show signs of being such a little lover as he flirts with my brother's girlfriend, promising that he "would really love her". NP, the youngest, is building up his vocabulary slowly. He can now call me "unka" for "Uncle". I think he might look a little like me when I was his age.

All this time around these little guys, and the few times I was around your little girls, makes me realize I am ready for that next step...I am ready to be a dad. I am ready to put my secret, silly walk to use for babies that are ready for bed. I am ready to put my arms to use for young ones that need hugs to heal a scraped knee or bump on the head. I am ready to put my heart to use relating to the delicate emotions of little girls. I am ready to put my feet to use teaching soccer to little boys. I am ready to put my brain to work helping with homework or inventing creative family activities. I am ready to put my pride, my selfishness, my stubbornness all aside so as to put my children, born of me or not, before all else.

And I am ready to do all of this because I am ready to be your husband. Well some things I've been ready for forever...

I miss you! I love you!

Yours Always,
J

April 6, 2010 – 8:31 PM

D,

It has come to the quiet part of the evening when I generally try to find some little piece of my day to spin into a relevant thought, an articulate wisdom, or even, when I'm really lucky, a few verses of silver-pronged poetry.

But tonight my eyes have daggers in them. To stare at this miniature, illuminated screen is to feel throbbing pulses of pain wash from my eyes back into my head. I can't be poetic right now. I have no wisdom. I can barely think.

I will lay my head down, hoping the pillow is cool, hoping the sleep comes quickly, hoping the dreams are of you.

I miss you! I love you!

Yours Always,
J

April 7, 2010 – 10:00 PM

D,

I had a conversation with my mom yesterday and much of it centered on "perfection". It is pretty well-known by most who know me how much of a perfectionist I can be. While outwardly it may appear I want to be perfect, inwardly I am fully aware that "perfect" doesn't really exist. Where I differ from most people, my mom included, is that the recognition that one can never attain perfection will not be a deterrent. I am still going to pursue perfection. The pursuit is the real point.

Plus, there may be differentiation to be made between perfect perfection and relative perfection. Can you and I ever have a perfect-perfect love? No. My idea of perfect would have seen us married years ago. Your idea of perfect probably would have had me more open to the church years ago. Neither of us would have likely chosen to be anywhere near words like "affair" or "divorce". But we can have a relatively perfect love. For all of our flaws or missteps, should we come to be together, it would be the most perfect love I have ever felt and even ever witnessed. And while these letters will soon come to an end, and this love will go dormant, it will never die. I will pursue it always...silently, methodically, patiently.

A similar story can be told for pursuing perfection in anything. The only perfect thing it requires is a perfect effort. Effort is a renewable resource. Know what you want...educate yourself on what it requires... and take every subsequent step to reach it. When obstacles arise, make leaps, take sidesteps, walk backwards for a time if necessary, but just keep moving with eyes never leaving the goal.

But it doesn't end at the goal. When you reach that goal, find a new goal. Even if the goal is to maintain, refine, elevate the new standard. What is so hard about that? Why can't more people do this? Or at least try?

Make it perfect.

I miss you! I love you!

Yours Always,
J

April 8, 2010 – 8:53 PM

D,

Just two nights ago I wrote of wishing to dream of you...and last night I couldn't get to sleep for chance to do so. My waking mind was overrun with thoughts of you. It would not stop, it would   not   rest. I can't remember the last time I had a refreshing, full night of sleep. I lay in bed most nights tossing, turning, and always thinking. I would guess most nights it takes over half an hour to fall asleep. I have to guess because I try to avoid looking at the time on the clock...it only keeps me awake longer. I sometimes feel like Goldilocks...as sleep won't come when I am too warm, nor too cold...it must be JUST right.

Once I do find sleep, it is never enough because the alarm clock buzz always arrives too soon. But even on weekend mornings when the alarm isn't needed, I find myself rising when the light breaks through the window blinds. The daylight always arrives too soon.

I wonder if more exercise could solve this...if exhausting my body daily might bring sleep closer to me nightly. I wonder if sex and the release it allows might act as some natural, biochemical sleep-aid. I wonder if a glass of milk before bed could calm me...is this something our bodies know and remember from our infancies when we would be nursed to sleep by our mothers. I wonder if my mind just needs to find some peace.

I will try all of these cures and more, but something tells me the one that will work best will be the last...and the last won't come without a love to have and hold.

You are my peace. Bring me to sleep.

I miss you! I love you!

Yours Always,
J

April 9, 2010 – 9:41 PM

D,

I have a problem with surprises. Or maybe it's more about change. Either way, I get my heart set on something, I prepare myself mentally and emotionally for it to occur, and when it doesn't, or it occurs with different parameters than I had prepared for, I become crestfallen.

This happened to me tonight. I was planning to make a late-season trip to go snowboarding with a friend tomorrow morning, but late tonight I found out there was an extra person invited on the trip. I don't know why, but it just bothers me. And it's not that I have a problem with the third person. If the trip had always been planned for three I wouldn't have objected. But something about planning for two and now having to adjust to three is uncomfortable for me.

Is this a subconscious desire to hold people to their word? Am I wishing people thought with clearer foresight? Am I just being selfish, or childish, or both? I often pride myself on my adaptability and performance under pressure...so why does this bother me? Is this another symptom of my constant over-thinking of every situation? I do generally run things through in my head with intense attention to detail. It's part fantasy and part planning. I don't know that I can turn it off.

What's worse is that as a result of my hangups, I end up being the guy that is the Debbie-downer...that can't go with the flow...and who removes himself from the new, surprise, unplanned situation. This cannot be healthy.

I miss you! I love you!

Yours Always,
J

April 10, 2010 – 8:36 PM

D,

I can't do this. I can't keep being this. Things have to change. I have to change.
I love you.

Yours Always,
J

April 11, 2010 – 9:01 PM

D,

I wonder how many women get married while they're in college.

I wonder how many have to drop out of college when they become pregnant shortly after getting married.

I wonder how many never have time to go back to school once they have children.

I wonder how many do some serious growing up after gaining the life experiences that marriage and motherhood create and demand.

I wonder how many find they aren't the same person IN the marriage that they were BEFORE the marriage.

I wonder how many want to leave the marriage.

I wonder how many want to leave the marriage but stay...terrified of the prospect of needing to work but having no college degree, and/or worried about their ability to balance work and being a good mother.

I wonder how long most of these women live that life.

I wonder if any of this is you.

I wonder if you'll break from this pattern.

I wonder if, in spite of all your fears, you'll give us a chance.

I miss you! I love you!

Yours Always,
J

April 12, 2010 – 9:14 PM

D,

Somehow we will always be united through "House". There will be nights we both sit down to watch at the same time, and some small little detail of the storyline will be eerily reminiscent of our moments together. That is, if you can still bring yourself to watch it. If you aren't watching, here is a recap:

Tonight, there are Robert and Allison...Drs. Chase and Cameron...married previously, now separated. She wants the divorce because she has been objecting to the fact Chase killed an evil man...he, unlike your husband, gave her a reason for her to leave the marriage without guilt. He wants to know that Cameron even loved him in the first place. She says she doesn't know. Which, of course, means she didn't. Perhaps she is incapable of love. Perhaps she loves House. Is this who you are?

Meanwhile, House, with his steely blue eyes and two days growth of beard covering his thin, pale cheeks, speaks of a woman he loved but who left him. He speaks of isolation. He says, "I like being alone. At least I've convinced myself that I'm better off that way." Is this who I am? Someone who makes decisions to chase a married, long-lost love, or who alienates the single, highly attractive woman who offers to take him snowboarding, all in the name of loneliness? To remain the strong, proud, impenetrable rock that never sheds a tear? A man who keeps himself untethered to any real responsibility or line of thinking, so as to always be able to turn on life or logic in an instant. Is this who I am?

If so, I should like to change the channel. What channel is "Survivor" on? Or "Who Wants To Be a Millionaire?"...is that show still airing? Let me be on one of those shows...but only if I get to play the title character...

I miss you! I love you!

Yours Always,
Gregory

April 13, 2010 – 9:21 PM

D,

Happy Anniversary. Last night marked the 14th Anniversary of our first date. Before that night we had only known each other through work. Before that night I had never been on a date with anyone. Technically it wasn't even a date as you were in a relationship with a guy from your school.

But somehow the stars aligned...you, a shy and reserved young woman with a boyfriend, agreed to go to a concert with me, a shy and introverted young man who had never gone on a date but who found courage enough to ask this stunning beauty out. I was brave enough to ask and you were trusting enough to say 'yes'...both things so out of character for each of us.

We went to the concert...so many moments from that night are now etched in my memory. The moment our hands touched while simultaneously reaching for the car stereo and I could swear there was a literal spark...a shock that made us both jump. I remember walking from the car to the arena and you tearing off the false fingernails you must have worn just that one time for me. I remember seeing you in regular clothes...a tanktop...inside the concert...it might have been the first time I had seen you out of your work uniform...you were perfection. I remember standing on your right in the stands...the Red Hot Chili Peppers playing to our left. I remember looking at you...watching you watch them. I remember you turning to me...for no apparent reason...and asking me, "what are you doing?"...it never made sense to me that you asked that...maybe I didn't hear it correctly over the sound of the music...but that's what I heard...and the answer that immediately ran through my head was, "I am falling in love with you!" I can still see it. I can still feel it. I still feel it.

They say when you fall in love, you'll know cause it just feels different. Well I knew it immediately. I know it still. 14 years later...through long-distance separation in college...through your engagement, marriage, and having a family with another man...through our affair...through the end of that affair and the indefinite silence that has resulted...through all of this, I love you. It is the nearest to unconditional love I have ever known. And now that love lives parallel to an unconditional pain. It is physics...for every joy, there is an equal but opposite pain.

556

April 13, 2010 – 9:21 PM

But it has an end. It can be sutured. It can be healed. It can return to love and love alone. Come back to me...heal my heart. Let our 15th Anniversary, and all others that follow, be spent in each other's arms. Fulfilling the promise that was made by the stars...the stars that wrote of this girl and this boy...the stars that tell all stories of love that is true.
I miss you! I love you!

Yours Always,
J

April 14, 2010 – 9:54 PM

D,

There can be no more horrible person than the person who does not laugh...who has no sense of humor. No, that's not complete. The worst people are those that have no sense of humor AND that wish to deprive others of laughter, of playfulness, of fun.

Of all the things I've tried to express to you over this year...all the shades and tones of who I am...perhaps the most lacking has been my sense of humor. I guess it has never seemed appropriate under these circumstances. But it has long been one of my favorite traits, my greatest sources of self-pride. It can come in the form of high-brow wit, it can come across as silly or crass, or it can spiral and flow from one sensibility to another...beginning as something senseless but building and shaping, one non-sequitor on top of another, until suddenly we find ourself back at the beginning...realizing I was always two steps ahead, and that all the nonsense might have secretly had a very specific sense all along.

One of my favorite places to be silly is on the distant and faceless Facebook. There, every conversation begins with a non-sequitor and ends whenever we choose to walk away from our keyboards. There is a certain thrill I find in not only entertaining my friends but also entertaining the friends of my friends who I really know not the first thing about. Every interaction lives in a vacuum...with no known history, no known politics, no bias or prejudice. It is simply, "here is a thought...take it in and react." And I get some great reactions.

It is a simple pleasure...one that keeps me going on these lonely nights without.

I miss you! I love you!

Yours Always,
Charlie Chaplin

April 15, 2010 – 9:49 PM

D,

Tonight I am restless, anxious, and eager...for events tomorrow, this weekend, and beyond. We will be freed from a shackle and allowed to take the next step...and the first step is a doozy...

I miss you! I love you!

Yours Always,
J

April 16, 2010 –

April 17, 2010 –

April 18, 2010 – 10:00 PM

D,

I know I haven't written you in a couple days. It has been my birthday weekend and I've been very busy. That isn't entirely true. I haven't really known what to say. Or I haven't wanted to say the things I've said before. For me, part of this process and this work was to do something epic and beautiful and always original for you. When it began to feel labored and repetitive I felt like I had fallen short of my goal. And then, for a time, I was scared off from doing this altogether. That was definitely a failure of my original intentions. But I always fought back...returning to seek redemption...to persevere and overcome.

So here I sit tonight...watching the clock tick down on the lingering moments of the last day of my sentence...tomorrow marking the anniversary of the first day I wrote you a letter...knowing I have fallen short of one goal. It is less than what was planned...but then again, maybe it is more.

Maybe somewhere in the midst of all of this I have done something right...something lasting and universal and true. Maybe in this creation I have done enough to show you how much I love you...enough to compel you to be with me...to let the world know that love can conquer all things...that faith and hard work are rewarded when true...and that, maybe, our love can be a shining example to all of this.

But these are all "maybes". They are unknown. They are still questions. Just a few of the many questions that have concerned and puzzled, intrigued and obsessed my daily life for all of this year. Most of these questions will live on. Questions of faith, questions of science, questions of progress, questions of stasis, questions of colors, questions of seasons, questions of pasts, questions of futures, questions of mankind, questions of motherhood, questions of vulnerability, questions of strength, questions of life, questions of love.

All have been asked...few have been answered. But only one question remains...only one question matters...only one question's answer can answer all others. I ask this question now with hope and with fear, with promise and with absolute perfect sincerity...

April 18, 2010 – 10:00 PM

Dawn you are the most incredible woman I have ever known, you are the greatest thing to ever grace my life, you are my best friend, you are my soul mate, you are the love of my life...

My Lovely Dawn, will you marry me?

I Am Yours Always,
Jared Christopher"

...I didn't know if she would answer...so I clicked "send"...

...and waited.

LaVergne, TN USA
13 October 2010

200535LV00001B/5/P